# TWO SHADOWS

# TWO SHADOWS

*Desiree Jury*

*Naki Press*

Published by Naki Press

PO Box 5235

Lambton Quay

Wellington, New Zealand


Desiree Jury

desiree.jury@gmail.com

Website: www.desireejury.com

Author photo by *Photography by Woolf*


Copyright © Desiree Jury 2011


ISBN: (print) 978 0 473 18663 0

ISBN: (e-book) 978 0 473 18664 7

*For NFJ*

# Pointe du Raz, Brittany, 1793

*Breakers crashed white, clawing the towering brown rock of the headland. Out at sea a russet-sailed fishing-boat made its steady way, standing well clear of the English frigate anchored offshore. In a cove shadowed by the cliffs, a shore party, six men and a tall officer, worked through the wreckage of the storm, searching tangles of cordage and shattered planks. Limp as seaweed, a corpse swayed in the shallows, caught by the pulse of the waves. An old sailor stooped, legs planted against the drag of glistening shingle as he raked over ribbons of sticky yellow foam. He tugged away a scrap of canvas.*

*"Major Fairfax, sir! Here's another!"*

*A dark-haired lad lay huddled and still. As the red-coated officer turned the body over, the light strengthened through a break in the cloud. It was not a boy he held but a fine-featured girl in boy's clothes, her black hair raggedly cut short, sleek against her skull.*

*"This one's alive," he said. Sand creaked beneath his boots as he stood, cradling her against his shoulder.*

*The sailor peered, grinning. "'Tis a silkie you have there, Sir Everard—a seal-woman."*

*Woken by the movement and the warmth of his body, her eyes opened: grey, dark-rimmed, huge in her thin face.*

*"Do you speak English? Who are you?"*

*Her voice was a whisper. "Je suis Marie-Claude de Josserac." Her eyes flickered to the red jacket, laced with gold. "They are all gone. 'Je n'ai pas un prisonnier à me reprocher. J'ai tout exterminé.' That is what he said."*

*"'Not one prisoner is on my conscience. I wiped out the lot'. Who said that?"*

*"That Jacobin murderer. Westermann."*

# 1

## *England, 1815*

He was not ready for this.

Longhallows loomed in the darkness, its long lines blurred by the lancing rain. Ralph, stiff from two weeks of hard riding, swung down from the saddle. A cold runnel snaked down his neck. The familiar stone lion snarled on its pillar, guarding the shield with its coat-of-arms.

A triangle of light spilled across the dark slick of the paving as the panelled door opened. Beyond its heavy bronze bosses he glimpsed the great staircase with his father's portrait. Was he still alive? Have I come too late? It would be easier if he were not. But there are words I need to say, to heal the breach.

His stomach clenched as though he were walking into an ambush. Squaring his shoulders, he strode inside.

The bedroom was stuffy, overheated from the crackling fire. The face of the man propped against the pillows had sunken into its strong bones. A deep sabre-slash carved a frown up his forehead, a purple seam running into his once-gold hair.

As the dark-haired young man approached the bed, he caught the sour mingled taint of sickness and unhealed wounds. Ralph had learned its meaning in Spain. His father was dying. But there was no point asking about these things. Sir Everard never confessed to pain or admitted failure.

The sick man's eyes opened, still fiercely blue, taking in the sodden grey riding cloak slashed with mud.

"Ralph. You are late. You may sit." Ralph tugged with numb fingers at the wet leather of his riding gloves, moulded and clinging. With each intake his father's breath whistled, where four months ago a Polish lance had pierced his lung at Waterloo. "How goes it in Vienna?"

Ralph shrugged. "We talk; we dance."

"At last your position is worthy of your rank. Better than Spain. I purchased you a commission, lieutenant in the Light Dragoons. All for you to skulk about in stinking rags!" The scar darkened as Everard's face flushed.

Only reproaches, even now. With an effort Ralph kept his tone calm, reasonable. "Father, it was an honour to serve with Colonel Grant. He ordered me behind the lines. They needed an Observing Officer, a good horseman with fluent French. This is not the time to discuss it again."

Everard's reply caught in his throat: he was seized by a rasping dry retch. Ralph stood and leaned forward, but a manservant appeared noiselessly at the bed, bearing a basin and towel.

"Excuse me, Mr Ralph, but you had best leave for now. The surgeon has made up a sleeping-draught. He suggests you return in the morning."

The woman poised at the dressing table was no longer young. But with thick coils of blonde hair piled high, her face still traced the classic lines of a cameo against the blue brocade of the wall.

"Robert!" Dorothea Bromley turned as her son entered, tall and fair-haired. "I was not expecting you in London. What brings you from Ash Park?"

"Everard Fairfax is dying," Robert Bromley replied gravely. "It was better you heard it from me."

Her rings flashed as she clasped her hands, closing her eyes as memories welled back. Everard as she first saw him, smiling, beautiful as Apollo; marvelling with her at the sunset on the Wengen Alp; reading Goethe together by the thunder of the Lauterbrunnen. For he was Werter to her Charlotte, promised already to a man in trade, twice her age. But Everard had such glamour about him. *I want only him*, she vowed, and gave herself willingly. With what ardour he swore to marry her, and acknowledge their child as his heir!

Then came the night they were discovered: shouts, the humiliation, the tears. By next morning her lover had gone, and she was packed off home, sold like a chattel. All so her father could settle his debts, and an artisan dignify his riches with gentle blood.

Dorothea twisted to face her son. "You are handsome and clever; you excel in all you turn your hand to. What more could he want in a son? Fourteen years I clung to hope; he had no wife, and no sign of one. I would have taken you and left Josiah, gone to Everard, anywhere. Then whom did he marry? That scrawny castaway he dragged back from France! Much good it did her."

Robert reached to still his mother's hand. The familiar rancour stirred: news of a child, a boy; and his utter disbelief, a sense of falling, gnawing hurt souring into hate. I should be standing at my father's deathbed, he thought, acknowledged as his heir. Not that half-French brat. He could have died in the wars easily enough. What had he ever done, to deserve Longhallows?

"Robert! You are hurting me!"

His fingers flared as he released his grip. "I am sorry, Mother. I must go. I will tell you as soon as I have further news."

Dorothea turned back to the mirror. Gathered in its lustrous curve were flasks of crystal, finely chased boxes, silver with blue enamel. With a sweep of her hand she knocked them clear.

The sickroom fug was thick now, with a stench that not even the fire of sweet applewood could disguise. Beneath the careful wrappings the putrid flesh had blackened, turning to decay. After hours of sitting, half-awake to the restless murmur, Ralph eased his weight onto his elbows, stretched his legs. He started at the voice from the bed.

"I never could understand you. You're a dreamer, like Marie-Claude."

Ralph had a sudden recollection of a small boy snuggled up warm against his mother, rapt as she recounted with shining eyes the *contes* of her Breton childhood, tales of mares that could speak and enchanted quests with magical names: the Castle of Crystal, *la Princesse de Tronkolaine*. Sir Everard was drifting again. His fingers twitched; a glint of gold from his signet ring caught the light. Ralph moved his hand towards the bed and let it drop. He had his father's powerful hands, but Everard's were wasted now, the sinews standing clear of the slack skin. The fire flickered. Ralph, his mind kindled still by deep memories, sensed a movement in the shadows: the *Ankou*, black and stark-ribbed, the Dancer of Death. Marie-Claude's tales had grown darker as she sickened. *'Il faut que je l'aie pour mon mari, ou je mourrai de douleur.'* What had she meant? She had married her handsome rescuer, just as in the story; why should she die of sorrow?

Everard turned his head away, his eyes half-closed. His voice was so low that his son had to lean close to catch it.

"I treated her badly. And the boy."

Ralph felt a rush of anger. Too late for apology now. His mother had been dead these ten years. He had been dispatched to school to make way for Everard's mistresses. Ralph stood up abruptly and walked out.

At the end of the garden, high brick walls and a line of cypress muted the rumble of the city beyond. Within the unlit grotto, Dorothea sat unmoving, her face ivory-pale in the gloom. Robert had expected, when he brought the news, a rush of tears. But his mother's face was set. Within her sable muff, her grip tightened on a worn little book.

"Never forget who stole your heritage. Had he perished in the wars as so many did, your father would have turned to you. Now Everard Fairfax is dead, after I waited my life for him, and Longhallows lost."

The setting sun lanced through the open porch, striking to cold fire the facets of amethyst and many-angled quartz. For a moment the Falls roared before her, all-encompassing, sublime, the myriad prisms casting splinters of light, the pink glow suffusing the snow-cliffs beyond. Then the light died, and all was shadow.

Six hundred years ago the White Monks of Cîteaux had come to this valley to build Fontclaire. So her father had told her, often enough. Flavia wondered ruefully what the Abbot would have thought if he could see her now, a tall girl crouched awkwardly, her ear pressed to the cold brass of a lock, straining to hear over the November hail clattering on the windows.

*"Don't lie to me!"*

She snatched at the candlestick as the door flew open. Hot wax stung her fingers.

"Flavia! It's bad enough being lectured by Father, without you eavesdropping as well. I was not lying! Get out of my way." Her brother stalked past.

Pushing back a lock of chestnut hair, she scurried along the dark-panelled corridor after him, but he was already halfway down the stairs. She leaned over the balustrade.

"Lucius! Wait for me!"

He pulled up abruptly. "You heard what he said?"

"Some of it," she admitted.

"One more gambling debt and he will stop my allowance!" His face reddened. "In two months I'll be twenty-one. Yet still he treats me like a boy!"

He looked up at her, demanding her assent. Though he was the older by almost two years, it was the practical Flavia he had turned to ever since their mother Emily died. Lucius had inherited her golden hair and delicate good looks; Flavia, her father's strong cheekbones and dark brown eyes.

"Lucius," she pleaded, "what can you do? It's Father's money."

"It will be mine one day!"

"Not if half the estate is mortgaged across a gaming-table."

"You exaggerate. You're as bad as he is." How could his invalid father and bookish sister understand the thrill of staking everything on a hazard, on a turn of the cards? "Go back to your pianoforte. I'm going out."

Foreshortened against the sandstone flags of the porch, he snatched his coat and hat.

"Where?"

Lucius paused, hand on the door-latch. "I have friends who will treat me like a man, even if my family does not." A scatter of hailstones rattled on the floor as he hauled open the thick oak planks, then the door resounded behind him, leaving an eddy of chill air. From upstairs she heard her father, knocking on the library floor with his stick. She turned back with a sigh.

Charles Stanton glared at her from beneath his shock of white hair. He jabbed his stick at his knee-rug, crumpled on the floor.

"It fell off," he said accusingly, then looked her full in the face. "I'm sorry, my dear," he said more gently. "The fault is none of yours. For years the estate was taxed to fund the war against Napoleon. Now we are at peace this endless rain has ruined the harvest. Lucius does not consider these matters. This is his second gambling bill this quarter; I will waste no more on his extravagances. I will not see Fontclaire pass to strangers so he may impress his wealthy friends."

Flavia tucked the rug about his knees and quietened the shaking, blue-veined hand with her own.

"I never defied my father so. Why is he not sensible like you?"

Poor father, Flavia thought, trapped in his chair, while Lucius fluttered like a bird at the window. She plumped the cushions. "Lucius has stormed off before. He always comes back. Now, what were we reading?" she asked. *The Vicar of Wakefield?*

She pulled the book from its shelf behind the fat-legged refectory table which served her father as a desk. Charles stroked the worn crimson binding with its faded gold tracery.

"This was the world of my childhood," he said quietly. "Things were different then, innocent, before all this tumult of revolution and war."

She adjusted the sphere of water before the candlestick to throw a better light. Behind her the faint glow picked out the pleated folds of

Tudor panelling, and the oak-leaves and stars of the plaster ceiling. Her voice slid easily into the cadences of this familiar tale of a kindly country parson and his family, some dutiful, some wayward. The lines of the old man's face relaxed.

Flavia awoke to the insistent yapping of a dog. She lay still a long moment, savouring the bed's warmth, studying the familiar pattern of flowers on the faded bed-curtains. Like most of the furnishings at Fontclaire, they had been new twenty-three years ago, for her parents' wedding. Lucius considered the old pieces shabby. He had decorated his own room in Napoleonic style: heavy dark green curtains massed with swagging and gold tassels. His latest purchase was a huge desk like an Egyptian temple, all papyrus-leaf columns and fierce brass claws. On seeing it, his father had remarked that he now lacked only an Imperial eagle perched on the bed-head and a marshal's baton over the fire-sill.

Flavia's mood of pleasant relaxation faded. Remembering last night's argument, she pulled back the covers. Despite her father's words, she felt responsible for keeping the peace. She dressed quickly, anxious to confirm that Lucius had returned; her father fretted when his son was out at night in bad weather.

In the hall, before the broad fireplace, Betsy Turner crouched on her hands and knees on the patterned tiles, plucking at cigar-ends as though they were so many cockroaches. The plump freckled pink of her arms showed where she had turned up her sleeves.

"No, I haven't seen Mr Lucius, or I'd give him a talking-to, leaving these smelly things about. You could try the kitchen, though. He's interested all of a sudden in the cooking, with that Simpson girl starting."

The kitchen lay at the end of a long corridor, with the scullery opening to the yard, the dairy and the old cellars beyond. Previously they had cooked as the monks did, on a broad open hearth with brackets for spit-rods above. Then three months before, Lucius had insisted that they fit a modern stove like the one at Ash Park. Now bacons and hams hung above the old hearth, while the bread-oven had been dismantled to make way for this shining, black-leaded apparatus with its gates and doors. As Flavia entered she smelt the savour of meat pastries fresh from the oven, lined neatly on a linen cloth along the scrubbed deal table. Against the light of the double row of windows, Mrs Wallace, thin and sharp, leaned over a girl with striking green eyes and dark, curling hair.

"Not like that, Molly! I'll show you again."

Mrs Wallace was fiercely proud of her new stove, regarding herself as the priestess of a mystery. Her acolyte must be the new girl from the village. The cook opened the upper oven door, and darted into it a small tin with a smudge of white. She clanged shut the door, and waited, arms folded.

"Now look close. If the flour is scarcely coloured, the oven is too slow and you need more wood in the firebox." A gust of hot air marked the opening of the second, larger door. "Hurry up!" she urged, her voice rising in exasperation. "You'll lose the heat!" The girl fed in two more billets. "Now give it another two minutes. When that flour turns a nice gold the heat will be just right. If it burns, the oven's too hot. *Are you listening?*"

Flavia moved, and the cook swung round. "Do go on."

The cook reopened the door, Flavia absorbed into her lesson. Mrs Wallace retrieved the tin and jabbed a finger into the golden pile. "Perfect. Off you go, Molly, and fetch more wood. 1 won't have my pies ruined by some lazy miss who lets the fire die."

"Have you seen my brother?"

"Not this morning." She darted a shrewd look at Flavia. "Have him and Mr Charles been having words again?" Flavia nodded. "That young man needs summat to do. It's a great pity he didn't join the Army."

"He's burning to go to London, but Father fears he'll get into more trouble."

"He'll get into it anyway, if he has a mind," Mrs Wallace replied, hauling the heavy bowl of dough closer. Punching it vigorously, she released a whiff of yeast. She went on in a lower voice. "I'd be happier if that young Molly was cross-eyed. Mr Lucius was down here twice yesterday, and the farm lads are hanging about like flies." Her face brightened. "Joe the Carter says young Mr Fairfax—Sir Ralph, I should say—is back at Longhallows. Could be he's gone there. But look, dearie," she added, "don't you worry. Your brother will come back in his own good time, and he won't like your father any the better for sending you to fetch him. Now have one of these, and take yourself off for a walk."

The pastry was crisp and fragrant, still warm. Flavia wrapped it in a napkin.

"Thank you, Mrs Wallace. I'll go up Beacon Hill."

She peered out the scullery door. The sky was still veiled, a pearly grey. She donned an old hooded plaid cloak and thick knitted red mittens. Outside the lawns shone emerald, and the ochre-to-grey of the ancient stone glowed in the soft light. On the side of the Abbot's Tower, an angled scar showed a white line, where the north transept of the abbey church had been. Flavia stepped out briskly past the herb garden, through the orchard, opened the gate in the high yew hedge and vanished into its black tunnel.

Here at Ash Park no-one treated him like a boy. The long pistol-barrel winked, damascened in gold. The weapon levelled, steadied. Lucius cocked it with a click. He took aim at his reflection in the wall-mirror and pulled the trigger. Grinning with delight, he set the pistol gently back in its walnut box.

"They are superb. Bromley! Are they really for me?"

His companion, older and elegantly dressed, leaned over and snapped shut the lid.

"Indeed. As for the other matter you mentioned: a bond for three hundred guineas, perhaps? Would that settle your most pressing needs?"

"But Father—" began Lucius, caught between embarrassment and relief.

"Let us keep this to ourselves," his host interposed. "Fathers do not always acknowledge what their sons have become."

How true, Lucius thought. His father would never think to buy him a set of duelling pistols. Some musty old tome, more like. It was bad enough that he had forbidden him from joining the Army. Sir Everard, over at Longhallows, had sent Ralph Fairfax off with his blessing when Ralph was what? Nineteen?

Lucius stretched his hand along the arm of the chair, in unconscious imitation of Bromley's pose. His host might have made his money in business, but there was plenty of it. His taste was impeccable, and he was sought out by important people in London.

Bromley rang for a servant. "More brandy, Stanton?"

"Oh—yes, please." He reached forward and fingered the satin-smooth walnut of the gun-case. "May I ask where you found these?"

Bromley gave a sardonic smile. "Call them spoils of war. I won them at *The Cocoa Tree*, when I was last in London."

Lucius had heard rumours from his friend Dacre about *The Cocoa Tree*. It shone in his imagination like the Promised Land: smart men-about-town, officers, lords even, making one casually welcome. He longed to join them, donning a broad-brimmed straw hat crowned with flowers against the glare of gaslights boxed in their long shades, low over the green tables; linked by the shared undercurrent of danger, insouciance, of courage displayed.

"I wish I had your luck at cards." Lucius's tone was more plaintive than he had intended. "Mostly I lose. Or if I win, it's only a little."

Bromley stretched out a booted foot to the fire. "My dear fellow, luck has nothing to do with it. If you want something badly enough, winning is a matter of determination. It depends how far you are prepared to go."

Lucius looked admiringly at his host. Bromley was beholden to no-one. His father, a self-made Manchester factory-owner, had died fifteen years ago, leaving a thriving business. Within five years Bromley had doubled his wealth and purchased Ash Park, the fine house where they were sitting now. Fifteen years: Lucius suddenly realised that was the same length of time his own father had hidden himself away in the country, a scholarly recluse, after his wife's sudden death.

"By the way, Stanton," Bromley added, "do not hasten to repay that bond. Your father is unwell, and should not be troubled by such things."

Lucius blushed. "But, sir—"

"My friends call me Bromley. Let us say that I was able to do you a good turn. Perhaps you can do one for me, sometime."

Flavia, sheltered within the tumble of old stones on the summit, licked the last crumbs from her fingers. She looked out from her vantage-point. In the soft light, neat hedged fields spread out below her to a vague horizon. Beneath lay Fontclaire Priory, with its tower, the ridged roofline of the great hall, the wing with the library and living quarters beyond, and its straggle of outbuildings: none of it symmetrical but sitting easily in the landscape as if it had grown from the earth and been there forever. To the west she could glimpse, over the trees, a distant glint from the windows of Longhallows, three miles away. Five miles beyond lay Ash Park, hidden by a fold in the hills. All she knew of it was what Lucius had said, that it was "very grand, and not old-fashioned like us."

At her feet lay the charred logs of the huge bonfire lit to celebrate the news, last summer, of Waterloo. Scores of folk had gathered on the flat summit, defying the darkness with a mighty blaze, the snapping flames leaping high. It was hard to believe that the war, a presence all her life, was truly over. Flavia had spent hours poring over small print in crinkling newspapers, following Wellington's marches and victories.

Now the threat had gone, but so too had the excitement of stirring encounters and great events.

Her foot clanked on a bottle, another souvenir of that evening. As she leaned to pick it up, a shadow fell across her. She straightened up, the bottle still in her hand. Before her stood, not Lucius as she had supposed, but a thinner-faced, dark-haired young man whom it took her a moment to recognise.

"Mr Fairfax!"

"At your service, Miss Stanton. A lively celebration, I see." He tipped his hat, grinning at her embarrassment.

"Still teasing," she retorted. "You and Lucius shut me once inside that water-butt, and Father sent me to bed without supper, for being so late home."

"I do apologise. How is Mr Stanton? I hear he has not been well."

"Not since September, before your father died." She glanced at him sideways, curious for a better look but not wishing to stare. Sir Everard had been a robust, splendid man. His son, more lightly built, had his father's long bones and strong nose, but the dark hair and grey eyes of his French mother. "Now you have taken up your inheritance, I should call you 'Sir Ralph.'"

He shook his head. "My inheritance! I knew before I left Vienna that the estate was encumbered. My father never told me by how much. He had Frewin put the balance of our money into bonds. The fool quit them at a loss in the panic before Waterloo. I thought the Roman bronzes would fetch a tidy sum, but they returned less than I had hoped."

"Lucius saw them at Ash Park." Flavia coloured as she realised her lack of tact.

Fairfax frowned. "Excuse my rudeness in dwelling on such matters. They are of no interest to you."

"You are mistaken," Flavia replied, her qualms at discussing family matters yielding to an urge to confide. "Perhaps you could advise me. Lucius is gambling, more heavily than he can afford. I have no idea how gentlemen manage these things, and father refuses to discuss it."

"You consider me an expert?" His lip quirked.

"Of course not," she floundered. "But I thought that as you had some influence with Lucius …"

"That was years ago. Improvident young men don't take kindly to good advice, even from friends," he said gently, "and especially not from their sisters. It is not a subject I could raise directly." Her face fell. "This is causing your father concern?"

"They quarrel incessantly. Father is very strict in money matters. I suspect Lucius owes rather more than he admits."

"And he has been seeing Bromley?" She nodded. "Bromley is quite out of his class."

"That is what concerns me. It flatters Lucius's vanity to associate with him."

"Let me think about it." He darted a look of mischief. "I'm a respectable landowner now. But I must be on my way. Good morning." He strode back down the slope to his horse, swung easily into the saddle, and cantered off with a wave.

Flavia set off down the path, mulling over her encounter. Perhaps, if Lucius resumed his boyhood friendship, he would be less susceptible to the allure of Bromley's ready wealth. She had been relieved to air her concerns, but hoped Fairfax would not consider her forward...The mittens! She stared at them in alarm. They were clumsy—hideous! What would Sir Ralph think, newly come from Vienna! Too late she yanked them off, and jammed them into her pocket. Still preoccupied, she reached the tunnel, and opened the orchard gate.

She jumped at a loud report and a tinkle of breaking glass. Lucius ran up to her with a smoking pistol in his hand.

"You're not hurt?" he asked anxiously. "You silly girl! They said you were out walking. I did not expect you back so soon."

"Obviously," she said, recovering herself. She reached out to touch the elaborate mounting on the pistol. "Where did you get this?" She was about to ask whether he had been gambling again, but kept quiet, mindful of Fairfax's advice.

"A gift." He smiled at her, good-humoured with relief. "From Bromley. Here: I'll show you how to fire them."

Beneath the bare branches of an apple tree a table was set up with pistol-case, powder flask, cleaning gear and a box of lead balls like grey peas. She rolled one on the palm of her hand, round and unexpectedly heavy. Strange to think so small a thing could kill a man.

"See that bottle? Take aim—no, not like that!" He stood behind her, took the weight of her elbow and squinted down her arm. "There."

Immediately he stepped away, her arm dropped. "It's heavy."

"Hold it with both hands. Aim low: it will jump as it fires. Remember to cock it first. Watch for the recoil. Go on: try."

Flavia screwed up her face in concentration. She steadied the long barrel, clicked back the hammer with her thumb, aimed, and squeezed the trigger. The kick of the weapon caught her unawares. The bottle shattered; she coughed at an acrid gust of dirty smoke. Lucius stared unbelievingly at the jagged base.

"By the deuce, you hit it! A lucky shot. Well done!"

Unused to her brother's approval, Flavia smiled, the red mittens forgotten. They turned back to the house. "I shall tell Father—"

Lucius turned to her quickly. "Better leave it be. Keep mum about the pistols. He'll worry about you hurting yourself with a misfire, or such."

Flavia shrugged, uncomfortable at the hint of deceit.

"If you say so."

A quick hug. "As good as the Queen of the Amazons, eh? What was her name? Penny-something?"

"Penthesileia," Flavia corrected automatically.

# 2

# *England, late 1815*

*Robert Bromley, Esq. requests the pleasure of the company of Lucius Stanton, and Miss Flavia Stanton at a Ball on* —the scrolled capitals jiggled as the coach ran over a stone—*Ash Park*—another jolt—*The favour of an Answer is requested.* The card was too hard to read by the faint light inside the coach. Holding it carefully so as not to smear the print against her new kid gloves, Flavia handed it back to Lucius.

Ever since the invitation had arrived, Lucius had been conspicuously polite to his father, showing a degree of meek forbearance that led his father to query dryly whether his son was perhaps considering taking Orders. Now here they were, the coach swaying as the horses halted, the step scraping as it opened out, its hinge in need of oiling. As Flavia stepped down, carefully gathering her skirts, she registered a symmetrical facade, elegantly severe.

"The fellow who built it went bankrupt, you know," Lucius remarked. "Bromley bought it for a song and added the wings, and this Greek triangle bit in the middle."

Lucius flourished the card at the footman, splendid in blue-and-silver livery. They passed into a circular entrance hall where fluted pilasters rose to a lofty dome. Bronze statues gleamed in alcoves around the wall, while in the centre a jet of water chuckled into a shell of creamy alabaster. Lucius nudged her. "A cut above our old place," he whispered.

In the ballroom massed lilies filled the room with a heavy scent. Around Flavia the other girls gathered like ducklings under the anxious eyes of mothers and aunts. Flavia did not often think of her dead mother, but she could have done with her now. Lucius was supposed to be her chaperone, but so far this had extended to a warning *en route* not to find a quiet corner and pull out a book. Despite his cheery assurance that her dress would do very well, her self-striped pale blue muslin felt very ordinary compared to the figured silk of the other gowns.

This must be their host approaching, a well-built fair-haired man in his thirties, his beautifully-cut coat and snowy linen achieving without visible effort the style for which Lucius strove in vain. Bromley bowed.

"Enchanted to make your acquaintance, Miss Stanton. Your brother has often spoken of your attainments."

Flavia had come determined to dislike Bromley for encouraging Lucius to gamble, but his compliments distracted her. She cast about for an appropriate reply. "Those statues in the entrance-hall, sir: are they Greek?"

"Roman copies of Greek originals, from Cumae. But come, Stanton: the music has begun. Time to lead your sister to the dance." Flavia's face blazed with embarrassment as she realised these must be the statues from Longhallows. Thank goodness their host had moved on.

Ralph toyed with his glass of wine, which was excellent, and stared morosely though the doorway at the bronze athlete on his plinth. He would have expected Bromley to have more tact than to set it there. He thought of the gaps in his own long gallery. Not that antiquities interested him in themselves. In Italy his father had laboured to induce in his son his own passion for collecting. But Ralph had slipped away from the tours of dusty churches, their ceilings cluttered with bulging cherubs and saints in ecstasy. He preferred the blazing sunshine outside, and live horses to bronze ones.

All this opulence brought to mind the weight of his debts. Not until Sir Everard's death had Ralph discovered the merchants clamouring for payment and the encumbered farms. Ralph had never previously questioned where his allowance came from. In Spain his energies had been fixed on carrying out his orders while staying alive. He suspected now that Sir Everard, always contemptuous of commerce, had been similarly careless of financial detail, intent as he was on maintaining the display he considered appropriate to his rank.

Everard had entrusted the tedious minutiae of finance to his diligent and long-serving factor Micah Frewin. But the elder Frewin had died two years before and been succeeded by his son Thaddeus. Ralph had picked up some knowledge of accounts while serving under Wellington, who insisted on well-established lines of supply. Young Frewin was proving sluggish in complying with Ralph's wish to see the books.

More alarming was the collapse of the market for wool and wheat. When Napoleon had been dispatched to St Helena, the government's insatiable demand for uniforms and rations had vanished over the horizon with him. Instead of a greedy commissariat supplying armies in Spain and America and a far-flung Navy, now there were thousands of officers on half-pay, tens of thousands of returned soldiers, laid-off sailors; all hungry enough, but lacking the money to buy.

Nor had Sir Everard ever bothered himself with modern theories of stock-breeding and crop rotation. To him the old ways were the good ways, when the lower orders knew their place, before the madness of Jacobinism had infected Europe. *'Look what happened to your mother's family, boy: drowned like dogs. So much for 'Liberty, Equality and Fraternity'."*

Ralph was annoyed with himself for accepting the invitation. He had felt obliged to set the estate on a new footing, and not be bound by his father's prejudices, which had been strongly held and pungently expressed. He had no good reason to stay away, other than that the two families had always avoided each other: Sir Everard's contempt for trade would in itself explain the coolness between the foremost houses of the neighbourhood. More particularly, Ralph had come here poaching as a boy, been caught by Bromley's gamekeeper, and given a sound thrashing, with another from his father when he learned where Ralph had been. After that he had hardly needed his parent's strict admonitions to stay away.

The musicians, two fiddlers, a sallow-faced fellow with a clarinet, and a sharp-elbowed flautist, struck up a gavotte. There was Flavia Stanton in emphatic conversation with an ample middle-aged woman whom he remembered as Mrs Dacre.

"Mr Fairfax, is it not? Or, I should say, 'Sir Ralph'. I suppose you are quite lost here, after so long away."

"Miss Stanton and I have already met," he said, making a fine Hapsburg bow. "I was about to ask her to join me for this dance."

"I should be delighted," Flavia replied, smiling with relief at finding someone she knew. Lucius was by now far down the room, leaning over a girl in palest pink satin, with bunched golden curls.

Trying not to appear self-conscious, Flavia moved into the steps of the dance. She felt the slight ripple of the parquet through the thin soles of her dancing-slippers. Light and balanced on its smooth surface, she was caught up in the sway of the music.

"You dance very well," she said, hoping not to sound too direct.

"A strict regime of practice in Vienna, at the *Palais Palm*," Ralph replied as he led her into a turn, recalling the Grand Ball at the Imperial

Riding School, rows of radiant chandeliers; the dazzle of sashes, orders and gems: emerald, diamond, ruby, sapphire. "I could circle the Moonlight Hall eight times without falling over."

Flavia gave an unladylike snort of laughter. Then her curiosity got the better of her.

"What was the Congress like?"

"A very grand ball that went on too long."

"But the Tsar, and Castlereagh, and Metternich: what were they trying to do?"

Ralph looked at her quizzically. This girl was persistent and read the papers. "It was like a magic cauldron, all swirl and glitter, into which the rulers and statesmen of Europe poured old forms and broken Empires, each hoping to conjure up the shape that suited him best." He paused as they ran through an intricate series of steps. "Then the evil wizard Napoleon reappeared, and it all exploded in a flash of foul-smelling smoke. Now they are at it again."

"Will they succeed?"

"Who can tell? The statesmen of Europe have never before been asked to rebuild a broken continent. Most of us have known no other state than war."

This conversation was taking him back to parts of his life he would rather forget. After years of being always alert to danger, it had been a relief to reach Vienna and lapse heedless into the affair with Laure. That had ended abruptly when he found her going through his papers.

He recalled himself to the present. The music had changed to a familiar one-two-three beat. "Do you dance the Waltz?"

Flavia knew that her father disapproved of it, but she was not going to tell her partner. Correctly reading this uncharacteristic reticence, he drew her closer. She felt the pressure of his hand on her back.

"Follow my lead."

Fairfax led Flavia in to supper. His easy manner had allayed her earlier fears of making a fool of herself, and she was not so unworldly as to ignore the heads that turned as she passed. As she reviewed the array of grapes, jellies and ices, a deeper voice spoke beside her.

"You are enjoying your evening, I trust?"

"Most certainly, Mr Bromley," she replied with enthusiasm. "Thank you so much for the invitation."

Bromley turned to her companion. "Fairfax: accept my condolences on Sir Everard's death."

Ralph did not usually insist on his title, but its absence grated.

"His courage was exemplary; to stay on the battlefield despite being thrice wounded."

"Twice," said Ralph, shortly.

"And you survived the day unhurt?"

"I was trapped under my horse."

Bromley moved smoothly on. "Do you intend to stay in the district long?"

"I think not," said Ralph tersely, wishing that Bromley would move away. "Once my father's affairs are settled, I may travel on the Continent."

"Do you intend to return to Spain?"

"Not to Spain." The words came out more emphatically than he intended.

"Italy perhaps?"

"I really don't know." Ralph resented this probing into his affairs.

The players were tuning up for the next set of dances. Waving, Mrs Dacre caught Flavia's eye, and impelled over her son, a hunting companion of Lucius. Edmund, a strapping youth with bushy side-whiskers, stood beside her breathing heavily as he built up the courage to speak. His mother seized the moment.

"Miss Stanton," she beamed, "might you join Edmund for *Sir Roger de Coverly*?"

Fairfax, the good humour gone from his face, nodded at her in acknowledgment and moved away. Flavia fought her sense of disappointment and stepped out with her new partner. His gloves were damp; his turns too sudden. He trod on her toe and his neck flushed pink. Lucius and the petite blonde girl swirled past. Her eyes, large and cornflower blue, were fixed on his face. More dances. Her new shoes pinched. Glimpsing the clock by the wall, Flavia saw it was now two in the morning. Unused to keeping such hours, she was flagging. The rich odour of lilies made her head ache, and she had accidentally brushed her glove against them, smearing on it a vivid orange pollen that would not rub off. She wondered when they would go home.

Ralph stared up at the bronze athlete. The light, reflecting from the pool of the fountain, caught the play of the boy's tensed muscles, the easy confidence of his grace and strength. Before Ralph had left for Spain, the statue had been unremarked, part of the background of his home. I had this picture in my head, Ralph reflected, all the years I was away, of coming back to Longhallows, and being reassured by what was familiar. But it had all changed.

Why did Bromley's questions rankle so? They were reasonable enough on the surface. But it pricked Ralph's pride to be reminded of the contrast between his father the Gentleman Volunteer, cut down heading the charge by the curved sabres and red-and-white pennants of the fierce Poles, white plumes nodding on their *czapkas*, while his son the Light Dragoon flailed uselessly under a dead horse, stopped by a lucky shot from a sweating foot-soldier of the Guard Artillery.

Ralph imagined the athlete propped beneath the jet in Bromley's fountain, apparently relieving himself into the basin. It was as well that the statue was too heavy for him to lift alone, for he was sorely tempted to shift it. Bromley would guess immediately who had done it. Sir Everard had warned Ralph more than once that his taste for practical jokes, what he called his "antics", would get him into trouble. He could hardly prove his father right with him only weeks in the grave.

Waking after noon, Flavia felt the dislocation which follows a long night and too little sleep. The dining room was the only one of the main rooms at Fontclaire in more modern style; Charles had decorated it to Emily's taste to celebrate the birth of his heir. Usually Flavia found it pleasing, with its light butter-yellow walls and fine Indian carpet, a wedding present from Charles's wealthy cousin Harriet. But today tiredness, and a vague sense of disappointment, made her terse.

"For the third time, would you please pass the sugar?"

Lucius's spoon stilled its tinkling against the side of the cup.

"Eh?" No doubt about it, Lucius was infatuated again.

"You are showing all the symptoms."

Lucius swivelled round in his chair and stared anxiously into the mirror. "But I drank very little last night."

"Not drunk, silly—in love!"

He swung back, his face alive with enthusiasm. "You did see Caroline Lennox? Does she not dance divinely?"

"Yes, she dances divinely, and no, you did not introduce her. You were too busy flapping around her in circles, like a moth around a flame."

"It's all very well for you to scoff," retorted Lucius, disgruntled. "I did look for you, but you had gone off with Fairfax. You really should be more careful, you know. You are supposed to change partners after two dances. People were taking notice. Bromley said—"

"Bromley said!" She repeated tartly. She had wondered at the time whether she should have mixed more generally. "I danced two sets with your lumpish friend Dacre. If he rides as heavily he dances he should have a cart-horse, not a hunter. All we ever hear is *Bromley said!* When are you going to form some opinions of your own?"

Lucius leaned forward, his face solemn. Flavia recognised the expression; a copy of their father's, about to deliver a lecture.

"Now Flavia—" Lucius began.

Flavia sighed. 'Now' was always a bad sign.

"You have no experience of the world. You should not show a partiality—"

"Lucius," she snapped back, "why can you spend all evening besotted with some girl you have barely met, while I must apologize for talking to a neighbour I have known since I was a child? And you still haven't passed me the sugar."

She knew how her brother's mind worked. There was more to this. Lucius hated confrontation, and would always bring up an unpleasant subject indirectly. What was he implying? Had the news of Fairfax's debts spread around the neighbourhood? Or was it something else?

Lucius shoved along the sugar-bowl in aggrieved silence. With Flavia you never knew where you were. She would sit like a mouse for days, never putting herself forward, then scratch like a cornered cat at some perfectly reasonable advice.

As the glow of righteousness faded, his own dilemma returned to his mind. Caroline's mother, Mrs Lennox, was just the type of commanding woman that Charles Stanton disliked. Lucius could not afford to have him take against her: Caroline was beautiful and fatherless. She needed protection. He must see her again.

# 3

# *England, Christmas 1815*

Flavia was pleased, in the days following the ball, to see her brother spending more time at home. Bromley had left for Manchester, Caroline and her mother had returned to Bath. Fairfax called briefly to pay his respects to Charles Stanton, and announce his departure for London on urgent business. His conduct, even to Lucius's critical eye, was unexceptionable. Lucius began to feel a little ashamed of his hard words to his sister. He would not like her to think he was jealous of Fairfax's independence.

In his pocket, creased from being read and re-read, was a note from Caroline. The Lennoxes were returning for what she called "the Yuletide Season," and Lucius was determined to present them to his father under the most favourable auspices.

Two weeks before Christmas the sky closed over, lowering and dense. Snowdrifts blocked the roads. It was four days before the filtered half-light brightened. Scraps of dirty white cloud hurried before the wind.

Swinging his arms against the cold, Ralph looked back at Longhallows, past the lion on his pillar, wearing a crown of snow, to the mullioned windows glinting in their rows. Above ran long balustrades, dark under a crisp white rim. Ranks of tall chimneys marched across the roof, dominated by the corner towers with their elaborate Dutch gables. It was a proud, even arrogant building. It had fitted his father well.

Now Longhallows was his. Ralph felt its massive façade weighing on his shoulders. Somehow he must hold the estate together. He owed that both to his father and to his name: his Fairfax ancestors, staring out, demanding, from the long gallery. Only with Longhallows secure could he consider his own future.

Ralph had been away four years: first in Spain, then Vienna. Now he kept thinking of questions he wanted to ask his father. He would never know the answers. He grieved that Sir Everard had never reconciled himself to Ralph's transfer from the orthodox Light Dragoons to Colquhoun Grant's handful of officers, riding behind the lines. Disguised as a poor Spaniard, or passing as French, Ralph had mapped the roads and noted the movements of troops and cannon.

His father had taken that choice as a deliberate slight, a conscious rejection of the military career he had planned for his son, intended to culminate in high rank and a peerage to restore the Fairfax fortunes. Sir Everard had a quick temper and cutting tongue, both of which he had passed on to Ralph, whose first and only home leave had ended abruptly with a public row in his father's club. Since then they had communicated only formally by letter, until the summons to his father's deathbed.

Now Ralph's resentment was coloured by regret. Would he have felt less of a fool over that business with Laure had he discussed it with Everard, man to man? And that night in the citadel? What would his father have made of that, the trapped, terrified boy trying to close his ears to the shrieks that still echoed in his sleep? Ralph had never told him, afraid he would be despised as a coward. He remembered the derision in his father's last words: *"You're a dreamer, like Marie-Claude."*

Now it was over; part of another life. Ralph walked faster, concentrating on his surroundings, gaunt hedges, snow and trees: dark, fissured oaks, some older than the house, their branches sketched in Indian ink against the grey sky.

I shall ride over to Fontclaire, he decided. It was time he became better acquainted with his neighbours. There was Flavia Stanton, too, with her fine dark eyes and pleasing smile. His conversation with her had been the one part of Bromley's ball he had enjoyed. Her frankness was refreshing after the equivocations of the sophisticated women of Vienna, whose every gesture was calculated, and whose every exchange came at a price.

He jumped up to snatch at a dangling bough; the sudden jerk sent the branch swaying. He skipped out of the way, dodging the shower of snow. Here he was, striding over his own land, on a day when each breath invigorated like iced wine. Perhaps, he conceded as he took the path to the stables, he was at last beginning to enjoy his inheritance.

Lucius watched from his bedroom window as Ralph slowed from a canter to an easy trot, with the effortless grace which came from spending days in the saddle. Not for him the frustration of being fussed over by a sick old man. Fairfax's father had bought him an officer's commission. Now he was master of his own estate. No subterfuges for him; he could do what he liked.

Flavia sat at the kitchen table, checking the household accounts. Her mind was elsewhere. She had been flattered by Ralph's attention at the ball, and enjoyed his company. But she was surprised how vehemently she had reacted to her brother's censure. She was confused by the inconsistency of her feelings. She had been delighted when Ralph had last called, and felt immediately at ease. But why had she been so disappointed when he said he was going to London? During the years he was away scarcely a thought of him had crossed her mind. Had Lucius been less disapproving she would have confided in him, but their present relationship was wary. She chose to muse over her confusions alone.

When the visitor was announced, Flavia glanced down, flustered, at her plain brown dimity. Should I keep him waiting while I change? Suddenly she must see him immediately, as though he might evaporate. Ralph turned as she entered, his face kindling in a smile. The warmth of her obvious welcome matched his mood. He could think of nothing to say. Here we are, he thought, gaping at each other like a pair of owls.

Flavia broke the silence first, on a sudden impulse. "Sir Ralph, would you join us for Christmas dinner? My father cannot easily go out. He would enjoy the company."

"I should be delighted, Miss Stanton. How kind of you to ask." He had the satisfaction of seeing her blush. He took her arm. "Come, we had better let him know."

What was Ralph to do about Frewin? From the first meeting with his agent after his father's funeral, he had found the man glib. He eyed Frewin as he came in, noting the silk waistcoat and elaborate neckcloth. With a wife and a gaggle of relations to support, how could he afford to dress like that on a hundred guineas a year?

The factor smiled deferentially. Ralph came straight to the point. "How came Bromley by my bronzes?"

"You authorised me to sell the collection, sir. His was by far the best offer, and I would have been failing in my duty not to accept it."

And the *douceur* that accompanied it, Ralph thought. "I left the matter to your discretion. Did you have to advertise my impoverishment? I assumed you were dealing with a discreet auction house in London. I intend to sell two of the farms. If Bromley gets his hands on them, or on anything else of mine, you will be dismissed. Don't think you are irreplaceable, just because my father in his decline placed an exaggerated trust in you." Good, thought Ralph; that has wiped the smile off his face.

Frewin was startled into apology. "If you have any complaints, sir—"

"I have. There is a shortfall of two hundred pounds in last month's accounts."

Frewin clasped his hands. "I must apologise for my tardiness in completing them, sir. I was busy all Tuesday arranging the sale of wood—"

"The payment was due three weeks ago."

"The corn returns have been lower this year, with the season wet and mildew in the wheat," Frewin returned, fluently.

With each successive excuse Ralph's suspicions grew; but his father had been happy enough with his agent, even riding to hounds with him. He would hardly have done that, had he suspected Frewin of embezzling his money.

Frewin took Ralph's silence as encouragement. "The new Corn Laws will improve the returns substantially. Let me explain how the duty will operate."

Ralph cut in. "I read about it in *The Times*, in Vienna. I am well aware of the importance of this measure to the landed interest. I want that money settled within the month. That will be all."

The factor bowed with a tight smile, and left.

Christmas Day dawned crisp, with a layer of fresh snow. Lines of footprints converged on the grey-walled church with its crooked spire. From under the lych-gate Molly Simpson, in a new green bonnet, darted a smile at a gypsy-dark young man. Lucius flourished a fine new riding-coat with seven capes. Their edges flapped as he waved his arms, directing the awkward business of transferring his father from the carriage into a Bath chair.

Flavia was pleased her father had agreed to come. He had been in a difficult mood lately, suffering more pain than he would admit, and needing to be cajoled into coming to church at all. "The neighbours scarcely ever see you," she had urged. "A change of scene will do you good." Then, as the weather had settled in, Lucius had sought to keep him at home, for his health. This had provoked his father's determination to go.

Lucius had sulked. Why should his father insist that Lucius obey his commands, while his son's advice, given for his own good, was so readily ignored? Despite his retiring disposition, Charles Stanton could be obstinate as a mule.

Flavia, covertly watching the Fairfax pew, saw Ralph arrive. He smiled at her across the aisle. Her attention kept straying past the thick pillars and granite arches to the dark head three rows ahead. Usually she threw herself wholeheartedly into singing the old carols. Today she was suddenly conscious of the *timbre* of her voice, bouncing off the white plaster ceiling with its network of dark ribs, as if she were being overheard by the odd figures carved into the bosses: the stocky knight, the raven, the hare with staring round eyes, and the sinister figure of three legs interlocking, which had scared her as a child.

In the chill little porch after the service, Flavia felt a touch on her elbow. She turned with a brilliant smile. But it was Lucius, aglow.

"Caroline: meet my sister, Miss Flavia Stanton. Flavia; Miss Caroline Lennox."

Miss Lennox's cheek snuggled against the white fur lining her rose velvet hood; her dainty hands were exquisite in palest grey gloves. Flavia, a good three inches taller, felt awkward beside her.

"Mother says it may come on to snow," said Caroline, with the demurest of smiles. "But I am sure your brother will protect us from the weather." She looked up at Lucius.

"Indeed," he beamed. "I should feel obliged to take off my coat and spread it over that puddle, like Sir Walter Raleigh."

"Don't ruin your new Benjamin, Stanton," cut in Ralph's voice. "I saw a dead hedgehog there yesterday." Flavia half-turned. "I trust your father is safely settled in his carriage? Then we may go." As they neared the door, he added in a lower voice: "I'm sure your brother—"

Flavia felt a sudden sharp pain as a solid, handsome woman trod heavily on her instep. Flavia stared briefly full into her face. The woman's mouth crimped in annoyance as her eyes sought some point beyond. She strode past without apology. Fairfax guided Flavia over to the bench.

"Here: sit down. Did she hurt your foot?" he asked.

Her foot throbbed. She rubbed it and winced. "I had no idea she was there." She looked out to where the woman had joined the group around her brother. Fairfax followed her gaze.

"Unlike the Iron Duke, your brother is so set on his objective that he has failed to ascertain what lies on the reverse slope. That is Alicia Lennox, Caroline's mother."

A plump goose, redolent with herbed stuffing, was followed by a dark spicy pudding luscious with currents, sultanas and flecks of peel, ablaze with brandy. To Flavia's relief, Mrs Lennox appeared not to recall the incident in the church. She spoke at some length about Caroline's father, the late Major Lennox of the King's German Legion, "a gallant officer, so dashing in his black uniform." The usually-reserved Charles Stanton, after an animated discussion with Fairfax on the battles in Spain, looked round the table with satisfaction. "It is a long time since I took such pleasure in company," he said. "Thank you all for coming. Flavia, perhaps you will play for us before I retire."

It had been in the back of Flavia's mind that her father would make some such request, but she had been too busy with the dinner to prepare anything in advance.

"*Herr* Haydn, Father?" she enquired as they entered the drawing room.

"That will do nicely, my dear."

She adjusted the stool, scanning the music in trepidation, as though it had transposed itself into some new and unfamiliar key. She ended the first page on a wrong note; but as her pleasure in the music reasserted itself she finished creditably, at least.

There was a patter of polite applause.

"Caroline plays also," asserted Mrs Lennox. "Have you the music for *The Downfall of Paris?*" she asked Lucius. "It was very popular in Bath."

"Indeed I have," agreed Lucius, riffling through the music. He had ordered the piece for Flavia but she thought it trite. As Caroline sat in her turn, arranging the fall of her skirt with a graceful gesture, Lucius hovered over her, ready to turn the pages. She attacked the march energetically.

Ralph looked up, amused, as Flavia resumed her seat. "An excellent piece," he whispered *sotto voce*, "for a military band."

Mrs Lennox looked around, frowning.

Lucius refused to perform, claiming with a smile to Caroline that he was merely a servant to the Muse.

Mr Stanton appealed to Ralph. "Come, sir. You used to play the fiddle, did you not?"

"Unfortunately it fell off a track in the Pyrenees, along with the mule carrying it and most of my baggage."

"Then perhaps you could sing? Your father had a fine baritone, as I recall."

"I see a songbook on the music-stand," Ralph responded. "I will essay one of those, if Miss Stanton would be kind enough to accompany me."

He escorted Flavia to the keyboard. "Which would you recommend?"

She was grateful for his tact, allowing her to choose one she knew. "*John Riley.*" The song, with its haunting melody, was a favourite of hers. Confidently she gave out the chords of the introduction.

*As I walked out one morning early*
*To breathe the sweet and pleasant air*
*Who should I spy but a fair young maiden*
*Whose cheek was like the lily fair.*

*I stepped up to her and kindly asked her*
*If she would be a sailor's wife.*
*'Oh, no, kind Sir, I'd rather tarry*
*And remain single for all my life.*

Sir Ralph sang with an ease that showed this was not the novelty for him that it was for her.

*I'll not go with you to Pennysylvanny*
*I'll not go with you to a distant shore*
*For my heart is with Riley and I can't forget him,*
*Though I may never see him no more.*

His voice lingered on the simple words. Flavia caught the pulse of the music, as she had when they danced.

*Now when he saw that she loved him truly,*
*He gave her kisses, one, two, three,*
*Saying, 'I am Riley, your long-lost lover*
*Who has been the cause of your misery.'*

"I fear I must retire," Charles said. "You young folk must stay on. Lucius, see to our guests."

Lucius wasted no time settling Mrs Lennox and her daughter in front of the fire. Flavia sent for a tray of nuts and dried fruit, happy to stay with Fairfax by the piano.

"Thank you for your patience with my father tonight. He took an interest in the war in the Peninsula and followed it closely in the papers."

"And you also: *'But what were they trying to do?'*" Ralph teased. He enjoyed her sudden smile.

"I have read about the guerrillas and the victories," she acknowledged. "What was it like?"

"Would you prefer the newspaper version," he said dryly, "or the truth?"

"I have read the newspapers already. I have never had the opportunity to ask someone who was there."

As he collected his thoughts Ralph cracked half-a-dozen walnuts between his palms. Relaxed by his welcome, and encouraged by this vital girl's curiosity, he felt free to speak honestly.

"There were good things: the mountains, each with its fort and little town; the superb views over the plains; the hot summers smelling of oranges. A good horse under you, and a new world to explore. But set against those the interminable night marches and freezing winters.

"War is not glorious. Much of it is boring and uncomfortable, with bad food and scant. You have no idea what a luxury it is to eat a well-prepared meal, or sit down in a room with a whole roof and furniture that hasn't been broken up for the fire."

He set the walnuts in a line.

"Waiting for the cannon, trying to suppress the thought that someone you have never met wants to kill you, unless you kill him first. Then the din of the cannonade. You can't see for powder-smoke. The blood, and the cries. Afterwards, counting the friends you have lost. I am glad to be finished with it."

"And the battles were not the worst. Much has been made here in England of the *Guerrilla,* the Little War. Dreadful things were done in Spain, by both sides. Don't be misled by the twirling mustachios and fringed sashes. These are men who have not washed in a very long time, and have very unpleasant ways with strangers." He looked up. "I apologise. I should not discuss such things with a well-bred young woman."

"Thank you for your honesty. My father says it is better to know the truth than be protected from it."

"You are fortunate in such a father." He felt himself on the brink of uttering things better left unsaid. "But I see Lucius is gathering his charges. I too must be gone, while there is still a moon to see my way home by. Please thank your father for a rewarding evening." Lightening the mood, he scooped up the walnuts and stuffed them in his pocket. "Rations for the road home. Good evening, Miss Stanton."

Ralph had not meant to speak so openly, but had found himself responding to Flavia's eagerness to learn. The silent trees of the avenue jogged past. He remembered those other groves, by the ruined and smoking villages; the ones he feared to enter, knowing what he would find: dead women used and tossed aside; chunks of what had once been men, impaled.

And Charles Stanton: Ralph had been too young when he left to appreciate what a fine man he was, with a resolute honesty and power of mind. Would that his own father, for all his courage and code of family honour, had been as open to hard truths.

I am Sir Ralph Fairfax of Longhallows. The words were still new enough to have a ring to them. As he passed the wrought iron gates at the limits of the Fontclaire park he remembered the walnuts and munched, musing as his horse, familiar with the road, settled into an easy trot. The fields were open here, bare to the grey vault of the sky. Above him the moon shimmered, a disk of beaten pewter. A fox barked. For the first time it occurred to him that his father, too might have had secrets he was ashamed to acknowledge. Had he known how badly his extravagance and rash investments had diminished his patrimony? Was this why Everard had volunteered to fight at Waterloo?

Ralph knew that pride. Better to seek an honourable end in battle, to die gloriously for the code of honour he had lived by all his life. For the first time Ralph pitied his father. He had misjudged even his death.

# 4

## *England, January 1816*

"Flavia!"

The girl, reading in the orchard, lifted her head.

"Flavia!" Lucius, louder this time, bounded down the path. "We are going!"

"Where?"

"London, of course!" He vaulted over the garden-seat. "Father is sending us to stay with Cousin Harriet. We leave in two weeks." He seized his sister by the elbows and danced her round, then dashed off down the path to the stables.

Flavia felt as though she had been turned upside down and shaken. Why had Father so suddenly changed his mind? At last she would see London, and meet her formidable Cousin Harriet, whom she knew only by repute. Then a qualm: why leave Fontclaire now that Sir Ralph was back? Should she decline the offer? But she suspected she was being sent in part as a rein on her brother. Should she withdraw, her father might cancel the entire scheme. This would hardly be fair to Lucius, who had set his heart on it, driven to revolt by what he saw as the tedium of country life.

She must speak to her father. This would not be the first time Lucius had misinterpreted some remark and set himself up for disappointment.

Charles Stanton sat by the oriel window, the pale winter sunlight leaching what little colour there was from his face. She felt a surge of mingled pity and affection.

"I wondered how long it would take you to query the news."

"We may go to London, then?"

"Yes." He took her hand and patted it. "Come, you need not look so out of countenance."

She phrased the next question carefully. "How will you manage?"

"My dear Flavia, I shall manage perfectly well. Mrs Willis will stuff me like a capon, and Betsy Turner will guard me as the lioness her cubs. Of course I shall miss you both, but I have been selfish long enough. Listening to young Fairfax recount his travels, I realised that although I am content here, there is a wider world which you and Lucius should enjoy while you are young. You have spent long enough acting as nursemaid to an invalid. I can spare you for three months: come back in the spring. Then it will be warm enough for me to venture outside."

She bent to kiss him. "Thank you, Papa."

"Besides, it is time Lucius met his cousin. You know Harriet's father was a Nabob and she his sole heir. While she has the use of the capital during her lifetime, her estate is entailed and will pass to the male line; as she never married, that means your brother. She is a woman of great good sense, and he can learn much from her. You, I am sure, will like her. She is not afraid to be different."

"By the way, Sir Ralph has sought my permission to call on you in London. I found him an intelligent and observant young man; rather more so than his father. I have assured him I have no objection. By your expression, neither do you."

Charles insisted on standing at the door to see them off, his stooped, white-haired figure frail against the dark timbers. Flavia's eyes blurred with tears. "You must write each week, and describe your adventures." She had seen the effort it took him to smile. She watched until the curve of the drive shut him off from her sight.

They passed the park gates. Fontclaire was lost behind a spur of forest and Beacon Hill shrank behind them to a bump on the horizon. At the town they joined the glossy black mail-coach with its crimson wheels, Lucius preferring to sit outside teetering on the roof. Flavia could not understand why, until the stuffy smell of leather and the uneven sway of the coach brought on a malaise that worsened with every mile. By the time they stopped at an inn-yard to change horses, and for the passengers to dine, the mere thought of food repelled her.

"May I help you to a slice of the pork?" her brother suggested maliciously.

She shook her head, seeing only bubbles of fat swirling on top of the gravy.

Her stomach heaved. Lucius, alarmed at her pallor, relented. "Come outside. The fresh air will revive you."

Away from the odours of the dining room, sipping a mug of lemon-and-ginger, her queasy stomach settled, and she could face a plate of bread-and-butter. When they resumed their seats she changed, facing forward, and travelled more easily. In the course of the afternoon her appetite returned; when they stopped for the night she enjoyed a roast of mutton and went straight to bed.

Next morning, accustomed now to the motion, she could enjoy her new surroundings. The hours passed; villages and towns clustered more closely, and the traffic on the road thickened. Lucius tapped her arm and pointed at the blur of the horizon. After her mother had died there, her father had never returned to London. *"He who is tired of London,"* she remembered reading, *"is tired of life."*

She heard the din of the city well before they reached its outskirts, and smelled the sour tang of smoke from innumerable coal-fires. Now the iron wheel-rims of the coach rattled over cobblestones. Shops and houses passed in unending rows, seemingly identical except that some were brick and some plastered in white stucco. Rivers of people flowed down both sides of the road, loud with the clatter of coaches, glossy barouches, heavy wagons, curricles, drays. Her ears buzzed with shouts and cries, and the clopping of hooves echoing back from the walls. As she craned to see the vast dome of St Paul's, looming at the end of the street, they turned into a broad archway and pulled up in a galleried courtyard.

"Where are we?" she queried.

"At *The Bull and Mouth* in St Martin-le-Grand," Lucius replied, proud to air his knowledge. Already the sweating team had been unharnessed, dwarfing the skinny youth who led them down a ramp. Flavia tried not to gape as the ground appeared to swallow them up. A passing stable-boy grinned at her. "Plenty of room, Miss," he said cheerfully. "We got four hundred horses down there."

Four hundred! Flavia had never seen so many horses together above ground, let alone below.

By the time they reached their destination, off Fitzroy Square, the short winter day had faded into a starless darkness, punctuated by house-lights. Travel-weary, Flavia climbed the marble steps. As the door opened a large white dog dashed out and almost tripped her. Flavia found herself drawn forward to kiss the dried-petal cheek of a hawk-nosed woman in late middle age with heavy-lidded eyes, dressed in old-fashioned billowing skirts topped with a fine lace *fichu à la Marie Antoinette*.

Harriet, after one searching look, exclaimed "Poor girl! You are quite done in! Off to bed with you! We will sort out your things in the morning. Wardell: see Miss Stanton up to her room."

Flavia followed the butler up two turns of narrow stairs, the light from the wall-brackets reflecting off his bald pate. He bowed her into her room, then left. Candlelight picked out the pale lemon stripes of the wallpaper and glowed on the folds of the heavy silk curtains. On the bed lay a fresh nightgown, blissfully warm. She climbed under the thick covers and closed her eyes, but jostling images crowded her head: solid rows of houses winding past, each joined to the next; a sweating cart-horse leaning into the collar, hauling a massive dray stacked with barrels; the green line of countryside, blurred by the glass; her father, frail and stooped, alone. The motion of the coach still rocked in her bones. She turned over to the other side of the bed, softer than what she was used to. From beyond the window came the unceasing rumour of the great city.

Flavia was disconcerted by Harriet's abrupt manner and odd appearance. Never before had she seen an elderly gentlewoman arrayed in Indian jewellery: necklace of chased gold, studded with tiny turquoises and rubies; and a bracelet, all twistings of gold, ending in monster-heads with pink eyes that glowed in the light.

Lucius did his best not to gape at their surroundings, but Flavia could see how he carried himself with an added spring in his step. Flavia feared that their hostess might find his manner over-familiar.

"Lucius," she urged, *sotto voce*, "stop staring like a bailiff making an inventory. And that story at breakfast was quite unsuitable."

Her brother dismissed her concerns with an insouciant wave and sauntered off. To Flavia's embarrassment, Harriet had overheard. She caught Flavia's eye and gave a dry smile.

"Your concern does you credit, my dear. But I am not yet so old that I cannot enjoy a little impertinence from a handsome young man. Besides, Lord Byron put it very well in *Don Juan.*"

"I have not read it," Flavia confessed. "Father refused to have it in the house. He considered it scandalous."

"You will find it in the library, on the third shelf from the door: Canto I, verse one hundred and twenty-five."

Flavia went straight off to look it up. As she read she laughed aloud.

*"Sweet is a legacy, and passing sweet*
*The unexpected death of some old lady."*

Her father had been right. She was enjoying Harriet's company already.

Lucius had set his heart on an outing to Vauxhall Gardens, but Harriet pointed out that at this time of the year the Gardens would be much too cold, and they were in any case unsuitable for young girls. She suggested instead Astley's equestrian display at the Royal Amphitheatre. Flavia's initial enthusiasm for the scheme waned when she heard Mrs Lennox was to accompany them as chaperone, but revived when Ralph Fairfax arrived unexpectedly to join them.

Flavia's eyes shone as she watched the horse Pegasus, so agile and clever that its attached feathery wings might almost have been real. And not even Mrs Lennox's reek of Attar of Roses could spoil Flavia's enjoyment of the skill of the Russian acrobat, who, reeling in feigned drunkenness, rode six horses at once. Ralph, who had studied Pegasus with a close eye, excused himself and disappeared to speak with the proprietor.

"I was right," he said on his return, showing an enthusiasm Flavia had not seen before. "Our Pegasus is an Andalusian." At her look of incomprehension, he went on to explain. "They are an old Spanish breed, magnificent creatures, intelligent, swift and enduring. I rode many in the Peninsula. They are not so tall at the shoulder as our thoroughbreds, but they are compact and better suited to this work." He stopped. "When I grow tedious, raise your hand."

"Like Pegasus, I am schooled to it. Lucius also discourses on horseflesh: hunters and carriage-horses, for the most part. You may rattle on about pasterns and fetlocks by the quarter-hour."

She was rewarded by his easy grin. "Once I convinced young Astley that my interest was genuine, he told me how hard it is to find good Spanish horses. So much breeding stock was sent to the Army, and all the shipping taken up with returning soldiers. He has planted the seed of an idea." He shook his head at her evident curiosity. "Not yet. It needs refining. Ah, here is the opera."

As Lucius guffawed at the burlesque, Ralph reflected. He had been looking for some purpose, something to set his ownership on Longhallows. What if he imported quality Spanish bloodstock and established a stud? To fund it he would need to part with more of the forest-land. But for the first time, he had a picture in his head of himself at Longhallows, doing what he wanted, rather than what the ghost of his father expected of him.

On the way home, giving in to Caroline's pleas, they stopped at the Frost Fair. The bright lanterns, the colour and bustle, stood out crisp against the winter night. Flavia was surprised at the number of men in uniform, many with bold, brightly-dressed young women beside them. Ralph held her arm firmly. "Stay by me." He guided her over to a stall. "Oysters a penny a gulp! Baked taters all hot!" Ralph bought her a paper twist of chestnuts, steaming in the cold night air.

He slipped the change back into his pocket.

"A penny for an old soldier!"

A hand tugged at Flavia's skirt. On the ground slouched a lank-haired man, with a patch over one eye, and a faded red coat. A thick stump swathed in dirty bandages stuck out where his left leg should have been.

Ralph tugged Flavia free and propelled her away.

"Don't give money to beggars," he said, "especially in a place like this. They'll swarm after you like flies."

"But how can he work, with only one leg?" She felt Ralph was being unfair.

"It may simply be bandaged back to look like a stump," he said reasonably. "That eye may not be blind. You would be amazed at the tricks old soldiers get up to. He may not even have been in the military. Beggars can be very plausible." He pulled out his watch. "We had better go. I promised your cousin we would be home by midnight. We can't have her coach turning into a pumpkin."

"Just one more." Flavia had just caught sight of a hoarding. "I have never seen a Monster Woman before."

"Yes you have," he countered. "One stood on your foot at Christmas."

"You should not be so unkind. I am sure Mrs Lennox is not as bad as you make her. Lucius finds her very civil."

Ralph had his own opinion of Lucius's powers of discrimination, but now was not the time to give it. Better the Monster Woman. He paid over his shilling and they entered a tent, smelly and poorly lit. At a table before a screen there sat hunched a figure of massive bulk, whose tiny eyes, deep-set behind round spectacles, occasionally caught the light. A grotesquely flattened and projecting nose rose to a low forehead; greasy curls straggled from beneath a limp bonnet.

Flavia's eyes widened.

"Stay here," Ralph whispered into her ear. "Watch." He slipped out through the crowd. She was wondering where he had gone when there was a tremendous roar from the "Monster Woman". The table with its concealing cloth tumbled over, and the "woman" leaped upright, shedding hat, curls and most of her dress, to reveal the shaven face and small furry ears of a bear.

Ralph reappeared in the hubbub, ushering her out as the enraged customers demanded their money back and the beast, excited by the din, reared to the full extent of its chain, the stool still strapped to its massive hindquarters.

They squeezed through the crush to a bench outside where Ralph collapsed, shaking with laughter.

"*You* did that!" she accused him. "You prodded it with a stick! You knew before we went in that it was a fraud, yet you sat there and let me make a fool of myself!"

"It was worth a shilling—you looked so serious —"

Her eyes glinted with anger: Flavia hated being made fun of. Had it been Lucius, she would have slapped him.

Ralph pulled out a crumpled handkerchief, dabbed his streaming eyes, and blew his nose loudly. He glanced warily at her. Another bubble of mirth welled inside him.

"It was more—" he struggled to get the words out "—it was more than I could *bear*!"

She gave an unwilling splutter of laughter in her turn, then realised with sudden astonishment that the rumpled and undignified figure doubled up on the seat beside her was suddenly, frighteningly, very dear to her.

Back in his rooms, toasting his legs in front of the fire, Ralph sipped a glass of port. He had enjoyed the evening far more than he had expected. Watching Flavia's pleasure in her surroundings; being sufficiently at ease to tease her; were new experiences for him. It was like having a younger sister. He had often wondered what it would be like to be one of a family, rather than the only child; to have someone of shared blood who knew you well, to laugh with, someone you could trust.

His mother had been quick to laugh; mercurial in her changes of mood. She had been very young when she bore Ralph, little more than a girl, buoyant with the hope of more children to please the handsome Milord who loved her so passionately. But child after child had miscarried, each further draining her health. After the fourth, the doctor had told Sir Everard, ever a proud man, that there must be no more pregnancies. She had always been prone to odd bouts of silence and sadness. Now the laughter faded and the sadness deepened. Ralph remembered once trying to ask her what was wrong.

*"There was once a fairy seal. She lived where the grey waves dance around the rocks. One day a handsome prince saw her. 'Will you leave the sea and be my bride?' he asked. 'But of course,' she said, for he was fair to look upon and he had stolen her heart. So for seven years they lived together in joy. But a curse had been laid on her that all she most loved would be taken from her, and each night the spell faded that held her to her human form. So at length the prince turned his face away, and she returned to her rock. But she could never be happy again, for with him he had taken her heart."*

*"Pauvre Maman,"* the boy had said, consoling her as best he could. She had died three years later. Ralph had always assumed this *triste* little fable was a Breton folk-tale told by her nurse. Now he wondered whether it had been her way of telling him what went wrong with her marriage. He downed the rest of the port in a toast to her memory.

Harriet, determined to expand the range of their entertainments, secured them invitations to a rout graced by an Italian soprano. The room was crowded; Flavia was cornered by a pale young man who declared himself a poet, with carefully-dressed curls, an open-necked shirt and embroidered Greek jacket.

"And what is your theme, sir?" she enquired politely.

"Liberty, Equality, Fraternity!" he proclaimed. Ralph, three feet away, looked around. "The defeat of Napoleon was a fist in the face of freedom."

Ralph was beside them now, with an expression she had not seen before. "You would feel differently," he interrupted sharply, "if *Liberty, Equality and Fraternity* were three moustachioed Hussars billeted on you, requisitioning your horses, guzzling your family's food and wine, and taking liberties with your daughter."

The poet stood his ground. "Napoleon swept away what was priest-ridden and inefficient."

"The French carried no stores, you mean, and paid for nothing. What they ate, they stole."

His antagonist reddened. "You have no idea what you are talking about," Ralph snapped as he turned away. "Keep to swans and sunsets." He took Flavia's arm. "Come, Miss Stanton. There must be more intelligent conversation elsewhere."

Flavia, taken aback by his rudeness, was unsure what to say. He stopped in an alcove and turned to face her.

"I am sorry if I offended you, but I have no patience with such dolts and their slogans. My mother's family were Breton nobility. When the Vendée rose against the Revolutionary government, all Royalists were driven from their homes. My mother escaped on a fishing-boat, disguised as a boy, but her health never recovered. Thousands were harried, starving, along the banks of the Loire, then exterminated like vermin; loaded onto barges and sunk. *Vertical Deportation*, they called it. My grandparents and my uncle were stripped, bound and cast into the river to drown by the Jacobins who went on to refine their skills in Spain."

"I knew only that your mother was French, and died young," said Flavia quietly. "It must have been hard for you."

"A month after the funeral Father sent me off to school. Let us say it facilitated his domestic arrangements. I was forever getting into fights. They called me Frog. But I see *La Signora* has arrived. Your cousin will expect a detailed account: we must not miss her performance."

By the time they made their way to the concert room, most of the seats were taken. Mrs Lennox, some distance away, was deep in conversation with a tall bewhiskered Colonel. Lucius and Caroline were not to be seen. Ralph found a place for Flavia at the end of a sofa and, following several other of the young men there, lounged Turkish-style on the carpet, leaning back against the sofa with his head on a cushion. His earlier grimness had passed: he looked up and smiled. The soprano was in fine voice, but he paid little attention to her. His mind was on Mrs Lennox's laxity in her duties. Not that he was complaining. He could feel Flavia's long leg warm against his arm, and catch her faint scent of lily-of-the-valley. For her part, Flavia was acutely aware of the weight of Ralph's shoulder and the sleek dark head just inches from her hand. She longed to reach out and stroke it.

She wrenched her attention back to the song. Just now she could not have told Harriet what language it was in.

# 5

## *England, January 1816*

Ralph pushed back his chair with a sigh. After so much writing his shoulders were stiff: he flexed them to ease it out. He folded the last letter and sealed it with his signet ring. It had been his father's, and his forefathers for three generations. The stone was chalcedony, "bloodstone", deep green speckled with flashes of bright red; its gold setting smooth with the lustre of long wear. The device stood sharp against the hard red wax: a mailed glove clutching a sword, encircled by the motto: *Fortiter Ad Finem*. Resolute to the End.

He surveyed the pile of letters and heaped documents with weary satisfaction. The estate would survive, less the town house, two farms and half the forest-lands, but there would be no more lavish house-parties and splendid balls. He had had his fill of those in Vienna anyway. No wonder his father had been so urgent in his demands that Ralph marry a rich heiress. But his upbringing with an invalid mother and no sisters, joining the Army at nineteen, had provided few opportunities to meet women of his own class. Eligible heiresses were thin on the ground in Spain, and the women he had met in Vienna had consumed money rather than provided it.

Ralph had sent Frewin away to make an inventory of the remaining farms. Such accounts as his factor had provided to date were in a fine, clerkly hand, meticulously set out. Indeed, as examples of calligraphy they might have been framed and hung on the wall. But like Frewin's appearance, they were too neat by half. How far they reflected the true state of affairs was another matter.

Ralph could not rid himself of the suspicion that his servant was taking such pains because he had something to hide. Was it carelessness or outright theft? Once the final settlement went through in a few weeks, given the reduced scale of the estate, he could dispense with Frewin altogether.

Then Ralph could do what he wanted with his life. He would look seriously at building up a stud at Longhallows. His father might have despised anything that smacked of commerce, but horse-breeding was a gentlemanly activity, and it would be better to see the stables at Longhallows used to good purpose than see them empty. He had been forced to sell off most of his father's hunters already.

Ralph's mind turned to Flavia. He remembered the concert: the smooth skin of her arm, so close. He had not seen her for a week. Really, he had seen very little of her at all; yet he felt easy in her company. During his years abroad he had missed the warmth of such simple activities as a family dinner. Was it because he linked her in his mind with the surroundings of his childhood? It was something deeper than that. He relished her curiosity and quick humour. He smiled, remembering the bear. It had been appallingly bad manners to tease her like that. But it had seemed such a good idea at the time, and she had taken it like a trooper.

Alone in his room Lucius hugged to himself what had happened. He had visited the Lennoxes at their lodgings. Caroline had been at her most enchanting; his eyes had followed her all evening. Then her mother had been called away. He had longed to tell Caroline how much he loved her; if he might just touch her hand, kiss her, as he had so often imagined... but the kiss, when it came, was real, moving from lips, dizzying, to shoulders, to breast; Lucius waiting for her to protest, and feeling instead her body move against his.

He had never meant to go so far. It had happened so quickly, so unexpectedly. He should feel ashamed of himself for taking advantage of her, but triumph pulsed with every heartbeat; he was afire with exultation. She loved him; there was nothing more she could have done to show it. With what pride he cradled her repentant head on his shoulder afterwards, kissing away her tears. He had met her mother's gaze when she returned. Had he not promised Caroline he would marry her?

In the drawing room Flavia was playing with the dog, tossing a leather ball for Hester to catch, and trying with varying degrees of success to induce her to give it back. The dog, a white Arabian hunting-dog named for Lady Stanhope, was one of Harriet's Eastern trappings, along with her Indian jewellery, the inlaid cabinets, and the curved daggers on the wall. That Hester chewed the peacock-feathers in their brass vases, and shed hairs over the Persian carpets, her mistress did not mind.

Lucius looked in. Flavia had just retrieved the ball, but it was tacky with dog-spittle. Had she been more observant, Flavia might have noticed that her brother had taken particular care over his appearance.

"Have you seen my new gloves?" he queried, peering down the back of a chair.

"No," she said, looking around for something to wipe her hands on. Then in an effort to be helpful: "Have you asked Wardell?"

"He says he gave them to that maid of yours to sew on a button. She vows she gave them back. Simpson has been quite surly since we came to London."

"Perhaps she misses her family."

"Give a country girl the chance of a lifetime and she sulks. Some people are never satisfied," snorted Lucius, with the vigour of an uneasy conscience. He had tried to steal a kiss from pretty Molly; she had slapped his face and told him to keep his hands to himself. Heading back up to his room he reflected that his sister, with her experience in running a household, was normally quick to register such undercurrents.

There was a murmur of voices in the vestibule. Flavia darted to the top of the staircase. It was not Ralph, but Bromley, come to collect her brother. She hoped her disappointment did not show. With Harriet resting in her bedroom upstairs, and Lucius not yet returned, she must act as hostess.

"A fine morning, Miss Stanton. Would you care to ride with us?"

"Thank you, sir, but no. I am expecting guests." Well, one, anyway. She was hoping Ralph had returned to London, and did not want to be out if he called.

"Another time, perhaps."

To her relief she heard her brother's footfall on the stair. "Here is Lucius now." She rose, ready to usher them both out, when Wardell announced the arrival of Sir Ralph Fairfax.

Ralph nodded in curt acknowledgement as the others passed, then turned on her as the door closed.

"What was he doing here?" She was nettled by Ralph's brusque tone. She had so looked forward to seeing him; now she was being snapped at for no reason.

"I fail to see that it is any of your business." Then, just as she was reproaching herself for her hasty tongue, his expression eased.

"I beg your pardon. It was unmannerly for me to say such a thing. I forget I am not still in an Army camp." The moment had passed, but he could see her constraint remained. "A thousand pardons? Twelve hundred?" Her face softened in the beginnings of a smile. He had not noticed before that one of her brows was level, the other slightly flared. "Let us see if your cousin can spare you for three hours. I have hired a boat to row you downriver to the Tower."

Seated on the thwarts of their elegant varnished skiff, with a freeboard so low she could touch the water, Flavia stared at the bustling river-traffic. They overhauled a long, black, bluff-bowed barge, its stubby masts growing treelike from either end of a sloping mountain of hay. Nimbly Ralph slipped between two sturdy open boats, their heaped cargo of fish glistening silver against the dark red of gaff-rigged sails. The long overhanging bow of a wherry drew up alongside: the two gentlemen passengers doffed their hats to Flavia as they passed. Wharves and jetties lined the banks, with slick barnacled piles, black with age. Here loomed the sterns of great ships, their masts and rigging a tangle of ropes and spars; there gangs of men hefted bales bigger than themselves, bearing them, like ants, down impossibly narrow gangways.

Flavia was impressed by Ralph's dexterity in threading amongst the throng of vessels. "Have you spent much time on the river?" she asked curiously.

He gave a wry smile. "My mother grew up on the Breton coast. Her brother Alexandre taught her to swim and sail. She said the sea saved her life, and was her friend. From when I was a boy she insisted that I learn to swim and handle boats. My father was happy to humour her, so long as I was taught to ride."

The light, and the activity around them, were cut short. Now they were in the gloom of the Tower. Seen from the level of the water, the pallid cliff of ancient stone reared and tilted against the sky. A chill gripped her. Twin mighty turrets, the nearest only feet away, rose sheer from the water, their deep arrow-slits and tiny square gridded windows a brutal declaration of royal power. Here prisoners of state were brought to learn the folly of defiance. The hopelessness of their coming, the pain of their torment and the despair of their deaths had seeped into the stone.

They pulled in beneath the archway of Traitor's Gate. In the dank tunnel the imprisoned water slopped and fretted. She shivered.

"You look unhappy. What is the matter?"

"This is a horrible place. It weighs upon the spirit. May we leave now?" As he turned the boat, she tried to lighten the mood. "You will think me childish to be frightened so. I daresay you saw many such castles in your travels."

He was silent for some moments as he guided the boat back. His reply when it came was unexpectedly serious. "Like this? Not really— only one. It is not a story I have told anyone else." He found a sheltered spot in the lee of some stairs, and rested on the oars. "I knew a castle haunted by cruelty. It was in Spain, at a town called Badajoz, three years ago.

"We were besieging the city; our Colonel had gone to meet someone beyond the lines, and not returned. I was sent into the town in the guise of a peasant, with a Spanish guide, to discover where the French were holding him. We were challenged and taken to the citadel for questioning by a French officer. I was very young, very dirty, and very frightened, dressed in rags that stank of incontinent donkey. They took Juan first; he was older and looked to know more. They tied my hands and set me under guard in the next room. I have never forgotten his screams. The guard was laughing. *You next,* he said.

"As an English officer out of uniform they would have hung me. I was desperate; I rushed him. He slashed my shoulder but I was taller; I caught my foot behind his heel and threw him. As he tried to call for help, I set my roped wrists across his throat. Horsemen have strong hands." Involuntarily Ralph glanced down at his fingers, seeing again the dark eyes beneath him, widening in terror; bulging: then blank and staring in death. "I cut myself free with his bayonet and took his gear." He remembered clawing through the man's pocket for the key, locking the door behind him, trying to block out the shrieks from the other room.

"I knew I should rescue Juan, but there were three of them in there. Then the attack came. There was a great roar over the din of the fighting as our army forced the breach. I slipped out the castle gate, down to the city. They chased me, but it was dark and pouring with rain." He remembered the shouts, the sky ablaze, the whining fragments of an exploding shell, his astonishment, light-headed, as he realised the blood tracing down his arm was his own. "Somehow I managed to swim the river and cross the lines without being shot by my own side. We went back the next day and found Juan's body. They had put out his eyes."

Wavelets slapped the side of the boat.

"Did you find your Colonel?" she asked, gently, to bridge the silence.

"In time. He and his Spanish companion had been betrayed. A squadron of French hussars was waiting for them. He was in uniform, so they tied him up, then tortured his friend to death in front of him. After many adventures, he escaped."

He looked at her directly. "To this day I question myself about that evening."

It was not courage as Sir Everard understood it. But then this new war of all against all was not campaigning as he understood it, either. Ralph doubted his father had ever gone to battle without a dozen changes of silk stockings. "Thank you for having the patience to listen." He pulled out his watch. "We should return."

The topic was obviously closed. Flavia wondered how it would feel to kill someone. The most frightening thing that had ever happened to her was her horse bolting when she was fourteen. She had taken the comfort and safety of her upbringing entirely for granted. Thank God the war was over and all that horror now in the past.

They journeyed upriver in shared silence. Back at the jetty Ralph secured the rope to the mooring-ring and reached down to hand her up. As she stepped the boat rocked to a ripple, and she stumbled. Catching her body against his to steady her, he was startled by a quick stab of desire. She felt his hands tighten around her. He cupped her face in his hands and drew her to him in a gentle embrace. Her immediate response to his kiss threw her into turmoil. Between one instant and the next her skin had come alive. She could feel the rise and fall of his breathing. Then a long sigh.

He gathered her hands together, kissed them, and let them fall. Carefully he stepped back, leaving her reluctant and breathless.

"I must take you home."

"So he disapproved of my purchasing the bronzes?"

"Indeed, Mr Bromley," said Frewin, with a hint of indignation. "Sir Ralph fair flew at me when I told him. He has sold the town house already, and plans to sell two of the farms, to raise capital. But he has stipulated—begging your pardon, sir—they must not go to you. I'm sorry, sir; I did my best to change his mind."

"Do not trouble yourself with excuses," Bromley said.

"Our dealings were far easier, sir, when Sir Ralph was overseas," said Frewin with feeling. "He even threatened my position, after all the years my father and I have served them! And I hoped to approach him about a family matter. He was less than accommodating." Frewin paused.

"Go on," said Bromley, with a faint smile.

"My wife has a cousin, sir, as close to her as a brother. This gallant young man, just back from the wars, got into a scuffle in London. Trying to protect a young lady of his acquaintance, he most unfortunately injured a ruffian, who subsequently died."

"And the cousin?"

Frewin went on, reluctantly. "He was found guilty of murder, from perjured evidence by a criminal gang. He has been consigned to the *Justitia* hulk, awaiting transportation. I withdrew a small loan, to ease the conditions of his imprisonment."

"And now Fairfax wants his money back?"

Frewin looked down at the table.

"How much?"

"Two hundred pounds." He hurried on as Bromley's eyebrows rose. "Payment for easement of irons, sir, then a doctor when he caught the gaol fever, and warm clothes and some decent food; my wife is quite sick with worry. Sir Everard was not so hard-hearted. He knew that generosity becomes a gentleman."

"And what is this young man's name?"

"Fletcher, sir. Ralph Fletcher. He served bravely in the Seventh Division in Spain."

There was a silence.

"Ralph, eh?" Bromley sat back, considering. "Meet me in the City tomorrow."

# 6

## *London, January 1816*

Ralph stared into the fire. A number of unexpected things had happened that afternoon. Telling Flavia about Badajoz had eased some of the guilt and dread which so burdened his memory of that place. He had not meant to speak of it: the words had flowed, responding to a sensibility he and Flavia held in common. He felt a wash of gratitude to her for hearing him out without revulsion. He already acknowledged her intelligence and eagerness for experience. But this was something more.

The past was behind him now; the terrors of Badajoz and the follies of Vienna together. It was time for a new start.

Then, more urgently, he remembered their shared intimacy: the kiss; her response; the flood of his own desire. He had not planned that either. Clearly he could not go on thinking of Flavia as only his neighbour's daughter. He felt a burning impatience to see her again. He wanted to explore that long body; he could have gone further, much further.

*I am no longer bound by my father's ultimatum to wed a rich heiress. I could marry Flavia.* The notion, initially so surprising, had a rightness to it. He grinned at a sudden incongruous picture of the squire and his lady, with a brood of little Fairfaxes in their best clothes in descending order of size, with a dog on either side; in the background the Longhallows stud, with a groom holding a grey Andalusian with liquid eyes, strong arched neck and flowing mane.

Here was the answer to his discontent. No longer need he resent his father's demands and infidelities. He was dead now: they belonged to the past. For the first time Ralph pitied his father, caught in an appalling dilemma. So attractive to women, passionately desiring his wife, he knew that if he made love to her, she would die. No wonder Marie-Claude had pined away. Everard's mistresses had been a simulacrum for what he craved but could not have. And then his career had ended in a botched attempt to die with honour.

Ralph ran his thumb over the face of his signet. Let the dead bury their dead. It was time to marry Flavia and begin their life together. He would leave London tomorrow to settle the few details remaining at Longhallows, and seek out the ring Everard had given his mother: a superb sapphire surrounded by brilliants. His fine-boned mother had found it heavy on her hand, and rarely wore it. Flavia's long fingers would set it off to perfection. He could see himself now, slipping it on her finger, relishing her joy.

Her face highlighted by a single candle, Flavia stared intently at her reflection in the oval glass. Ralph's touch had woken a promise of fierce delight, tantalising and dangerous at the same time. Excited, scared and ashamed, she was overwhelmed by feelings she did not understand. Gentlewomen who acted on such impulses were disgraced, or disappeared into a half-hinted underworld of mistresses and street-women. What was wrong with her? Had her mother been still alive, she could have sought her counsel. But Flavia was too embarrassed to confess her concerns to Harriet, elderly and unmarried as she was. What would her cousin think? In all likelihood she would send her straight home.

Robert Bromley looked around his mother's salon. No jarring vulgarity betrayed the origin of the fortune that paid for it.

Dorothea Bromley, reclined on a sofa, looked up at her portrait: a strikingly beautiful young woman on horseback, beside her a handsome blond-haired boy on a dappled pony. Robert settled the lace shawl where it had slipped from her shoulder.

"How close is he to settlement?"

"Three weeks, Frewin says."

"And what do you propose to do about it?"

"He has barely arrived back in the country. We men of business keep track of our competitors. He has been showing an interest in the Stanton girl."

"*He* has not wasted his time, at any rate," she countered. "Should he marry her, and father a child, all my sacrifice and your efforts will have been in vain."

"Mother, you must invite Ralph Fairfax to your ball."

She pushed her embroidery-basket aside. "Why? It would be an insult to me to have him in my house. You should be master at Longhallows, not he."

"I hold information to his disadvantage. If you will agree to bring him here, I will so compromise him with Charles Stanton that there will be no marriage."

"Is this the best you can do?" she goaded him. "Your last chance to redeem your inheritance, and you trust in a few words? After all these years of being sneered at as *Josiah the tradesman's son?* You will only scotch the snake, not kill it."

Robert's expression tightened under the familiar weight of her demands. He pulled up a chair, sat beside her, and took her hand, heavy with rings.

"I will do better than that."

"But what?"

He smiled, once more in control. "Wait till it is done. When have you ever known my undertakings to fail?"

She looked up with a sudden qualm. "Robert, you would not. You would lose all in the discovery."

He stood up, tall, reassuring. "Do not distress yourself. It will take time; I must act circumspectly; but I will succeed. I will welcome you to Longhallows to take your rightful place, as my father should have done."

He smiled at the elegance of his plan. The Law had deprived him of his inheritance; the Law would give it back.

Ralph had run out of excuses. He must honour his overdue promise to see Lucius. For all his growing pleasure in Flavia's company, he found Lucius awkward. Ralph was too young to act the uncle, yet too remote in experience to play the older brother. In Spain you grew up fast, or not at all. He settled on Harry Angelo's. It was time he worked off the *Sahnetorten* he had scoffed in Vienna. A few bouts with *epeé* and sabre should satisfy the joint requirements of refreshing his fencing skills and being adequately civil to a puppyish neighbour. After all, acquiring some gentlemanly polish was one reason Lucius had been sent to London.

In the event Lucius gave a good account of himself; the proprietor dropping an approving nod and some tips. When Lucius rejoined Ralph, he was glowing with exertion and pride. As Ralph fastened his shirt, Lucius's eye fell on the faint puckered line along his collarbone. Ralph had no intention of disclosing to Lucius, as he had to his sister, how he had come by the scar. He would rather make a joke of it. He leaned forward and lowered his voice to a whisper.

"I got that in a duel over the love of a beautiful woman."

Lucius jumped as if stung.

"Come on, Stanton, where's your sense of humour?"

"I thought—" Lucius shifted uncomfortably.

Ralph scented more than youthful prudery. "What did you think?"

"Nothing. Just something I heard." He tried to turn away.

"From whom?"

Lucius's face was burning. "It doesn't matter... I'm sure they were mistaken."

Ralph's voice took on a military edge. "About what?"

For all his embarrassment, Lucius resented the cutting tone. "Some fellows at the Club. They saw her last week, here, in London. The—" he almost said '*woman you were with in Vienna*' but amended it hastily to "—Laure Augsberg."

Ralph, stony-faced, finished dressing in silence. Lucius could tell he was angry, but the voice, when he spoke, was cold.

"I might point out that in all my dealings with the King's German Legion I never heard talk of a Major Lennox. Perhaps I should tell your father. Good day."

Ralph worked off his temper in a long gallop in the park. So Laure had followed him. Damn the woman. News of her arrival would spread quickly. How long would it be until Flavia knew? Would Lucius tell her, in a fit of misguided zeal? Would their father get to know of it, and forbid Ralph to see any more of his daughter?

The sooner Ralph settled his affairs the better. Only then could he ask Flavia to marry him; with her consent, he would be in a much stronger position to talk her father round, should he raise any difficulty. Meanwhile he must send Laure packing. So flamboyant a woman would not be hard to find. He sighed, angry at himself for getting entangled with her in the first place, annoyed at Lucius making him feel a fool, and irritated at this unsavoury complication just as he saw his way clear. Unwillingly he recalled his last interview with Laure. The next would be equally unpleasant.

Flavia was reading to Harriet in the morning room when she caught snatches of argument from the vestibule. She went to investigate, pulling her shawl tighter against the chill air seeping round the open door. Wardell was waving away a shock-haired youth.

"I must apologise for disturbing you, Miss Stanton."

"Stanton?" The boy stepped up to the porch. "Know a Mister Lucius Stanton, Miss?"

"Of course. He's my brother."

"Please Miss, give him this?" She took the letter from his outstretched hand; by the time she looked up, he had gone. Puzzled, she told Harriet what had happened.

"Lucius will thank you for that, my girl," Harriet said dryly. "I am willing to wager that you have just accepted on his behalf a summons for debt."

Not gambling again! "What shall I do with it?" This was quite outside Flavia's experience.

"Set it by his place at dinner, my dear," Harriet replied with relish, "and prepare for a display of temper."

The summons lay like an accusation between them.

"Why did you take it?"

"It was addressed to you."

"Why do you always have to interfere?"

"I am not as familiar as you are with such things," she snapped back, refusing to take the blame for his misjudgement. "You should have considered how much money you had before you hazarded it."

There was truth enough in this to hurt. Lucius had been alarmed at how quickly his pile of ivory fish had shrunk. He was only playing short whist. He knew that debts over a hundred pounds must be paid in full the next morning. He had hoped to make up his losses at *écarté*, but they were playing too high. Still, he was in no mood to be lectured by his sister.

"Tattle-taleing to Father again, I suppose? How I spend my time is none of your business! Point the finger at my friends, and we shall see what we can discover about yours!" He snatched up the envelope and strode out.

Flavia was shaken, both by her brother's vehemence and his implied threat. Lucius knew something; that was sure. He could only mean Ralph. Little doubts flared up, like flames in tinder. Then she remembered their afternoon on the Thames, when she had felt so close to him.

Wardell returned, with another note on a tray. This was addressed to her and her brother together. She opened the seal. On an embossed card was an invitation to a select ball, at Bromley's town house, to celebrate his mother's birthday.

She sighed. It would, she knew, be the highlight of their visit to London. Lucius would demand to take Caroline, and expect Flavia to accompany them. But would Ralph be there? However impolite her action might be, she could not go without him, to dance all night with other men.

The next morning Lucius left early. She was staring out the window at the dull brick buildings under a grey sky when Ralph walked in.

"I have been invited to Bromley's ball. I take it you have also."

Her pleasure was so transparent he gave a rueful smile. "And here was I, hoping you would not want to go."

"Why not?"

He made a face and shrugged. "In all honesty I could not tell you. I don't like the man. Ever since I came back he has been under my feet, like a rucked-up carpet. But given his standing, and the proximity of our estates, I cannot avoid dealing with him. My father despised old Josiah because he made his fortune in trade. I suspect he was jealous of his wealth. I had better attend, in the interests of civility."

He grinned at her delighted smile. "And I shall have to pay my respects to his harpy of a mother. She never could abide me, from the day I startled her horse with my slingshot and she came off in the ditch."

"You didn't!"

"I was aiming at the dog, and missed."

Her smile faded. "Has Lucius said anything to you about money?" She looked crestfallen as he shook his head.

"Is he in debt again?"

She told him briefly what had happened. "Lucius holds it is none of my business, but sooner or later Father must come to hear of it, and there will be the most dreadful row. It was bad enough last time." She did not add that the first consequence would be their immediate return home.

Ralph considered the problem. He reproached himself for not taking up Lucius sooner. By providing the older companionship he craved, he might have distracted him from the high-flyers with tastes beyond his pocket. London and Bromley's patronage had gone to his head. And the Lennox girl: how far had that gone? Mrs Lennox was keeping a suspiciously lax watch over her daughter's virtue. That was the real reason Ralph had decided to attend Bromley's ball: to ensure that someone looked after Flavia other than her negligent brother. Unfortunately, after Ralph's harsh words, it was doubtful that Lucius, headstrong at the best of times, would listen to anything he had to say.

But he owed him some gesture. Lucius would shortly become his brother-in-law. Better to heal the split now than let it widen into an open breach.

"Could you at least speak to him?" pleaded Flavia.

"I can but try." As he left, he felt a reluctant sympathy for Lucius, so desperate to be accepted as a man among men, but lacking an opening to prove himself. A pity his father had kept him out of the Army. He was warm-hearted, with pleasing manners, and looks better than were good for him; he would have profited by a challenge other than that of spending money not his own.

His sister: it was time to declare himself. Why not at the ball? It would be totally unexpected, seizing the initiative, taking the first step in his new life. That Flavia would accept he had no doubt.

Gently he brushed away her anxious frown.

"Don't worry. All will be well."

# 7

# England, February 1816

From his Grand Tour, Everard had brought back four magnificent cabinets, two from Italy, two from France. He had installed them in a room opening off the first-floor landing. As a child Ralph remembered running his palm over the cool panels of many-coloured stone, fingering their twisted columns of gilded bronze; his father barking at him for leaving smears on the glass. Inside Everard had locked the family treasures. Now Ralph held the keys. His mother's ring would be here somewhere.

He found it at length in a faded velvet box, together with a shabby book, *Sorrows of Werter*, and a coiled shell. He tilted it: gritty sand trickled onto his hand. Ralph had a strong sense that he was intruding. These oddly-assorted objects had been precious to his father. Why, he would never know.

Carefully he lifted out the ring he had last seen as a child. The deep blue fire lit as he held it to the light. What a superb stone: the long curves and pointed ends of the marquise-cut sapphire glowed against the surrounding ripple of *pavé* diamonds. He could see it now on Flavia's hand, glinting against the rich chestnut hair tumbling loose over her shoulders. This line of thought was distracting. He must press Charles Stanton for an early wedding.

Lucius sat astounded. She had drawn him aside as soon as he arrived, to pour out her momentous news. He was at once delighted and appalled.

"With child?" he repeated. "Are you sure?"

Caroline blushed. "It is beyond the time of the month. I have been ill in the mornings."

Lucius felt a rush of annoyance with the girl for having got with child. They had made love only the once! Then he reproached himself for being so heartless; it was he who had seduced her. Staring down into her tear-brimming eyes, he could repeat his folly on the instant.

"Don't worry, my darling. We will work things out. And you may yet be mistaken." He said this only to cheer her; he was as ignorant as she of the mysteries of growth and birth. They exchanged tight, worried smiles.

What would Caroline's mother say? And his father? Lucius was smitten by a further qualm: had Fairfax passed on his innuendoes about Major Lennox?

At the sharp knock on his street door, Ralph set down his towel. He was not expecting any calls so early in the morning; he had just finished shaving, and was still in his shirtsleeves. Now he was back in London, and his affairs at last settling into some order, he really must do something about hiring a valet. With his mind on placing an advertisement in *The Morning Post*, he opened the door.

"What are *you* doing here?" he burst out.

Laure Augsberg, resplendent in burgundy velvet, was the last person he expected, or wanted.

She pouted. "*Mon chère* Ralph, are you not happy to see me?"

"I don't tell lies," he retorted. "You do, fluently. I have nothing more to say to you. Go away."

As he went to shut the door she slipped in an elegantly-booted foot. "Do you want *tout le monde* to hear?" She drew out a pretty enamelled watch. She had wheedled him into buying it from Neuling's the jeweller, whose *clientèle* had much deeper pockets than his; startled at the price, he had all but collided with the resplendent figure of Eugène de Beauharnais, erstwhile Viceroy of Italy. The memory did nothing to improve Ralph's temper. "It is cold outside. Give me ten minutes only. I have a proposition to make."

He stood back with an ill grace. "That, and no more. You have taken up more than enough of my time—and money—already."

She brushed against him as she entered. He remembered that heavy perfume. Then it had seemed exotic and alluring. Now it was cloying and stale.

"Do you remember the Palais Palm, and the nights after? I am free this evening." She moved closer.

"Never 'free'," he replied cuttingly, as he pushed her away. "All your lovers got from you was a bill in the morning for more pleasure than they received."

Her smile abruptly faded. "Do not think you were the only one. There are stories I could tell—"

"'I thought you had told them already, to Baron Hager of the *Oberste Polizei.*"

She coloured, but quickly recovered her composure.

"Money for services rendered?" he taunted. "Or more specifically, blackmail? Why should I pay, even if I wanted to? I could not trust you to keep your mouth shut for a week. You would be back after the next jeweller's bill. Your ten minutes is up; I suggest you leave."

She made a show of consulting her watch, then turned and blew him a kiss from the doorstep. *"Wiederschauen."*

In the passing hackney Bromley let fall the corner of the blind.

"Those are Fairfax's rooms. That woman is Laure Augsberg, his mistress in Vienna. This is an early hour for an unchaperoned woman to be leaving a gentleman's chambers; particularly one of her reputation. Fairfax has an interest in your sister, has he not? Have you seen him of late?"

Dumbfounded, Lucius shook his head. That had been Ralph at the door, all right, with the white of his shirt against the jamb betraying his undress.

Bromley's smooth voice gave shape to his thoughts.

"He has been keeping other company, perhaps?" He knocked on the glass.

"Drive on."

"Simplicity, my dear!" Harriet smiled at the girl hovering anxiously over the gown laid out on the bed. "You have youth, fine eyes, and that splendid hair. The white silk will set them off. I will lend you my Kashmir shawl for a touch of colour, and my mother's diamond *aigrette* to set off your *coiffure*. Do not fret over fancy gowns and elaborate jewels. You have no need of them."

Flavia had felt on edge all week. Lucius had twice sought her out with the air of having something to impart, then veered off into commonplace remarks. She was once more apprehensive, suspecting it concerned Ralph. Her feelings for him were new and intense; she would see him at the ball, she knew, but needed the reassurance of his presence. Her future happiness depended on someone she barely knew. This awareness, powerful yet undefined, frightened her.

On the night of the ball, Flavia felt lethargic and out of sorts, a touch nauseous: the wrong time of the month, just when she needed all to go well. She dressed with unusual care, conscious of the grand company she would be keeping. The shawl glowed with lustrous silks patterned with silver and gold thread; she had never seen so beautiful a fabric. The *aigrette* was a delicately crafted spray of flowers picked out in diamonds, mounted on a tortoise-shell pin. Harriet set it in place in her hair.

"Take good care of this, my dear." She stepped back. "Turn around," she commanded. "Drop a curtsey. Splendid. Now off you go, and enjoy yourself. Dorothea Bromley may be frosty, but you can be sure of an excellent supper."

Flavia gave her cousin a nervous smile, and descended the main staircase, remembering Harriet's advice not to dash. Ralph, in a smart new coat she had not seen before, stood by the hall table, fingering something in his pocket. He turned and gave her an appraising stare. She felt his eyes travel down the length of her body.

"How well you look this evening, Miss Stanton," Ralph said as he handed her into the carriage. He longed to run his hands up that slender neck, to where the jewels nestled, to feel the weight of those dark tresses. I want to ask her to marry me now, slip the ring on her finger... But her nuisance of a brother was right beside them, and he saw how tense she was. Better do it later, when she is more at ease, and we can be alone.

The carriage set off. Lucius sat absorbed in his own thoughts. Ralph whistled as he looked out of the window. Flavia watched the stripes of light and shadow from the streets outside chase each other across his cheek and jaw. He turned suddenly.

"A soldier's song from Spain. Does it bother you?"

"No," she said hurriedly, though in her touchy mood, it had grated.

They stood in line at the top of the staircase. The banked candles and brilliant chandeliers glared in the long mirrors. The press and heat, after the chill of the air outside, made Flavia feel slightly ill.

Lucius nudged her to where Bromley stood beside his mother, exquisitely dressed, younger-looking than Flavia had expected, with the classic features she had passed onto her son. Flavia was disconcerted by the simultaneous glances of two pairs of strikingly blue eyes. She dropped into a curtsey, as Harriet had taught her. Her murmured words of welcome were ignored as both heads turned towards Ralph behind her. Flavia passed on into the ballroom with a sense of relief.

"Does she do that to all the guests," murmured Ralph as he caught up with her, "or only old acquaintances? She looked fit to turn me into stone, though Bromley was very civil. He has a plan for bridging Whitmonk's Brook; it would save four miles getting our wagons to market. He will show me the details on Tuesday. Wait here while I get you a card."

Flavia followed him with her eyes through the throng, to see him waylaid by a bewigged foreign-looking gentleman, his coat covered in orders, who clapped Ralph on the shoulder. Ralph was at ease here; he knew these people.

"My dear Miss Stanton!" Mrs Lennox rushed up, shining in dark green satin with a tambour trim. "You must meet these charming people from Bath. They knew your father, in his younger years."

Lucius, fetching Caroline a glass of water, stopped short. Surely that was not Laure Augsberg, in a distractingly low-cut dress and a set of fine rubies. He put down the glass before he spilled any more of it. He must warn Flavia. It was his duty as her brother to let her know what was going on. The cheek of it! Fairfax parading his mistress at a select gathering like this, under the eyes of the girl he was courting! Such behaviour might pass muster in Vienna, where morals were notoriously lax. He would not tolerate the insult to his sister; not here in London.

It took Ralph ten minutes to escape the garrulous Count. As he cut back across the room a familiar voice pulled him up.

"Good evening, *milord*. I said we would meet again." Laure glanced down at the dance-card in his hand. "You will write me in for the waltz?" She pressed close, brushing a speck of dust off his collar.

"I told you: not another penny." The Count had eyes like a hawk, and knew Laure of old; he would make a fine morsel of scandal of their meeting. And where was Flavia?

Laure pouted. "Good enough for the officer's mess, but not for fine houses?"

He remembered these tirades. His temper rose. "There is nothing for you here. If you need money to leave the country, I will provide it."

"So you have made other arrangements. Some fresh country girl, perhaps?"

He fought an urge to slap her.

"Go!" he snapped.

Flavia sat aghast. "I'm sorry," Lucius said quietly. "But you had to know. I considered it was merely Club gossip until I saw her myself the other morning, leaving his rooms. I never thought for a moment he would have arranged to meet her here."

She stared across the room at Ralph with this strange woman, their heads so close; saw her reach up and touch him in a gesture of casual intimacy, almost a caress. From this new, raw part of herself, an ugly question sprang out: this woman, older, so beautiful, so assured; had Ralph kissed her as he had kissed Flavia by the river? She shied away from the thought. She must keep calm, take it in her stride, but it mattered too much. She felt clumsy, inadequate, out of her depth.

"I am your brother. It was my duty," Lucius repeated, confirming the purity of his motives. It had just occurred to him that with Ralph out of the picture, the slur about Major Lennox would never reach his father. Flavia felt she had swallowed a stone. So this was what Lucius had been hinting at! The dark coat and crimson gown had drawn apart. She must pretend she had not seen them. She tried to blank her mind, but jealousy swamped her. Those intimacies she so longed for, and was afraid to admit to herself: he had shared them with this woman, and was doing so still.

She darted to the other side of the pillar, and leaned against it, faint with shock. How could she not believe it, when Lucius had seen her leaving Ralph's rooms? Tears pricked her eyelids. She must not cry, not here, in front of all these people.

Ralph shoved through the press, his rage kindling. He remembered Lucius's innuendoes after their fencing bout. Had Stanton set this up, to humiliate him in public? There she was.

"Flavia! I must speak with you." He laid his hand on an arm as stiff as wood. Surprised, he looked at her face; it was set and unyielding. He swore under his breath. She must have seen them together; here there would be no shortage of gossips to provide the name of his *confidante*.

"Call a carriage. I want to go home."

"You cannot leave so early. People will talk."

"They already have. She followed you from Vienna, didn't she?" She could smell the musky perfume on his clothes. Flushed and close to tears, Flavia blazed with hostility.

Not more weeping women and public scenes. He bridled at the accusation. His pride had been mauled enough. His temper flared.

"Well-bred young women do not concern themselves with such affairs."

She retorted, too hurt to be careful. "Well-bred young men should not indulge in them!"

He gripped her wrist hard. "Look, my little Methodist, what right have you to lecture me in this fashion? No wonder your brother resents your interference in his affairs! I have not yet proposed to you, that you might reproach me with my infidelities!"

His anger scared her. All her surety had been knocked away. How could she trust him? A dreadful weight of loss dragged her down, distorting everything around her. Acid with hurt, the words spilt out: "Nor would I accept if you did!"

"Very well, then: I see I have my answer."

They stared at each other, appalled by the chasm which had opened between them. Flavia pulled away from his grip, white-faced. All the promise of their lives together, gone.

"You will regret this," she said quietly.

She pushed through the knots of people, her limbs working mechanically, like a puppet's. Some string pulled from outside caused her to smile at one, curtsey at another. She reached the vestibule and summoned Harriet's coachman. He looked startled, but her evident pallor convinced him of the urgency of her request.

During the ride home she felt only numb horror. Harriet, thank God, had fallen asleep in front of the fire. Flavia tiptoed past. Not until she gained the privacy of her own room did the enormity of what she had said, and done, strike her. The tears that had pressed hot behind her eyelids spilled out. It was a long time before the angry words echoing inside her head died to a bleak calm. Dragged down at length by her own heaviness of heart, she fell asleep.

The footman at the door, concerned by this sudden departure, reported back to Bromley. Robert was buoyed up by the gambler's instinct; Fortune was running his way. Within the next hour, it lay within his power to rid himself of the usurper. With his message the footman had brought a shawl, and a diamond brooch with a loose pin, their loss unremarked in the girl's distress. He rang a bell.

"Fetch Mr Stanton. Immediately."

Where was Flavia? Surely she had not left by herself? Now his temper had cooled, Ralph bitterly regretted his outburst. He had behaved like an oaf.

He searched everywhere, desperate to ask her forgiveness. But there was a curse on this evening that blighted everything he put his hand to. At least there was no sign of the hateful Laure.

There was Lucius. Ralph swallowed dislike and pride together.

"Stanton! Have you seen your sister?"

Lucius gave him a strange look. As well he might, Ralph reflected with bitter self-reproach. Lucius drew a folded paper from his pocket.

"I have a note for you." He handed it over, hesitant. Ralph snatched it and strode off to a corner. *"Meet me at the grotto."* He let out his breath in a long sigh of relief.

The night air broke over him in a cooling wave. His spirits soared as he hurried down the deserted path: he would explain everything, tell Flavia the truth about Laure, as he should have done before.

The windows of the house glowed behind him. Ahead, through a dark latticework of boughs, he glimpsed a row of cypress, a single candle flickering inside the mouth of a little cave, its walls set with crystal: the shimmer of light on an Indian shawl; a glitter of diamonds.

His hand closed over the ring in his pocket. He drew it out as he ran. *She must still love me, to come out alone like this.*

Then the shock of a blow, and a blaze of pain.

The sapphire ring rolled forward on the gravel. Robert picked it up. He smiled in satisfaction. Here was an unexpected prize. Kneeling by the sprawled body, he stripped off Ralph's signet and quickly emptied his pockets.

He stood again and dusted his knees. "Here, take this," he said, tossing a *rouleau* of guineas to the woman staring down at the lover who had despised her. "Draw the balance upon my bank in Paris. Now be gone. Stay out of England, lest the climate damage your looks."

She pushed the brooch and shawl into his hands, picked up her skirts, and fled through the open gate.

With a crunch of footsteps Lucius arrived, panting.

"Have you seen Fl—" His query died as he gaped at Ralph's inert body. "What happened?"

"Your sister went home. Return these to her as unobtrusively as you can. She would feel badly about having mislaid them." Robert thrust the bundle at him. Lucius started as the pin of the brooch pricked his thumb. Robert looked down.

"Don't worry about him; he will wake up tomorrow somewhere unexpected, with a sore head. It is time someone took that arrogant young man down a peg."

Two rough men stepped from the shadows. They hauled Ralph upright. There was a coach at the gate. Bromley turned and held out his hand.

"Thank you Stanton, for your assistance, and—" the grip tightened "—your confidence. Your prompt action has saved your sister from severe embarrassment. I will meet you on Tuesday to discuss the other matter you mentioned. Now," he said pleasantly, "I must give my mother her birthday gifts." Both of them: the one he had planned, and the other which had fallen into his hand.

# 8

# *"Adelphi", at sea, early 1816*

*Running: must explain... branches, a flash of diamonds; his head... A coach jarring over cobbles; his skull pulsing. A hard rim; swallow or choke; bitter aftertaste. His shoulder-blade prickled. A low laugh. Then a torch flaring in his eyes; the stink of mud. A thwart dipped under his weight. Head forced back, spluttering raw spirit. Voices, drifting. Remember, a long time... Another creak, closer.*

The floor lurched.

The slap of waves and groan of stressed wood: at last Ralph placed it, a ship under way. The *Countess of Perth*, carrying him to Spain. His first impulse was to lapse back into its familiar rocking motion, but something was wrong. He smelt close air, musty with stale sweat and the stink of a latrine bucket. With a huge effort, Ralph opened his eyes. His temples throbbed. A wave of nausea caught him and he retched. He blinked; his vision swam. Surrounding him in the gloom were loose trousers, clumsy shoes, all the same. His hands, grit beneath his palms, were braced against worn boards. His signet was gone. Instead, a pale stripe of skin.

"Must you cat on my foot?"

Ralph tried to speak. He croaked and gestured. A hand appeared in front of him with a pannikin, which jolted against his teeth as the planking tilted.

"What—" he coughed, cleared his throat, and started again. "What's this all about?"

"Prinny's yacht, out of Brighton." There was a bray of laughter. Ralph's skull ached. Gingerly he lifted his fingers to touch it. His hair had been chopped short. He went to wipe his mouth with the back of his hand and felt stubble. Vomit fouled the sleeve of his coarse shirt.

"The joke's gone far enough, lads," he said, as levelly as he could manage. "Will someone tell me where I am?"

"You don't know?" The voice rose in wonder. Ralph did not see the speaker tap his forehead. "He'll be telling us next he's forgotten his name!" More sniggers. "Macey, you're Mess Captain: you give him the good news."

A burly man with a pock-marked face and broken nose bent down and spoke slowly, as to an idiot. "Your name's Ralph, right? Well, Mr Fletcher, we've lumped the lighter."

Ralph looked at him stupidly. The words made no sense. "All of us, Teddy-my-godson," Macey repeated in a parody of Ralph's accent, "are convicted felons aboard the convict transport *Adelphi*, outbound for Botany Bay."

"Don't be so bloody ridiculous." Ralph pulled himself up. "Get out of my way." He shoved through the men penning him in. The ship moved beneath him and he pitched forward. At a sudden stab across his palm he recoiled. The bulkhead was studded with nails. He slumped back onto the decking.

I am Sir Ralph Alexandre Fairfax of Longhallows, Ralph told himself. This is not a dream. He sucked his finger, tasting blood, warm and salty. This was real. A felon on a convict ship? How? Who had brought him here?

Confused and suddenly afraid, he forced himself to remember: the ball; Laure; his quarrel with Flavia. Lucius bringing her note. Just as he glimpsed her, pain bursting across his skull. Then—nothing. His fingers went to his pocket, but these trousers were canvas. His mother's ring was gone, along with everything else. Robbery? There were desperate men aplenty in London, lurking in the shadows.

A savage practical joke? What name had they called him? Who was Fletcher? His abduction had been organised: he had been knocked senseless and drugged. Enough men arrived in gaol pickled in gin or stupid with laudanum for one more to attract no attention.

He had no enemies! But what of Lucius and his hints about Laure, his eyes watchful as he handed over his sister's note; Flavia, her face mask-hard. *You will regret this.* She would never do such a thing! She loved him!

And Lucius, besotted with that Lennox girl; how far had he gone to stop Ralph passing on his gibes about her father? Every gambling club had its disreputable hangers-on, violent for a fee. Had Lucius paid to protect Caroline's reputation by having him dispatched to where he could do no harm? Had Flavia agreed to act as bait? Surely not! But he remembered a flash of diamonds and the play of light on a rich shawl: the last thing he saw before the darkness.

He woke again to a rattle of wooden bowls. Ralph caught the smell of food; his stomach growled. Macey, seeing he was awake, passed him a bowl and spoon. The meat was salty and tough. He set it down.

"Which hulk were you on?" asked a slight, dark man, with a sing-song accent. Ralph could feel the eyes of the others on him, eager as dogs in a kennel. The silence lengthened as they waited for him to answer.

Time to bring this nonsense to an end. "I didn't come from the hulks," Ralph snapped. "I am not a convict."

"As Turpin said, afore he danced the hempen jig," chirped a voice from behind, to a burst of raucous laughter.

The bulkhead, pierced with loopholes, ran across the width of the between-decks. Behind the heavy iron-barred door in the middle he glimpsed the red coat of a sentry, and thumped on the bars.

"Soldier! I must speak with the captain. There has been a mistake."

The guard's nose was webbed with purple veins. He looked at Ralph consideringly. Expertly he spat a stream of tobacco onto Ralph's foot. "Shut your trap."

"But I'm innocent!" Ralph burst out.

"You and all the rest. Any more cheek and you'll speak to the captain all right, in a strait waistcoat. Stand back." The muzzle of the musket jolted Ralph's breastbone.

"He's a guinea a minute, this one." The men sniggered.

Ralph stood rigid, resentful at being made a laughing-stock, until the men around him fell to talking among themselves. Macey tugged his sleeve.

"We don't look, or smell, like the company you're used to," he said quietly, "but whatever you were before, you're a convict now." He gestured at the double row of deep shelves running astern, untidy with sprawled men and shapeless bundles. "Till we reach port we're all the company you've got." He glared at Ralph, to see that the message had sunk in.

Feeling obscurely rebuked, Ralph retrieved his wooden bowl. He tripped on a sturdy ringbolt screwed into the upright of the bunks. Macey caught Ralph's puzzled look.

"Eighteen months ago the master of the *Chapman*, new to the game, took a notion his convicts were about to mutiny. Four were shot, and another twenty wounded. The bolts are there to run a chain through, to put us in irons. Don't let it put you off your victuals. It's pease porridge tomorrow."

That night, as the others snuffled and snored, Ralph wrestled over what he should do. His claims of innocence had got him nowhere. Mocking echoes came back to him of the excuses he had heard from defaulters in the Army. The soldiers on prison ships were notoriously the worst in the Army, the King's hard bargains, scarce two steps ahead of the rabble they guarded. There would be no gentry here. And even in the unlikely event that the ship's master checked his story, for how long would he languish, awaiting a reply? Unless by chance he met someone he knew, or someone sympathetic to his plight, he would excite only more derision.

Crammed in the bunk with Macey, the Welshman, and a sharp-featured fellow with a twitch, Ralph curled himself tightly on the edge. The back of his right shoulder itched, just where he could not reach: he must have scraped it, in whatever rough ken he was held. The scab caught in the rough wool of his blanket. Perhaps, when they made landfall, he could escape, or win his freedom by some lucky chance. His musings tailed off into dream: he was on deck when up went the cry: "Man overboard!" He dived in, neatly as a seal, and hauled the struggling man to the surface. It was the Captain. "What can I do for you, my man?" "Sir, there has been a terrible mistake…" He felt a wash of relief.

By next morning his headache had eased, and his eyes adjusted to the gloom. He swung his legs out onto the floor.

"Ware head!"

Ralph checked just in time. The deckhead was too low for him to stand to his full height.

"Thanks. You're Macey, aren't you?"

"That's right. What hit you? A coal wagon? You were acting odd yesterday."

"I'm new to this," Ralph said, honestly enough.

Macey looked at Ralph curiously. "We don't get many fellows in the 'tween-decks who talk like you." He paused. "I'm Mess Captain, so I draw rations and keep order. These are your duties. Up on deck at first light to wash—that's a bucket of seawater. Collect rations at six and stow the beds. Scrub decks, breakfast at eight; then back on deck with the holystones.

"Davies you met last night: he's Welsh. Thomasin!" He shook the humped figure. "Show a leg, lad." The blanket stirred as Thomasin peered out resentfully. "Kemp and Poole are up top. The other two are in the hospital. That's why you ended up here. Give me a hand with the water-tub."

Ralph counted three locks as they passed through the door in the barricade. They climbed in single file up a ladder. A heavy grating blocked the hatch. Ralph followed Macey, ducking out through a small port guarded by two armed sentries. Beside them stood a stocky, grizzle-bearded sailor with keys dangling in bunches from his broad leather belt. Macey nudged Ralph. "That's Morgan, the bos'n. He holds all the keys. Better not lose him overboard."

The prisoners milled about abaft the mainmast, shut off from the forward part of the ship by a wall topped with spikes. Ralph glanced up at the quarter-deck and pulled up short. Squat and foreshortened, a cannon's blank mouth pointed straight at him. Another matched it on the other side.

"You thought they were for Boney and his Frogs," Macey said in his ear. "Now they're aimed at you, double-shotted, to drive any thought of mutiny from your mind."

"Move on there!"

Through the jostling crowd Ralph saw the purposeful clutter of stacked spars; a longboat, raised in its cradle; the splayed ends of rigging, running down to neat coils of rope; a row of belaying pins, each set in its hole. Chickens squawked on the other side of the barricade. Ralph picked up a wooden bucket, and joined the line. He looked behind him. Watchful marines blocked the two companionways up to the poop.

Those few narrow steps now marked the door to another world. Two officers stood at the rail. The older was a beefy Major of Marines; the other, much Ralph's own age, was brown-haired, lean-faced, with a firm mouth. He wore a naval lieutenant's uniform, the blue faded, and the gold braid dulled by sun and salt.

The water-tub slopped, full. Ralph hefted the rope handle. Back at the hatchway he took a last lungful of the salt-tanged air, balanced the tub to pass it to Macey below, and descended into the crowded stink of the prison.

It was a relief to return topsides. Slopping water over the striated timbers, swinging the weight of his body into the worn sandstone, Ralph had at least fresh air to breathe and some room to move. Something about Macey's manner was familiar. As he worked his way, caterpillar-like, along the wet deck, Ralph tried to remember what it was.

Then he placed it: Macey had the unruffled air of a good sergeant, treating Ralph like a raw recruit who needed to be shown the ropes. Ralph had to smile at this curious inversion of roles and was tempted to ask Macey outright if he had ever been in the Army. He was checked by sudden reticence. Each man here was convicted of some crime. What was Macey's? What, for that matter, was Fletcher's?

Macey pulled up his shirt to wipe the sweat from his eyes. Across his back Ralph glimpsed fearful scars, not yet faded. Officers could not be flogged. The world in which he now found himself ran to different rules.

To his left Thomasin kept up a continual fidget. His fingers kept fluttering away from surfaces as he touched them, as if they would contaminate him. He edged closer to Ralph and spoke in a conspiratorial whisper.

"I am a lawyer's clerk, a Special." For all the man's air of self-importance, Ralph had no idea what he was talking about. "I can see you are a gentleman. People of our sort should not be bullied by such louts." He jabbed an elbow towards Macey. "I have letters of introduction to men of business in the colony. Assuredly we—"

"You are mistaken, sir," Ralph cut him off icily. It irked him that that this snivelling clerk should presume an acquaintance, and parade some advantage of which Ralph was ignorant. Thomasin gave an involuntary grimace at the rebuff and turned away. Ralph saw that his fingernails were bitten to the quick. The man was terrified. But just now Ralph was in no position to extend patronage, preoccupied as he was in trying to make sense of his own situation.

The exchange gnawed at him nevertheless. He queried Macey as they returned their holystones to the store.

"What's a 'Special'?"

"You don't know? You are a rum 'un. Specials are convicts with education. They think they're a cut above the rest of us. Thomasin will land an easy billet pushing a pen while the rest of us sweat." Macey looked around to make sure they were not overheard, and dropped his voice.

"Watch him; he'll make trouble. Whatever you said to him before, he didn't like it. He's a toady; I've come across his sort before. They're all over you with tales of you and me against the other fellow. Next thing they're sneaking up to someone else to gang up on you."

Ralph frowned, disconcerted to discover there was a hierarchy among the convicts, in which the rest knew their place, but he did not.

That night he dreamed he was rowing a little skiff, heading for a light on the shore. Each time he turned the boat's head towards it, he was beset by a hidden rip and drawn further out to sea, until finally the light vanished and he was adrift, alone.

At some unknown hour he stirred. What was Flavia doing now? He remembered the touch of her skin, the fall of her hair across his fingers. Did she miss him? He felt a sudden aching need for her. Macey's elbow jammed into his back, provoking him back to the present. Tense and angry, he lay awake in the darkness.

His mood soured. She betrayed you, out of a young girl's spite. She had hardened her heart against any explanation you might give. What happened in Vienna was none of her business. You were wasting your time. For all you know, Lucius told her about Laure weeks ago, when he first found out, and she had been pretending ever since. Had she and her brother got the whole charade up between them?

His surge of anger subsided. Ralph reproached himself. Such cruelty was not in her nature. Where was she? The ship might founder; even if he escaped or was immediately released, he could be months returning to tell her what had happened. But the taint still lay in his mind that perhaps she knew already. For whatever reason, he was here.

He gave an explosion of breath, part snort, part sigh. Macey turned over.

"Can't sleep?" His words were just loud enough to carry.

"No."

"What are you thinking about?"

"A girl."

There was a scraping in the darkness; a tiny glow. Ralph caught the sharp scent of tobacco.

"Here: have a puff. The sentry won't be back for a while yet. It's Oakley tonight, the lazy bastard."

Ralph was startled out of his self-absorption. "You know him?"

Macey chuckled. "Know him? I taught him all he knows. Not that that amounts to much. He always was fonder of his bottle than his drill."

"You were in the Army, then?" Ralph's voice was carefully neutral.

"Six year. I came back home in '14 and settled to peacetime soldiering. Met Biddy. She was different from the others; we were wedded. Then Boney slipped away from Elba and my battalion was recalled to the Low Countries. By then she was with child, close to her time. We tried to hide it until after the ballot—"

"The ballot?" Davies' sing-song whisper broke in. "What is that?"

"When the regiment's posted overseas, there is a ballot in each company to decide which wives can go. Only one woman can go for every ten men, and those with children—" his tone flattened "—cannot go at all."

"But surely," Davies insisted, "a wife's place is with her husband? My Megan has come with me, to the other side of the world."

"Perhaps we need more Methodists in the War Office," Ralph put in, dryly.

Macey took a pull on his pipe. "Biddy had no family and I had lost touch with mine. I couldn't leave her penniless and sick. She went into labour the day before we were due to embark. I damned the Army's eyes and went to her. By the time they caught me, she and the babe were both dead. I would do the same again. At least she died my wife, not a pauper on the parish."

"And what happened to you?" Davies asked the question, but already Ralph knew the answer.

"I was broke —lost my stripes — and sentenced to five hundred lashes for desertion. I was lucky. My mates spoke up for me after two hundred."

A silence fell. Ralph had never paid much attention to the ballot. Now the stories crowded his mind: a sergeant in the Rifle Brigade cutting his throat rather than leave his wife behind; a distraught wife giving birth to a dead child in the street; the regimental band blaring on the quay to drown out the screams and wailing of the women left behind. How had they coped on their own? How many had seen their menfolk again?

Macey was a deserter. The officer in Ralph condemned him. Only the man's previous good service had kept him from a crippling punishment which could have killed him. But Ralph admired the raw courage of the choice he had made.

The heavy tread of the returning sentry interrupted his thoughts. The smell of tobacco still hung pungent in the air. Macey hastily knocked the dottle out of the pipe and ground it underfoot. He need not have bothered, thought Ralph sourly; Oakley's reek of rum drowned out any other. He lurched past, a drunken sot. Ralph glanced from him to Macey. *I know who is the better soldier. I must see what can be done about Macey's case...*

The ringbolt stood stark against the faint glow of the sentry's lantern. *What use is your interest here? First prise yourself free of the law: if you can.*

The next morning brought grey skies, a chill wind and a muscular sea. The convicts on deck were cold and subdued. Ralph stared out over the rail. His initial confused disbelief was giving way to frustrated anger. His house, everything he owned, all that made up his life were hundreds of miles away, falling further behind him by the hour.

"Fletcher!" He turned to face Oakley. "Report to Captain Jamison."

He felt a rush of hope. Here was a chance to argue his case. With growing eagerness he followed the soldier's red jacket up the companionway, to the officer's quarters, where he belonged.

Ralph stooped at the low lintel. Jamison sat at his table, his long nose and fierce eyebrows silhouetted against the grey overcast from the sloped stern windows. A clerk beside him opened a massive register with thick boards, its pages written close.

"Sir—" Ralph began.

"Keep silence! Doff your hat when an officer addresses you. As you were brought on board insensible you missed your interview with the Superintendent of Convicts. This is now in session."

Jamison cocked a finger at the clerk, who passed over a paper.

"Fletcher, Ralph," Jamison read out, "ex *Justitia* hulk, Woolwich. Age: twenty-three years. Religion: Church of England. Marital Status: single."

"There has been a mistake," Ralph interrupted. "I am no convict. I am a gentleman, kidnapped in London. Until two days ago I had never heard the name Fletcher. I respectfully submit that you investigate my case and expedite my release as soon as possible."

Jamison's eyebrows shot up. "What proof have you of this extraordinary tale? You are a gentleman? Then you have letters of introduction. Show them."

"I have explained why I have no letters."

"Come, man; you expect me to take you at your word, in a shipload of liars? I was there when you came aboard drunk. All you had in your pockets were a set of marked cards and a dishonoured bill from *The Split Crow* in Whitechapel, a notorious gaming-house. Take off your shoes and stockings. And that shirt."

Ralph went to protest. Oakley started towards him. He had no alternative, humiliating as it was, but to undress before these men. "Stand up straight."

Smirking, the clerk unfolded a wooden ruler. Ralph felt like a horse being measured in hands.

"Five foot eleven inches, sir."

The captain went on. "Hair, black. Distinguishing marks—" Jamison checked his papers— "*scar on left collar-bone.*"

"There it is, sir," the clerk confirmed.

"Also *tattoo on right shoulder-blade.*"

"No!" Ralph exclaimed. This was ludicrous.

"I take it you can read?" The Captain's voice was heavy with derision.

Ralph leaned over the book. He saw the entry neat and clear: *Badge: VII within Shield.*

"I was with the Army in Spain. But not the Seventh." This made no sense. What was happening to him?

A hard finger jabbed his back. "Why deny it? I can see it here, even if you have somehow forgotten it in your recent delirium. What were you about to say? That you were on the Duke's private staff?"

Ralph opened his mouth and shut it again. The gibe was too close. His words were invalid before he spoke.

"Claim what you will, the facts are here in your record. You are a cardsharp who knifed a pimp in a squalid brawl. You may have escaped justice with your glib tongue and cozening ways in the past. Now your crimes have caught up with you, and you are transported for life. You will learn to treat your betters with respect." He shut the heavy book with a thud.

Ralph stood light-headed with shock. The sense of nightmare flooded back. He cast about with increasing desperation for something to say, but his mind froze before Jamison's intimidating stare. He felt the other's cold wash of contempt as he scrambled to recover his miserable clothes.

"I have no time for such cock-and-bull stories. I have a ship to run. Take him out."

In the narrow passageway he passed the naval officer from the day before. Ralph caught his glance in an instant of entreaty, before Oakley pushed him along.

Back in the waist of the ship, Ralph slumped in the angle of a bulwark. He was a man with two shadows: his displaced Fairfax identity, and this malign Fletcher-self who had somehow appropriated even his very skin. He stared out at the grey sea, merging imperceptibly with the grey sky. "But it's the truth!" he repeated to himself.

A seabird, high above, screamed in parody.

# 9

## *"Adelphi", at sea, 1816*

*Ting-ting, ting-ting*

The ship's bell roused Ralph from uneasy sleep. Bare feet thudded across the deck over his head. The flapping sails cracked; as the wind filled them, the ship heeled over on a new heading. Ralph stared up at the rough-sawn boards shutting him in. Though Thomasin had decamped to the upper bunk, his hissed arguments with Kemp and Poole still kept Ralph awake. The place stank like an ill-kept stable. From the stench of urine, Thomasin had pissed his bed again.

Ralph heard the skitter of rats' feet along the boards. Increasingly bold, they came out at night, seeking scraps. Sharp claws prickled across his arm; a smooth belly flowed over his hand. Ralph snatched at the writhing fur and flung it squealing upwards. Above him the boards creaked to threshing and curses. A crunch. The rat's body flopped messily onto Ralph's face, with the crushed head spat after.

"I were a rat-catcher," Poole's voice came lazily out of the darkness. "Don't need no terrier."

Ralph scrubbed at his cheek with the blanket. He was angry at his squalid surroundings, at himself for his naivety in his interview with Jamison. Every phrase of the disastrous exchange echoed in his mind. It was bad enough being branded as a liar; worse, being so casually dismissed as an object of contempt. In Spain he had taken on characters other than his own, but these roles had been freely chosen, and discarded at will. This despicable Fletcher-creature had been forced upon him. As long as he was on board ship, no-one would believe a word he said. Would it be any better once they landed?

Should he have given them his name? To these people it would have meant nothing. In this place where he had so little, his name was his talisman. It was all he had left. He would not expose it to further scorn.

By night he summoned up Longhallows in his mind: the lion keeping watch on his pillar, the embossed door, the double staircase sweeping up to his father's portrait, splendid against the battlefields of his youth; beyond, the cabinet room with its treasures and trophies. Threatened as he was, he drew reassurance from the remembered weapons around the wall. The sleek steel pike with its narrow damascened blade, so intricately crafted, had fascinated him as a child. Next to it hung his grandfather's sabre, heavier and straighter than the modern style. His father had carried it to war thirty years before; Ralph in his turn in Spain, preferring it to the lighter curved blades which were regimental issue: pretty on parade, good for nasty gashes: useless at stopping a charge. On this subject, he and his father, for once, had agreed. His hand flexed around the imaginary hilt. He could still be Fairfax inside his head.

*"You're a dreamer, like Marie-Claude."*

In this place, what else did he have? By day his ill-assorted companions grated increasingly. For Macey he felt a certain respect, even liking. The man had a shrewdness that made up for his lack of polish. But the big ex-sergeant kept order in their mess as he had in the Army, with his fists, and was as ready to clout Ralph as the rest.

Davies was no problem; a decent fellow who belonged to some abstemious Methodist sect, bowed down by disgrace and concern for his wife, up in the forecastle with the other free passengers. Macey treated him with genial tolerance; Thomasin sneered at his sing-song speech. The bandy-legged ostler Kemp and his rat-catcher mate Poole called him 'Welsh runt', and teased him mercilessly in their thieves' cant.

"Hey runt! What's *morts* and *blowens* in your lingo? *Quims? Whore-pipes?* Can't you speak the King's English?" They pranced about, jiggling their hands obscenely.

Davies' narrow face reddened. Ralph shared his disgust. These people were savages. How he yearned for a newspaper, or ten minutes of civilized conversation. The only use Kemp and Poole would have for the exquisite works of craftsmanship that Ralph treasured in his dreams would be to fence them, or smash them up to burn.

As far as he could, Ralph kept to himself. He had found a cranny behind one of the ship's boats, the closest he could manage to solitude. One afternoon his messmates had got there before him. Poole rocked with laughter as Davies spluttered on the deck, Kemp on his chest forcing gin into his mouth.

"You don't know what a 'shit-sack' is?" Kemp taunted. "There was this preacher, a Methodist, just like you. He was so scared he—"

"Leave him alone," Ralph snapped. "You know he doesn't take drink."

"And what are you going to do about it, Mr Smart Jemmy? Run off to your mate Macey?"

"You can take your filthy hands off him, for a start."

Kemp let the Welshman go, and swung the square bottle at Ralph's head. Ralph punched him clean on the point of the jaw. The grin on Poole's face faded. Ralph slung the dazed Kemp aside and threw a bucket clattering after him. He helped Davies to his feet. "Clean yourselves up, both of you." Poole scuttled off. My manners are getting as rough as Macey's, Ralph thought wryly as he shepherded the Welshman away.

"Fletcher! Message for Lieutenant Hunter. I'm busy." Pushing a note into Ralph's hand, Oakley turned back to his cards. Whist again, on a winning streak, Ralph thought, glimpsing the stack of shillings.

Ralph read the name: *Lieutenant Edward Hunter.* Here was an opportunity to turn this errand to advantage, and salvage his reputation yet. He rubbed his hand over a bristly chin. His twice-weekly shave was not due until tomorrow. His plea from one gentleman to another might sound more convincing, were he more presentable.

Ralph tapped at the door. "A note for Lieutenant Hunter, Sir."

Standing in the doorway was the naval officer he had seen outside Jamison's cabin. Briefly startled by the mismatch between Ralph's voice and appearance, Hunter took the note and walked—with a heavy limp, Ralph noticed—over to the light. Ralph had sensed a spark of sympathy at their previous meeting. Now he addressed him as frankly as he dared.

"May I take a moment of your time, Lieutenant?"

"I saw you with the Captain, did I not? What is your name? Fletcher?"

"Yes, sir—no, sir," Ralph returned, clumsily. "It is of that I wish to speak." The lieutenant's scrutiny made Ralph intensely conscious of his shabby clothes, but he held the other's glance.

"Don't expect me to do for you what the Captain would not. I will condone no irregularities," Hunter said sternly.

"Thank you, Sir. I will be brief. My name is not Fletcher; I am innocent of any crime. I was kidnapped. I am a gentleman, not a murderer."

"A gentleman? Can you prove it?"

At least Hunter had not dismissed him out of hand.

"I was an officer with the Army in Spain."

"Spain? I was on the American station, until I was invalided home." His expression eased, as Ralph moved impatiently. "By your speech you are a man of education. Your present surroundings must be distasteful to you."

"But I swear to you—" Ralph's voice sharpened in desperation as Hunter raised his hand.

"You obviously believe this extraordinary tale; I overheard some of what you said to the Captain. But look at the evidence. Your record states that you were convicted at the London Assizes and sentenced for life. You came aboard rotten with gin and laudanum— I did ask—too drunk even to know where you were! Why should I believe you?"

*"Because it's true!"* screamed the voice in Ralph's mind. He stood with shoulders hunched with tension, his knuckles white. He wanted to hammer the table, shake the man; anything to convince him. He made a last effort.

"If I gave you a letter—"

Hunter's face hardened. "You know I cannot carry private correspondence. I must follow the Captain's decision in this matter, as in all others to do with the running of the ship."

All the excitement went out of Ralph in a rush. It was hopeless to go on.

"You think I'm crazy, don't you?" Ralph said, bitterly.

Hunter turned away. "You are dismissed."

Ralph stared out through the knotted web of the ratlines. Without warning, Poole shoved him up against the bulwarks, while Thomasin made an elaborate bow.

"If you please, Milord..." Kemp capered before him with exaggerated respect.

Other men joined the circle, unknown but equally hostile.

"What have you been saying to the officers?"

"Was it you who told them about my rum?"

"Pity your mother forgot whose bye-blow you were."

Ralph's fist jarred on the jeering mouth. The knot of men closed and Ralph went down in a flailing tangle. A kick caught his face. Cold seawater sloshed over him and his attackers.

"Worse than a pack of dogs, you lot!" Oakley yelled. "Now clear off, quick! Fletcher, keep your fists to yourself."

Macey strode up. He hauled Ralph over to the rail. Ralph wiped his bleeding nose on his sleeve.

"What was that about?" Still too angry to speak, Ralph stared at the sea. Macey shook him. Ralph staunched another crimson gout.

Macey bent closer. "Don't humbug me! They were out for your blood. If I am to keep any sort of order in my mess, I need to know why. I've made allowances for you, but if I find you've not been honest with me, you can spend the rest of the voyage down the coal-hole, for all I care."

"Kemp called me a bastard," said Ralph tightly.

"They were after you for more than that. 'Turning stag,' Davies said. They're calling you an informer."

Ralph's truculence gave way to amazement. "Why would they think that?"

"Someone heard you talking to the naval officer with the limp."

Macey was an ally he could not afford to lose. He would only be satisfied with the truth—or most of it.

"I was trying to get my sentence quashed," he said shortly.

"You're hopeful. On what grounds?"

"Unlawful arrest."

Macey regarded him for a moment without speaking. He drew himself up.

"Now listen, my lad. You still don't understand: this is a prison ship, not a palace If these fellows think you've been peaching on them—and somebody has, as you would have noticed if you thought of anybody but yourself—they won't cut you at the Club; they'll slit your throat. So get down off your high horse and leave your gentleman friends alone. And watch your step."

He gave Ralph's shoulder a final shake and walked away. Ralph grimaced at his red-streaked sleeve.

"An interesting case, this Fletcher." Jamison surveyed his guests, Hunter and Mellors, the major of Marines. Here he was, master of his own ship, with a contract to transport a commodity which would never be in short supply; while this naval fellow would limp to the end of his days on half-pay, with a mother and sister to support.

Hunter, glass poised just above the table, looked at him expectantly.

"Obviously a fellow of some education," Jamison resumed, "before he fell from grace. He has the air of some gentleman's bastard. His father must have had conscience enough to pay for his schooling, for all he lacked the will to marry his mother, having taken his pleasure."

Hunter swirled the Madeira, the colour of old blood in the candlelight, and set it down. Fletcher's case troubled him. He had raised it, seeking to put forward his remaining doubts in order to see them resolved.

"But he seems so earnest— even desperate."

Mellors, a florid-faced veteran, leaned forward on one elbow.

"You're new to this game, Lieutenant. When I was your age, we had an Irishman aboard. He had all the bog-trotters convinced he was the last High King of Ireland. The closest he got to a crown was the mark on the spoons he stole." Hunter smiled despite himself. "Fletcher would not be the first bastard whose mind was eaten by jealousy for a life he felt entitled to, but could never share."

"Aye, his father thought he did well," Jamison weighed in, "when all he did was plant ambitions above the boy's station."

"As for desperate," added Mellors, "so would you be, transported for life. Whoever his family, he'll not see them again."

An awareness of the peculiar fate of their cargo chilled their mood. Mellors was the first to recover.

"Tell me; do you know this song? *In Rheims was a strumpet, a fine strapping wench...*"

The stiff breeze thrummed in the rigging. The paper in the sergeant's hands flapped as he straightened it out, holding it stiff at opposite corners. "Now listen here," he bellowed above the wind, continuing his monthly litany. "*All living and sleeping quarters to be swept daily. All bedding to be aired on deck each day. Air scuttles to be kept open in fine weather.*"

He folded back a section of the notice and went on. "*Bottom-boards of the beds to be scrubbed with seawater. Prisoners to be allowed on deck no less than twice every twenty-four hours. These regulations to be observed by order of the Surgeon-Superintendent.* You that can read can explain it to the rest." With four sharp taps he tacked the new copy over the tattered remnant on the wall.

"Not much use you looking at it, Keogh, you can't read anyhow."

"I can remember more of it than you can," returned Keogh, unruffled.

"Aye, because you've done this journey before at the King's expense," came the response.

"Sure, and wouldn't His Majesty be knowing the sea air is good for my health?"

Keogh had shoulders like a beam. Little wonder, thought Ralph, that he had been transported again for useful labour in New South Wales, rather than wasted on the rope.

"These regulations: how strictly are they observed?" Ralph queried.

"Jamison runs a tight ship. He'll batten down the hatches in rough weather. You'll not need your bed-boards scrubbed then." A laugh rumbled in the cavernous chest. "They'll wash themselves. No: they had a fright last year with the *General Hewett* and those two other ships, with scurvy and gaol-fever." He looked at Ralph curiously. "Aren't you the fellow that came on board sick?"

Ralph shook his head a fraction.

"One of the orderlies said there was a prisoner brought late, just before we sailed. They left him awhiles in the cable-locker, for fear of the typhus."

Ralph remembered the boat and the voices. Another piece fell into place.

"But back to your question. The worst passage was my first one out, in Governor Hunter's time. Two hundred and eighteen days it took; and at the end there were ninety-five dead. It was a death-ship, that one; there were those as said there was a Jonah on board." He stared again at Ralph. "What did you say your name was?"

"Fletcher." The alien name slipped more easily now off the tongue.

The Irishman's brow wrinkled. News of Ralph's visit to the quarterdeck must have spread. Beneath the loom of the mainsail yard he glimpsed Thomasin whispering urgently to a new crony; the latest ally, Ralph supposed, in his campaign for respectability. Someone pushed in to ask Keogh a question. Ralph slipped away.

Around him the ship creaked in the darkness. The first month of the voyage was almost over. The days were warmer now and the motion of the vessel easier. Recalling his humiliating interviews with Jamison and Hunter, Ralph acknowledged that however unwillingly, he must play at being Fletcher, at least until they made landfall. Now he knew the ship's routines, and resolved to bring himself as little as possible to the attention of the authorities.

Meanwhile he savoured the irony of his situation, envisaging the faces at his club as he explained how he courted the opinions of an illiterate Irish navvy, and quailed at the disapproval of a disrated sergeant. No, that was unfair. Macey was a decent man, who had risked his life to uphold what he saw as his duty to his wife. How many of Ralph's acquaintance would have done as much? And even Keogh had a quality about him that Ralph could recognise, beyond his size; in the topsy-turvy world of the convict ship, it was to him that people deferred, not Ralph.

For the first time since he woke up on board, Ralph felt he had reached some kind of balance. Once in New South Wales he must surely find someone who would believe him, and clear up this ridiculous imposture. Grasping this confidence, he fell asleep.

Beyond his prison, the stars he could not see wheeled above the ocean's rim, pricking the dark vault of the sky with white fire, silvering the arrow of the ship's wake, driving always south.

# 10

## *"Adelphi", at sea, 1816*

"One day's biscuit."

"Two."

Come on, thought Ralph, it's hardly a Stradivarius. "One, and a quid of tobacco. It's only for an afternoon."

"Done." The violin's owner, a dancing-master before he forced his attentions on one of his pupils, passed across the scratched instrument and its bow. However reluctantly, Ralph had accepted the truth of Macey's reproach. He should indeed pay more heed to his surroundings. Making music was better than enduring the endless squabbles of bored men pressed too closely together. He looked round the deck. What to play? Three sailors, clutching their cards like fans, were preoccupied with able-wackets, the winner administering the forfeit of mighty thwacks across the loser's palm with a knotted handkerchief. This was no Viennese *salon*.

The first songs that came to mind were French, from his time in Spain. *Chant du Départ* had a certain appropriateness, and *Le Chat dans la Marmite* was a jolly tune, but there would be more than the cat in the cooking-pot if he played either of them here. Safer to start with *The British Grenadiers*, and *Rule Britannia*. Seated on an upturned crate, he tuned up and began. As he played his audience grew.

"Give us *Boney's Lament!*"

A Scot's voice, stronger. "Gi'e us *Bonnie Doon*."

Ralph started casually enough, but as he played, the words formed in his mind, and the yearning he dared not admit to himself poured out in the music:

> ... *Ye'll break my heart, ye warbling bird*
> *That wantons through the flow'ring thorn*
> *Ye mind me of departed joys*
> *Departed never to return.*

Around him the men stood silent.

*...Wi' lightsome heart I stretch'd my hand*
*And pu'd a rosebud from the tree;*
*But my fause lover stole the rose,*
*And left, and left the thorn wi' me.*

From the back of the row a gaunt Scotsman bestowed a quiet smile of approval. One of the sailors tossed a shilling at Ralph's feet. But Ralph could take not joy from his success. He would not play again.

Thomasin's flashy shuffling and dealing had obviously been perfected in loftier surroundings. Ralph had grown up playing cards by the hour with his invalid mother, who would regain in the excitement of play the wit and spirit of the charming girl she once had once been. She had taught him *écarté* and *vingt-et-un,* and the games she learned from her brother Alexandre, a *lieutenant de vaisseau* in the Bourbon navy. Ralph's familiarity with these games, his dark hair and Breton-accented French, had enabled him to pass muster behind the French lines.

Formerly Ralph had regarded cribbage as a pleasant way of passing the time. But the convicts played it continually, with ferocious absorption. He had never seen grown men staking on it the clothes off their backs, or the food from their plates. These gambling sessions, in the half-light of the prison, were taken as seriously as anything Ralph had seen in more fashionable gaming-hells.

Despite the heat of the 'tween-decks Thomasin wore a blue velvet coat with deep buttoned cuffs, trimmed with tarnished silver lace, won four nights before and paraded ever since. It flattered Thomasin's idea of himself as a gentleman *manqué.*

Thomasin and Macey were level-pegging on the last hand. Thomasin scored first.

"Fifteen two, fifteen four, six for a proil," he called. He counted off the holes with satisfaction and stuck his bone peg into the winner's hole at the end of the board. "Ten! I win!" His hand moved towards the pennies on the floor.

Even in the poor light, something about the movement caught Ralph's eye. He reached over and caught Thomasin by the wrist. Thomasin struggled but could not break his grip. Ralph twisted his hand up and back until a card tumbled from the cuff: the knave of spades. Ralph picked it up and slapped it down with a flourish.

"And one for His Nobs."

The cabin erupted in laughter.

"Game over," said Ralph, pushing the coins back to Macey.

Thomasin muttered something under his breath.

"Speak up, Nobby," said Macey. "I can't hear."

The others hooted and guffawed. Thomasin's pale face flushed crimson. He had never spoken about the crime that had led to his being transported. Ralph suspected it had to do with gambling: he could easily see Thomasin, the ill-paid lawyer's clerk, running deeper into debt, striving to be accepted by some raffish clique of gentlemen, envious all along of their ease and style. Ape them as he would, he lacked both the breeding and the income. Even Lucius Stanton—Ralph wrenched his mind back to the present. That topic was too raw. Better to wall off the Stantons altogether.

Ralph looked back at Thomasin, tense with humiliation. His wealthy companions would happily have relieved him of all he stole. If in his desperation he had tried the same tricks with them as he had here, they would have tossed him out. Gentlemen would forgive many things: drunkenness, infidelity; a fair measure of stupidity, but not a gamester who cheated.

The next night Ralph was asked to join the play, while 'Nobby', as he was now known throughout the mess, sulked in a corner. Ralph had always had a good memory for the run of the cards. His opponent was Kemp, who relied overmuch on native cunning. Ralph found it easy to put him off: he held his discard ready to put down before Kemp played his turn. Despite his good hand, Kemp lost, disconcerted by Ralph's ploy. Macey caught Ralph's eye as he gathered up the cards and gave an almost imperceptible nod. At last, thought Ralph, I am doing something right.

In the Captain's cabin, Jamison and Mellors studied the open book between them. The light from the stern lantern threw latticed shadows across Mellors hand as ran his thick finger down the page and jabbed. "Here he is: *Fletcher, Ralph: ex Justitia hulk.* This pleading his case with Hunter: I don't like it."

Mellors pencilled in a thick cross. "I've had sea-lawyers make trouble before. It's my duty to keep order on this boatload of scoundrels. The last thing I need is some resentful gentleman convict stirring them up."

Jamison poured a generous glass of port, and passed it to his companion.

"He's plausible enough to have young Hunter worried."

"Hunter's served in fighting ships in the regular Navy, not convict transports. I'm sure he's had rascals among his crews, but not two hundred and twenty of them, all unhappy with their lot. Fletcher's way with words is his profession. He's good at it—or was, until his temper got the better of him. I daresay he's excellent company until he gets a gutsful of gin and a knife in his hand."

Jamison topped up his own glass, and took a meditative sip. "The best way to deal with trouble is to make sure it never gets started."

"A cutting-out raid?" Mellors grunted. "My thoughts exactly. That lanky Special Thomasin's in his mess. Get your clerk to let slip that Fletcher is a card-sharp. Thomasin hates gamesters with a passion; they put him where he is. He'll spread the word out of spite. All true—" he tapped the page "—and it won't cost a penny."

They were becalmed. Sweat trickled down between Ralph's shoulder-blades to soak into the waistband of his trousers. He flapped a hand in the foetid air. Shut in the dark like cakes in an oven, the prisoners ached for air; but each breath brought only the smell of sweaty bodies, the stink of the night-tub and rotten bilge-water.

Ralph mopped at his face. What a waste of his three quarts of water a day, brown with peaty Thames sediment; no sooner did he drink it than it poured through his skin like a sieve. Images of past banquets floated unbidden into his mind. Quail glistening in aspic. Succulent apricots, nested on ice. He swallowed uncomfortably.

He turned over, carefully avoiding the tacky puddle of pitch which had dripped down between the planks of the decking above. Yesterday Poole, to general amusement, had caught some on his bald patch, oozing into in an angry black question-mark as he leapt about, swearing.

Boots clattered as Oakley approached the door, lamp in hand, another redcoat behind him. Ralph sat up.

"Captain wants extra men."

Ralph shook the dozing Macey awake. "We'll do it," he said, pushing himself forward, eager to get topside. The bolt shrieked as the door opened. Macey was already half up, rubbing his eyes; Ralph paused only to grab his shirt. As he stepped out into the corridor, Thomasin stirred, peering over the edge of his bunk.

"What's up?"

"Special working party," grunted Macey.

"I'll come too." Thomasin made to rise.

"No you won't, Nobby," said the other guard, pushing him back. "The Captain wants men who'll work, not skulking Specials."

Following the guard, Ralph grinned. Had he not been forced to share Thomasin's company, Ralph might have felt sorry for him. In a place where strength conferred authority, the gangling clerk was tentative and quick to take offence. Even his sentence failed to impress, a miserable seven years. He had made no friends among his cellmates, despising those sent out for fourteen years, or for life. He too obviously saw himself as free, and established in some profitable business, while the rest still toiled out their time.

After the fug below, the fresh air on deck was a blessing. A knot of sailors chatted idly by the glow of the binnacle lamp; above them loomed the masts, their sharp lines obscured by the swathes of useless sails. Without the usual background murmur of a ship under way, every noise sounded clearly: the squeak of an officer's leather sole; a sudden cough. The slack tracery of rigging grew more distinct as the sky lightened. It flared in the swift tropical dawn.

At a sudden shout of command the sailors leaped into activity, scampering aloft, agile as spiders. Their task was simple, if laborious; the captain reckoned on an early morning breeze and had ordered the sails wetted, to increase their drawing-power. Two sinewy old hands with tarred pigtails worked the handles of the wood-and-leather pump, which clattered and wheezed as it spouted sea-water into the waiting buckets. The sailors passed them hand to hand across the deck and hauled them up to the yards, working fast, racing the sun.

Ralph climbed out on the end of the mizzen yard, as far away from the crowded, stinking, noisy ship as he could get. High above the sea with his bare feet braced on a loop of rope and the comforting solidity of the spar pressing his midriff, he was at last alone. Between him and the faint curve of the horizon stretched an infinity of water. Ralph felt as remote as a seagull. As the world's edge blazed with light, he willed the distant silhouette of a ship to appear, bearing letters of release.

"Bucket ahoy!" Ralph grabbed it, dashed the water onto the discoloured canvas, passed it back. Hold; pour; return; he lost track of time. The fierce light on the huge expanse of sail made his eyes ache.

The sailor next to him pointed down. No more buckets. Stiffly Ralph edged his way back to the mast. This was the first chance he had had to see the ship in its entirety. The slab-sided *Adelphi*, built for the convict trade, lacked the grace of her fighting sisters. She was merely a floating box, designed to jam in as many unwilling passengers as possible, the after-deck seething already with convicts moving about, foreshortened, queuing like ants. All too soon the familiar clatter rose to meet him.

Swinging nimbly down onto the deck, Ralph almost ran into the lieutenant. He caught the regret in his gaze. Not for the crippled Hunter the exhilaration of climbing aloft. Ralph checked, speaking to ease the other's embarrassment. "Will this succeed, sir?"

Hunter stared appraisingly at sea and sky. "It is a week since we crossed the Equator. A good breeze would bring us shortly to the southeast trade-winds. With such a swell as this, we may catch one before the morning is out."

Even as he spoke, a tremor ran through the rail beneath Ralph's hand. The dampened sails caught and held the light airs.

Hunter turned to Ralph with a quick smile. "Would that all my prophecies came true! You worked well. Good day to you, Fletcher."

"Good day, sir." Ralph saluted without resentment. There was much to like about Lieutenant Hunter. None of the other officers would have thanked a convict for his efforts. Certainly not Mellors, he thought as he caught sight of the broad, red-coated back. From what Ralph had seen on his way down Mellors was more interested in the women passengers than the men, anyway.

After a gulped breakfast Ralph made his way over to his messmates. Kemp was dealing out a hand. He looked up as Ralph joined the circle.

"I wouldn't play against him," Thomasin said silkily. "You'll not win."

Ralph bridled. "What do you mean by that?"

Thomasin smirked. Ralph's fingers flexed. Macey, seeing a fight brewing, intervened. "Fletcher, keep your hands to yourself. And you," frowning at Thomasin, "keep a civil tongue in your head." He turned back to Kemp. "Now deal."

Reluctantly Kemp resumed dealing out the cards. Ralph won the hand. Thomasin gave the crestfallen Kemp a nudge.

That evening, Kemp and Poole refused to play.

They had picked up a steady wind. Soon they were spanking along parallel to the coast of South America; they passed Tristan d'Acinta, its mountain wreathed in cloud. That same week the sailors caught an albatross, lured down with a hunk of greasy bacon on a tin triangle. It tore its webbed feet, threshing in the line; a smear of crimson marred the dazzling breast-feathers. It fixed the craning onlookers with its fierce accusing eye.

Suddenly the mood changed. The cabin-boy darted forward and cut the bird free. Everyone was caught up in the drama of returning it to its proper element. The great bird stood, poised on its long, impossibly slender wings, taking up half the deck; dominating its surroundings like an archangel. Then the wind veered and it dived into the sea. It ran over the water, flapping its wings, spiralling up, glowing white against the sun, until it was a remote speck: alone, of all the creatures on the ship, free.

As they made their southing towards the Roaring Forties, a chill set in. Within three weeks they were east of the Cape of Good Hope. The men who had sweated in the tropics now froze in their thin clothes and single blankets. The others huddled together for warmth; some for more than warmth, as the frustration of months without women began to tell. Ralph wrapped himself as best he could in a corner of his own.

Daily the weather grew colder. Damp and dejected, the convicts lapsed into sullenness. No one had the energy to fight. They invented excuses to skulk below deck rather than face the biting air. Even the sight of a whale roused little interest.

Ralph's companions were for the most part silent. The prospect of landfall, and its uncertainties, filled their minds. For all the discomfort of the ship, it had become familiar. Davies wrapped himself up in his blanket like a sheepdog sheltering its nose with its tail; Thomasin, fidgety despite his heavy coat, complained endlessly.

After a week of cold weather the ship's motion abruptly changed. Overnight she bucked and tossed, then developed a lurch which left the stomach poised on the crest of a wave while the rest of the body raced down the slope. No question now of their going on deck; the hatches were battened down; lamps and galley fires extinguished for fear of fire. Cold, bruised, and sodden, the convicts were flung from bulkhead to bars. The anxious men knew nothing of what was happening outside their prison, as the ship ran before the gale under close-reefed topsails, but their alarm rose as freezing seawater sluiced in from above.

Caught in the trough of one wave, ambushed by another, *Adelphi* was flung over on her beam ends. As she righted herself sluggishly, a wall of water broke over her deck. A broken spar speared through the hatch-cover, cracking the wooden grille. A torrent cascaded down the companionway, sweeping the men off their feet. Tumbled with the others into a heap, Ralph remembered stories of the *Pandora*, foundering with the prisoners from the *Bounty* locked in cages on the deck. An older nightmare stirred: his uncle Alexandre fighting his bonds as he sank, until his eyes fixed, staring, and his black hair floated like seaweed in the current.

They hammered at the door. Through the bars they saw Oakley lurching towards them, sodden and scared.

"Let us out, man!"

"Bos'n's down and I can't shift him. He's blocking the ladder."

Macey spoke with reassuring authority. "Ask Morgan to give you the keys. Let us out and we can help you."

Oakley's silhouette turned away. Runnels of water slopped at Ralph's ankles. Thomasin's laced cuff pawed his elbow.

Oakley was back. "Only two, Morgan says." Ralph ducked as the musket-barrel slewed past his face. "Don't move, the rest of you."

"Keogh!" Macey shouted as the gate opened. "Hold them back. We'll return for you others as soon as we can. Remember the *Chapman*. If you rush the door he'll fire, or they'll shoot you down at the hatchway."

Macey and Ralph edged out and the door slammed to. Behind them Oakley snicked the lock, swinging his musket to cover them. Don't trip, Ralph prayed. Morgan, his knee twisted under him, lay at the foot of the companionway.

"Keys," he grunted, snatching them back. "Get me topsides."

Macey seized his shoulders, Ralph his legs. They squeezed past the splintered end of the spar and worked their burdened way awkwardly up the slick ladder with its cracked and broken treads. Another wave doused them. Ralph took Morgan's weight as Macey tried to shoulder aside the wreckage blocking the top. The timber shifted abruptly, moved from above. Three muskets poked down.

"Don't fire, you goddam idiots! Bosun's hurt."

They clambered through the shattered grille. The wind, as they peered over the coaming, drew their heads from their bodies. Ralph, screwing up his eyes against the stinging spray, felt his burden lifted. The ship yawed.

Ralph knew boats. He looked aft.

"Steersman's gone." Before the soldiers could halt him, he was halfway across the foaming deck, with Macey behind. Together they raced up the unguarded ladder to the quarterdeck. Ralph slithered on the slick planking as green water roiled. The steersman was gone, washed overboard. Four men, unrecognisable in the flying spray, were caught in a tangle of cordage from a fallen sail.

The loom of another great wave gathered to port. Hunter's voice shouted. "Turn her stern to the waves!"

Macey grasped the blurring spokes of the wheel on one side, Ralph seized the other, hauling with their joint strength until they felt it answer. The tilt of the ship's deck altered as her head came round. The oaken circle strained against his braced body. The stern lifted as the wave, now behind them, picked up force. A dark blur flashed past; the wheel dragged as Macey slumped. Ralph dodged the loose block as it swung back. Two sailors dashed across to secure the wheel. Ralph was wrenched away.

Mellors roared in his face, "Who gave you permission to come aft?"

Ralph tried to turn back to Macey, crumpled on the deck.

"Fletcher! Stand to attention! You'll get no help from your mate. His neck's broken. Keep this man under guard until the Captain's free."

Jamison glared, grimmer-faced than ever from the strain of the storm. "I give the orders around here, not some cardsharp bastard. The bos'n and Hunter spoke up for you, or you'd be in irons, charged with breaking gaol."

He turned to Mellors. "I don't trust him back with the others. Insubordinate, and too clever by half. Lock him down the orlop. He can share his bread and water with the rats."

# 11

## *England, February 1816*

Flavia awoke with a sense of unease. Fragments of nightmare still clung, vivid and disturbing. She stood on the jetty as Ralph paid off the boatman; but when she looked back the scene had changed; he had gone. In the failing light the lane, though she knew the name, was strange. She turned to ask for a direction, but none could hear her, and the faces about her were unknown.

She sat up in bed, her stomach cramping. During the night her monthly bleeding had started. She felt heavy and oppressed. Her quarrel with Ralph rushed upon her; she remembered her precipitate flight. What had possessed her to behave like that? She had no memory of changing out of her gown, or of what she had done with Harriet's shawl and diamonds. She started out of bed, fearful she had lost them. Her gown lay crumpled on the floor where she had discarded it. The shawl was folded on her dressing-table, with the *aigrette* on top.

Her relief was short-lived. Lucius's accusation; the sight of Ralph and that woman together, the lingering taint of her perfume which had provoked Flavia's jealousy, rushed upon her. All too clearly she recalled the grief which overwhelmed her, her desire to retaliate, the hurtful words that rose to her tongue.

Before last night it had seemed so simple: she loved Ralph; from their growing ease in each other's company, he loved her in return. By some process she had never stopped to consider, she had assumed they would grow closer; he would ask her father for her hand; they would marry.

How wrong she had been. I made a fool of myself, letting my feelings run away with me.

She could not sit in bed all day, moping. Perhaps a hot drink would ease her discomfort. She had missed supper; not that she felt hungry. She rang for hot chocolate and toast.

When Molly Simpson appeared with the tray, the girl's pallor startled Flavia out of her self-reproach.

"What is the matter? You look unwell."

"It's all right, Miss. A bit of a cold." Molly gave a vehement sniff and withdrew.

Flavia relapsed into brooding. She did not trust Lucius's judgement sufficiently to turn to him for advice. Besides, he would only say *I told you so*.

The hot drink eased the ache in the pit of her stomach. She had better dress. Once Ralph had slept on his harsh words he would surely regret them, and send some message of apology. He had been so perceptive, beneath the walls of the Tower. But she had seen him flare up before. She remembered how he had turned on that poet, a harmless enough fellow, if naïve. Perhaps she had been naïve in her turn.

The day was overcast and grey; she tweaked the curtain to let in more light. The diamond spray twinkled fitfully. She must return it and the shawl to her cousin. As she picked them up she saw her reflection in the mirror, puffy-eyed from last night's crying, with her hair hopelessly tangled. Angry at herself, too impatient to call the maid, she dragged at the knots.

The house was very quiet. She sat at the piano, but was all thumbs. Wardell arrived with a message from Harriet: would she like to view the latest paintings at the Academy? Flavia declined, pleading a headache. She knew Harriet would be eager to know how the evening had gone. Just now it was too painful to talk about. More immediately, she could not risk being out if Ralph came.

Hour followed hour. Consumed by impatience, she willed him to appear, so she could turn back the clock, explain, be reconciled. Her heart leapt at a knock on the street door, but it was only a footman, presenting a card from one of Harriet's friends. Wardell brought the morning's letters on a silver tray. One was addressed to her, but the handwriting was her father's. She tossed it aside unopened.

With each empty hour her uncertainty grew. Please don't let me have lost him. Harriet returned, took one look at Flavia's face, and tactfully left her alone. The early evening came, no darker than her spirits. She felt the slow welling of anguish.

Another day passed; three; a week, with no visit, no word of apology or reproach. The carefully-rehearsed scenes faded from her mind, replaced by the hard, aching certainty of loss. By the time Flavia could bring herself to tell her cousin what had happened, Harriet had heard already, the tale embellished by gossip. You poor girl, Harriet thought, hugging her fiercely; innocence was a much over-rated quality, which did nothing to protect young girls from the pain of the world. Men did these things, Ralph's father more than most; nothing drove them away quicker than scenes in public, no matter how justified.

Harriet was deeply disappointed in young Fairfax, nonetheless; for him to acquire a flashy mistress in Vienna was understandable; to parade her before a gentlewoman, whose affections he had engaged, was both ill-bred and cruel. Such *louche* behaviour surprised her. She could only blame it on some change wrought by his experiences in the wars. He was not the first pleasant young man she had seen return warped by battle.

On Wednesday of the second week Bromley called briefly to see Harriet. By his close look as he left, Flavia knew his visit concerned her.

"Flavia?" The usually confident voice was hesitant. "I fear I have some bad news, child."

"Is it about Ralph?"

"I fear so. Fairfax has left the country."

"There must be a mistake!" Flavia cried.

"I fear not. We must face the facts. Bromley had business at the Ship Inn in Dover. A waiter there described a dark-haired gentleman in the company of a showy foreign woman; they left last Monday, booked on the Calais packet. The likenesses were exact. Bromley remembered the Augsberg woman clearly, from her intrusion at his mother's ball. He checked on his return to London. Fairfax's rooms are up for lease."

Flavia felt as though a huge hand was crumbling the bones inside her. She sat mute.

"I am so sorry, my dear. I thought you well suited. I had never reckoned him to have Everard's wildness." Harriet dabbed at her nose with a handkerchief.

Flavia was touched, despite her pain.

"I was once in love with Everard, when I was old enough to know better. He was a dreadful breaker of hearts. I had cut my hair, intending to dress as a page, like poor silly Caro Lamb, and run off with Everard to Rome." She pronounced it the old-fashioned way: *Room*. "Papa found one of my letters and gave me the most fearful dressing-down. He locked me upstairs until my hair grew again. I had hoped you might find happiness with that family where I had not." She patted Flavia's hand. "Go off and weep. You will feel better for it."

Flavia went up to her room, but no tears came. She was too angry. How could she have been so wrong? She had felt so sure of the depth of Ralph's affection. Had he merely been amusing himself until his mistress could rejoin him? Were they laughing at her now?

When she told Lucius he looked surprisingly relieved.

"If he has run off with that woman to the Continent, you're better off without him. The Fairfaxes always were a tetchy lot. You can't say I didn't warn you."

Oblivious to her misery, Lucius offered some brotherly advice. "Remember when I fell in love with Georgiana Wilcox? When she married that naval officer I was heartbroken for a week. Then all I could remember was her irritating laugh. Now I am relieved I did not pledge myself to her, or I would never have met Caroline!" He squeezed her hand and tried to coax an answering smile. "London is full of eligible young men. You will feel better by the fortnight's end."

She did not. Her brother's well-meaning attempts to distract her failed. They merely emphasised how much of her pleasure in London had been delight in Ralph's company. She finally took up Harriet's offer to attend the showing at the Academy; one painting depicted a square in Madrid. The thought flashed through her mind: I must ask Ralph if he was there. Then the blankness: she would not ask Ralph anything, ever again. Once more she felt regret: for the betrayal of a promise never made.

A fog settled for three days, the thick, tainted air pressing against her window, leaking its tendrils into the house whenever the door opened. Flavia stayed in her room, trying to reconcile her instinct with the tawdry reality of what she had been told. What had felt so right and true and full of promise was now revealed as a cheap flirtation. What confidence could she have now in her own judgement?

By day she tried to reason her way out of her distress. But at night she missed Ralph passionately. Tense, angry, rebuffed, her body cried out for what it could not have.

Worst was when she tried to sleep. She blew out the candle with a sharp whiff of beeswax, and lay back on the pillow. She was more than tired, but the crisp linen of the sheet felt as stiff as paper. She closed her eyes, but instead of a warm easing into rest, she felt a weight of gloom. The tick of the clock on the landing, once reassuring with its steady measure, now goaded her awake. She fought the urge to get up and check the hour. Briefly she drifted off, to be woken by the cry of the night watchman. Preliminary niggles crept into her mind, the questions she thought she had settled during the day: what had attracted Ralph to that woman? What had he wanted from Flavia? Would he have come back to her, had they made love? It only made things worse to recall how reluctantly he had drawn away that day on the landing.

As the half-hours crawled past, each marked by its muffled chime, her sense of malaise grew, and her questions multiplied. Would Ralph have stayed in London had she not made that scene at the ball? Could she have accepted the humiliation of his keeping a mistress? At last her tears rose, but rather than easing her distress, they confronted her with what she had irrevocably lost. Seeping tears grew to uncontrollable sobs; a profound and hopeless sadness. If only she could have spoken to Ralph once more. Never again. At length this tide of grief receded, leaving her devastated, eyes hot and swollen, scoured out.

Next morning she tried again to come to terms with his desertion. She chided herself: *I can't go through the rest of my life with tears coming to my eyes every time I think of him.* She was frightened by her lack of control, this deep sadness that welled up within her; her abiding sense of worthlessness and loss. She toyed listlessly with the rolls on her breakfast tray.

As day succeeded day, her betrayal reopened an older pain. Ralph, like her mother, had vanished without explanation. She remembered the line her father had marked in his copy of Chaucer: *Worldly blisse hangeth but by a wyre.* Now the wire had snapped for her, as it did for him. She could understand now why her father had closed up within himself and shut out the world. She had made the same mistake: committing herself profoundly, more deeply than she had realised at the time, to someone who had disappeared, taking her happiness with them.

Lucius said no more about Bromley's ball. Flavia was grateful, interpreting this uncharacteristic silence as tact. Harriet, although obviously concerned by Flavia's ongoing misery, did not intrude. As the already brief winter days grew shorter and colder, Flavia nerved herself to return home. She felt badly that she had written her father only one brief note, saying that she was out of sorts, kept indoors by the weather. She found his unopened letter under a half-read book.

*Mrs Willis continues to feed me well. Last week one of the old oaks lost a bough in the storm. It came down upon the stables and damaged the roof. I enjoyed your description of your evening at Astley's Circus; young Fairfax always had an eye for a good horse. I am pleased that you have a stimulating guide to London's sights...*

She could not bear to read any more, and screwed it up.

In the course of another sleepless night she steeled herself to a resolution. Her father had to be told what had happened; and the news, however unwelcome, must come from Flavia herself, not wagging tongues. Her father had always prized honesty, no matter what the cost; it was one of the reasons he had found Lucius's evasions so hard to comprehend. That her father had obviously been happy, in his undemonstrative way, for Ralph to see more of his daughter, made her task no easier. She did not want to burden her father with her own disillusionment. But he deserved the truth, no matter how painful for them both.

Lucius urged her to stay in London, largely, she suspected, because he resented any time away from Caroline. But now that she had made her decision, Flavia was ready to go home. She hoped that after the sting of the initial confession, she would find comfort in the familiar round of her household duties. Anything was better than the constant prick of memory; waiting for the door to open and Ralph to walk in.

The issue was suddenly resolved: their father had suffered an apoplexy.

On the hurried return journey Flavia's anxiety over her father pushed her mourning for Ralph to the back of her mind. She was too preoccupied to notice the motion of the coach, despite the rutted and muddy roads, though the maid Molly Simpson was ill at their noonday halt. Flavia was cold and stiff when they stopped for the night. In the poky, dark parlour where they had supper she sat before the fire feeding wood into the flames, watching the play of colour as it caught, glowed and finally subsided into embers.

Lucius stood beside her, warming his hands.

"I hope Father is all right," he ventured nervously. He meant *alive*, but shrank from the word.

"We are travelling as fast as we can; we can only hope the physician has better news when we arrive."

"It's not only that," he burst out. "I have important matters to discuss with him."

*So have we all*, she thought. "Do they concern Caroline?"

"Yes." He turned to face his sister. "I want to marry her. I could not discuss it before; with you being so unhappy, it hardly seemed fair." He fidgeted with the poker, and the fire flared. "I want Father to accept her."

"What are you afraid of? He was most polite to her at Christmas. Why should he take against her now?"

Almost Lucius confessed the truth: that Caroline was carrying his child, and his father, whose judgement was severe in moral matters, would not look with favour on his son's taking advantage of the girl. Nor, though Lucius hesitated to admit this even to himself, would Charles Stanton welcome a liaison with a family of dubious antecedents. Lucius needed his father's approval. Should their child be a boy, he would be the heir: he must be born legitimate. Furthermore, thanks to his evenings at Hazard at *The Cocoa Tree*, his debts had grown. Bromley had helped him over the worst of them, but Lucius knew his father would be withering in his condemnation, not just because of the gambling, but because of the obligations he had incurred to their wealthy neighbour.

He could be honest, and brave his father's wrath, or hide Caroline's condition, press for an early wedding and claim the birth to be premature. Then there would be no disgrace.

There was a further reason for his reluctance to parade his happiness with Caroline. He had seen how wretched Flavia had been since Fairfax left. Lucius felt a certain guilt at his part in the affair. Bromley's hint of ruthlessness, his air of being a man of the world, had drawn Lucius along on the night; all he did was carry a note. He had been protecting his sister. Sometimes strong measures were called for, to defend family honour. Fairfax must have provoked Bromley as well; obviously he had come to no lasting harm. But while Lucius had been quite happy to see Fairfax taken down a peg, he had never thought he would go as far as leaving the country—or that his sister, previously so dismissive of the young men of her acquaintance, had become so attached to him. She was moping like a sick cat.

As Flavia's question hung unanswered in the smoky air, she drew her own conclusions. There was no doubting the strength of Lucius's attachment: he was in love with all the ardour of his impetuous nature. How that felt, she had now painfully found out. Her brother at least could be happy. Caroline's feelings Flavia found it harder to judge; she was so young, and Flavia had done little more than exchange commonplaces. She was pretty, and appeared eager to please. Certainly her company gave Lucius a confidence he had lacked before.

Caroline's mother Flavia frankly disliked. She shrank from the prospect of entering into terms of close obligation with someone whose company she so little enjoyed. Still, Mrs Lennox lived in Bath; removed from her mother's influence, Caroline might grow less tiresome.

Flavia felt suddenly very weary. For weeks she had teased and worried at her thoughts. How she longed for things to be simple and clear. She ached for the reassurance of Ralph's arms about her. Don't fool yourself; he has gone and he is not coming back. Your father is dying and you must face this test alone. Tiredness weighed like a bar across her shoulders.

"Good night, Lucius."

"Oh? Good night," he responded absentmindedly.

The doctor's solemn face gave little hope.

"Your father is alive, but only just. He cannot speak. He can move his left hand; that is all. He was bled yesterday, but there has been no improvement."

Charles's slack face frightened them. He looked like a stranger. His skin was waxen against the white pillow; his hair, usually so neatly dressed, fluffed out as delicately as a child's. His breath snored faintly in his throat. Flavia was the first to step forward.

"Father?" she reached to touch the inert hand, skin fragile as tissue paper. "Can you hear me? It's Flavia and Lucius." Had she felt a faint pressure against her finger?

Lucius was scared. This mute helplessness reproached him; he could think of nothing to say or do. He did not want to touch the body on the bed; in some obscure way he feared his own vitality would be drained by the contact. A forgotten dread assailed him: the terror of a small boy being led up to a bed to touch a shape that looked like his mother, but was cold and hard as marble.

He was relieved when Flavia stood up and he could follow her out of the room. He gulped down a brandy. "I never thought to see poor Father in that state. Surely he can't last much longer like that?"

The doctor shrugged. "He may recover a little. Sometimes the natural forces rally and some movement returns. If he is no better in two weeks, he will probably die. He will need constant nursing." The doctor looked at Flavia. He gathered up his bag and made ready to go. Lucius saw him to the door.

"Without distressing you further, Mr Stanton, there is a further consideration. Your father is incapable of conducting business in this state. You will have to undertake the management of his affairs. Have you a power of attorney?"

Lucius shook his head. The doctor went on. "I suggest you arrange one as soon as possible. I will be happy to sign the necessary papers. It is as well not to let these matters slip."

Lucius returned, preoccupied, to the library. His father's pipe lay across the pages of the book he had been reading. Estate and household ledgers ranged along the shelves, each meticulously labelled in Charles Stanton's clear hand: *Farm Rents Quarterly, Household Expenses, Bank Correspondence, Accounts Payable, Estate Repairs.* Lucius drew down the last and opened it. *£5 15s 6d: replacing slates on Stable Roof.* It hardly seemed worth the trouble. That whole block was falling to pieces anyway. He shut the book and pushed it back on the shelf.

Lucius had so longed to be treated like a man, with a man's responsibilities. Now he had his wish. He regretted not paying more attention when his father had tried to interest him in the running of the estate. He was buoyed by a sudden thought: if his father was incapable, and Lucius should succeed to his father's legal authority, then he need not seek formal approval for the marriage. He could scarcely be disinherited by a father who could not speak. He felt a twinge of guilt at such disloyalty. Yet even so, he left the library more confident than when he went in. He was not entirely on his own; he could seek Bromley's advice on business matters, and Flavia would run the house. It would take her mind off Fairfax. She was well rid of him. One day she would come to realise it.

Flavia spent most of the next week in anxious vigil. She read aloud to the still figure in the bed, unsure whether the sound of her voice was penetrating the silence in which he lay. She could not bear to think of him lying there disregarded while the life of his house flowed unheeding around him. Betsy Turner helped her lift and wash, fetch and carry. Mrs Willis plied them with chicken broth and warm gruel which Flavia spooned carefully into the slack mouth. She felt an enormous gratitude to them both, and to the elderly and rheumatic manservant who relieved her at night.

As her days settled into a routine, she was haunted by the pain of her abandonment. She needed now a helpmate and companion, someone to share her burden. Lucius had withdrawn behind a show of business. She could have poured out her feelings to Ralph; she ached for comfort. A sound of hoofbeats on the gravel of the drive would draw her to the window, hoping against all logic that Ralph had returned. She lectured herself on her foolishness, but still her heart thudded.

One afternoon she went riding, unable to tolerate the sickroom any longer. Outside it was keen and fresh. She followed unthinking the old bridle-path through the woods, and drew rein when she realised she was at the edge of Longhallows Park. The grey bulk of the house lay as still as her father, shuttered and lifeless, against the dull sky. No lights glowed in the windows; no smoke issued from the chimneys. She chucked the horse's rein and turned back. She had been finding excuses to put off telling her father about Ralph's desertion. It was time to face the truth. She went straight up to the sickroom on her return. She weighed her words carefully, keeping her tale as simple and unemotional as she could.

"I took great pleasure in Ralph Fairfax's company in London. But we had a disagreement. He has decided to travel abroad."

Her father's fingers twitched. She gripped his hand. Her words tolled in her mind like a funeral bell. She felt she was killing a part of herself. They had to be said. Her father was on his deathbed and she could not let him go to his grave believing a lie.

As the physician had so cautiously suggested, the ninth day brought some improvement in Charles's condition. The grasp of one hand grew in strength. Propped up, he could view the world from one eye as the lid of the other drooped. One side of his mouth, too, was dead; his speech was slurred and difficult to understand. He needed a napkin round his neck, to catch the saliva he could not control; he suffered fits of silent, uncontrollable weeping.

Lucius was horrified. While his father had been at death's door he had been able to adopt a dignified anticipation of mourning. He did not know how to act towards this shrivelled creature hunched in his chair, helpless as an infant, with all his defining qualities of intellect gone. Only Flavia seemed able to pretend that nothing was different. She still read to him patiently from *The Vicar of Wakefield*, hour after hour.

After dinner Flavia cornered Lucius in the library. Burdened as she was by her father's illness, she resented having to carry the weight alone.

"Why don't you spend more time with Father?"

Lucius bridled at her directness. "I have been busy."

"Too busy to visit your own father, when he is desperately ill? You owe him more than that!"

"What point is there in my coming?" he returned, exasperated. "I can't understand what he tries to say, and the effort makes him cry. Better that I stay away."

Flavia too had been distressed by the frequent tears, but she scented an evasion.

"I don't know why he weeps. I doubt he has any choice in the matter. But it pains him to be shunned. Do you think he doesn't know what he looks like?"

Because his father looked senile Lucius had assumed that his mental faculties were similarly decayed. Now he realised that his father's intelligence might still be trapped inside that stricken body, like a survivor pinned alive under the ruins of his house.

"I'll see him tomorrow," he promised, shamefaced.

Before the interview, Lucius nerved himself to raise the matter of his marriage. How good it would feel to have it resolved, the date fixed, his father's blessing given, even if only by a clasp of the fingers! But face-to-face with his father, Lucius's courage failed. He had only to declare: *"I want to marry Caroline Lennox."* But he feared another gush of tears. Father looked so frail; a sudden shock might kill him. Better arrange a small, private wedding, soon. He could drag on like this for months; Lucius's son must not be born a bastard. Father could hardly be disappointed not to be asked to the ceremony when he was too ill to be moved, anyway. They could visit him after. So he reasoned as he smiled and nodded at his father's grimaces, impossible to understand.

As he stood to go, the wasted hand, with its raised purple veins, sought his own in its feeble grip. His father tried to mouth three words. "God bless you?" "Please come back?" Lucius could not tell. His father wept. Lucius felt his own eyes prick with tears.

That evening Lucius wrote to Caroline, setting a date for the wedding. Next day he carried the letter to meet the mail coach. Passing the jeweller in the High Street, he went in on a sudden impulse and bought Flavia a gold locket on a chain. He visited the vicar on his way home.

Facing his sister would be less easy. As he rode into the stable-yard he glimpsed her russet cloak and hood disappearing into the orchard. He swung down from the saddle and dashed after her.

The apple trees were gaunt and bare. Gravel crunched under his boots.

"Wait! I have something for you." He caught up and handed her the little box. "You have done so much for Father. I thought you deserved some thanks." Her face lit to a spontaneous smile of pleasure. It was the first time in weeks he had seen her happy. He congratulated himself.

She fiddled with the little brass hook, hard to open with cold fingers. So that's what Flavia needs to cheer her up, Lucius thought: someone to buy her pretty things and make her smile. She had smiled for Fairfax, a voice in his head reminded him.

She cupped the little torrent of gold links in the palm of one hand, and squeezed his arm with the other.

"Thank you, Lucius. That was kind of you. I did not realise you had noticed; you have been so preoccupied with business."

"I have some more news to brighten your day. There is to be a wedding in the family."

"A wedding?" she repeated. "Whose?"

"Mine, you goose! Caroline and I are to marry within the month."

He smiled down at her, willing her to swallow the conversational hook and give her felicitations.

But she had tasted the metal and spat it out. She swung round to face him. "Does Father know?"

"Not yet."

"A wedding? At this time? And without letting him know?"

"Why not?" Lucius resented her prods to his conscience. "Father could drag on like this for months! Why delay my wedding indefinitely? Must I wait for him to die first, and then add a year for mourning?"

"You can't treat him as if he is already dead! This is still his house and he is still the head of the family! He deserves respect. He has a right to know what is happening under his own roof!"

"The physician said not to excite him. The shock might be fatal."

"It would not hurt him nearly so much as learning he had been ignored," she retorted. "How would you hide the preparations from him? Wall up the door of his room?"

Lucius's temper snapped. "Don't be ridiculous, Flavia. Other people have the right to be happy, even if you are not!"

He would have recalled the words the instant they were uttered. They hit her flushed face, cold and stinging as a handful of the icy gravel on which they stood. She turned and blundered down the path beneath the barren trees.

"Flavia!" he shouted. But she did not stop. He wanted to apologise. His sense of irritation flooded back. His sister was so provoking: she would hit you with a string of accusations, burst into tears when you retaliated. She had always been the same, even as a child.

He was suddenly fed up with the whole hopeless tangle at Fontclaire: his father's condition, neither alive nor dead; Flavia's reproaches; the endless pettifogging queries about the estate. How should he know whether to drain the river meadow, or whose breeding ram to buy in spring? A gentleman's place was hunting, or administering the law as a Justice of the Peace, not stamping around muddy fields with dung on his boots.

He must see Caroline. He worried about her; she was so delicate. Was she eating the right food? Had she money enough for new dresses as the child grew larger? The knowledge that deep within her body his child was growing filled him with amazement and pride. They would have a boy, a fine, handsome son: as soon as he was big enough, Lucius would buy him a pony, and teach him to ride.

It was time to consult Bromley; get his advice on how best to run the estate under the power of attorney. It had suited Father to handle all the administration himself. He liked to have everything under his control, his son included, Lucius reflected resentfully. That was why Father had taken so against his gambling: to him it had been not just an extravagance, but an affront to his authority. Now things were going to change.

Poor Flavia: she needed a holiday too, but she was so good with Father, and they could not both leave the invalid at the same time.

# 12

## New South Wales, Summer 1816

Dazzle: a furnace-hot sun, beating on his skin. As he came on deck Ralph tripped on the lip of the hatch. He sat down, filtering the blaze of light through his fingers. As his eyes adjusted he lifted his head and looked around.

Below a cloudless blue sky, *Adelphi* rode at anchor; one ship of several in a sheltered cove. Bright sparks struck off the water. On his far left a low rocky point ran down to the harbour. From a narrow jetty a lane climbed past lawns and gardens, brown in the summer heat, to a white house clustered in trees. A row of windmills defined the skyline, and the scaffolding of a long, unfinished building.

A small fort commanded the left side of the cove; involuntarily his eye sought out the matching battery on the right: there it was, on the point. Two tall warehouses and another wharf dominated that side of the cove; behind them cottages clung like barnacles as the ground rose to a headland of shelving rock.

Ralph turned around. Behind him long fingers of grey-green foliage reached down to a bay, another anchorage cross-hatched with masts and spars. On both sides of the immense harbour, further coves and headlands of tawny stone receded as far as he could see. Set against this breathtaking setting, the makeshift town looked poky and inadequate. There was nothing familiar to reassure him in this huge landscape of blank sky, raw sandy rock and dull trees.

"Cheer up, lad!" Ralph looked up as a heavy hand clapped his shoulder. "You'll get used to it." His comforter was a stout red-headed woman with muscular freckled arms, pink from the sun. "Here: have this." She handed him a peach.

"I cannot pay." His voice croaked from lack of use.

"Give us a kiss, then, chuck." She turned her cheek to his quick peck.

Ralph bit into his peach. It was delicious: plump, juicy and warm. He savoured every bite, licking the sweet sticky juice off his fingers. No-one had given him the simplest acknowledgement for two solitary weeks; cheered by this encounter, he looked around for someone to talk to. He glimpsed Keogh and walked around the cradle of the ship's boat to greet him: not there. Strange: so large a man was not easy to mistake. Kemp, then, joking with a knot of men by the rail.

Kemp looked round; the humour died from his face. Deliberately he turned his back. So did his companions.

That snivelling Thomasin was behind this. What story had he spread now? Ralph tapped Kemp's shoulder.

"Where's Thomasin?"

"What's that to you? We were locked down for a week after you played the hero."

"What possible fault was that of mine? I've been down the orlop since Macey died."

"I'm pleased to hear it."

Ralph, exasperated by the other's rudeness, was angrier at himself for being goaded into what sounded like excuses. He was tempted to punch Kemp for his insolence. This satisfaction was denied him by a throaty-voiced cabin-boy.

"Fletcher? Muster-Master wants to see you, as soon as you've cleaned up." He gave an exaggerated sniff, and grimaced.

Ralph made to clip his ear. He did not need some cheeky urchin to tell him he smelt of a fortnight's sweat and dirt. But the boy dodged, and laughed in his face. Ralph made his way back to the mess. The others were still up on deck. He reached beneath the bunk to where he kept his gear. It was all gone, spare shirt, tobacco, his little cache of money won at cards; and Macey's kit as well. He had no time for a thorough search. Swearing, he pulled off his grimy shirt, doused his head in the water-bucket, dunked the shirt and used it to quickly scrub off what dirt he could. He wrung it out and pulled it on again, wet as it was. As he left he upended the bucket over the upper mattress.

In the great cabin Jamison, in the centre, was flanked by an unusually-tall man with iron-grey hair and a hard, keen glance. Next to him a secretary copied details from Jamison's ledger to an even fatter one beside it.

"Name?" the Muster-Master demanded. The secretary dipped his pen into the ink, hand poised.

Ralph stood disreputable, damp, and silent. The ink gathered on the quill, ran down the nib and splotched the carefully-ruled page. The writer gave a *tch* of annoyance.

"Name?" the official repeated, more forcefully this time. "Speak up, man!"

Ralph addressed the Captain. "Sir, we had this conversation before. You didn't believe me the last time."

Jamison let out a long breath. "Don't push your luck. Any credit you might have earned was spent saving your hide." He turned to the secretary. "Write: *Fletcher, Ralph; per Adelphi*. Not *FitzClarence*, as he would have you believe." Ralph coloured. "One of our more difficult passengers. *Sentence: Life*. You may add for the benefit of anyone foolish enough to employ him: *Temper: Proud*, and *Manner: Insolent*."

The Muster-Master fixed Ralph with pale blue eyes. His voice was as chill as his stare.

"I've dealt with your sort before. You will find we have your measure. You are dismissed."

Outside the door Ralph passed Mellors, who gave a knowing smile as he entered his cabin. From within Ralph heard a muffled voice: Thomasin.

How unwittingly Ralph had played into their hands! Of course: each meeting with an officer had been followed by some discovery by the guards. Thomasin had turned the men's growing anger, against Ralph, painting him as the informer who deserted his messmates to save his own skin. No wonder the others had shunned him.

Ralph berated himself for his conceit. Disparaging his shipmates for their lack of education, he had let himself to be outmanoeuvred by a rat-faced clerk and an oafish Major of Marines. Then his anger faded to a seeping sense of helplessness as the Muster-Master's words echoed, in all their authority. In this alien place Ralph Fairfax of Longhallows was invisible. Now he was *Fletcher per Adelphi*, a name on a list, trapped inside an identity which, like Hercules' shirt of Nessus, clung more tightly as he tried to shake it off.

After their midday meal the prisoners were counted off. Washed, shaved, and with their hair cut, they were issued new clothes, and lined up on deck, on their best behaviour: Governor Macquarie himself was coming on board to address them. Ralph, squeezed into the back row, glimpsed a lean-faced man who carried himself upright, his sallow skin accentuated by the bright crimson of his uniform, and the sun flashing on heavy gold epaulettes.

What manner of man was the ruler of this remote prison? What powers did he enjoy, and how did he exercise them? He looked to be in his late fifties, a Scotsman, by his accent. His words, so far as Ralph could hear them, were encouraging: praising the country they had arrived in and offering them opportunities to improve their lot if they behaved well. He did not look or sound like a cruel man, but one who would not take kindly to being crossed. The boots of the guard thudded as they stood to attention; the bos'n's pipe twittered; the official party filed ashore.

It was a long, empty afternoon. Small boats criss-crossed the harbour, tiny as waterbugs on a pond. A schooner passed *Adelphi's* stern, gliding towards the sentinel cliffs of the heads. The prisoners were sent back below, lest any should be tempted to brave the sharks and swim ashore.

Kemp swung up onto his bunk and checked.

"What bastard poured water all over my bed?"

Ralph looked up with an expression of polite concern. "Must have been the one who prigged my gear."

The night dragged by; another day. At least they now had fresh food and clean water. To Ralph's relief, Poole and Thomasin left in the morning. Davies' wife, young and pretty, came to meet her husband, greeting him with evident affection. Ralph wished them well as they departed. Recalling the Governor's speech, he reflected that the taciturn little Welsh sheep-stealer might have better prospects here, providing he kept out of trouble, than he had back home. Kemp went off an hour later with the owner of a livery-stable, seeking a groom.

Evening came on. Ralph lay back solitary in the now quiet mess. The Captain's bad character had had its effect. He was unwanted: an item of flawed merchandise. When would they put him ashore? What would he do once he got there? The bulk of the world lay between him and those he held dear. What was Flavia doing now? Was she thinking of him? A desperate longing for her company, the comfort of her presence, rose up in him.

The wave of longing ebbed, replaced by guilt. During the long nights in solitary when his body ached, it was not of Flavia he had dreamed, but Laure. As the night wore on, his sense of uncertainty grew. He had lost every prop of class and station. He felt like a man who all his life has been walking on water, and has suddenly begun to sink.

Early next morning the unassigned convicts were assembled on deck and escorted ashore. After so long at sea, the earth rolled under Ralph's feet. They mustered in front of the gaol and marched over a bridge to the lumberyard. The grass crackled under his feet, brittle with high summer. The sun tingled pleasantly on Ralph's skin; after the roll-call and yet another reading of regulations the prisoners were issued passes, and to Ralph's surprise, were dismissed. "Find your own lodgings. When the bell rings in the morning, report here for work."

The soldiers who had been standing to attention sauntered off; the line of convicts broke up into eddies. Friends sought each other out, and old hands lounged over to trade the newly-issued clothes for drink. From down the street came a rhythmical chinking. A file of men appeared, moving in a peculiar shuffling run, all with long chains running from belt to ankle-irons.

On the ship Ralph had heard talk of Government Men "on the chain". Now he was seeing them. He remembered similar sights in the grubby plazas of Bourbon Spain. These men looked better fed, but were linked alike in servitude. Ralph could not imagine a similar scene in the bustling streets of London. Was this why England's human refuse was sent to the end of the world, because such sights could not be tolerated at home? The men rattled off into the distance. No one else paid them the slightest attention.

The encounter, flawing the perfect summer day, left Ralph disturbed. As the bite of the sun grew fiercer, he looked for shade, following a path planted with trees. At the end was a little beach carved out of a hollow in the long layers of coarse sandstone, where waves flopped lazily on the pale sand, leaving a darker slick. The harbour beyond glittered like a jewel. The water, clean, cool, enticing, lured him to dive in, free as a seal. At the edge he sat on a convenient rock and pulled off his rough shoes and new stockings. He was tugging at his shirt when he heard a shout.

"Oi! You!"

Ralph looked around. Two soldiers stood alert at the top of the path.

"Come back!" Their muskets were at the ready.

"I was only going to swim." He tried to keep the anger out of his voice.

"*Sir.*"

"Sir," he added reluctantly.

"Where's your pass?"

Ralph fished the square of paper out of his pocket. The soldier scrutinised it with the exaggerated care of one barely able to read.

"Just landed, eh? Well, stay away from the beach." He gestured to where the anchored ships shimmered in the late afternoon heat. "Don't take any foolish notions. There's a guard on every gangplank, and all the ships are searched before they sail. I'll let you off this time because you're new, but next time you won't be so lucky. You're coming back with us."

"Yes, *sir*. Thank you, *sir*." Ralph looked down so they would not see his resentment at being frustrated in a perfectly innocent activity. The cool promise of the lapping waves taunted him as he headed back up the track.

*Rule Britannia, Britannia rule the waves*
*Britons never, never, never shall be slaves*

So much for the years I spent fighting Napoleon with his military dictatorship and secret police. Here the voices and uniforms are English, and the flag that flutters overhead is a Union Jack. But any man can be stopped and his identity challenged; I must show my pass on demand, and files of chained men rattle through the street.

Ralph's unwelcome guardians deposited him where he had started, back at the lumberyard. He felt stuck in a recurring dream. The scene around him was the same as before, except that the shadows had shifted, and the air beat on his skin even hotter than before. He did not know what to make of this place. It looked normal on the outside, but it was two things at once: a town and a gaol. The transition from one to the other was as abrupt as moving from sun into shadow. Ralph could understand the notion of a prison as a specific building. Here the whole colony was a prison: its styles of clothing, authorities, rules for walking from one place to another; all governed by this single purpose. It was disconcerting to realise that *Fletcher per Adelphi* was already an unwilling citizen of this bizarre polity.

Unsure where to go next, he moved to the shelter of the trees. The grey-green leaves were thin and tough. The slender trunks and boughs had startlingly pale bark, smooth as skin. He rolled one of the leaves between finger and thumb; it was brittle, with a pungent scent.

A little black dog trotted towards him, a mongrel bitch with a round barrel body, alert prick ears and a docked tail. She stopped in front of him, sat up on her hind legs and begged. She wore a collar and lead of braided red cord; holding the other end was an old man, short and bald, with a wizened face and practised whine:

"Got some baccy for my Gyp?"

Ralph, who disliked beggars, was about to say "no" when he noticed the set of the man's head. The man was turning his ear for the sound. He was blind.

The dog, still squatting on her haunches, stared up at him reproachfully from lambent brown eyes. Her pink tongue lolled over a fringe of black lip. Ralph felt in his pocket.

"Shall I give it to you or the dog?"

"She fetches it for me," the man returned pertly, "but I won't have her chewing the stuff." He slipped the quid deftly into a pouch, tilting his head like a sparrow.

"Thankee, sir. You're toney-tongued to be with these lags."

Ralph crouched to fondle the dog's ears, soft as warm velvet. It was a long time since he had patted a dog.

"Staying long?" the old man continued.

"Life," Ralph replied bluntly. He straightened up. Unperturbed, the man addressed his next remark to the dog. "Chatty new chum, ain't he, Gyp? We'd best be off."

Ralph regretted his curtness. "What's your name?"

"Clancy to you, sir, and I've a card to prove it, though I can't read it meself." He ferreted round in his pouch and drew out a small oblong of pasteboard, curled at the corners, printed in copperplate, "*Jas. Clancy, late of London, and his Performing Dog, Gyp.*"

Ralph smiled, won over by the man's cheerful persistence. "Ralph—" a fractional pause "—Fletcher at your service, Mr Clancy." He sketched a bow to the dog, who not to be outdone, rolled over and played dead.

"Got somewhere to stay?" Clancy enquired. "You have to find your own bed at night; the barracks for the Government Men ain't finished yet."

"No."

"You can stay with me, then, till you find a place of your own. I'll be glad of the company."

"Thank you," he replied. "I will."

"Is it always so hot?" Ralph asked, as they headed down the road.

"Last year were as dry as a whore's—sailor's throat," said Clancy, recalling his company. "But the drought has broke now, and about time. It were getting on everyone's nerves. Old Sandy and the big-wigs bickering and squabbling—"

"Old Sandy?"

"The Governor. You heard his welcoming speech? He meets all the ships new in. Him and the Judge-Advocate have a feud going, and he's at daggers drawn as well with that crummy-guts parson Marsden. He's Principal Chaplain for the colony, with a big spread out at Parramatta."

As the dog led them unerringly through a warren of cottages, pubs and steep narrow lanes, Ralph reflected that this raw town, small as it was, was as faction-ridden as the great cities Ralph had left behind.

"Where are we heading?"

"The Rocks. Most of the Government Men lodge here. Remember, you're free to work from three o'clock till sunset, to earn the money for your board. Keep your nose clean, and once you've done enough of your time a smart lad like you should get a ticket-of-leave. Then you can move about and earn some money."

Ralph was encouraged. It would seem that the lot of the transported convict, particularly if skilled or educated, was not as desperate as he had at first assumed.

"Some Emancipists, them as have worked out their sentence, are rich men, merchants with big houses, as keeps their own coach. Mr Redfern the Assistant Surgeon, he's an Emancipist, and a friend of the Governor, no less. Dines at Government House, he does, though the Colonel over at the barracks and the Exclusives cut up rough about it. They wouldn't be seen dead at the same table with one of us. No problem here, though," Clancy added, patting Ralph's arm. "I can't see anyways. I'll take your honest face on trust."

Dinner was corn soup seasoned with onion and a scrag-end of mutton, with stale bread to dip in it. Ralph, curious by now about his garrulous companion, asked him how he fetched up in New South Wales.

"I were a cracksman," he said with pride. "I could crack a crib in ten minutes. Housebreaker to you," he explained. "You don't need no eyes to pick a lock. Here, I'll show you." He reached up behind his chair to a shelf, and felt around for a leather bag. He tipped onto the table a padlock, a house-lock, and a smaller lock from a bureau drawer. Drawing out a ring hung with narrow rods, he demonstrated with an expert's delight in his craft how to release the mechanism without breaking it, or leaving tell-tale scratches. "You try, now. Learn something new every day, my Ma said." For the next hour he tutored Ralph in the finer points of lock-picking, beginning with the little bureau lock, until his pupil had the knack.

Ralph's eye was caught by a movement beyond the window. A dark cloud drifted past, like scraps of burned paper: bats, from their erratic flight. As the light failed, the room dimmed. Of course: his host had no need for a candle. Ralph sat on the floor, where he would sleep, listening as the shadows lengthened and the tone of Clancy's tales grew darker.

Echoing the soldiers' unwelcome advice, Clancy quashed any hope of a quick escape. "All the outgoing ships are searched," he explained, "by soldiers with a nose for convicts like an Exciseman's for brandy. There's some as get away, with sealers bound for New Zealand or American whalers, but most of them are scarce better off than if they stayed here, what with hard captains serving short victuals, and shipwrecks, and cannibals. I heard of one," Clancy said, his voice dropping, "as ran four year ago with a sealing gang. One of his mates saw him a year later, in a shipload of goods bound for London."

"In?" queried Ralph. "Surely you mean 'with'?"

"No, he was 'in' all right," retorted Clancy, with gloomy relish. "One of a basket of shrunken heads, he was, shrivelled up no bigger than your fist, with his cheeks carved in circles and his eyes sewn shut and his lips back from his teeth, like a dog that's going to bite. Reckon those New Zealanders must have eaten the rest of him."

The old man puffed contentedly on his pipe. He could not see the revulsion on Ralph's face. What a barbaric place.

Next morning Ralph made his way back along the dusty road. None of the roads here appeared to be paved. It was easy to find his way; the main part of Sydney town consisted of a coarse weave of streets running back a mile or so from the cove, clinging to the edge of this vast unmeasured land like a scrap of sacking flung down on a beach.

He was more alert this morning, and looked about as he went, noting a small ugly church with a squat tower, and the long line of the barracks with its flagpole on the crest of the hill. The familiar was jumbled with the strange. He was used to the red coats of the soldiers and the white square-set cottages with their pots of geraniums behind neat picket fences, but the sultry heat, the raucous cries of unknown birds, and the strange trees belonged to a jungle.

He checked in alarm. He had almost tripped over a lizard, about a foot long, banded in shades of slate grey, as thick as his wrist. It hissed at him, forelegs akimbo. Opening its mouth, it bared bony gums and a large tongue of vivid cornflower blue.

Laughing, he played St George to this indignant little dragon, picking up a stick and holding it in front of the creature's jaws. They promptly clamped shut, and Ralph lifted it, dangling and undignified, clear of the path.

At the lumberyard the convicts waited about. A squad of soldiers lounged, supervised, if the word could be used by anyone with such a bored expression, by an elegantly-dressed young officer on horseback. That should be me, Ralph thought, well-dressed, well-mounted. He loitered as he passed for a better look at the horse, a showy grey. It tossed its head, tugging the reins. The officer turned with an exclamation of annoyance. Ralph stared at him intently, willing him to see that he was not just a common criminal.

But while Ralph had regarded him with the frank look of an equal, the stare he received in return was both demeaning and disturbing. One might look so assessing a dog, Ralph thought, as the rider moved on. In London he would have been grateful to know me.

Ralph asked the man next to him for the officer's name.

"Devereux," replied his informant out of the side of his mouth. "Haven't been here long, have you?"

"Why do you say that?" Ralph was nettled.

The man turned to look at him. He was short and hard-faced, with tightly-curled brick-red hair; disproportionately broad in the shoulders and chest. "Don't draw attention to yourself, specially from the likes of him." He spat dismissively.

Ralph felt a burst of impatience. It was all very well for these criminals to skulk about; that frizzy-haired fellow looked as though he had not done an honest day's work in his life. But Ralph had business to attend to back home. He could not afford to moulder here in New South Wales.

# 13

## *New South Wales, Summer 1816*

"Fletcher? Beckworth?"

Ralph and the rusty-haired man stepped forward.

"Josiah Barrett's my name." The farmer towered half a head above Ralph. He was broad in proportion, his girth emphasised by a wide leather belt. He clutched a permit in fingers like sausages. "I need extra men to finish the harvest. Work hard and you'll be paid fair. No loafers."

"What's the rate, sir?" Beckworth enquired politely.

"One shilling and threepence a day, with rations found."

"Top rate's one-and-sixpence, sir," Beckworth replied. "There's none left off *Adelphi* but us." He smiled, reasonably.

Barrett gave him a sharp look. "Very well; one-and sixpence. I need one more—" he checked the list "—Kennedy." A bony Irishman lumbered across.

Barrett filled in their passes and handed them over. As they followed their new employer Ralph had to compress his lips so as not to smile. One-and-sixpence a day, he thought wryly. Even as a newly-joined subaltern, his allowance had been—he searched his memory—ten, no, fifteen times that amount. And here he was, about to work harder than he ever had before, for a fraction of what he had received at nineteen.

They passed houses and a brickyard; then an undulating landscape of farms and trees. The track was surfaced in gritty sand which dragged at his feet. He had to watch where he was going, so as not to trip.

The farmer set a brisk pace. After months of confinement, Ralph at first relished the exercise, running through marching songs in his head. The sun rose higher in the cloudless blue dome of the sky. Flies plagued them; small, tough and persistent, hovering around his face, crowding into his mouth and eyes, settling on the trickles of sweat, regrouping for another attack every time he flapped them away. The air grew fiercely hot.

As they left the town further behind they were surrounded by trees, but there were no glades of green shadow. The thin trunks rose high above the men's heads before separating into skimpy foliage; sun poured through every gap, burning his skin. To his right glinted the seemingly endless inlets and bays of the mighty harbour. Ralph was grateful to stop for a drink of water and a quick meal. Once more he was surprised by the seemingly casual nature of his imprisonment.

As he rested his aching feet he turned to Beckworth and asked quietly: "What's to stop us running away?"

"Where to?" Beckworth retorted. "Into the bush? Back to Sydney? A Johnny Raw like you would be nabbed within the week. Then it would be a flogging and six months in an iron gang. You're better off here. At least when we get to Concord tonight, we'll be fed."

After this discouraging reply, Ralph trudged on the rest of the day in silence.

After a night under guard, they set off early, jeered at by flocks of raucous cockatoos. Ralph reckoned they had made some dozen miles the previous day; and the same again by the following afternoon when they reached Parramatta. Barrett's farm was some distance yet. Ralph had made longer marches in Spain, but not when he was so unfit. His legs were stiff; every step was an effort. Beckworth loped on easily. Ralph, not to be outdone, ignored his burning muscles as best he could, and picked up his pace.

Sunset was vivid and sudden. Stars sprang out overhead, in strange patterns, Orion and Sirius upside-down. A bright constellation wheeled above, four points of a kite, held by two bright stars as a string. Beckworth saw the movement of Ralph's head as he looked up.

"That's the Southern Cross. You'd better get used to it. You'll not see your Pole Star again."

The moon hung huge and luminous above the edge of the world. Ralph's attention wandered. He was very tired. His feet burned; the rough boots had raised ferocious blisters. Would they never stop? He remembered a night march in Andalucia...

"Wake up, man! We're here."

A lamp swung in front of his face. He fumbled up a ladder into a rough loft, hauled the boots off his throbbing feet, and threw himself down onto a paliasse of sacking stuffed with corncobs. Sleep engulfed him.

Roused by the clang of an iron bar, he woke, ravenously hungry. Around him the others grumbled into wakefulness. Over his head was a sloping roof of saplings, criss-crossed by rough cords. He washed as best he could with the meagre water available; the others watched his ablutions with amusement.

"Why weren't you listed as a Special?" Beckworth queried. "What did you do? Get caught rove up one of the stable boys?"

Kennedy joined in. "The Colonel's fat wife?"

There was a bray of laughter.

"Happen it were his sister!"

Ralph restrained himself with an effort. If I could put up with my father calling me a stinking stable-boy, he thought, I can put up with this. Every word he spoke marked him as different. And there was no Macey here to take his part.

Kennedy spoke out, his pale eyes bright with malice. "A little bird told me he stuck a knife into some pimp down Whitechapel way."

Who had told him that? Thomasin, thought Ralph.

"They're a right bunch of scoundrels in the Seventh," said another. "They don't call them Mongrels for nothing."

Ralph stayed stone-faced. The anger he could not express boiled inside him. They must have seen that damned tattoo. He was acutely conscious of it: an irritation out of all proportion to its importance, like an obscenity daubed on a wall. It galled him that they could see it and he could not; incised into his skin in a land without mirrors.

Climbing down the ladder from the sleeping-loft, he saw it was already late afternoon. The barn clustered with other outbuildings around a yard. A long, low cottage built of rough slabs formed the front wall. Beyond this lay an extensive field of standing wheat, dotted with tree-stumps like the stubble on an unshaven chin.

Ralph followed the others to a trestle table. There was salt pork and cabbage, pumpkin and coarse bread, plenty of it, hot and fresh; nectar of the Gods after the monotonous fare on the ship. Ralph wolfed it down.

Barrett arrived as they finished. "Sleep during the day and work by night. Here is a scythe for each man."

Ralph took up his allotted place in the line. He swung the scythe, awkwardly at first, then with greater assurance as his body found the rhythm. His pride was at stake; he would not be bettered by these scrapings of the gaols. He was determined to keep pace with the others, though unfamiliar muscles were burning across his shoulders and the small of his back, and a blister was opening on his palm. He was grateful when they stopped. Water sluiced, deliciously cool, down his dry throat.

They worked into the evening. After the next break Ralph felt his muscles stiffen as he went to stand. Beckworth and the others got up easily; Kennedy looked over and laughed.

Ralph's muscles eased again after the first painful strokes. The night scene stood out around him, etched by moonlight; the stubble sparkled; he heard only the rustle of the falling sheaves, and the occasional mutter of words further down the line. After the incessant clamour of the last three months, he welcomed the silence. Above them, as they worked, the moon swung against the broad path of stars.

As the night sky paled, they stopped for breakfast. This was normally a meal Ralph took alone, after an hour's riding, at nine in the morning; not at five, after a night of heavy labour.

His stomach was pleasantly full; his hands and forearms prickling from the sharp ends of the sheaves, and his body buzzing with tiredness. He lifted and stacked the bound sheaves as the light around him strengthened into full day.

The sun was well up when the signal to stop was finally given; its growing warmth released a heady scent from the stubble. On Ralph it acted like a sleeping-draught. He fought to stay awake long enough to gulp down a final drink and climb up to his bed.

He dreamed that he was back in Bromley's garden at the ball. He glimpsed Flavia's shawl through a grid of boughs, and the glitter of the gems in her hair. Relief surged through him. She was still there. There was still time, to make all right. He reached out to touch her, but was distracted by Lucius tapping his shoulder. *No Mongrel will marry my sister.* Lucius would not let him go, he did not understand how important it was to find her, and explain …

With sour regret, he felt Beckworth's hard fingers shaking him out of sleep.

"Wakey, wakey!"

Every muscle—legs, arms, and back—had seized up. Should he stand suddenly, he would crack, like a flawed piece of metal. He sat up gingerly, his palms stinging as they took his weight. He looked down at blisters the size of shillings.

"Wearing our kid gloves today?" Beckworth gibed.

Ralph ignored him and got up. The paliasse was alive with fleas. He scratched, fiercely and surreptitiously.

After his breakfast—in this inverted world, with the shadows lengthening into afternoon, should he call it dinner? —his mood improved. Again Barrett was handing out the tools.

"You're new to farm work?"

Ralph, his mouth still full of a last grabbed crust, gave a nod.

"I've been watching. You put your back into it. I've had trouble with lazy Government Men before."

Ralph tried to work out whether this statement, delivered in a gruff monotone, amounted to a compliment or a warning.

"Show me your hands." Ralph turned them palms-up. The farmer grunted. "They'll harden up, but you could use some salve. Jane!"

A girl came across from the cottage.

"Fetch the salve and some clean rags."

Ralph suspected that the farmer's concern arose not from any feeling for him, but from a need for his labourers to be fit, as one must have healthy animals if a farm is to prosper. But his hands did feel better for the pig's grease, and once he had worked off the initial stiffness his body limbered up.

> *As I went out, one morning early*
> *To breathe the sweet and pleasant air*
> *Who should I spy but a fair young maiden*
> *Whose lips were like the lily fair.*

That was the song Flavia had played. The melody stayed with him as he worked up one row, and down the next.

> *I'll not go with you to Pennysylvany*
> *I'll not go with you to a distant shore;*
> *For my heart is with Riley and I can't forget him,*
> *Though I may never see him no more.*

All at once the song cut too close to the bone. Did you betray me that night?

He straightened up as a sudden movement in the moonlight caught his eye. He had disturbed a snake, which poured itself away into the shadows. Clancy had warned him of poisonous snakes, and spiders with fangs that could pierce your toenail. It was impossible to watch out for them in the dark. He finished as fast as he could and moved on.

When next he went over to the water-bucket, he found Beckworth, noisily gulping more than his share, splashing his face and head. He flicked water at Ralph, and jabbed him with his elbow.

"So sorry, *Mister* Fletcher. The gent's in a hurry. He'll do his guts a mischief, if he keeps on at this pace."

"My pace is my business," snapped Ralph, and made to turn away. Sharp nails pulled him back. His eyes followed the glittering edge of the scythe held upright, point towards him, like the beak of some enormous bird of prey.

"What you do here is everybody's business. We're happy to work, nice and comfortable, on the Government Chain. Whose side are you on? You might like being Barrett's blue-eyed boy, but it makes the rest of us look bad, see?"

Ralph pulled away from the other's grip. Bone idle, the lot of them, said the Fairfax voice inside his head; too lazy to do an honest day's work, and too sly to let anyone else show them up. No wonder they had fetched up in a penal colony. As the others sauntered away, Beckworth called back:

"This time we're asking you nicely."

The whetstone rasped as Ralph sharpened his scythe. Why should he collude with these shysters to cheat Barrett of a fair day's work? The farmer reminded him of one of his father's tenants; a Quaker of unyielding rectitude who touched neither liquor nor loose women. Ralph tested the edge of his blade. A Fairfax worked as he pleased.

The next day passed uneventfully. Ralph worked quickly, deliberately leaving the others behind. As afternoon darkened into evening, he strove to maintain the gap between himself, isolated on the edge of the field, and the gang of dark figures whose scythes glinted behind him in the moonlight. As the midnight meal approached, Ralph remembered men like Beckworth he had known in the Army, tough, sour, lazy old hands. He could do what he liked, so long as Ralph had a decent meal first. Even so, he scanned the path for likely points of ambush as he walked back to the cookhouse.

The workers ate under Barrett's stern eye, like recalcitrant boys under a master. The pork and pumpkin brought renewed vigour. There was even a mug of hot tea. Never had Ralph felt a keener appreciation of food. In Vienna he had been cloyed with chocolate and cream, his appetite dulled by hours of sitting in gilded chambers.

A clatter of dishes startled him. The others had already gone. That was foolish; he had meant to leave first. With his scythe at the ready, like a sentry's musket, he traversed the rows of stubble. The others were binding and stooking now; he set down the scythe reluctantly, missing the reassurance of that smooth shaft of seasoned wood.

Behind him the stacked sheaves of wheat marched like pawns on a huge chessboard. He worked automatically, bending, tying, stacking; pausing occasionally to rub his nose where the chaff tickled. A welter of ideas drifted through his mind. He would begin to follow one through, when imperceptibly it would change into something else. Halfway through one of these vague transitions he realised suddenly where and when the others would attack.

Around him the darkness blurred into pink-edged dawn. As soon as Ralph saw the signal to stop, he slipped back to the kitchen. Only the farmer's daughter was there, ladling stew.

"Excuse me, Miss," said Ralph at his most polite, "would you have any pepper?"

She smiled shyly and pointed to a jar.

"Thank you," he said and, blocking her view, tipped half a handful into his palm. He was seated at the table outside by the time the others arrived. The Irishman, pretending to stumble, kicked at Ralph's stool, but Ralph had anchored it with his full weight. The other stubbed his toe and cursed.

"I'll have no foul language here," rumbled Barrett. "You, Kennedy, eat with the pigs if you cannot take your meal in decent fashion."

The Irishman limped away, glaring.

Ralph ate quickly, his mind on the outbuildings he must pass on his way to the barn.

"That's enough for tonight." Barrett's deep voice lingered over the prayer of thanksgiving.

Ralph strode briskly across the yard, conscious of Beckworth behind him and Kennedy ahead. Once round the corner he would be out of Barrett's sight.

He called down the empty alley as he turned. "Enjoy your meal, Kennedy?"

"I'll lend you a poke!" Into his path sprang the furious Irishman, wielding a fencing stake. Now the trap would close from behind.

Ralph feinted to dodge past. Kennedy swung; Ralph flung the pepper full in the Irishman's face as his club whistled past. The man fell back with a cry, hands to his face. Before Ralph could follow up his advantage, Beckworth was upon him. Ralph doubled over with a fist in his belly, dropped, and rolled. His foot caught the other's knee with a satisfying jar. He twisted round and grabbed Kennedy by the belt, hauling him off-balance into his leader, who tripped as well. The three of them fell in a flurry of arms and legs.

Ralph flailed with his arm to block another punch. He heaved to dislodge the man sitting on top of him. For all his bony frame, Beckworth weighed heavy as a sack of bricks. Ralph threshed again and felt him give; drew his knee up for leverage and flung him off. A boot crunched where his hand had been.

There was a low whistle: "Barrett's coming!"

Ralph lurched to a valedictory kick; his attackers fled, swift as cats. He was squatting unsteadily on his haunches when Barrett appeared, tight-faced, gripping an axe-handle. He loomed above Ralph like a tree.

"You been fighting?"

His tone warned Ralph that it would be better if he had not. He lied with a fluency forgotten since his schooldays.

"I tripped on that wood there." There echoed in his mind a series of excuses, each more ludicrous than the last: I dropped my snuffbox. I have mislaid the diamond pin from my cravat. The corners of his mouth quirked.

Barrett looked unconvinced. "Get to sleep, then," he snapped. "There's more work tomorrow."

Ralph stood, spat the grit from his mouth, and headed for the water-trough. The others stood around Kennedy, his eyes screwed shut, dabbing his crimson face. He looked like a small boy who had been crying. Ralph laughed.

"What's so funny?" asked Beckworth, sourly.

Ralph shook his head. "If I told you, you wouldn't believe me."

# 14

## *New South Wales, Summer 1816*

After their failed attack, Beckworth and the others left Ralph alone. By fighting back he had drawn a line in the sand; his assailants returned to the loft as if nothing had happened. Ralph slept soundly, but woke to a rough prodding. It was still full night. Barrett, a lamp bobbing in his hand, was rousing the men himself.

"Get up, the lot of you. The corn needs loading. Who can figure and write?"

Ralph sat up, half asleep, staring at the farmer until he realised that only he, of the five, could read. He ventured a hand. Barrett stared at him piercingly, as if to seek out any mischief lurking within. "I need a clerk to keep tally. No tricks, now; I'll be checking the numbers at the other end."

Ralph resented Barrett's unremitting suspicion, though he had to admit he would not trust his companions an inch. He soon learned the reason for Barrett's haste. The next day but one was Receiving Day. They needed to start early because no more grain would be accepted after the Government Store was full.

After a quick breakfast, they loaded the sacks onto two-wheeled drays as massive and unwieldy as the bullock-teams that drew them. Their drivers, in clothes whose original shape and colour were long forgotten, cursed as they prodded and heaved. Their beasts were as solid as mountains. Ralph swore as one backed onto his foot, and limped for half-an-hour after. He could understand why the bullockies blasted and goddamed as they did.

Eventually the last knot was pulled tight. As Barrett's unofficial secretary, Ralph was to accompany the load. Barrett handed him a folded paper: his pass, entitling him to be absent from his place of assignment for four days.

"The pass is for four days only. Show this to the constables when they ask for it, or any soldier. Lose it and you'll be straight in the lock-up."

Ralph was neither a fool, nor a child. Why should his every movement be subject to mistrust? Their journey was hardly a major undertaking. As he well remembered from Spain, bullocks travelled so slowly that he could walk the distance in the same time. The long train of animals started out to the crack of whips and the thwack of long sticks. Ralph stretched himself along the top row of sacks, and with the sky lurching from side to side above him, drifted back to sleep.

When he awoke, the carts had stopped and he could smell smoke. He sat up, yawning. A billy steamed over a fire. Ralph jumped down as the bald-headed bullocky ladled him out a pannikin of tea, and handed him a hunk of bread.

"How long do we stay here?"

"Why, for the night, of course. We don't run these beasts in stages, like the Exeter Mail. I can just see old Blossom pounding along like a rum prad at eight miles an hour." He grinned toothlessly at his own joke.

Ralph sighted Barrett further down the line. Recalling his duties, he started to count the sacks on the load. The bullocky called from behind him.

"Hey! Here's a friend to see you."

A friend? His heart leapt: someone who knew who he was; who could speak to the authorities, so he could go home...

"You are Fletcher? Davies said—"

Davies! Hope wilted. He was foolish even to entertain such thoughts.

"Over there." The man pointed to a stand of stringy trees. Ralph saw as he approached his Welsh cellmate of the voyage out, brindled in the shadows. With his thin face and dark brown eyes, body taut with anxiety, he looked more like a sheepdog than ever.

Ralph remembered how quiet he had been on the ship. Now he poured out a torrent of words. His voice was so soft, and his speech so heavily accented, that Ralph had to ask him more than once to slow down.

His story was simple enough. Mellors, the Major of Marines, had taken a fancy to the pretty Megan. Instead of husband and wife finding work together, as he had intended, Davies had found himself assigned to the holding of Mellors' brother, thirty miles out. Meanwhile the Major tried to coerce Megan to accept a post euphemistically described as "housekeeper", at the barracks in town.

"Like David and Bathsheba, it is," finished Davies bitterly. "I am Uriah the Hittite, to be sent out of the way. What can she do? She has none to care for her but me." His hands tightened on the stick he used as a crook. His expression was fierce for so mild a man. "If he lays a finger on her, I will kill him." He lapsed into a stream of Welsh.

Ralph sipped at his now-cold tea. Ralph knew the Major's cunning from his own experience. Nothing a lowly convict-shepherd could do would stop him. Nor could Ralph see how he could help.

Davies turned to him, pleading. "You are a *chentleman*. They will listen to you where they would laugh at me." Ralph went to protest; Davies clutched his arm. "Please, sir." The honorific came naturally. "You know Lieutenant Hunter. Perhaps he can put a stop to this."

Ralph's ready excuses failed. The man was desperate; he had no other recourse. In his present mood he was capable of any folly. Hunter just might intercede on his behalf. Besides, Ralph was flattered by Davies' appeal. For the first time since he woke on the ship, someone had seen him as other than a criminal.

"Do you know where he is lodging? Mind, I can promise you nothing."

He clapped Davies on the shoulder. "Come on, have some tea." Or, as he realised just what he had taken on, something stronger, if the bullocky had it.

All the next morning was taken up completing the slow journey into Sydney, re-checking the load, and transferring it to the Store. Not until late in the afternoon could Ralph set off, having begged leave from Barrett to attend to business for a friend. He was under strict orders to be back at the inn by sunset. Only the mention of Hunter's name dispelled Barrett's suspicion that Ralph aimed to find a grogshop, or women, or both. Not, Ralph thought sourly, that he could come to any harm without so much as a penny in his pocket.

Ralph arrived at the direction he had been given, in a row of square-built sandstone cottages. He knocked on the green door. It was opened by a flaxen-haired girl barely tall enough to reach the latch.

"Does Lieutenant Hunter live here?"

The girl stared wordlessly up at him out of enormous grey eyes.

"Who is it?" Hunter himself appeared, in his shirtsleeves. "Fletcher! Your pass?" His eyes scanned the paper and he looked up. "If this concerns your case, you know I cannot discuss it." He went to close the door.

"It's another matter, sir, of some urgency." Ralph tried to keep the exasperation out of his voice. He was fed up with being scrutinised like a counterfeit coin.

"Very well," the officer said crisply. "Come in."

Hunter's room held a bed, a sea-chest studded with nails, a bookshelf topped with brass navigational instruments, and a table with two chairs. Hanging behind the door was his uniform coat. The light caught a shiny patch where the scabbard of his sword had rubbed; Ralph's own regimental jacket had worn likewise. Hunter sat down behind the table, Ralph standing like a defaulter before him.

"This concerns the wife of a Welshman named Davies, who was on the ship with me."

"Davies?"

"A little, quiet, narrow-faced fellow," prompted Ralph.

"Indeed. I have him now. Go on."

"Davies' wife, young and pretty, took passage on the ship. Major Mellors—" he chose his words with care "—has taken an interest in the girl. On landing he has so contrived matters that she is to take a domestic position in the barracks here in the town, while her husband herds sheep on a distant farmstead."

"His wife is not a convict?"

"No. She is a decent free woman, and by all accounts devoted to her husband. But Davies fears that Mellors will force his attentions on her. And after *Adelphi* sails, her prospects will be bleak indeed."

Ralph hoped he had not put his case too boldly. Fortunately for him, Hunter was recalling his hours as unwilling audience to Mellors' boasts of amorous conquest.

"Even supposing this were true," he said, with an expression of strict naval severity, "what do you propose I do about it? Why should I interfere in the affairs of a fellow-officer on a word of a convict? What is your interest in the matter?"

Ralph was too angry to be prudent. "I have no interest in the woman myself, if that is what you imply. I shared a cell with Davies for three months. He is unfortunate rather than vicious, a man who would be honourable and hard-working if given a chance. He came to me because he thought I might help him, and it was he who suggested your name because you struck him as fair. I would not want any woman of mine in Mellors' clutches. But perhaps I have been wasting your time."

He turned to go.

"No—wait." Hunter struggled to make up his mind. "Have you spoken to anyone else?"

Ralph shook his head.

"I shall have to investigate the matter, if only to ascertain that you and Davies have not concocted the whole business out of malice. If so you can expect to be punished."

"Will that be all, sir?" Ralph struggled to keep the edge out of his voice.

"Yes." Hunter looked up, stern-faced. "Remember: this must go no further."

Ralph left with a sense of relief.

He wandered down towards the harbour, drawn by the ships and their promise of freedom. He must have been mad to let Davies talk him into arguing his case. He would make an enemy of Hunter if it failed, and of Mellors if it succeeded. Why, Hunter was probably writing a letter at this very moment—

A letter! If he could write a letter, to tell someone where he was! It would take time, of course, for matters to be sorted out—he would have to allow from three to six months each way—but once someone in London knew the truth, there must be an inquiry, followed by a free pardon and his immediate release. Perhaps one of the sailors...

*"Out of the way!"*

He blinked as a team of horses clattered past, their hooves throwing up showers of grit. Get run over by a half a ton of horse and your release will be permanent indeed. As the thudding of his heart subsided, his daydream began to fall apart. Whom could he trust? Lucius, the author of his exile? Flavia, whose note had lured him into a trap? Frewin, for whom Ralph's disappearance could only have come as a relief?

Friends, then: but they had been in the Army; cheerful Crowther, with his puns and sudden fits, shot in Spain; Munro, the apprentice surgeon who had sewn up his shoulder, posted to America together with his vile tartan waistcoats, and dead by now, for all Ralph knew. He had fallen through a hole in the bottom of the world.

His mind was going round in circles. He stared at his rough boots with their thick leather laces; his palms hardened by the scythe. How was he to write a letter, with no paper, no pen, no ink, and no money to purchase them? He had never lacked so simple a thing as a piece of paper. He recalled the useless reams of embossed note-paper in his library at Longhallows. Why had he not thought to palm a sheet off

Hunter's desk? At least, he reflected, the thieves I live among know their craft.

And who would frank the letter for him? Here was another problem he had never grappled with before. Others had brought their mail to him for that all-important superscription. He could hardly front up to the Muster-Master and say: *Excuse me, Sir, but I have here a letter incriminating you in a gross miscarriage of justice; will you post it to England for me?*

A breeze came up off the harbour; the afternoon was fading into evening. I had better get back to Barrett, he thought listlessly.

As he hurried past the park, a dog romped out to greet him, waggling its barrel body as hard as its stub tail: little Gyp. She dabbed her nose wetly on his hand. The old blind man stood waiting patiently.

"How are you, Clancy?"

"Why, if it isn't Mr Fletcher!" Clancy sounded genuinely pleased. After the awkwardness of his last interview, Ralph felt himself relax. It was a gift the old man had, of giving simple pleasure. "Got a position, then?"

"I've been in a gang harvesting out Parramatta way, but that's almost finished. I don't know what will happen after that." His tone betrayed the studied cheerfulness of his words.

"Now don't you worry. A polite, well-spoken young fellow like you, who can read and write; you'll have no trouble. Some gentleman as needs a secretary will snap you up like a cake at a christening."

"Thank you, Clancy. When next we meet I'll buy you a quid of tobacco, and a bone for Gyp here. And I owe you for a night's lodging. Goodbye."

He waved to the old man as he walked on. Not that he can see it, he realised.

Outside the inn Barrett scowled at the angle of the sun.

"You're late."

"I met a friend," Ralph said shortly. The farmer sniffed as he passed, to check whether he had been drinking.

Ralph did not join the others in the bar-room. The hubbub leaked through the thin walls as he lay with his face turned to the shadows. He willed himself to sleep while the events of the day churned inside him. Never before had he felt this constant tension, this fear that things were happening faster than he could make sense of them. Black against the sputtering flame of the tallow candle, Barrett, huge and disapproving, pored over his Bible.

# 15

## *New South Wales, Summer 1816*

Reaping, threshing with awkward wooden flails; winnowing, measuring the last of the grain into sacks to sell locally; at length the harvest was done. They worked by daylight now, cleaning and greasing the reaping-hooks, sickles and scythes. In the yard Ralph stopped to wipe the sweat from his eyes, as the sun poured heat like a furnace from a cloudless sky. The others were already resting some distance behind him. The farmer's daughter, Jane, carried a bucket towards them from the house; Ralph watched her approach. He would have put her age at perhaps sixteen. With the collar of her dress white against her sun-browned skin, she looked like a milkmaid from a fairytale.

He grinned at her, and was rewarded by a shy smile. The girl's face tightened. She picked up the bucket and turned to run. I haven't had my drink, Ralph thought, and reached out to stop her. A swipe to the side of his head sent him sprawling. He landed on his back, winded. He fought for breath on the hard-packed earth while Barrett raged above him.

"I'll have no croppy near my daughter with his whoring ways. Keep away from her, d'ye hear?"

Ralph's astonishment gave way to anger. Any fool could see he meant the child no harm. He had regarded Barrett as a fair-minded man, within his narrow limits. The man had a fist like a blacksmith's hammer.

Ralph felt his cheek and winced. Fuming, he picked himself up, aware of Beckworth and the others, smirking. He recovered the scythe. All his pleasure in his work was gone. The side of his face throbbed. Stupid boneheaded oaf.

*Whoring ways!* Little chance of that over the past months, unless one's taste ran to other men. He had seen enough of that on the ship.

The scythe jarred against a stone. Ralph flung it quivering to the ground. Should Barrett's tools get blunted, well and good. Beckworth sauntered over with a pannikin, sharp with anticipation.

"Master can't strike an assigned man. You could report him to the magistrate."

Ralph gulped the water and shook his head. He felt humiliated enough already, without advertising it further.

Beckworth shrugged. "Have it your way."

What remained of the harvest Barrett arranged to sell to a contractor in Parramatta. Ralph walked along the yoked files of shaggy, patient beasts, checking the tallies. The lead bullocky waved his long whip.

"Oi! Fletcher! I got a message from that Welshman. He says thank you from him and his missus. Pretty little tit she is too."

"She's back with him, then?"

"They were packing up as I came through. He's assigned to some Navy cove out West. She's going too."

Ralph was cheered by the news. Hunter must have acted; that was one confidence not misplaced. He returned to counting, his mind half on Davies, and had already moved to the next wagon when something struck him as wrong. Surely there had been another sack? Kennedy had loaded it, but he was not to be seen. Barrett was some yards away, deep in discussion with another driver.

Ralph slipped back to their sleeping quarters. The light from the doorway picked out a tell-tale scatter of flecks across the floor. Where could you hide anything in this unfurnished loft? He poked about experimentally; kicked at the palliasses. Three yielded with the dry rustle of corncobs. On the fourth the surface layer of husks parted, and he felt the flowing resistance of grain.

He squatted and probed further. The inside was filled with long cloth pipes filled with wheat. These must have been carried inside the men's trousers. Ralph's eyebrows rose. No wonder they had tried to frighten him off. They certainly were an enterprising pack of rogues. He dusted his hands and stood up. Beckworth and his cronies were stealing Barrett's property. His duty was plain. He turned to go.

His finger strayed to his discoloured cheek. What if he simply went back to his counting? Barrett regards me as a felon like the rest: very well then, I will keep this to myself. He could feel the attention of the others as he resumed his place. Beckworth caught his eye. Expressionless, Ralph looked away.

Choosing not to tell Barrett was a petty freedom, but a freedom all the same. Tomorrow he would leave this place, and go back to Sydney with money in his pocket; a pittance indeed, but enough to buy him the services of a barber, and some better clothes. Next time he might find the congenial position Clancy had anticipated. Let Barrett moulder among his clods.

When Ralph returned to the hut, the floor had been swept and the grain had gone. What Beckworth and the others had done with it he neither knew nor cared.

The working party was consigned to a detachment of soldiers returning along the Parramatta road. Ralph's wages lay in a hard lump against his chest, in a little bag he had contrived and hung on a string around his neck. He did not trust his companions to keep their agile fingers out of his pockets.

Already this stretch of road had become so familiar he paid it little attention. His mind wandered as his feet followed the dusty hollows. He reflected on Davies and his wife with satisfaction. It boded well that so unlikely an enterprise should succeed. Perhaps in some position of trust, Ralph might be able to state his case with some hope of being believed, and gain the free pardon he deserved. Then home to England, to get to the bottom of this whole malicious business: his kidnapping; the mystery of the tattoo on his shoulder.

He had learned much from his months of seeing society from the wrong end of a telescope. At the very least, he thought as his coins jingled, he would raise the wages of his harvest help—and keep an expert eye on them himself, after his companions' lessons in shirking and theft.

The marching column moved at a brisk military pace. Ralph suspected that the sergeant had an assignation in Sydney; but by the time they reached the outskirts of the town, even he was flagging and called a halt. The day had been long and hot; the sunlight was thickening to gold as the sky showed the first tinge of evening.

Ralph stared languidly along the thread of road, and combed the sticky hair back off his forehead with his fingers. A familiar tubby shape trotted out from under the trees: the dog Gyp, leading his master. Ralph had remembered his promise to the old man, and bought a twist of tobacco off one of the soldiers. He stood up.

"Here, Gyp!"

The dog's ears pricked; she cast back to her master enquiringly. He urged her on. She moved out onto the road, her eyes on Ralph. Scarcely had the old man stepped after her when Ralph felt a drumming on the dry turf. Two horsemen raced around the bend at full gallop.

"Run!" Ralph yelled. Clancy faltered, unsure which way to go. The lead horse's powerful shoulder sent him sprawling. Gyp jumped snarling in his defence. The rider wrenched the big bay back on its haunches. Iron-shod hooves drove the dog under, yelping, as Ralph leapt at the reins, dragging the horse away from the beggar cowering on the ground. A riding-crop slashed Ralph's knuckles. He ducked a second blow.

"The man is blind!" he shouted, as the horse plunged and sidled. "You must have seen him!"

The rider, a sparely-built man of middle age, soberly dressed, leaned forward as Ralph frowned enraged into the glare of the low sun.

"Must?" It was a precisely-enunciated voice used to authority. The cold tone hit Ralph like a bucket of water. "You forget your station. Next you will say that I rode him down deliberately. Well?"

It had been on the tip of Ralph's tongue to say just that. The sergeant, awakening to his responsibilities, seized Ralph by one arm as a soldier grabbed the other, and forced him back to the side of the road.

The bits jingled as the horse shook its head. Ralph knew he should abase himself and apologise. The words stuck in his mouth. The man had run Clancy down.

"I see we will have to teach you manners. What is your name?"

The sergeant shook him.

Ralph was so beyond himself that it took him a moment to recall his convict identity. "Fletcher." His arm was twisted painfully. "Sir."

The rider switched his attention to the sergeant. "This insolent fellow attacked me. He should be charged."

"Aye, Mr Masters."

Ralph stood rigid with resentment as the bay and the other, a grey whose rider he now recognised as Devereux, turned away. His gaze flicked back to Clancy groping, calling with increasing desperation for his dog, which lay six feet away, broken in the dust. Ralph surged forward. He was wrenched back.

"You're not going anywhere," the sergeant growled. "You've got us all into strife. I hope you get something to learn you to keep your mouth shut. That's the whole bloody evening gone. Stick your hands out."

"Why?" He was genuinely perplexed.

"To clap the darbies on, you mooncalf! You're under arrest." The fetters were cold against his skin. That's all it means to him, thought Ralph; his plans for the night are ruined. Ralph's hands hung clumsy before him as he was marched away. The other convicts burst into a flurry of conversation.

"Damned lucky not to spoil a valuable horse," muttered the sergeant.

The door clashed behind him. The sunset branded a barred rectangle on the wall. Ralph moved beyond it, into the comforting darkness, and sat down on the edge of the bunk. The cell was stiflingly hot. He longed to pull off his shirt, but the handcuffs hampered him, so he tugged it loose and undid the buttons. He longed for a bath, a shave, fresh clothes. A hollow ache reminded him that he had missed dinner.

Ralph could not forget his last sight of Gyp and the old man. Had he checked the road was clear before calling the dog, this would never have happened. He knew how hard it would be for Clancy to manage without her, locked in his world of darkness.

His little hoard thudded against his breastbone. Perhaps he could bribe the turnkey to bring him some food. He hammered on the door for attention. In his mind he haggled over the price of a loaf of bread and a jug of water. The jailor, when he appeared, asked twice that, but Ralph was in no position to argue.

When the water arrived he drank half of it straight off, ate the bread, washed it down, and used what was left to clean himself up. His hand was bleeding again, so he tore off a strip of shirt with his teeth and bound it round his knuckles.

The sun had set now but the room was no cooler. He was surprised that the death of a mongrel dog should touch him so deeply. He mourned the loss of her friendliness and loyalty. There was little enough of those qualities in this place; that one man's carelessness should destroy them was wasteful and wrong. The cell door creaked open.

"You may wait outside, sergeant. I will be quite safe."

What was Devereux doing here? Ralph stood up, conscious of his dishevelled appearance.

Devereux's stock was untied and his breath smelt of rum. He held a bottle in his hand.

"Ah, Fletcher. Thought you might be thirsty. The others have all gone off to bed. Have a drink."

Ralph shook his head. He had learned in the last months the gap between convict and officer. Devereux was too ingratiating.

"No need to be shy, man." He patted the bench beside him and caught sight of the rough bandage. "Let me see that."

Devereux took a pull on the bottle, set it down, and came over. He laid a hand on Ralph's shoulder. Ralph pulled away. Devereux leaned closer.

"You're in a heap of trouble, Fletcher," he murmured. "Anyone can tell you're a cut above the rest. I need an educated man as a secretary. I could get you off this charge."

This was more than casual drunkenness, Ralph realised, with a shock of revulsion; it was lust. Only the remnants of commonsense restrained him from smashing Devereux in the face, handcuffs and all, and flinging him against the wall.

Ralph did not lower his voice. "Go seek your catamites elsewhere!"

Devereux's eyes widened. He reached for his sword-hilt, but he had come unarmed. His mouth compressed; he snatched up the bottle and Ralph feared he would hit him with it.

"You'll suffer for this, you ungrateful guttersnipe," he hissed. "Guard!" Ralph glimpsed the sergeant outside, trying to keep a straight face. Devereux lurched out the door, slamming it behind him.

He could at least have said something original, Ralph thought. With the tension broken, he was overcome by the incongruity of the scene. He rested his head on his forearms, shaking helplessly at the recollection of Devereux sidling up to him like a lecherous old squire, while Ralph defended his virtue like a village maiden. As his mirth subsided, he felt the stirring of unease, and his mood chilled. Devereux could hardly take the matter to higher authority. But Ralph knew that by tomorrow the sergeant's version of their *contretemps* would be all over the gaol, and Devereux would never forgive Ralph for making him look a fool. Masters had put him on a charge. Now Devereux had a grudge against him as well.

Ralph could not have stood by and watched a helpless old man run down. Nor could he so degrade himself as to prostitute himself for favours. What galled him was the knowledge that if Fairfax had acted thus, back home, his actions would have been applauded. That sordid interview with Devereux, in the unlikely event of it happening at all, would have been grounds for a duel.

When a gentleman stands up for himself, Ralph thought bitterly, he is upholding his rights: a convict is threatening the King's Peace.

So much had happened on that one day; the next three crawled by, as Ralph awaited the next sitting of the Court of Petty Sessions. He felt the yawning impatience of a spectator at a bad play, waiting for the curtain to come down so he might go home. He would have liked to shave; his half-grown beard gave him a villainous look which, along with his shapeless prison clothes, would do nothing to impress a magistrate. He remarked on this to the jailor when the day came round for his trial.

The turnkey gave a sharp bark of laughter. "You'll need more than a natty barber to get a good hearing from the beak. That Mr Masters you had your little spat with has a big holding up Newcastle way. At Coal River they don't take kindly to cheek from the likes of you."

Inside the courtroom, Ralph felt an odd sense of dislocation. Ralph Fairfax, displaced gentleman, looked out through the holes in a mask: everyone here, looking back, saw Ralph Fletcher, an unkempt convict charged with assault. The sergeant, red-faced in his high stock in the heat, gave his evidence: the accused had hurled himself at Mr Masters, seized his horse, and shouted abuse at him when he tried to defend himself.

The magistrate took off his glasses, and rubbed the bridge of his nose with finger and thumb, like a man with an incipient headache. He closed his eyes a moment then turned to Ralph in the dock. "What say you to this?"

"Not guilty, Your Worship," Ralph replied firmly. "An old man was run down. I tried to stop it."

The magistrate turned back to the witness. "Was the man seriously injured, Sergeant?"

"No, sir. He was only knocked to the ground. But his dog attacked Mr Master's horse, a fine animal, which could well have bolted, at great risk to his rider."

The magistrate addressed himself again to Ralph. "Did you shout at the complainant, as alleged?"

"I did. I was trying to get his attention. Clancy was blind. His dog was only protecting him. The rider came on at full gallop, and made no attempt to rein in."

"So you consider yourself an expert in equestrian matters?"

Ralph recalled the thousands of miles he had ridden in Spain, in all weathers, on every degree of horse, from proud Andalusians to broken-down nags. "As it happens, I do."

Too late, he realised the question had been meant as irony. His inquisitor's face hardened. He leaned forward.

"I see that you have but newly arrived. Your speech shows you are a man of some education. Taking into account your evident, if misplaced, concern for the old man, I have dismissed the more serious charge of assault."

Ralph's shoulders relaxed.

"However," he went on, "a declaration of Governor King permits the destruction of cur dogs flying at horses. In view of your arrogant demeanour, towards both the complainant and the Court, I have no hesitation in sentencing you to twenty-five lashes for insolence. This will encourage you to remember your condition, and keep your opinions to yourself when addressing your betters. You may stand down. Next!"

At a touch on the elbow, Ralph stepped down. Again he felt the dislocation of being two people at once; one inside his body, trying to absorb the magistrate's words; the other detached, watching. Back in the gaol he sat silent, his mind crawling with questions. Until now he had regarded his exile as a temporary inconvenience. But tomorrow opened like an abyss.

None of the others looked concerned. They diced, laughed, drank. He dreaded the sentence, and the deeper shame of letting his fear show. He felt again the apprehension of an imaginative boy with a father for whom courage was easy as breathing. Everard had "bottom"; he was "game".

On the battlefield, there was a shared fatalism. In the castle at Badajoz, facing the deliberate malice of torture, Ralph had been terrified. Please God, don't let this happen, he prayed, groping for words. I have done nothing wrong. I'm not asking for a miracle; only common justice.

A short, ugly man, arms blue with tattoos, got up from his dice and came over. "Have a swig, lad. You'll sleep better with some rum in your gut."

Ralph took the proffered bottle. The raw spirit clawed into his stomach. Imperceptibly he relaxed.

The scene was familiar from a dozen military punishments. He did not want to look at the convicts, ranked in line, for whom he was to provide a salutary example; still less at what had already begun, in the middle of the yard.

He could hear cicadas chirring, so loudly his ears throbbed. The sky was an open, guileless blue. The line shortened by one, a wide-eyed youth, who sobbed and cried out from the first touch of the cat. Then all too quickly the man ahead of Ralph was shrugging on his shirt with a fine show of defiance and swaggering off. His feet left red prints in the dust. Ralph swallowed.

He walked across the open square, his legs moving as though they belonged to someone else. He reached the triangle. In the strong sunlight, it threw a sharp black shadow. His nostrils flared as he stepped within its wooden arms.

A voice droned to his left. I know what they are about to do; I have watched it often enough, upholding discipline, shutting off disgust behind compressed lips. The old hands took it phlegmatically enough.

The soldier reached over to pull off his shirt. A faint breath of air tickled his skin. He took his place, feet straddling the clotted sand. Ropes bound his ankles and his body tilted forward as his wrists were lashed above his head. His weight dragged on his shoulders. He felt uncomfortable and ridiculous, like a skin pegged out to dry.

The guard offered him a length of strap. His first instinct was to spit it out. But he remembered the derision which had greeted the boy's cries, and mouthed it distastefully.

The soldier stepped back and lifted his hand. Ralph glimpsed the bored sergeant beyond him, his finger marking the place on the punishment list, and the eyes of the prisoners beyond.

"One!"

The thongs whistled across his shoulders, stinging. The first blows were no worse than the beatings he remembered from school. But all at once Ralph jerked forward and bit into the leather gag. The pain was suddenly sharper. The flogger had found his rhythm now and was drawing blood. Don't flinch. It's worse if you move.

The hiss of breath, the blood singing in his ears, the dispassionate counting voice, the *whitt* of the lash, pulsed together.

Cry out, release some of the pain. His mind clouded in panic. No, said a colder, clearer voice above the tumult: don't give them the satisfaction. Remember you are Fairfax: *Fortiter ad Finem*. It is your body, not theirs. He breathed out in a soundless whine. Fight them! First you must control yourself. Count; think of anything to blank out the pain. Don't cry out. The bones of his skull and jaw ached with the effort of fierce silence.

A gap in his hearing: the drumbeat had finally stopped. He had bitten deep into the gag; he worked his jaw to free it and spat it out. It left a foul taste in his mouth. The voice in his head instructed him: don't fall over when they cut you down. Put your shirt on. He was surprised how easy it was; his back was quite numb. How clumsy his fingers were. Right turn: he swayed and regained his balance. He felt suddenly very cold.

# 16

## *England, Spring 1816*

Poised at the raw edge of the freshly-cut grave, Flavia stared down at the coffin. The silver cross and name-plate glimmered against the dark wood. As the sexton held out a shovel piled with earth she grasped a handful and tossed it down, rattling on the lid in a dry tattoo of farewell. Slowly she walked back up the path, dusting the dirt from her gloves with a wrinkled ball of damp handkerchief.

Caught by the sun, the fresh spring leaves of the old oak danced vivid in the breeze. Around the leaning tombstones rusty with lichen, daffodils bunched, bright yellow; blue forget-me-not lay in soft swathes against the grass. Beyond, smoke rose lazily from the distant cottages. It was too benign a day for black mourning clothes, thought Flavia. Her father would have loved it, sitting out like an old dog in the warmth.

She was relieved that Lucius had finally told his father about the wedding. As far as they could tell, the invalid had appeared to welcome the news. It had obviously been a comfort to him that Lucius was at last settled, and with the news of the pregnancy barely a month after the wedding, the family name secure.

Ribbons of dark crepe stirred against the yellow varnish as Lucius handed his sister up into the new carriage. Flavia, in defiance of convention, had insisted on attending the interment. Caroline, just returned from her honeymoon in France, waited more properly back at the house. With her delicate build, her condition was already starting to show.

How strange it was to walk into the house and know Father was no longer there. His favourite paintings still hung on the walls; the familiar furniture stood still in his preferred places. The library door was ajar; his last parcel of books, pages still uncut, cluttered the table. Flavia had the uncanny feeling that if she looked up she would see him seated in his chair. The notion half comforted, half frightened her. She pushed the door fully open. Her brother's new desk sat against the wall until a space could be cleared. Lucius was master of Fontclaire Priory now.

Over the next weeks there were visits from neighbouring gentry and notes of condolence from others further afield, Cousin Harriet in London, Bromley in Manchester. But the letter Flavia most hoped for never came.

Only now, with her father dead, did she realise how much of her time had been spent in nursing him. She filled the gaps in her day supervising a belated bout of spring cleaning. Curtains were taken down and washed; carpets beaten; mattresses turned out, their feathers aired, and restuffed. There were clothes to sort and give away; chests and cupboards to empty and tidy.

Flavia had Molly Simpson to help her, but the girl seemed increasingly indolent and withdrawn. One afternoon Flavia turned to ask her help clearing a cupboard, and found her asleep on the bed. Her first impulse was to shake her awake and rebuke her, but looking at her, she checked.

Molly was noticeably fuller in the face. As she lay, her arm outflung, Flavia saw an elongated diamond of fresh fabric set into the side-seam of her dress. The girl was pregnant.

Flavia remembered Lucius's interest in Molly. She stood up abruptly; the girl woke.

"I'm sorry, Miss," she apologised, colouring. "The heat must have come over me." She sat up with the awkwardness Flavia had come to recognise in her sister-in-law.

Gripped by a sensation almost of dread, Flavia blurted out: "You are with child, aren't you?"

The girl's lips shaped a denial, but she could not give it voice.

"Who is the father?"

She stayed silent.

"Is he in a position to marry you?"

A shake of the head.

"Have you told your family?"

The girl was scared into speech. "Dad will beat me if he finds out. Please don't tell him!" Flavia recalled Simpson from the village, a dour, stalwart man, given to violence in his cups.

"How could you do such a thing!" Flavia exclaimed, exasperated. Had her father known of Molly's condition, she would have lost her position forthwith. Lucius, as head of the household, must be told; but given her suspicions of the child's paternity, Flavia shrank from the task. The matter was beyond her experience. Molly, now the shock of discovery was over, sobbed noisily into her apron.

Flavia needed someone to talk to, but she was loath to approach a stranger with what might be a family scandal. What of old Sarah Rusden? Though ancient now and crippled, she had for many years been the village midwife. More to the point, she never betrayed a confidence.

Sarah's cottage looked picturesque from the lane. Its grey thatched eaves and strongly-marked timbers would make a pretty watercolour, Flavia thought, with the row of hollyhocks up the path adding daubs of colour. On closer inspection the garden gate hung awkwardly on one hinge and the plasterwork beside the door had peeled, exposing the lathes beneath.

The old woman was sparrow-spare, so tiny that Flavia towered over her.

"Ah, Miss Stanton. You'll be wanting to come in."

The room was dark after the bright sun outside. A small fire burned in the grate, yet a musty smell of damp pervaded the tang of wood-smoke. As Flavia's eyes adjusted she saw tell-tale dark streaks down the back wall. She was surprised; she had not remembered the cottage being so shabby.

Flavia worked the conversation through the prescribed sequence of topics the old woman regarded as good manners: the weather, her grandson Luke, the latest events in the village.

"Mr Charles was a good master to us until he fell ill," Sarah observed. "He let me stay on here when my Tom was lost at sea."

"I am sure Mr Lucius will follow in his footsteps. I will ask him to send round the carpenter."

"Mr Charles would not have needed telling," the old woman replied.

Flavia felt the rebuke. There was little hope, she knew, of inducing her brother to visit what he would call "a smelly old woman in a smellier cottage."

"It's about the house I came to see you," she said. "Not this house," she corrected herself nervously, "but Fontclaire. Molly Simpson is with child."

A quick flash of the eyes, as quickly hidden, told Flavia this news came as no surprise.

"I hesitate to tell my brother," Flavia continued, disconcerted, "because Molly will not name the father. If we send her back to her family I fear she will be harshly treated."

"Happen she should have thought of that before," the old woman observed. "But she's not the first maid in this village to get herself in the family way, and she won't be the last. She's a strong girl; she'll bear her bastard with no trouble."

"But who will care for her?" Flavia exclaimed, taken aback by the old woman's callousness. "She cannot stay at Fontclaire in her condition."

Sarah leaned forward to stir the fire. "She has a sister in service in London," she remarked at length. "She can stay with her till the child is born, and put it out to nurse. She's a fool, that girl; with a face like hers she could have wed any of the local lads. Now no one will have her."

Poor Molly, Flavia reflected on her way home. The whole course of her life was changed; the stigma of bearing an illegitimate child had set her beyond the pale.

What had Sarah meant by that look? Did she know more about Lucius than she was prepared to say? And there was the state of that cottage; standards had slipped during her father's illness. He had always prided himself on his care of the older tenants.

Now these obligations were her brother's responsibility. Her father's table had gone from the library now, and in its place was Lucius's broad desk, spread with architectural drawings.

"Flavia! Excellent: I wish to seek your advice. Here are the plans for my new coach-house and stables, to replace the orchard. Which do you prefer? The Palladian or the Gothic?"

"If you have money for building," Flavia replied, "please spare a few pounds to repair Sarah Rusden's cottage. It's a disgrace."

"Cottage?" retorted Lucius. "We have needed a new coach-house for years. It was all very well making do while Father was alive; we had only one carriage, and he rarely used it anyway. But now there is my phaeton, and the new team of bays, prime horseflesh, far too valuable to risk in that dank old shed." He waved a dismissive hand. "No proper ventilation—that patch on the roof—poor drainage—their hooves will be rotten by autumn."

It was pointless to reason with Lucius in this mood. Flavia felt an edge of anger. She had as much as promised Sarah that the work would be done. Perhaps she should leave it till tomorrow, when the first rush of her brother's enthusiasm had passed. It would be tactful to show an interest.

She studied the two drawings. "I prefer that one," she said, handing back the Gothic. "It accords better with the house."

Lucius looked crestfallen. "I thought the other more modern. But Caroline agrees with you. She says the Gothic has more *feeling*."

Flavia went outside, hoping to enlist her sister-in-law as an ally in Sarah's cause. Caroline was resting on a swinging chair in the orchard. With the tendrils of leaves and blossoms behind her, she looked like a shepherdess in a Watteau painting. Even her black mourning-dress, its sash tied high, only served to enhance her fragility. Her condition became her, Flavia thought; not for her Molly's mopings and distress.

Caroline looked up from the pages of her magazine as Flavia approached.

"Now I am *enceinte*, Mother says, I must dress with particular care." She teased out a blonde ringlet with her fingers and looked at it critically. "Perhaps I need a rosemary wash for my hair. Have you tried it?"

Flavia ran a dismissive eye over the extravagant claims for Godfrey's Cordial and Daffy's Elixir. "Lucius showed me the plans for the new coach-house."

"Did you like the Gothic?" said Caroline, brightly.

"Yes," said Flavia with a smile, pleased to find something on which they could agree. "I know Lucius has his heart set on this project; but one of the estate cottages is sadly in need of repair. It will cost very little. The tenant is an old widow who has always looked to the Stantons for support. Now you are a member of the family, I hoped you might raise it with Lucius."

The girl looked at her blankly. "But we must start the coach-house before Mother comes. I told her it would be ready by the winter."

Flavia reminded herself that Caroline had not lived all her life among these people; she could not be expected to feel the same sense of responsibility. Then the words sank in. "Your mother is coming? When?"

"Three weeks, she said."

Flavia, alarmed at the prospect of sharing the house with Mrs Lennox, did her best to look pleased. "Her company will be a great support to you."

"Yes; she means to stay till after the baby is born."

Flavia's heart sank.

Each day the carter delivered more trunks and portmanteaux, piled in a growing stack in the hall until Flavia could prepare rooms for the visitors. She was too busy sorting through the old furniture in the tower and mending sheets for the extra maid and coachman to discuss Molly Simpson with her brother. She lightened the girl's duties as far as she could while she wrestled with the problem of how to raise such a delicate subject, made even more embarrassing by the possibility that Lucius might be the father.

Mrs Lennox and her entourage swept in like an occupying army. Besides the guests Flavia had expected, there came also a cook to provide Caroline with special dishes, a nursemaid for the baby, a cheeky groom, and a brilliantly-coloured, raucous parrot.

The extra numbers threw out Flavia's careful planning. She had to ask three of the Fontclaire servants to double up, to make room. The new groom lounged about the stables, picking fights; the cook clashed with Mrs Wallace, jealous of this intrusion into her domain. The parrot got loose and chased Betsy Turner's cat up a tree. Wailing, the cat clung beyond the reach of the longest ladder, until retrieved by Molly Simpson's young brother Sam, at a cost of three scratches and a shilling.

In the midst of all this Flavia noticed some money had gone missing: two guineas which she was sure she had left on her dressing-table. She wondered whether the parrot had taken them, attracted by the bright shine of the gold. The bird was surprisingly dextrous with its strong hooked beak and agile claws.

Meanwhile Mrs Willis and the new cook wrangled over who should first use the stove in the morning. Wearily Flavia adjudged their complaints. When the decision went against the newcomer, she went to Mrs Lennox, who appealed to her daughter. Caroline then used her influence with Lucius to override Flavia's verdict. Flavia tried to convince herself that it would all pass over as the visitors settled in.

Lucius could see nothing wrong; in her condition, his wife should have familiar faces around her. This did not stop him querying the increased bills. "A gross of beeswax candles? In a month?" At the expression on his sister's face he wrote out the cheque with no further comment.

It was Molly who brought matters to a head. Flavia returned one day to find her maid bedraggled and red-eyed, with Mrs Lennox, hard-faced, shaking her by the shoulders.

Flavia's frustrations of the last weeks boiled over. "Leave the girl alone!" she snapped. "You have no right to manhandle my servant. If you have any complaints, bring them to me."

Mrs Lennox turned to Flavia with a sneer. "Have it as you will. She is a thief." She pointed to the table. There lay the two missing coins. Flavia turned to Lucius for support.

He shook his head. "It's true, Flavia. We found these in her room."

Flavia, appalled that the girl had betrayed her trust, stared at her, unbelieving. Molly stood defiant beneath the tears.

"She is a slut to boot!" added the older woman, pulling Molly's dress tight to betray the unmistakeable curve of her belly. "Do you tolerate such conduct in your servants?"

Flavia's temper rose. "As a guest here, you might have raised the matter more courteously," she said, as levelly as she could.

Embarrassed, Lucius intervened from behind his imposing desk. "I sent for you earlier, but you were out."

"Send her to prison!" exclaimed Mrs Lennox. The girl's pupils widened in fear.

"No!" Whatever she had done, Molly did not deserve this onslaught.

"Mrs Lennox is right, Flavia," Lucius said gently. "She must be made an example, to teach the house servants respect for property. They cannot be allowed to thieve with impunity."

Flavia felt the prick of angry tears. Had she no authority at all in her own home? For the theft of two guineas, Molly would be hung, or at the least transported. Flavia turned to her.

"Why did you take the money, Molly?"

The girl looked up, shamefaced. "I meant to run away," she muttered, "and use it for me and the baby."

"A likely story!"

Flavia ignored the interruption. "You have a sister in London, do you not?" The girl nodded. "Have you taken anything else?" She shook her head.

All at once Flavia knew what she would do. "It is my money. I will not press charges. Molly will go to her sister."

Mrs Lennox swung round to Lucius. "It is not Miss Stanton's place to make that decision. Caroline is mistress in this house."

There was a moment of silence. Flavia's eyes blazed. "Then I shall take Molly to London myself, and stay with Cousin Harriet."

"But—" began Lucius.

"Come, Molly," said Flavia, her heart pounding. "We have trunks to pack."

# 17

## New South Wales, Autumn 1816

Ralph stared at the sandstone wall, dinted and seamed, which shut off the narrow yard from the bustle of the cove beyond. Behind him lay the hospital, a long, segmented building with poky rooms and mean windows. The fierce heat of summer had faded; the breeze on his face was cooler, with the first hint of autumn. The cut across his knuckles was healing, and would leave only a faint line. His back still burned at every movement. He would carry those scars to the end of his days, branded by them as a felon.

And what of Flavia? On his first night in the hospital Ralph had been consumed with piercing regret that he had not followed his impulse and made love to her that afternoon, while his body was still unmarred. She would have accepted him then, and not betrayed him. No gentleman's daughter would want him now. The very whores in the street would despise him.

His initial distress had soured to a corrosive bitterness, the weals eating into spirit as well as flesh. Had Flavia's warmth been only an illusion? Perhaps he had imagined it all. Under the cuts of the lash, in the measured half-minutes between, the beliefs that had shaped his life had crumbled. Love, hate; true, false; just, unjust: sounds with no meaning. Worse than the physical pain was the loss of self-respect, displaced by self-loathing. He raged at his own helplessness.

As soon as they were fit, the convalescents were set to light work. Ralph found himself cleaning boots, a mindless task which left him free to brood. He had no choice now but to accept that his real life was here. His clothes, his future, the welts which disfigured him, were those of Ralph Fletcher, convict. It was his memories of England that were insubstantial.

Ralph found himself working on a riding-boot of Spanish leather. He had seen that stitching before: only inches from his eyes, the day

Gyp died. The fine silver spur had been strapped on—there. He traced the mark on the leather.

What could he do with a pair of boots? He spat on them, with a curse for every rub. The battered wicker hamper had a paper tag: *Cumming's Hotel, Macquarie Street*. So Masters was still in town. Ralph had teased out some more information about him from the infirmary clerk.

"Masters? Him from Newcastle? From Canada, they say; family Empire Loyalists, or some such. Very sharp."

That night, as he lay unsleeping, he remembered a story his father's gamekeeper told him, about his revenge on the farmer who shot his dog. The next morning Ralph spent most of his small store of money, bribing the clerk to buy him aniseed.

Friday came; a different hamper this time, of shoes. Perhaps Masters had left. But on Saturday the boots were back.

On Sunday Ralph, buoyed by excitement, joined the line of fellow-prisoners for compulsory Divine Service, shuffling along the gallery of the ugly church he had passed the day he landed. The parson was a short, dumpy Yorkshireman, his tightly-pursed mouth dragged down by deep lines to a small fleshy chin. Ralph found his sermon hard to follow; the Catholic Irish next to him, here under duress, kept up a resentful fidget.

The clergyman's eyes bulged with divine wrath: *"Satan's kingdom … depravity and vice … nay, the very prayers of the wicked are an abomination unto Him…"* No consolation here. The coarse shirt chafed Ralph's shoulders; he eased his weight to the other foot.

"Who's that?" he whispered to the little Irishman next to him.

"Marsden, the Flogging Parson," his informant mouthed back. "Don't get athwart him! *'The Lord have mercy on your soul,'*" he quoted, "*'for the parson will have none.'* He's magistrate at Parramatta."

So this was Clancy's "Crummy-guts". Ralph composed his features attentively as the preacher glared up at the gallery.

*"What lamentable depravity pervades every part of society! There is no sin, however serious, which is not practised without remorse amongst us. Lying and perjury and theft, and whoredom and blasphemy and drunkenness are daily committed amongst us…"*

A ripple of distraction played along the men to Ralph's left. Masters, arriving late, pushed his way along a pew. From outside the church door came a scratching and whining, muffled by the thick wooden panels. A soldier opened the door a crack; a grubby mongrel scurried through, yapping, bounded up the aisle, then leaped and fawned at Masters' knees. More barks and yelps announced other dogs outside, their entry thwarted. The congregation's enforced solemnity quickened to curiosity, then a rustle of laughter.

Masters, goaded out of his reserve, kicked at the vagrant, but it was a nimble cur and kept up its dervish prancing until a corporal of the 48th grabbed it by the scruff and bore it out, writhing, at arm's length.

The Irishmen beside Ralph had the high colour of suppressed mirth. The sermon was forgotten. Masters sat coldly and rigidly angry.

Ralph hugged his satisfaction to himself. He had meditated on his text for the day: *an eye for an eye; a tooth for a tooth; a dog for a dog.*

The charge was unexpected: the theft from Barrett of five sacks of wheat. Ralph had counted on Masters' fear of ridicule to protect him. Adulterating boot-polish was hardly an indictable offence. Masters lived a long way out, and Ralph might reasonably have expected never to have crossed his path again.

Well, he was wrong. He had plenty of time to dwell upon his miscalculation as he was confined in a solitary cell. The warder was impervious to conversation; the bed had bugs, black and shiny; they scuttled away into the cracks when he tried to catch them, like his disconnected thoughts. How had Masters found out about the stolen grain? What would happen to him now? Ralph's mind shied away from this last question, but it returned to haunt him in the grey hours of early morning, when hope sleeps.

Two days before his trial the warder changed to one less forbidding, who hinted he might be willing to carry messages, for a fee. Ralph was ready to snatch at straws. Hunter, who had intervened for the little Welshman, would surely not believe him to be a common thief. The note and a bribe to the warder took Ralph's last shillings. All the next day and night he waited.

There was no reply.

It did not help that he was up before the same magistrate as before, who looked up sharply at the name "Fletcher" and consulted his notes. Beckworth grinned at him across the courtroom; Kennedy slouched, his mouth hanging open; Barrett hulked over a bench. Hunter sat, arms crossed, in the gallery, wearing the severe expression of a presiding officer at a court-martial.

Barrett repeated the oath in a loud monotone. Yes, he recognised the accused as a Government man hired for the harvest. He had set him to keep the tally, but Fletcher's manner had made him suspicious. The final payment from the Commissariat had been short. On enquiry he had found the load was five sacks down. He had not been able to find Fletcher, but had tracked down Beckworth, who had initially denied all knowledge of the theft.

Beckworth was surprisingly cheerful. Yes, he had lied to begin with, to protect his friend Kennedy, him being a little simple and Beckworth feeling responsible for him. He had changed his mind (a week ago, guessed Ralph) after he heard the Parson's sermon. Now he understood that honesty was the best policy, and it would be better for his future in the colony to admit his sins and turn over a new leaf. After all, it was Fletcher, the educated one, who had put them up to it. No, he did not know what had become of the corn or the money as Fletcher had taken both and kept all the proceeds for himself. Ralph rose to refute this slander, but was slammed painfully back by the guard.

Barrett confirmed that on the day after the wheat was delivered Fletcher had been gone some hours, and that later he and the other men had been fighting, though Fletcher would not admit to it.

Ralph was appalled. It sounded so plausible. He stared over to where Hunter sat, willing him to provide an alibi. But Hunter would not meet his eye. Their business could hardly be made public, and by Barrett's calculation, accurate as far as Ralph could recall, he had been absent rather longer than his errand to Hunter required.

Now it was Ralph's turn; hand on the creased black leather of the Bible, he swore to tell the truth. Had he known about the theft? He hesitated. He was perjured if he said no, condemned if he said yes. He was on oath, and could not go against the habit of a lifetime.

"Yes. I knew." There was a murmur around the court. Then why had he said nothing? Another damaging pause. "Barrett and I had a disagreement." What about? How best to put this? Barrett stirred, glowering. "He said I was making advances to his daughter." Did he consider he had been fairly treated in this matter? "No."

The magistrate leaned forward. "You have admitted yourself that you knew a theft had occurred, and held a grudge against your employer. Now you expect me to believe that although you were in a position of trust where you had access to the load, and had fallen out with your companions, that you are innocent?"

"Yes!" His answer was sharp. The magistrate stiffened.

"Will you tell me what you have done with the stolen property?"

Exasperated, Ralph snapped back: "How can I, if I never took it in the first place?"

"Do you wish to face an additional charge of contempt of court?"

Ralph restrained himself with an effort. "No, sir. I beg your pardon, sir."

"You may stand down."

The Irishman took the stand. Ralph veered from anger to fear. This attack was being orchestrated by a subtler mind than Beckworth's, whose cooperation had doubtless been bought. Ralph felt in its full intensity the convict's loathing for an informer. So much for any gratitude Beckworth might have owed Ralph for not turning him in.

Down the room, Hunter's taut frown betrayed his growing doubt. By now he must be asking himself whether Ralph's visit had not after all been intended as cover for other, more dubious purposes. Fiercely Ralph willed him to understand.

He heard his name and stood up. On the prisoner's first appearance before the Court, barely a month ago, he had been given the benefit of the doubt, and convicted of only a minor offence. The scale, and degree of calculation involved in the current case were altogether more serious. Taking into consideration the value of the stolen wheat; the prisoner's abuse of trust; his obduracy in the face of the evidence, and his refusal to admit what he had done with the proceeds, he was sentenced to fifty lashes. In addition he would receive a further twenty-five each day until he confessed where he had hidden the stolen grain.

Ralph felt the blood drain from his face. *Barbaric!* He must have spoken the word aloud, for the magistrate glared at him. Thereafter he was to be sent to a place of secondary punishment for a year.

He fought and bucked as they dragged him away.

They would not believe that he could tell them nothing, and persevered till the fourth day, when the surgeon said they had better stop. They flung him back into the hospital, cursing him for an obstinate dog.

Hunter stood in the empty office, eyeing the yellowing regulations pinned to the wall. He wished that he had not come; yet something about Fletcher made him uncomfortable.

He had pondered, when he received the note, whether to intervene: but by then the case was *sub judice*. He had been taken aback by the severity of the sentence. Upon enquiry he had found that several such had been handed down in the last year. Indeed they were favoured by no less a personage than the Reverend Marsden himself.

The door opened and Fletcher entered, stiffly. His face was sallow, thumb-smudged under the eyes.

"You took your time," he said bitterly.

Hunter found himself apologising. "No visits were permitted before. Are you well?"

"Do you expect me to say yes?"

Hunter was stung by the other's tone: he sat down.

"Let me give you some advice. Whatever you may have been in England, here you are merely a convicted felon. Your only hope of improving your lot is to conform to the conduct expected of you. A reputation for intransigence will do you no good at all. Look at you!" Hunter was almost pleading. "You simply cannot continue to defy authority."

Ralph leaned forward across the desk, bracing himself with both hands against the tide of platitudes. His voice was strained.

"Damn you and your authority!"

The legs of the chair screeched as Hunter erupted in a single violent gesture. Ralph crumpled to the floor under the blow.

Hunter looked down at the man on the floor. "You'll need to be tougher than that to survive where you're going."

Leaning heavily on his stick, Hunter limped out.

# 18

# *England, Spring-Summer 1816*

This time it was Lucius standing framed in the door, lifting his hand in an awkward gesture of farewell; Flavia remembered her excitement when last she left Fontclaire for London. Such hopes, so ill-formed. At a brisk trot they passed the lodge gates. She did not look back.

They jarred down the rutted lane. Molly hunched uncomfortable, withdrawn, an enigma, her newly-rounded face and body giving an air of maturity. How odd, Flavia thought, to have another little body jouncing inside your own. Molly still had not named the child's father. Was it Lucius?

There were other, deeper questions Flavia did not want to acknowledge. What was it like to lie with someone you loved? How would she have felt, alone with Ralph, feeling his touch? Discomforted, she wrenched her mind to the road ahead.

Towns and signposts rolled by, familiar from her previous journey. This time she was a seasoned traveller; when they stopped Flavia recommended the restorative effects of lemon-and-ginger to a lady in the dinner-room, a Mrs Backhouse from Manchester. As the miles passed Flavia felt her cramped spirits ease. So much had happened since her first visit to London. Now she was leaving behind her not only her childhood home, but, she hoped, the sadness of her father's untimely death, and, not before time, the goading Mrs Lennox.

At *The Bull-and-Mouth* Molly was met by her sister, none too pleased to have added to her responsibilities a pretty younger sister carrying a bastard child. Flavia made up the balance of Molly's wages, adding extra towards her keep. She had done all she could to help. She was relieved to see them disappear into the crowd.

A frenzy of barking announced Flavia's arrival. Hester burst through the half-open door, twining about her knees, nails clattering on the chequered marble.

"Welcome, my dear!" Harriet crushed Flavia against the lace on her bosom.

"I trust I have not put you to any trouble."

"Not in the least," Harriet replied in her forthright fashion. "Thank goodness one of you has taste enough to be revolted by that Lennox creature. I cannot imagine what Lucius sees in the daughter, but he never was a boy of any perception. Besides, Hester enjoys your company." She caressed the long, narrow head; the bitch lashed her feathery tail in delight. "Now up to your room; you will be tired from your long journey." Abruptly she took her leave.

Again Flavia followed Wardell up the staircase. Here she had stood on Ralph's first visit; she remembered the turn of his head as he greeted her. This long glass had caught her reflection on that last, disastrous evening, the candles in their brackets picking out the flash of diamonds in her hair and the lustre of her shawl.

She took a deep breath. Resolutely she ascended. That part of her life was over.

That evening she joined Harriet in the library, a fitting place for Flavia to recount her father's last illness, with the gilt-embossed spines glimmering in the sheen of the fire.

"Poor Charles," Harriet observed. "At least he was spared the misery of dwindling into a drivelling dependant. That would have been intolerable to a man of his spirit. He always was sensitive to what people thought of him."

Flavia had never considered her reclusive parent in this light. "You knew him when he was young," she said. "To me he seemed always to keep the world at arm's length. He was happier with books."

Harriet gave one of her sharp glances. "He was a different man before your mother died. Emily was pretty, to be sure; your brother has her features, as you inherited her gift for music. But she had a steadiness and inner strength. From her unfailing support Charles drew a confidence he had never enjoyed before."

Encouraged by this vein of reminiscence, Flavia asked shyly: "What caused her death? Father would never speak of it."

Harriet stared into the fire. The lines of her face deepened in an old grief.

"It seemed nothing at the time. She had come to visit, so the floors had been polished with particular care. Emily slipped on a rug in the hall. She fell heavily, but appeared to have taken no hurt except for a bruise on her leg. It pained her, so she rested the next three days. Then, with no warning, she took an apoplexy and died within the hour." Harriet sighed. "She was not yet thirty. Charles was left with you children to care for. He was devastated. For him, the sun had gone out. It destroyed his belief."

"So that is why he never went to church, and would not have the vicar in the house!"

"He could not reconcile her pointless death with the notion of a loving and merciful God. Neither could I, though it was not an opinion I advertised among my friends. Poor little Lucius; he was only six, very close to his mother. When Charles withdrew into himself, Lucius was left rudderless. I have sometimes thought this lies behind his yearning for approval, and his susceptibility to influence by an older confidant like Bromley." She snorted. "It may even explain his tolerance of his mother-in-law."

Harriet's face eased. "You were different: a clever child, bookish, like your father. He was at ease with you."

Flavia absorbed these new insights. From the other side of the hearth, Harriet studied the girl's face. She had her mother's quiet determination, allied to her father's capacity of thought. But the spirit and eagerness of her previous visit had been quenched.

Her father's loss would account for this in part. Charles was not a demonstrative man, but there had been no doubting his affection for his daughter, or his pride in her abilities. Harriet suspected this grief went deeper; that Flavia had been pining ever since young Fairfax had left so abruptly. Harriet had seen her come alive under his attention. First love and heartbreak were never easy, particularly for a girl of her loyal temperament. When she gave love, she would feel it was for life. They had seemed so well suited. He had appeared lively, intelligent, and ready to settle down after his return from the wars.

It was a long time, Harriet reflected, since had been so mistaken in her reading of character. She might have expected Fairfax to be rash, even reckless, like Everard. But she had not believed him capable of callous disregard, or outright cruelty. Perhaps, like many a young man before him, he had simply sought a woman more immediately available. Well, there was nothing she could do about that now. It was time for Flavia to move on. Harriet would make it her business to provide the stimulus of new faces and ideas.

Two days later a visitor was announced. To Flavia's surprise, it was Bromley.

"Please accept my condolences on your recent sad loss, Miss Stanton," he said. "Your brother said told me you had returned to London. Feel free to ask for any assistance."

Flavia had felt constrained in her previous dealings with Bromley. Now she was touched by his solicitude.

"You are most kind," she replied warmly.

"Not at all. Lucius is a friend; courtesy to his sister is the least I can offer. Perhaps you would care to join a family party to visit the Houses of Parliament? My cousin, Mrs Backhouse, has just arrived from Manchester."

"But I met her yesterday!" Flavia exclaimed.

"So she said," Bromley replied. *"'A most helpful young lady'."*

Flavia coloured. Bromley's manner might be stiff, but after the sting of Ralph's desertion, and months of her brother's neglect, she appreciated the compliment. "I should enjoy it very much."

"Very well then; we shall collect you tomorrow at two o'clock. Good afternoon, ladies." He bowed to each in turn, picked up his hat and gloves, and left.

Harriet eyed the door speculatively as it closed. "I wonder what prompted his call?" she remarked.

"Perhaps he was merely being polite," said Flavia. "I thought his manner much improved."

"He certainly was making an effort to please," Harriet said. "He seemed almost human. But I must not tease. You had, I think, some prejudice against him before?"

"Ralph disliked him— Sir Ralph Fairfax," she corrected. She felt the force of Harriet's too-penetrating gaze, and hurried on. "Besides, I believed Bromley was a bad influence on Lucius, encouraging his gaming."

"And when Lucius came into his inheritance, was it noticeably diminished?" Harriet queried.

"No; that is the surprising thing," Flavia replied. "Father was so distressed about it at the time, but Lucius must have made up his losses. Perhaps Bromley advised him on some profitable investments." Flavia looked puzzled. "It scarcely matters now; the estate is his anyway."

Flavia was visibly cheered by the prospect of an excursion; Harriet smiled at the resilience of youth. Unexpectedly she found herself grateful to Robert Bromley; should this Mrs Backhouse prove a suitable chaperone, Flavia would be able to get about to many more places than Harriet could take her.

She had sensed the distress behind Flavia's plea to return. Every time she walked into the library at Fontclaire, it would bring to mind her dead father. The execrable Mrs Lennox would offer no solace, and Lucius had room in his head for only one idea at a time. He was obviously too preoccupied with his wife, and the novelty of playing the squire, to consider his sister at all.

Mrs Backhouse, when she arrived, was a good inch taller than Flavia, and some ten years older, with an air of quiet authority. Her simple dove-grey silk dress set off corn-coloured hair and blue eyes.

"As we shall be seeing more of each other, I suggest you call me Marianne; and I shall call you Flavia, with your permission, of course."

Flavia responded to her grave smile, and the offer of friendship behind it. She discovered that Marianne's husband, a Nonconformist clergyman, ministered to a parish on the outskirts of Manchester, where they lived with their three children. She had been summoned to London to help care for an aunt recovering from a riding accident. Flavia had never had an older sister; she warmed to Marianne's kindliness.

The gothic halls of Parliament were dark after the sun outside. Around them voices reverberated from the high vaulted ceilings. Bromley was obviously known here; Flavia was impressed by the alacrity with which they were attended.

She had pictured the House of Commons as a mighty hall, fit for the soaring oratory of Pitt and Fox. But the chamber, when she peered over the balustrade of the gallery, was smaller than she had expected, meagre in its proportions, with its three awkward round-topped windows. On the floor of the House below, a handful of members lolled at their benches, ignoring the droning speaker; one was reading a newspaper, three others deep in conversation.

Her disappointment must have shown. Bromley looked down at her, amused. "Did you expect more reverence?"

"I have seen better behaviour in the village school!" she exclaimed.

"They paid more attention to the Game Laws," Mrs Backhouse remarked, with an intensity which Flavia had not expected. "At the moment they are merely setting up some Board or other. To animate your country gentleman, you must touch a subject close to his heart, like grouse or rabbit."

Flavia remembered how indignant Lucius had been when poachers raided his pheasants. "Any law on the preservation of game would touch my brother's heart. May I assure him his covert is safe?"

"Game is to be hunted by the squire or his eldest son only. Anyone else caught with guns or snares will be transported."

"That is harsh!" Flavia exclaimed. "If I were to trap a rabbit on Priory land, would that make me a criminal?"

Bromley gave a tolerant smile. "Only if you were to act without your brother's permission. But I hardly see a young lady of your attainments setting up as a poacher."

He offered Marianne and Flavia an arm. Leaving the stuffy chamber, Flavia considered what he had said. Their villagers had always enjoyed a little rabbit. She remembered seeing the long furry corpses hanging behind the doors in pairs, like strings of onions. Always the tenants claimed they were 'took on the Common.'

But there was no common now; it had disappeared under an Enclosure Act. The villagers' common rights had gone with their beehives and little Kyloe cows. Charles Stanton had never pressed the matter, saying he did not begrudge his tenants a little meat in the pot in a cold winter. Why, there had been a hare inside Old Sarah's back door when Flavia had gone to visit. She could not accept that one dead hare made the old woman, or more likely her grandson, into a felon.

Outside they joined the crowd promenading along the riverside terrace, beneath the fresh green of the plane trees. Bromley indicated the buttresses and spires. "The House, and its institutions, go back to the Middle Ages. We can thank the Iron Duke for ensuring the safety of our freedom and laws. Without last year's victory at Waterloo, we would not be strolling here in the sun, free from the twin evils of revolution and tyranny."

Mrs Backhouse turned to her cousin. "But Robert, what of those workmen driven to riot? A labourer must pay one and twopence from his eight shillings' wage for a single loaf of bread. What satisfaction does he gain from the law, in particular the Corn Laws, driving up the price of wheat?"

Flavia's father had fully supported the Corn Laws. She was astonished to hear them attacked from such an unexpected quarter.

"Come, Marianne," Bromley said reasonably. "As a factory-owner I appreciate that foreign wheat would feed my hands for less. But these broils are simple lawlessness. You cannot excuse attacks on honest millers and corn-merchants, and the whole of Ely in an uproar. Your Christian sympathy for the poor does you credit, but you must not let it distort your judgment. Living as you do in Manchester you fail to see how important this measure is to the landed gentry. Their very position depends on it."

"The men in Littleport were desperate. They said they might as well be hanged as starve." This argument had been aired before. Flavia admired the restraint with which disagreements were conducted in this family. In a Stanton debate tempers would have flared long since.

"There are institutions to cater for paupers," Bromley retorted, with a hint of asperity. "Law and order must be upheld."

"By condemning twenty-four men to death?"

"Leniency would only encourage them further. Besides, you neglect to mention that nineteen of those convicted at Ely were reprieved."

"Transported, you mean," Marianne corrected him quietly. She turned to Flavia.

"In our parish I see such want. Robert means to make a career in politics; we have long disagreed on these issues."

Flavia glanced at the tall, self-assured man beside her. He looked down at his cousin with an indulgent smile. "This is too fine a day for dry debate. Come: here is an excellent vantage-point."

From beneath the latticework of branches, Flavia looked out over the broad reach of the river. Idly tracing the roofs and buildings ranked along the further shore, she saw in a flash of memory the slime-rimmed walls of the Tower, and felt the rocking of Ralph's boat on the restless water. The breeze flurried; the air filled with a sharp prickling, stinging her face, catching in her throat.

"My dear Flavia!" Marianne's voice exclaimed. "You are pale." A hand on her elbow directed her to a seat.

"Forgive me," Flavia murmured, her hand over her eyes. "Some chaff in the air... the heat..."

The sense of being in two places at once subsided. When she dared look up, red-sailed barges and bustling wherries crowded the face of the river, oars twinkling in the sun.

"It is some stuff from the trees. We have walked you too far. Robert, I shall accompany Miss Stanton back to her cousin's."

Flavia, still faint, sat back gratefully onto the soft cushions of the carriage. As they drove home Flavia rebuked herself. She had not realised with what force the scenes of her previous visit would strike her. *I must not shrink away from society as my father did. I will not fall back through that hole in the middle of myself, into that terrible sadness.*

Caught on her sleeve was a miniscule dart, with a hard needle and fluted body, ending in a tuft. It was these that had blown into her face from the trees, and so distressed her. She flicked it off with her finger.

Flavia told Harriet what Marianne had said about conditions in the North. "I should like to learn more about these matters," she said to Harriet. "I had no idea about them before."

Good, thought Harriet. My plan is working. This is just what the girl needs; a new interest to occupy her mind.

"I shall subscribe to the *Political Register*," Harriet replied. "You are old enough to shape your opinions for yourself. But don't leave it where Wardell can see it. He won't allow it below stairs."

Filled with a sense of daring, Flavia unfolded her first issue. She was promptly roused to indignation. "The Prince Regent is in debt for three hundred and forty thousand pounds! And this at a time, as Mr Cobbett says, when a skilled workman must support his family on fifty-five pounds a year!"

"Turn radical, and you will scandalize your brother," Harriet remarked. "But it is time you broadened your knowledge of affairs. I shall recommence my Tuesday *salons*."

Flavia had feared appearing *gauche* before her cousin's clever friends. But the first Tuesday went better than she had expected. Both Bromley and Mrs Backhouse were there; Marianne's calm settling Flavia's nerves. And now that she was seeing Bromley more frequently she found more topics for conversation, and his manners, though lacking in natural warmth, were impeccable.

On her first visit, every part of this huge metropolis had been equally unknown. Over the succeeding weeks, she gained in confidence, as with Marianne to accompany her, Flavia began to find her way around London. More significantly, from Harriet's Tuesday guests, she learned something of the country's leaders: Castlereagh, Sidmouth, Wellington, reformers like Wilberforce, previously only names on a page Mrs Backhouse in her turn introduced her to the strange new world of Manchester, whose hundreds of thousands of inhabitants lacked a single member in Parliament while the hamlet of Old Sarum returned two members for its seven voters. Flavia, impressed already by her friend's interest in politics, was startled to discover she was a member of the Manchester Female Reformers, arguing for wider representation for the seven millions of Englishmen who as yet lacked the vote.

Bromley dismissed these as "Marianne's band of Amazons", countering that political power was best exercised by educated men of property with experience of affairs.

"You are old enough to remember what happened in France," he said to Marianne. "There such Jacobin notions, spread by an unregulated press, led first to the Terror and then to Bonaparte's tyranny. Why expose England again to these dangers? We have just ended one war. Why start another with our own people?"

Flavia lacked the nerve to contribute to this debate. Later she confessed her timidity to Marianne. "You are not afraid to contradict him. He tolerates from you notions which he regards as heresies."

"His father was my uncle; I have known him all my life. Also, you forget that to him my opinions pose no threat. He refuses to take them seriously. He regards women meddling in politics in the same light as Dr Johnson, invited to hear a woman giving a sermon : '*A woman giving a sermon is like a dog walking upon its hind legs: one did not look to see it done well; it was a marvel that it was being done at all*'. But enough of these matters. You have not yet visited St Paul's. Shall we go tomorrow? I shall be free in the afternoon."

"How many steps?" queried Flavia, her feet still tender from their last excursion. "More than The Monument? After three hundred I stopped counting."

"Many more. In fact, twice as many. But the views from the dome are superb and the singing accounted very fine."

How Father would have enjoyed reading about it! But Father was dead. All these remarkable places, Flavia thought: I could have brought them alive for him. The pain was less now, as ripples grow smaller with distance. Yet it caught her unexpectedly. She squared her shoulders, clad still in the black silk of mourning.

"I shall wear my most comfortable shoes."

# 19

# *New South Wales,*
# *May–November 1816*

The axe-blade flashed, slicing down; with a crack the tree toppled, branches flailing, shaking the ground as it fell. Braced at the two-handed saw, Ralph drove his weight into the gauging iron teeth as they severed the top-hamper, then set down his end of the long saw and stepped into the leather yoke.

"Two, four, heave!" Muscles trembling and shoulders raw from the rough logs, Ralph hauled, one of six men in harness dragging the massive trunk. For the abuse heaped on them, they might have been the bullock-teams whose work they did. The chief overseer, a stocky disrated boatswain, bald and one-eyed, improbably named Nelson, kept discipline on his blind side by striking out vigorously with his starter, a length of stout knotted rope. The other, Roberts, thin and taciturn, left the work of organising their charges to his companion as he slipped away, and returned smelling of rum.

It was winter now, a strange mild winter without gales or snow, but cold enough in the raw bush. The fetters around Ralph's ankles, and the chain between, looped to his belt, chilled where they touched. The irons had been riveted on when he left the hospital. Every time he stood, walked or turned to speak, their weight reinforced Hunter's bitter lesson. He was a felon twice-convicted: none would speak on his behalf.

Ralph clutched the wooden bowl and headed off on his own. Here was none of the rough camaraderie of Sydney gaol. He had nothing in common with the surly Devon farm-labourers transported for rick-burning, murmuring among themselves of *emmets* and *bee-bows,* or McCrae the gaunt violent Scot, with a huge indented scar across his scalp, or Stingo and Jazey, pickpocket twins from the London slums, supple as weasels.

Initially Ralph was so tired that he crawled off to sleep as soon as he had eaten. But as his muscles hardened he watched the others playing hand after hand of greasy cards, first abel-wackets, the sailors' game he remembered from the ship, then whist. McCrae, whose temper was uncertain at the best of times, flung down a poor hand, cursing, and retreated to his bunk. As the others wrangled over whose turn it was, Ralph silently picked up the discarded cards. He had always had the knack of remembering the run of play; he continued the rubber, and won. His prize was a quid of tobacco, useful when trading for extra food. He tied it on a string round his neck.

During the night he stirred and found it gone. From close by came the rustle of somebody carefully settling their weight. Ralph was suddenly filled with a searing fury. His arm snaked out and grabbed Stingo. He wrenched him out of his bed and flung him to the dirt floor.

"Give it back!"

"I haven't got it! Honest!" Ralph, so angry he wanted to break something, seized Jazey from the bunk above.

"Don't ever touch anything of mine, ever again!" The bones of the scrawny shoulder worked under his grip.

"Don't look so cutty-eyed! Here it is."

Ralph snatched his prize and let Jazey go. He had no idea where this sudden rage had come from. For an instant he had almost become the Ralph Fletcher who had jammed a knife between a pimp's ribs in a Whitechapel tavern. And all over a quid of tobacco. Tired as he was, it was a long time before Ralph could sleep.

But there was no more stealing.

So far he had avoided further punishment. The memory of those mornings in the prison yard, and the salt dressings of the nights between, burned yet. Confused by the Antipodean seasons, and the perpetual grey-green of the leaves, Ralph found it impossible to keep track of time. He was too proud to ask what month it was. From a scrap of the *Sydney Gazette*, wrapped around a twist of tobacco, he discovered it was now August at least. He had served less than half his sentence on the timber gang. Dispiritedly he schooled himself to patience.

McCrae was getting worse. Previously he had sat in gloomy silence, lashing out if anyone got too close. Now he huddled over his food, muttering angrily to himself. Even the overseers were nervous of him, and set him tasks away from anything sharp.

One morning the ground was wet from overnight rain; already one of the farm-boys had cut his hand to the bone when he missed his footing and fell onto the pitsaw blade. During the day the ground was trampled to a slurry, slick with wood-chips. Someone slipped, driving in a wedge. It sheared; Ralph jumped. There was a roar from behind him. Ralph turned to glimpse McCrae, a bloody line across his cheek, snatching an axe from Stingo, next in line. McCrae swung a great blow that would have sliced the head off anyone in its way. Ralph, dodging as best he could, reversed his axe, and with the blunt head caught the Scotsman behind the knees. McCrae went down in a heap and started to tremble. Nelson stepped forward with a raised length of wood.

"No," said Ralph. "He's having a fit." He knelt beside McCrae, turning his face out of the mud so he could breathe, and forcing a stick across his mouth in case he bit his tongue. He looked at the shuddering body, and the livid four-inch scar, clearly visible now as they had just had their heads shaved.

Nelson peered down with his one good eye. "And where did you learn that?"

"I had a friend in the Army who took fits when he was tired. Till he stopped a musket ball."

The overseer gestured at the man on the ground. "He were foretopmast hand on *Macedonian*. A spar clipped him on the head. Now he thinks every shadow is a Frenchie, come to kill him."

McCrae was still now, his lined face gentle. Two men came over to pick him up, but Ralph waved them back. "Let him sleep. He will wake soon and remember nothing."

As the others rustled and snored, Ralph's mind raced. What manner of man had McCrae been before the plunging beam destroyed his mind? Foretopmast hands were the most agile sailors in a ship. Now he was a clumsy menace, imprisoned with his terrors, a threat to his fellows, or a joke.

This work was not only hard but dangerous as well. Should one of the towering trunks fall the wrong way, or an axe-head glance off a knot in the timber, Ralph could be crushed in an instant, crippled like the boy from Devon, or ruined like McCrae. And beyond the obvious threats was the more subtle one from within. His outburst the other night had shaken him. He must get out of this place.

The winter was turning. As the weather warmed he noticed spindly red flowers, like bunches of crimson bristles, enlivening the drab bush around him. The fall of a tree would dislodge flocks of noisy parrots, their cries as strident as the vivid blues, reds and greens of their feathers. More than ever, the constraints of camp life oppressed him. He resented being chained like a dog, the incessant clinking, the ludicrous gait he was forced to adopt. In his rare moments of privacy he levered at the fetters with lengths of wood, trying to oval them and work his foot out, but always the wood splintered. He hammered at the links with rocks, but the soft sandstone shattered in his hand.

Then one day, as they were clearing up, he stubbed his toe on something hard: he reached down to feel the broken iron wedge. He clenched it in his hand, and surreptitiously lashed the length of metal to his leg. He would be off at the first opportunity, like a fox loosed from a trap.

He slipped the wedge inside his straw paliasse. All next day he brooded over it. What if one of the others found it first?

Roberts joined the card-table. Ralph knew a gambler when he saw one; the first three nights he let him win. It took all of Ralph's previous winnings, but it was worth it once Roberts started to lose, and staked his bottle of rum. When the squat dark flask shifted to Ralph's side of the table, he could see the strain on Roberts' face. The overseer was grateful when Ralph proposed that, rather than keep it for himself, they should share it round. So they did, except that Ralph did not swallow any. The rest would sleep deeply tonight.

It must have been a good half-hour since the two overseers left, slamming the heavy door behind them, and securing the padlock on the other side with a loud click. The rest of the gang had subsided into sleep. Ralph swiftly muffled his chains with strips torn off his spare shirt. He studied the untrimmed poles that served as rafters. Standing on his bunk, stretching as far as he could reach, he could just touch them. He took a firm grip and hauled his upper body up and over. For a second he swung, his weight across the beam, but slithered back. The muffled links chimed on the edge of the bunk. Trying to quieten his breathing, Ralph looked around anxiously. He caught the glint of open eyes in the gloom. McCrae was staring at him. There could be no doubt about what Ralph was trying to do. Then the Scotsman's hand came up in a salute; he turned his back and settled again with a sigh.

Ralph took a deep breath, flexed his hands and jumped again, shoulders burning, swinging his encumbered legs to follow. He poised, and this time twisted sideways, grabbing the corner brace to distribute his weight across it and the rafter. Carefully he twisted so he was lying on his back. He grinned to himself. Something useful had come out of his time in the camp. He could never have done that straight off the ship.

The wedge had cracked along a flaw in the metal. He used the sharp edge first as a chisel, then a knife, to saw at the bark lashings securing the thatch to the framework of saplings above him. He glimpsed a patch of sky. He worked at the opening until it was big enough for him to crawl through, replaced the thatch as best he could, and dropped to the ground.

Groping in the still-warm embers of the cooking fire, he found a hardened stone, then headed north into the bush. They would expect him to head for the coast; by making a wide sweep he hoped to evade pursuit. He walked until he had set two ranges of hills between himself and the camp. The moon, veiled before by patches of cloud, now rode cold and free. A faint haze in the dome of sky above glowed like mother-of-pearl; it was the best light he would get.

Ralph set his right foot on an outcrop of rock, held the wedge against the rivet, and struck it with the stone, hard, again and again. The tone of metal on metal changed. He swung the iron semicircles open, and set to work on the other foot.

He could move more freely now, but his hand was numb with the repeated jarring of the blows. He stopped and straightened up, stretching his fingers. He struck again. At the fourth blow his crude hammer flaked away.

After an initial surge of dismay, he used the broken fetter instead, hammering until the other leg was freed. He unlooped the chain from his belt, quickly covered up both chain and irons, and set off.

He lurched and began to laugh. From long habit, the muscles of his legs were still allowing for the ten pounds of metal that were no longer there. He capered and pranced. Deliberately he broke into an awkward run, and maintained it until his legs found their rhythm. As his stride lengthened and his breathing settled into a pattern, he exulted. He was free.

He curled up under a tree and slept, to wake hungry. In the middle of the afternoon he found a stream. Along the bank the vegetation was greener, wilder and more profuse. Tree-ferns crowded near the narrow watercourse; eucalypt and wattle gave off sharp, spicy scents. The soil—he sifted a handful between his fingers—was not the rich dark loam of the fields he remembered, but thinner and gritty.

By evening his belly was griping. There was a hut, black in the gathering darkness. He forced the door, looking for something to eat, but found only a neatly stacked pile of wood, a tinderbox, and half a dozen withered apples, which did nothing to allay his hunger. His stomach grumbled at him resentfully. He pocketed the tinderbox and went on.

It was now full night, but his way was lit surprisingly well by the huge full moon. He stayed with the watercourse, drank gratefully, and eased his aching feet in the water. Downstream the walls of the gully grew suddenly steeper and more rugged. The flow had undermined part of the bank and brought it down in a tumble of rock. Ralph was wondering whether to retrace his steps or attempt to climb the cliff-face in the dark, when he heard a scrabbling. He turned, crouching with his wedge at the ready, to confront a sheep, caught in the rocks of the shallows and struggling to heave itself free. It gave a faint bleat.

Savage with hunger, Ralph smashed the wedge down on the creature's skull and felt it give beneath the blow. He found a sheltered spot, lit a fire, hacked a leg off the beast and skinned it; a clumsy, bloody job.

Someone might see the smoke of his fire. He was too hungry to care. He ripped the meat into strips and hung them off a stick. They took an interminable time to cook, tormenting him with the sweet scent of roasting mutton. Little spatters of fat sizzled as they dripped into the flames. He turned the skewer over and tore shreds off the side that was done, ignoring his burnt fingers. The juices ran deliciously down his throat; he savoured the crust on the skin, and the tang of woodsmoke. Sated, he smothered the fire and slept.

He dreamed of hunting; the surge as rider and mount gathered for the leap; the baying of hounds as they poured down the slope. They sounded closer. He woke up.

A black and white sheepdog stood braced at the top of his hideaway, throwing its head back with each bark. Ralph glanced about in panic. In the bright morning light the debris of his illicit slaughter lay all about him, the bloody carcass stiff on the flat, stained rock like some primitive sacrifice. He snatched up a stone.

At a sharp whistle the dog streaked away.

"Don't you be hurting my dog." The voice, with its familiar Welsh lilt, came from above.

Ralph squinted up into the sun. "Davies." He let the stone fall. The other stood poised, gripping his staff. "Come down. I won't hurt you."

The Welshman slithered down with a crackle of snapping twigs. His wary expression eased into a smile. "I was beginning to wonder. It's a regular wild man you are now."

"I've run from an iron-gang. I killed one of your sheep."

Davies inspected the dead beast. In daylight Ralph could see a dash of blue raddle across its shoulder. "Not Mr Hunter's," Davies replied. "That's his boundary over there. Ours are marked in red. She must have strayed and fallen into the streambed. We picked up the scent where you left the water." He paused. "I owe you a debt, Fletcher. Come home for clothes and a meal. You've a set of ribs on you like a washerwoman's basket."

This kindness was painfully unexpected. Ralph flushed. "Thank you," he said in a low voice, suddenly ashamed. He gestured towards the dead sheep, now crawling with ants. "What shall we do with that?"

"Bury it," replied Davies, briskly. "What have you to dig with?

Ralph proffered his wedge, which had served him as knife, axe, and now spade.

"It will have to do." Davies whistled again to the dog, which slunk off close to the ground and set herself on guard.

Ralph set to work, gouging out a trench. He was amazed at the change in his cellmate. Their positions were reversed. Now it was Ralph who started nervously at every sound, while the once-diffident Welshman was quietly confident.

Davies' wattle-and-daub hut was touched with the loving details of home. The roof was shingle, the ground about cleared and fenced with stakes; the neat lines of a vegetable garden showed to one side. A row of peach saplings, barely a foot high, marked the path to the front door.

Davies' wife was gathering in washing. As she turned, Ralph saw she was heavily pregnant. Her expression kindled with pleasure at her husband's unexpected return, then set in alarm as she saw Ralph behind him. Her eyes flew to her husband's face. He spoke to her softly in Welsh. Ralph was not surprised at her misgivings. He was not at all the kind of companion a young wife wanted her husband to bring home, with his magpie trousers split up the sides and the marks of the irons still raw upon his legs. She darted ahead of him into the house like a minnow startled by the shadow of a pike.

While the dinner cooked, she unpicked a shirt and trousers of her husband's, to let them down for their taller guest. Davies whittled a slab of wood he was shaping as the end-board of a cradle. From time to time he would address a brief statement to Ralph, whom he seemed to regard as some sort of privileged confidant.

"We will never starve here; not like the hard winters in the valleys, with my Da too sick to go down the mine, and no money coming in. In two years I will have my ticket-of-leave. With the Governor opening up those new towns over the mountains, one day we will have a farm of our own."

He looked proudly over at his wife, who smiled in return. Her life, Ralph reflected, would be a hard and lonely one, but she trusted her husband and would follow where he led. Together they would toil to provide a better life for the child she carried, no longer Welsh, but a Currency lad or lass, born under the Southern Cross. Ralph had seen these young folk in Sydney, taller and stronger than their parents, untutored as yet but confident and free, healthy from clean air and sufficient food.

Ralph was humbled by Davies' hospitality. He was a danger to these good people, and must leave as soon as he could. He felt a tug of sadness.

In the corner lay a Bible on a wooden chest. After their meal Davies carried it over and asked Ralph to read. Ralph took the heavy book awkwardly, unsure of what to say. He could not visit upon his hosts his own disillusionment with the established church, his bitterness at Marsden's sermon. No more divine displeasure. These two would have troubles enough, half a world away from family and friends, threatened by snakes and fire, native spears and bushrangers. He flipped through the pages of heavy black text, looking for words of encouragement. He cleared his throat.

"*By faith Abraham, when he was called to go out into a place which he should after receive for an inheritance, obeyed; and he went out, not knowing whither he went. By faith he sojourned in the land of promise, as in a strange country, dwelling in tabernacles with Isaac and Jacob, the heirs with him of the same promise; for he looked for a city which hath foundations, whose builder and maker is God.*"

He looked up, and saw the glance of contentment that joined the two like a touch. To hide his intrusion he turned the page.

*"Be not forgetful to entertain strangers: for thereby some have entertained angels unawares. Remember them that are in bonds, as bound with them; and them which suffer adversity, as being yourselves also in the body."*

He snapped shut the heavy clasp and handed the Bible back.

Next morning Davies pressed him to stay, but he could see the relief in the woman's eyes as he bade them farewell and set off towards Parramatta. By and by the track broadened into a path, then a rough road; by afternoon he was passing established farms, some with substantial houses. Bullock-carts lumbered by, individual riders, teams of horses hauling drays; the occasional curricle and smart carriage.

In his clean, nondescript clothes and wide-brimmed straw hat, Ralph attracted little attention. Only once did he sense eyes on him. He glanced around to find himself watched by the leader of a party of natives. Down the man's chest ran a pattern of thick, symmetrical scars. The narrow-boned women squatted; their menfolk, dusky skins set off by bright red loincloths, stood thin and still as the tree-trunks behind.

Ralph caught a glint from deepset eyes. He suddenly remembered these tribesmen had remarkable skills as hunters, and were used to track fugitives. He turned from the black man's impassive regard and walked on.

# 20

## *New South Wales, Spring 1816*

It was dusk when Ralph reached the outskirts of Parramatta. He had refused the coins Davies had tried to press on him, so he would have to steal. Dressed respectably, with a little money, he could, in the character of a gentleman, bluff his way to Sydney and a ship.

Buoyed by the good meal inside him, decent clothes, and the unfamiliar warmth of friendship, Ralph felt his inner tension ease. He had forgotten the simple pleasures of being free to walk where he wanted and dispose of his own time. He could almost have been on leave, sauntering through some unfamiliar Spanish village as the sunset blazed a vivid salmon across the western sky.

Beside the river ran a path sheltered by trees. He hid behind a smooth pale trunk striped with long peels of bark. Dusk passed swiftly into night. Light steps approached; a girl hurrying home late, her nervousness betrayed by the clatter of the two empty pails against their wooden yoke.

He waited. Ripples flexed on the surface of the river. Strange stars pricked out above him. He recognised, upside down, the three bright markers of Orion's Belt. Orion was a mighty hunter; a good omen.

He huddled stiffly as the moon rose. From his right sounded the confident stride of a heavier footfall. The moonlight gleamed on a white shirt-front and glanced off a polished walking-stick.

Ralph flung a stone; it cracked against the bole of a tree. The man halted. Ralph, stepping out, hit him hard and clean as he turned, and caught him as he fell. Quickly he stripped his victim's coat and trousers, and bound and gagged him. His own gear Ralph weighted with stones and threw into the river, lest it be traced back to Davies.

Quickly he donned his new clothes. Months of hard labour had put on muscle across his shoulders: the coat was tight, but at least the shoes fitted. As he walked away he felt in the pockets: a key, which he threw away; a handkerchief; coins. These he counted eagerly, but they amounted to only ten shillings in florins; hardly sufficient to fund his escape.

The stick had a deeply-incised silver band. He twisted it. The handle came loose, followed by a long slender blade. A swordstick!

He followed the river downstream and settled down again to wait. He would try once more to raise the capital required to fund his restored gentlemanly self. He grinned at the prospect: faced by a sword, the mere threat of violence should suffice. Peering through the leaves Ralph was surprised to see a man already close. Bigger than the noise he made would suggest, he wore a coat and hat and carried some sort of pole. A watch-chain winked across his waistcoat.

Ralph darted out, snatched the chain, and fled. He expected a shout. Instead, he sensed two bounds behind him and felt the grasp of a strong hand as his feet were swept from under him. He landed flat on his back. His would-be victim poised above him in a partial crouch, pressing a hard point against Ralph's throat. He was too astonished to be afraid.

"Give it back." The voice was deep, with a strange accent. The face above him was dark, a fierce mask of elaborate whorls and lines cut into the skin. A white shark's tooth swung from one ear. Ralph remembered Clancy's story of the tattooed head. The man Ralph had tried to rob was a New Zealander; a cannibal, like as not.

Ralph gave a choked laugh. His captor's scowl deepened. Ralph remembered the swordstick.

"I'll fight you for it." A practised swordsman would easily prevail over a savage with a wooden paddle.

The brown man's teeth flashed in a fierce grin. He stood back. "Run and I, Te Hakuwai, will strike you down."

Ralph draped the watch-chain over a branch. He retrieved his sword-stick, executed a preliminary flourish, and faced his opponent *en garde*. The man was an easy target, square on and half-crouching, his staff gripped in both hands.

Ralph feinted. The other dodged the blow and turned with a dancing step. Ralph attacked, his point ripping the hem of the other's coat, but he had to recover quickly as his adversary struck at him from the other side. Ralph was watching the point, anticipating a downward stab, but it was the whirling shaft he had to guard against. He was being driven backwards into the trees. It occurred to Ralph that his adversary was more experienced than he at night-fighting, and undoubtedly stronger.

They circled, seeking an opening. Ralph lunged low, knees flexed and arm outstretched. Before the point could connect, the edge of the wooden shaft cracked down smartly on his elbow. His swordstick dropped from numb fingers. Ralph found himself back on the ground, staring at the carved tip of the spear.

"*The tongue of a woman in peace; the tongue of the taiaha in war.* The prize is mine."

Carefully Te Hakuwai reattached the watch-chain to his waistcoat. He picked up the swordstick.

"I wouldn't take that if I were you," Ralph retorted. "I've just stolen it, and the owner might want it back."

From where he lay it was impossible to read the expression on the other's deeply-incised face. Then the victor threw back his head and roared with laughter.

"Come, *e hoa*," he said, stretching out his hand. "You fight well for a *pakeha*."

Ralph sat up, rubbing his elbow. His coat had split along the seam.

"The clothes are stolen also? You are a runaway slave?"

"Here I am a prisoner, but I am a chief among my own people," Ralph replied with dignity. It was not something he would have said to anyone else in New South Wales, but his new companion accepted it without demur.

"I too was trapped by my foes at *Nga-tai-pari-rua*, the battle of the twice-flowing tide. Then my brothers came."

"And your enemies?"

"They filled our ovens."

A silence. Ralph reached for the wooden spear. "May I?" he queried.

"Do not touch the head," warned Te Hakuwai. "It is *tapu*."

Gingerly Ralph took the proffered weapon. His first impression of a wooden paddle had been quite wrong. It was light and slender, beautifully balanced, with a finely-carved tip shaped like an out-thrust tongue. Above a tufted collar, two inset eyes reflected the light. The long rounded shaft splayed at the butt into a broad, flattened blade. He would never have thought a native capable of producing something so elegant and apt to its purpose. He handed it back, and they set off down the river-path.

"Why are you here?" Ralph asked his companion.

"I stay with the *tohunga—Te Mihinare—*" he corrected himself. The word was obviously hard for Te Hakuwai to pronounce; it took a moment for Ralph to catch it. Missionary? Marsden! Here he was, on the run from an iron-gang, strolling about Parramatta with a house-guest of the flogging parson! What could his interest be in so remote a place as New Zealand?

Vigilant as they traversed the darkened streets, Ralph learned that his new acquaintance was one of several chiefs staying with the Principal Chaplain. Ralph was astonished by the contrast between his convict experience of the man, and that of the warrior beside him. Ralph had dismissed the dumpy chaplain as a callous hypocrite, amassing a fortune while preaching charity, a man of God notorious for the severity of his punishments. Yet here was a savage praising the man for his hospitality, and his willingness to pay the *Maori* hands on his ship the same rate as the English. As they turned down a side-alley, Ralph suspicions hardened. He hung back.

The chief grinned; a fearsome sight on that tattooed face in the dark. "I will not betray you. I do not trust this man like the other chiefs. They see only the wealth and power of the *Pakeha*. They invite them to their lands to win *mana* for their *iwi*. I fight for my *mana*. Soon I go to *Ingarangi*. There I buy *tupara*—muskets."

England! Ralph was flooded with desperate excitement. "When do you sail?"

"Five days."

Ralph's heart raced. He staked everything on a single throw. "Can you take me with you and hide me on the ship? In England I have guns —" here an incongruous picture of his gun-cupboard at Longhallows floated into his mind, with the two of them poring over its contents. "You could have as many as you wanted."

"How many?"

"Ten," said Ralph, mentally tossing in a brace of pistols for good measure with the eight fowling-pieces he had left behind. "And I'll buy you a musket from the best gunsmith in London."

Te Hakuwai considered the offer. He nodded approvingly. "*Ae.* I take you."

The chief stopped beside a wooden fence, pulled aside two loose boards and wriggled through. Ralph followed, to find himself in a hut stacked with rubbish. There was an unglazed window, high up, and a single wooden door.

"Stay," Te Hakuwai ordered. "Tomorrow I bring food and sailor's clothes."

"Take these." Ralph handed over half his florins. A sudden thought struck him. "Can you bring me some paper, and a pen, and ink?" This was too good a chance to miss: at the very least, the chief could carry a letter to England.

"I too can write," Te Hakuwai said proudly. Ralph's estimate of his versatile new friend's abilities rose yet again. "I see you at sunrise."

His breathing slowed as deep silence grew around him. He settled against the wall and allowed himself to dream of escape: to leave all this pain and humiliation behind, resume his rightful place, go home, back to Longhallows. In his mind's eye he saw the coast of New South Wales shrink behind him, until the tawny sandstone cliffs faded to a line in the distance, then vanished altogether, and all he could see was the blue arch of sky and the clean silver curve of the horizon...

"If I was an enemy, you would be dead." Ralph jumped out of sleep. Te Hakuwai loomed dark against the growing light. "My grandfather beat me if I did not wake at once. Put these on. I show you where we meet, at noon."

After being cooped up all night, Ralph was glad to stretch his legs. They headed back along the lane, across an open field where people were setting up a market. Ralph's buoyant mood of the night before had gone, replaced by the awareness, a habit now, of anything moving at the edge of his field of vision. Watching them was an older man wearing the badge of a constable. Ralph, acutely conscious that he lacked the all-important pass, met his gaze innocently and moved on, nudging his companion with his elbow as the man came up behind them.

Te Hakuwai drew himself up to his impressive height, and turned on the man the full force of his tattooed stare. The constable veered away, taking a sudden interest in a tray of apples. The chief took a resolute step towards him, and the man's ambling pace accelerated to a scuttle as he disappeared in the crowd.

Te Hakuwai gave a snort of derision. "*He hiore hume.* He is a dog with its tail between its legs."

The little scene had all the makings of farce. Had it happened anywhere else, Ralph would have laughed. But he was sobered by the knowledge of how close he had come to being caught.

They walked on for some time, past well-fenced fields and carefully-tended gardens. In the distance was a two-storeyed mansion, set back from the road.

"Here I stay," Te Hakuwai said. Ralph's mouth hardened. "I see you have no love for this man. Why does he treat strangers as his sons, but his own like slaves? And the people of this land, where is their standing-place? Where are their chiefs? Does your *atua*—your God—not look with favour upon them?"

"Has Marsden visited your country?" asked Ralph, feeling more comfortable now they were behind a grove of trees and out of sight.

"He came last year in his ship. Ruatara asked for his help, but died accursed."

"What happened?" Ralph could not see the dumpy Yorkshireman, with his round, choleric countenance, as a wizard.

"A man in Sydney said: Do not bring the *mihinare* to your land! Where one comes in peace, many soldiers will follow with guns. They will steal the ground from under your feet while your eyes are turned to heaven in prayer."

Ralph wondered who this might be, of such compelling candour.

"On the ship Ruatara felt great fear. The *mihinare* asked what troubled him, and Ruatara told him these words. The *mihinare* said: I will turn the ship back if you have any fear in your heart. So Ruatara believed him. But when they landed the sickness came on Ruatara and he died. Was this not *makutu*—a curse?"

"I do not know your gods," said Ralph. "But from what I have seen of Marsden, I would be very careful in my dealings with him. He may treat you well for his own purposes, but he is not a man to cross. When the convicts rose up at Castle Hill, he had a boy flayed from shoulder to heels, three hundred lashes, on mere suspicion of withholding information. Then sent him to the pepper factory afterwards, grinding cayenne, when he refused to talk."

They walked on in silence, stopping where the road met a stream.

"We will meet here. I will bring horses. Now show me you know the way."

Ralph retraced their steps without difficulty, and bade his companion farewell. He climbed back into his hut and ate his breakfast of bread and cold mutton, washed down by a bottle of weak beer. The light was now good enough to write by. He wiped his fingers on his trousers, and opened out the page on the dirt floor.

He kept the letter as straightforward as he could, a bare summary of what had happened since his abduction. Of the more squalid details he conceded only *"sentenced to irons in a timber-camp."* His pride demanded that he omit even that; but he let it stand. It marked the seriousness of his current plight, and the need for urgent action on his behalf.

The ink dry, he folded the letter—his quick-witted friend had even remembered a wafer to seal it—turned it over, and addressed it to Charles Stanton, care of Harriet's address in London. For all that Ralph had quarrelled with his daughter, Stanton was an honourable man. He would not tolerate this injustice. And by directing it to London rather than Fontclaire, Ralph could ensure Te Hakuwai would deliver the letter in person, so ensuring it would reach its destination.

From the angle of the shadow Ralph guessed it was still early, around nine o'clock. He still had three hours until his rendezvous. Again he felt caged in the little shed, one moment exulting at the prospect of liberty, the next afraid what might go wrong. He must get out into the open air, and dispel this unease.

He struck out briskly by a different path, keeping close to the trees, and taking particular note of the angle of the sun. The track ran for about a mile; he would turn back just short of the junction. But as he reached the intersection of the Western Road he saw a knot of people gathered. Ralph glimpsed the red coats of a party of soldiers. They were escorting a prisoner: Davies!

Ralph was shocked out of his silence. He tugged at the sleeve of the man in front of him.

"What happened?"

"That's a little Welshman, some convict shepherd. They've arrested him for killing a magistrate's sheep. The poor devil has a wife, too, close to her time."

The cavalcade moved on. Despite the mildness of the morning, Ralph felt a chill clutch at his gut as he returned to his lair. He crouched on the floor in the shadows, his head on his knees, rocking, wrestling with his dilemma. What did he owe Davies? He had done him one good turn already.

Yet the image of Davies' pregnant wife haunted him. She had known better than her husband the risk they ran, harbouring a runaway. She could have insisted that her husband hand Ralph over to the authorities; Davies would have won time off his sentence for that. Instead, she had let his charity outweigh her judgement.

He struggled, torn this way and that, his Fairfax-self upholding what was honourable; his Fletcher-self asserting shrilly that he was a convict now, only survival mattered, and Davies' arrest was his own bad luck. Then Ralph's bitterness at his own false indictment would rise up like bile, and the arguments would begin again.

He had been extraordinarily lucky to be offered this chance of escape: there would not be another. But if he let Davies suffer in his place, would he be any better than Beckworth and Kennedy, cynically standing by as Ralph took their punishment for stealing the corn?

The patch of light from the window touched his feet. It was time to go. The knowledge of what he must do lay on Ralph like a stone. He bundled up his meagre luggage and set off for the rendezvous. Te Hakuwai was there under the trees, holding the two horses.

Ralph handed over the letter. "Take this to London for me. I am sorry. I cannot come."

"Why?" For the first time since he had known him, Te Hakuwai seemed perplexed.

Ralph groped for words his companion would understand. "A friend has been arrested for something I did. I must turn myself in to the court and tell them the truth."

"This man is of your *iwi*?" Ralph shook his head impatiently. "This is a law of your *atua*?"

"It is a debt of honour. If I do not do this, I will feel shame for the rest of my life. Go. Thank you for what you have done."

Te Hakuwai looked hard at him. He uttered a low-pitched rhythmical chant, falling away at the end. "*Kia toa*," he said. "Be strong. *Haere ra, e hoa*. Goodbye, my friend."

He mounted and wheeled round, leading the spare horse.

Ralph watched until he could see only a cloud of dust on the road, then turned and walked heavily back to the town, consumed by a gnawing grief. He found the courthouse, still closed. Worst was the waiting. A boy whistling as he swung a bucket; a groom walking a pair of smart coach-horses; how long before he would enjoy such simple pleasures again? A milkmaid came past, selling new milk from a little donkey-cart; Ralph bought a cup. Her cheery farewell was a valediction.

Drawn by a delicious yeasty smell, he found a baker's. A curious regulation on the wall stated: "*No bread is to be sold until the same is twenty-four hours old.*"

"Two loaves, please," he asked the shopgirl.

"It's against the rules, sir. They're fresh from the oven."

He flashed a smile he was far from feeling. "Only two. I won't be here tomorrow." That much was true.

"Oh, all right, then," she replied, colouring.

The loaves were crisp-crusted, soft inside, almost too hot to touch. He tore them apart and wolfed them down, feeling like a guest at his own wake. He remembered from his regimental days that Irish wakes were always jolly affairs. In a grogshop he spent his last shillings on liquid courage. Anything to drown out the voice of reason that shrieked at him to run away, quickly, before it was too late. Giving himself up was the honourable thing to do. But never before had honour come at such a price.

After a bottle of rum and another of peach cider, he made his way unsteadily back to the courthouse. The scene within had the familiar quality of a recurring dream. Three magistrates sat on the Bench, red-faced in the heat. The prisoner cowered in the dock, with a broad-shouldered soldier beside him, like a mastiff guarding a mouse. Davies' eyes caught those of his wife; her pale face strained. Huge with child, she looked ready to faint in the crowded room.

Proceedings had just begun. Good, Ralph congratulated himself, smothering a belch. I can interrupt to good effect.

"How does the prisoner plead?"

Davies cleared his throat. "Not guilty, Your Honour."

"That's right," Ralph called loudly. "It was me." Every eye turned towards him. *I, said the sparrow, with my bow and arrow, I killed Cock Robin.* No, mustn't say that. He could see Davies' start of astonishment, and feel the pleading gaze of his wife. The crowd around him melted back as if he were suffering some potent contagion.

The magistrates conferred, frowning. "Stand forward and identify yourself."

"Happy to oblige, Your Worships." Ralph doffed his hat with a flourish and a titter ran around the room. "Ralph Fletcher, absconder, at your service."

The sergeant of the guard rushed to present his bayonet at Ralph, who airily waved the point away.

"Put that aside, my man. I kill sheep, not sergeants." He was enjoying himself, and the appreciative audience fuelled his recklessness with covert grins. He turned to the startled clerk of the court.

"Pray tell me, what day is it?"

"The fifteenth," the man replied nervously.

"I do hereby confess," Ralph recited, "that on the tenth *inst.*, or thereabouts, with malice aforethought—" he swayed and clutched the bar "—I did slaughter a sheep, of provenance unknown —"

"The sheep was mine," snapped the eldest magistrate.

"Indeed?" replied Ralph. "Please accept my condolences." Another ripple of laughter, louder this time. "Let that fellow go," he called to Davies' escort. "I killed the sheep. Smashed its head in, helped myself to an excellent leg, and buried the rest."

"Damn your impudence! The beast was butchered just so."

The clerk flourished a handbill at the magistrates, who scrutinised it keenly, glancing up to match the description against their unlikely catch.

"How considerate," called Ralph, as the sergeant snapped on a pair of handcuffs and hauled him forward. "A notice, just for me. May a keep a copy?"

"Do not mock the Law, Fletcher. Do this again, and you will assuredly hang for it. You will suffer for your effrontery in bringing this court into contempt."

The officials conferred again briefly, and muttered an aside to the harassed clerk, who waved Davies outside with an air of embarrassment, like a butler accused of setting out the second-best china. Davies' wife slipped towards the side door to join him.

Ralph stepped up into the dock. "I will suffer anyway," he replied more coolly than he felt. "I might as well enjoy myself."

One of the spectators leapt to his feet. "That is the thief who attacked me, two nights since!"

All eyes turned to Ralph. He was having trouble focussing that far down the room, but he could see the man was sporting a nasty bruise on his jaw.

"No offence meant, my good fellow," he drawled. "It was your clothes I was after. Though from the little money in your pockets you obviously frequent cheap tailors."

There was a surge of laughter. The courtroom was abuzz. The *thunk-thunk* of a gavel hammered silence. By now the senior magistrate was livid with rage.

"Ralph Fletcher," he cried, "you are hereby found guilty of sheep-stealing, robbery, and assault with violence. You are sentenced to fifty lashes for absconding, with a further fifty each for your criminal behaviour and contumacious demeanour. These will be delivered immediately, as an example to any fools who might feel tempted to seek similar notoriety. As this is not your first offence—" he shook the handbill "—you will be sent thence to a place of secondary punishment, to be decided, for two years. The court is adjourned!" he shouted above the hubbub. "Clear the court!"

A file of soldiers drove the spectators out, accompanied by whistles, catcalls, and a derisory chorus of *baas*. The uproar outside was turning into a riot. Soldiers issued from the side door at a disciplined trot, faces fixed beneath their shakoes, muskets at the ready, and clove the milling crowd.

Ralph, with a bayonet prodding his back, had no option but to keep up. "Hey lads!" a voice echoed in his mind. "Wait for me!" Better save his breath for what was to come.

Triced up in the gaolyard, he hung all afternoon as a bloody example, and into the early evening, so abject a figure that his guard slipped away for a quick pipe with his mates. When he returned, there was only a dog lapping furtively at the patch of fouled sand, with the empty triangles rearing above, and the cut ends of rope stirring faintly in the breeze.

# 21

## *London, Autumn 1816*

Flavia had heard no further news of Molly Simpson. A footman sent to her sister's address had returned with the news that both had left, two months since. So Flavia, coming downstairs on a September morning, was surprised to see Molly's brother Sam, squirming in the butler's grasp.

"Lemme go!"

"Out!" Wardell hissed. "Ow!" He dropped the lad, who dashed over to Flavia.

"What is this commotion?" she demanded. "Sam: have you news of Molly?"

"She's having her baby!" he blurted, his eyes wide. "She's got nobody to help her!"

"What about your sister?"

"Molly and Sue fell out," the boy muttered. "Sue's gone off with a feller up north. Molly said not to tell you, but it's coming *now!*"

Flavia was alarmed. The boy was distraught and obviously telling the truth. Harriet was out in the pony-trap. What could she do?

After a moment's hesitation, she turned to the butler. "Wardell: the carriage."

His bushy eyebrows rose in surprise. "Excuse me, Miss Stanton. You cannot think of following this urchin to the slums!"

"I can't leave the girl alone, perhaps to die," Flavia snapped, more sharply than she intended. What should she take? Her only experience of birth had been seeing lambs born on the farm. "Fetch a basin and ewer, quickly," she ordered, "and some towels, and sheets, and a pair of scissors to cut them up with. And soap. And a bottle of brandy," she added as an afterthought.

"You cannot go alone, Miss. Miss Harriet would never allow it. If you are determined on this, then let me accompany you, at least."

"Thank you. I would appreciate that."

She scribbled a note, and snatched up her cloak. The party gathered at the front door. Wardell, with an expression both fierce and disapproving, bore a heavy walking-stick. He handed Flavia into the dark, leather-smelling interior, hefted the bag of gear onto the roof, and sat up with the coachman, where Sam was giving directions.

They set off through the city streets, clopped over the Bridge and swung south. Here were none of the elegant façades Flavia was used to. The buildings grew increasingly shabby, the streets narrower. They passed the eyeless walls of a prison. Streets thinned to lanes, then a court, with barely enough room to drive through the gateway. The carriage lurched to a stop.

Wardell looked about suspiciously, grasping his stick. "Are you sure this is the place, boy?"

"This is it, Mister."

"Watch your feet, Miss," Wardell called back unnecessarily to Flavia, who had already lifted her skirts clear of the clogged gutter. She breathed through her mouth to avoid the stench. They entered a gloomy hall smelling of cabbage and grease. Sam led the way up the narrow staircase at the end. A slatternly girl in a red petticoat leaned against the wall; she made no effort to move as Wardell eased past. They toiled up two more flights of stairs; beneath their feet threadbare carpet gave way to creaking boards.

Beneath the grimy skylight, Flavia saw Molly, lying on a mattress. Her face was strained, her hair clinging with sweat. She moaned; her back arched.

"Miss Stanton," Wardell urged, "surely you must—"

A scream cut him off. Flavia fought an impulse to turn and run. What should she do? As she leaned over the girl, hesitating, Molly snatched her hand and squeezed it till it hurt. The girl was foundering, like a ship caught in a gale.

"Wardell," Flavia ordered, "find a doctor. Sam will know where to go. Don't just stand there!" Her voice rose in panic. She turned back to Molly, caught in another spasm. "What can I do to help?"

With her free hand the girl tried to twitch down the skirt that had ridden indecently above her knees.

"It hurts."

With the utmost reluctance, Flavia looked down. She was astonished to see between the girl's legs the hemisphere of a baby's head pressing out, dusky red and slicked with wisps of dark hair. There was another push and the opening widened.

"Molly!" The girl's head turned to her voice and her grip relaxed. "It's coming!" With another convulsive shudder the head came clear, turned to one side. With trembling hands Flavia reached forward and grasped the tiny shoulders, wet and streaked with blood. At the next great heave, she nerved herself to pull. Molly cried out as though she were being torn apart. Abruptly, the resistance holding the baby ceased, and it slipped out in Flavia's hands. The slick little body was followed by a glistening tangle. Flavia, alarmed, wondered what essential organ had come unstuck.

"What is it?"

The baby was purplish-red, covered with a fine wax. It squirmed and gave a high faltering squall. Flavia peered.

"A girl."

"The cord," ordered the faint voice from the bed. "You have to cut the cord."

Flavia thought of the heavy steel scissors and recoiled.

"You hold it," said Molly, "and I'll cut. There's a knife in that box."

Flavia was shocked into a reply. "You won't need that." She handed over the scissors and held the baby, feeling the fragile ribs beneath the too-large skin. She looked away, feeling sick. When she looked back, Molly was ineffectually trying to wipe the baby with a fold of her dress.

All Flavia had was brandy; she supposed that would do. She used it to wipe the baby clean, and wrapped her inexpertly in a piece of sheet. The child had fingers as tiny and perfect as those of a china doll. She nuzzled blindly at her mother's breast.

Flavia stared at the small, mysterious creature, gazing impassively out of cloudy blue eyes. Molly, who had so shortly before been screaming in agony, smiled.

"You didn't have to help," Molly said with incongruous dignity. "She isn't Mr Lucius's, if that's what you think."

Flavia suddenly felt very foolish. That was exactly what she had thought, or at least suspected. This child might have been her niece. Now she seemed clumsy, an intruder, stupid and hurt.

"We had better get you washed and away from here," she said with forced brightness. The door opened and Sam carried in a slopping jug of water, followed by Wardell, red-faced from running up the stairs, and a thin woman in a threadbare grey shawl.

"Young Simpson vouches for this person. She has five children of her own and knows what to do." Wardell kept his eyes averted from the bed. The woman glanced nervously at Flavia.

"If you gentlefolks will wait downstairs, I'll clean up," she said. She turned to Molly. "Got somewhere to go, love?"

Wardell opened his mouth to reply but Flavia forestalled him. "She comes back with us."

"Miss Flavia—" Molly called, as she turned back at the doorway. "Thank you for helping." Despite her ordeal, the girl looked radiant with some hidden power. Descending the stairs, Flavia felt obscurely that their roles had been reversed; Molly was the fortunate one bestowing a favour, and Flavia the supplicant, seeking some hidden boon.

Immediately upon her return to Harriet's house, Flavia called for a bath. Vigorously she scrubbed off the dirt, the blood, the smell of the slum. The episode had been deeply disquieting. The whole process of giving birth was so painful and undignified. She could not tell which was the more startling: the agony she had beheld or the joy that succeeded it. The change in Molly could not have been more marked had there been two women, one to bear the child and another to hold it after.

Molly had little enough to rejoice about. Her child was a bastard, its father unknown. Her only means of supporting herself was to go on the streets, or throw herself on the Poor Relief. She should give the child to a foundling hospital; but Flavia rejected this idea immediately. She felt somehow responsible for the baby's wellbeing.

Flavia answered her cousin's summons with trepidation.

"What is this I hear about your escapade?" Harriet boomed. "Wardell has recounted an unlikely tale of sudden journeys and incognito *accouchements*. He is not given to reading novels, or I would have dismissed the whole business on the spot."

Flavia's heart sank. Harriet was her only ally. Without her she was helpless to give Molly any help at all. Even worse, she might herself be banished back to the country.

"It was all my doing," she admitted anxiously. "I knew Molly from home, and her brother told us she was giving birth and needed help, so I took Wardell and—the baby was born," she concluded awkwardly.

"You delivered this child yourself?" Harriet exclaimed.

Flavia coloured. "I had to do something," she confessed into the growing silence.

"Then you presumed to bring the girl back here? With her bastard?"

Flavia did not look up to see what must surely be a frown of disapproval.

"You make very free with my hospitality," Harriet went on. "Can you imagine what tales will be spreading through the servant's hall by now? They will be claiming that the child is my granddaughter, at least. Such gossip will do your reputation no good at all. I have tried to find you a place in intelligent society. It was no part of my intention to train you as a midwife."

Flavia felt a tightness in her throat that presaged tears. She had acted on impulse, without the least thought of Harriet's acquaintance.

"I did what I believed to be right," she said stiffly. "Molly was alone and ill with nobody to help her. Since it was I who took her to London, I felt some responsibility. It was wrong of me to bring her back without asking, but you were out at the time, and—" a wave of loneliness overwhelmed her "—I had nowhere else to turn." She burst into sobs.

Harriet held out her arms. Tears sparkled in her faded eyes. "Here, my child," she murmured in an altogether softer voice, cradling Flavia awkwardly as the girl wept over her fine French lace. "It is what Emily would have done; she always had a kind heart. Do you feel better now?"

Flavia nodded wordlessly and sniffed.

"Sit down. Take my handkerchief."

Flavia dabbed her face with the square of fine lawn.

"Had you thought before you acted, this problem would not have arisen. But your heart is stronger than your head, as I knew when I asked you here. There was a time when I cared for the opinion of society, and these habits linger. Perhaps it does not matter as much as I once thought."

She sighed. "Your company means much to me, and I have not thanked you for it. If this waif is important to you, I am sure we can spare it a corner until more lasting arrangements can be made."

Flavia hugged the old woman with sudden affection.

Harriet fixed her with a sharp stare. "The child is not Lucius's, by any chance?"

"No! I thought so at first, but Molly assures me it is not."

"We can be grateful for that, at any rate," said Harriet.

In clean surroundings, with good food, Molly and her baby thrived. Flavia visited them over the next few days, drawn by this enigmatic scrap of humanity, with her solemn assured air. Her fingers, so tiny, so exquisitely articulated, clutched at Flavia's thumb.

"What will you call her, Molly?" Tentatively Flavia touched the child's downy head, with its blue veins more delicate than the finest thread.

"Maria, after my mother," said Molly. "I hope one day she'll see her," she added sadly. "Dad told me never to darken the door again."

"Once he learns he has a granddaughter," Flavia suggested, "perhaps he will change his mind."

From Molly's expression, she thought this most unlikely. "I wanted to call her after you, Miss, after all you did, but I wouldn't presume. I did wonder —" her face flushed "—if you would stand godmother. That is, with me not being married, and all."

Flavia was touched. "Why, I would be delighted!" This way she could maintain her interest in the child without appearing to intrude. She leaned over the crib between them, where Maria flared out a tiny hand, then settled again into her little universe of warmth and contentment.

# 22

## *England, Autumn 1816*

The next Tuesday afternoon, Flavia nervously awaited some reference to her unorthodox work of charity. She was relieved to see the guests turn their attention instead to a newcomer: a broad-shouldered, red-headed young man, good-looking in a rather coarse way.

Harriet called her over. "Flavia, my dear, may I introduce Mr William Charles Wentworth. Mr Wentworth: my cousin, Miss Stanton. Our guest has travelled a great distance to study law here in London."

"Have you come from Europe?" Flavia enquired, already kindly disposed to their visitor for providing distraction.

"No," he replied, with an easy laugh, "much further than that. My homeland is the other end of the world: New South Wales."

Bromley, whom Flavia had not noticed before, was at her elbow. After a brief but attentive scrutiny, he joined the conversation.

"Have you been long in London?"

"I left Sydney early in the year," Wentworth replied. "We were almost wrecked; the ship's hull was rotten. I could break off lumps of wood, just so!" He crumbled a ratafia biscuit in his fist. "At the Cape I left the vessel to her fate, and sought one more seaworthy and less crank."

As he recounted his quest for sandalwood in the South Seas, Flavia was struck by his self-assurance in this room full of older men.

"Are you by any chance related to Mr D'Arcy Wentworth, the Principal Surgeon?" queried Bromley.

"I have the honour to be his son," Wentworth replied.

"I was unaware, Mr Bromley, of your interest in New Holland," Harriet interrupted in her cavalier fashion.

"Mr Grey Bennet has several times raised the subject in Parliament," Bromley returned smoothly. "Since the wars ended public disorder has risen. A prison colony should deter lawlessness, but the laxity of the present Governor has encouraged crime, rather than deterring it."

The guest had a temper, which revealed itself in a sudden flush of colour. "Who says this?"

"My sources are my own," Bromley replied.

"I presume you allude to the Bent-Vale petition, which your Mr Bennet intends to present. The whole thing is a tissue of lies, concocted by Marsden and his cronies." Wentworth glared at Bromley, his big head hunching between his shoulders like a baited bear.

"But the Reverend Marsden is a pillar of the Missionary Society," put in Marianne. "Mr Wilberforce speaks highly of him."

By his expression, Wentworth did not share her opinion. Harriet interposed before her afternoon was spoiled by the fiery rejoinder he was clearly about to make.

"I have here Dr Shaw's *Zoology of New Holland*," she said. "Perhaps you can enlighten me as to the habits of that peculiar creature, the Water-Mole or Paradox. Does it truly have a duck's bill, and lay eggs?" She led him off to the reading-desk.

"That young man has a high opinion of himself," Bromley remarked.

"He said he was a connection of Earl Fitzwilliam," Marianne remarked. "He is confident of playing an important part in the colony's future."

"An important part!" echoed Bromley, with a derisory inflection. "Appropriate enough, for the future of a gaol."

Later, Flavia came upon Wentworth drinking claret in a corner. His audience had gone; he looked very much alone. She felt sorry for him.

"It must be hard, to have your family on the other side of the world. At least you can write to your parents, to tell them how you fare."

"My mother died when I was a small boy," he said shortly, then appeared to repent of his churlishness. "You are right, Miss Stanton. I miss the invigorating heat and the blue skies. Here it is forever damp and cold."

Perhaps, thought Flavia, Mr Wentworth is in love.

"Is there a young lady back in Sydney, who awaits your letters?"

Wentworth brightened. "I have an understanding with one of the Misses Macarthur," he said proudly. "Her father is one of the first men of the colony," he explained. "We hope to marry when I have completed my studies."

Poor Miss Macarthur, thought Flavia; waiting, while the days turned into months, and the months into years, as she had waited for Ralph. She lifted her glass.

"Let us drink a toast," she said, "to true love and a happy return."

On Friday Flavia decided to visit Swan and Edgar's to buy some material for Molly's baby. She was running some stuff over her hand to test its weight, anticipating how pretty it would look pin-tucked and threaded with ribbon, when she heard her name. She looked up, but could see only a tall cabinet stacked with bolts of fabric.

The voice on the other side hurried on, with the eagerness of one determined not to let a fresh piece of gossip go stale: "In a brothel, my dear, they say; with two of the girls in attendance! And the doctor was so outraged he refused to come!"

Flavia froze, straining to listen, with a yard-and-a-half of best Manchester lawn spilling from her hand. She burned with anger and shame. How dare that woman spread such lies! She was about to confront the speaker when the hand of commonsense held her back. This was what Harriet had warned her about.

A scene would only provide further bones for the jackals to gnaw. Her best hope was to lie low until some more diverting scrap of tittle-tattle took their fancy. But it hurt to be so disparaged, and she crushed the fabric in her hands so hard that the assistant leaned forward anxiously.

"This lawn is of the best quality, Miss, and will not crease."

Flavia set it down on the counter. "Yes—it will do very well."

"How much does Miss require?"

"Oh, the usual amount for baby-gowns—say half a dozen." Flavia murmured, acutely aware of her voice carrying.

"I beg your pardon, Miss? A dozen yards, did you say? Ten should be more than sufficient."

Flavia nodded. The assistant measured the cloth in a series of flourishes, tore it expertly along the line of the thread, and folded it into a neat square.

"Where do you wish it sent?" he continued, brightly.

If I had any courage, Flavia thought, I would speak my name clear and loud, for those old cats to hear. But she shrank from the thought of meeting their hard, mocking eyes as she left. Despising her own cowardice, she leaned forward.

"I shall write the direction so there is no mistake."

The assistant's accusing look was quite lost on her.

As soon as she arrived home, she burst in on Harriet.

"Someone has been spreading the most dreadful lie—" she exclaimed indignantly, then stopped short as Bromley stood and greeted her gravely.

"I am sorry to have taken you unawares. But it was about this matter that I called. These rumours must be stopped."

Flavia sat down nervously. She could think of nothing to say. Both the venom of gossip and its antidote were beyond her experience.

"I have a suggestion," Bromley went on. "As you know, Mrs Backhouse will shortly return to her family in Manchester. She has undertaken to take the girl and her child back with her. Once they are gone the whole affair will blow over."

He sat back with a faint look of distaste. Flavia realised bleakly how far-reaching were the consequences of Molly's transgression. It tainted even those who sought to help.

Harriet divined her mood. She spoke in a tone gentler than her words. "The dice of society are weighted, Flavia. No one can play against it and win. Even Lord Byron, for all his rank and fame, has found that to his cost."

Flavia's face burned at the implied rebuke, but she felt she could not let the subject lie. Molly must be supported somehow. "Will they be provided for?"

"She will not live at my cousin's house, if that is what you mean," Bromley replied disapprovingly. "But a position will be found for her. Marianne will ensure that she is adequately cared for."

Molly could expect no better, and was indeed fortunate to have done so well. Marianne Backhouse could be trusted to fulfil her charge; she would not let mother and child starve.

"Thank you, sir. You have been most kind."

"An honour, Miss Stanton."

After he left, Flavia flared up. "How can they be so cruel to a poor abandoned girl with a babe in arms!"

"In the eyes of those securely born in wedlock, the bastard is always fair game," Harriet observed.

Bastard! An ugly word to apply to a creature as delicate and innocent as little Maria.

"Where is the child's father?" Flavia cried. "I'll wager no one is treating *him* as an outcast!"

Harriet looked across at her. Her face was weary. "That is the way of the world, and thus it has always been. Your fretting will not change it. I am feeling tired this afternoon. I shall rest in my room."

Harriet set down the medicine-glass. It rattled against the table as her hand shook. The fierce pain, of knives stabbing her chest, eased as the laudanum spread its comfort. This was the second attack. The first had been sudden, at night. She had felt today's coming on. At least she had managed to get back to her room without Flavia noticing.

Harriet's fingers unclenched. The girl must not know she was ill. The doctor had said there were a few years in her yet; but she had not told him of these fearful cramps.

Flavia's life had been marred enough by illness. She was happy here. She had her father's intelligence; she would never be satisfied stitching at tambour-frames and exchanging social calls in the country. And here in London she was free from persecution by that Medusa, Lucius's mother-in-law.

I was more content as a selfish old woman, Harriet chided herself. I never had the patience for children, with their noise and mess. Now I have allowed myself to become attached to this *gauche* child. She has brought a warmth into my life which has been absent for years. I do not love her as a daughter; we lack the closeness and the spice of conflict that comes from shared blood. But I have set my mark on her, all the same, opening her mind.

Her father would have approved. A pity I could not do the same for Lucius; but he bores me. Besides, he has already chosen his mentor. True, Lucius sent me a fine Sèvres vase for my birthday; he would remember the proprieties better than his sister. But Lucius would never involve himself in a potential scandal out of goodness of heart, as Flavia had done. He lacked the imagination.

Harriet snorted fiercely. It was all very well for Lucius to be charming; when I die, he will inherit this house and everything in it. I shall add a codicil to my will, to ensure Flavia gets my jewellery.

That evening, Flavia took a last look at the baby. Molly was feeding Maria as she entered, and made to stop. The baby's face puckered.

"Please go on."

With a flush of embarrassment, Molly settled the baby again on her arm, covering her exposed breast as discreetly as she could. Maria returned energetically to suckling, her eyes closed and her tiny hands kneading.

Flavia laughed. "She looks for all the world like a puppy."

Molly smiled down at the child. "Reckon I'd look funny with half a dozen of them, like Dad's old Bess," she remarked.

Molly deftly detached the baby from her breast, rested her against her shoulder, and patted her back. The baby gave a minute belch. Molly changed her to the other side.

"You're very good at this," Flavia commented admiringly. "I would no more know what do to with a baby than an octopus!"

"I learned helping my Mam with young Sam," the girl responded. "And Betty, and Bob. It's a pity they'll not see their niece."

"Perhaps they can visit you in Manchester," Flavia suggested.

Molly flashed an impatient look. "How would they get to Manchester? But for Sam, there's none of them has ever slept a night outside home."

Flavia sensed the rebuke. It was all very well for her to talk about long journeys by coach. Molly's father was only a labourer, with a cow and a couple of pigs. None of his family would have the money, or the time, to travel.

"I'll miss the baby too," Flavia said suddenly. "I would have enjoyed watching her grow." She looked almost enviously at the tiny sleeping form. "If you need help, ask Mrs Backhouse to write to me. May I?" she reached forward at Molly's nod, and brushed her forefinger lightly over the baby's head, marvelling at the smoothness of her skin, her downy hair, and the faint, sweet baby-smell of milk.

"Goodbye, Maria. Oh, I almost forgot." Flavia handed the girl a package. "Here is some lawn, for baby-gowns."

The next day, Flavia started a letter to Lucius, but could not explain the sense of something momentous the baby had represented. She was trying to think of what to write when the door flew open, and her brother strode in.

"Lucius! Why didn't you tell us you were coming?"

"One thing at a time, little sister!" he replied breezily. "Caroline's baby is not due for another month yet, so I decided to attend to some business before her confinement. Why waste time writing, when I could be here in my new Tilbury quicker than the mail? I shall take you for a turn around the city."

He whirled Flavia into a hug. "On the subject of babies..."

Flavia coloured. "I suppose Harriet—"

"It was Bromley, actually. He considers your activities quite beyond the pale."

Flavia smiled. She was delighted to see her brother again, and his buoyant spirits lifted her own. She felt a rush of affection for him, and an urge to confide. "I had wondered at one time whether Molly's condition was any doing of yours."

Lucius looked startled. "Who have you been talking to in London?" he replied. "Whatever gave you that idea?"

"Oh, this and that. You showed a marked interest in her when she started at Fontclaire. In fact," she added, as it occurred to her, "was that why Mrs Lennox was so keen to see her gone?"

"It was unwise to let you stay with Cousin Harriet," Lucius observed ruefully. "She always was a sharp-eyed old bird. I confess all: I kissed Molly one day in the scullery, and she slapped my face. That was the end of it."

"I thought as much; the baby's hair is the wrong colour," Flavia said daringly. She enjoyed his discomfiture, and the sense of speaking as one adult to another. It would do Lucius no harm to treat her opinions with respect.

They spun along in fine style down Bond Street, along Piccadilly and the Haymarket, and crossed the Thames. It was such a pleasant day, and the horses were going so well, that they continued southwards. It was not until Flavia saw her brother swivel around as they passed through the junction of several roads, that she guessed he was lost. He tried to turn back, but the traffic behind them pressed them on. The dark walls of a prison were rearing in front of them, and Lucius was looking glum, when Flavia suddenly spoke.

"Turn left at the next street." She pointed. "After that coal wagon: quick, while there's a gap."

The long reins angled across the horses' backs.

"That will be the King's Bench Prison," she continued. They passed beneath the long shadow of the walls. Flavia was enjoying this.

"Turn here, and follow the main road left, you should come out on the way leading back to Blackfriars' Bridge."

Sure enough, they found themselves in familiar surroundings. She sat back satisfied. As the river came in sight, she laughed at the look on her brother's face.

"I never thought the day would come when my sister would guide me around the London slums," said Lucius with reluctant admiration. "And pray tell: what is your acquaintance with Walworth and Southwark?"

"We came this way to Molly. I remembered the prison."

"You have grown up since you came here," he said, his face serious. "London agrees with you."

Flavia was flattered and touched. She and her brother had disagreed in the past, but their relationship appeared to have settled on a new, more equal footing. "Just as marriage agrees with you," she replied.

As they turned back into Harriet's street, Flavia saw her standing on the front step, waving excitedly. "Let me be the first to congratulate you!" she cried, reaching up to clasp Lucius's hand. "You have a son!"

Still coated with the dust of travel, the Fontclaire groom answered their excited questions. Yes, Mrs Stanton was safe; the pains had come on unexpectedly and the doctor had been fetched; as there was no hope of Mr Stanton returning in time, they had decided to wait until the outcome was sure. The labour had been quick, for a first baby. Flavia found it hard to envisage Caroline in so messy and undignified a situation. Birth, she thought, was a great leveller.

The babe was a fine boy, well made and of good size, with flaxen hair and a lusty cry. A wet-nurse had been engaged from the village.

With each new detail Lucius looked more bemused. The messenger, clutching his five guineas, went off for food and sleep. Harriet had Wardell fetch a bottle of old French brandy, laid down to celebrate Trafalgar, and they toasted young Charles, as Lucius had decided to call his heir. Flavia was happy for him. No longer fretted with impatience, he was much easier and more confident. With the birth of a son he was truly established as the head of the family.

Lucius was all for dashing off upon the hour, but was prevailed upon to wait till the horses were rested and he had taken a good meal. Flavia had time to dash out and buy a gift, a silver rattle with bells, set with a peg of red coral on the end for teething. It felt strange to have it engraved *From your loving Aunt.*

When she handed it to her brother, he had tears in his eyes.

"You're a great girl, Flavia," he said in a low voice. "Will you come back with me?"

Flavia had foreseen this question and spent some time framing her reply.

"Thank you for asking, Lucius dear," she answered gently, "but no. I will come up for the christening, of course. But I am happy here, and Harriet has come to rely on me. Give little Charles a kiss from me."

Lucius stepped up into the seat and picked up the reins. He chucked the horses into motion.

Flavia waved till he was out of sight. It was true that she now felt at ease here, and enjoyed her cousin's company. But there was more to her decision than she was prepared to tell her brother. Here she had room to grow. London was Flavia's independence; she had no desire to give it up. Above the roofs the sky still carried the sheen of the long afterglow of sunset. She turned back into the house, reaching down to acknowledge Hester's lick of welcome.

# 23

# *New South Wales, December 1816*

A rhythmical jolting jarred Ralph awake. His wrists were tied; he could not ease the intolerable pressure rasping his back. He forced his eyes open, but was blind. Panicking, he struggled and lapsed back into darkness.

Te Hakuwai, riding one horse and leading another with a long roll lashed in a blanket, jogged steadily westward towards the mountains. The dusty road glimmered pale in the moonlight. Behind him confused soldiers scoured Parramatta, seeking the prisoner who had sliced his bonds and vanished. By the time the captain of the guard thought to call out a native tracker, the prison-yard and its surrounding streets had been so trampled as to obliterate any trail.

Candle in hand, Te Hakuwai carefully searched the back of the cave. In his own moist green land on the slopes of the great *maunga* Taranaki he knew every nuance of the forest, by night and day. But the realm of Tane held no legless lizards that bit and killed. In this harsh dry bush he was always careful.

He cut the lashing on his load, bore it inside, and unwrapped the blanket. How strange these people were! To kill in swift punishment he could understand. But beating men bloody, then shutting them in holes like kumara rotting in a damp pit, led only to hate, and the urge for *utu*.

He worked carefully, soaking away the bloody shirt where it had stuck to shredded flesh. The candle guttered low. He had to hand none of the healing plants he knew, but at least when his friend woke in the morning, his wounds would be clean. Lucky for him that Te Hakuwai, always curious, had turned back to see what happened.

Ralph jerked awake from his nightmare, shaking his head to dislodge the flies which had crawled incessantly over his face, into his eyes and his parched mouth. He supposed he was still in prison, until he made out the sunlit opening laced with trees.

His mind shrank from his ordeal. His duty had seemed so obvious at the time; the words had flowed so readily in his drunken recklessness. Now all he wanted was for the pain to stop. A shadow fell across him.

Te Hakuwai, with a bright red feather in the glossy black topknot of his hair, savoured Ralph's astonishment.

"Did you bring me here?"

"Who else could steal you from under their noses? I heard you in the court. You spoke well."

Ralph, his head still thumping from so much raw spirit, tried hazily to remember what he had said. He must have been mad! He had paid for every word in blood. Even so, he had enjoyed speaking his mind. He grinned faintly.

"Thank you." It seemed inadequate; he was ashamed that he had nothing to give in return for his freedom. "Where are we?"

"The Blue Mountains. Stay off the new road. There are huts where you pay money to pass. Sydney is back there." The Maori gestured over his right shoulder. "My ship sails tomorrow. There is water outside. I give you food and this *toki*."

There was an axe against the wall. What did he mean? With deepening dismay, Ralph realised that he was to stay behind.

"But you said—"

"Take this." Te Hakuwai held out the leather water-bottle, dangling from its strap.

Ralph went to reach out, but pain lanced across his lacerated shoulders. His arms were leaden, the muscles strained from the triangles. He dragged one hand around, tried to lean his weight on it, and fell forward.

"You see now why you cannot come?" said Te Hakuwai, not unkindly.

Ralph lay biting his knuckles.

"Wait till you are stronger," advised the voice above him. "Then you can make your *utu*."

"What's that?" Ralph muttered.

"Hate?" queried the other, tentatively seeking the right word. "Pay back?"

"Revenge," said Ralph.

A beam of sunlight woke him, warm on his face. Te Hakuwai had gone.

Ralph, desolate, curled up on the dusty bracken of his bed. He had been handed a chance to escape, and had been too feeble to seize it. The weight of the opportunity he had lost grew on him hour by heavy hour. Te Hakuwai would be on board by now, awaiting only the right wind to cast off and leave this vile place behind. Ralph should have been with him, going home. Despising himself, he wept.

By the next morning the water-bottle was empty. He must move or die of thirst. He crawled painfully out of the cave-mouth, like an injured lizard. Water fell in a long ribbon down the tawny sandstone cliff and gathered in a little pool, which flowed away in its turn; he could hear the rustle of its further fall. He must be on some sort of plateau. He crawled to the outflow and levered himself painfully upright, then stood rigid, amazed.

Below him, the spume of water vanished over a rocky outcrop which plunged, sheer and sharp-bladed as a knife, for hundreds of feet. Peering over the drop, he could see far below a knobbled pelt of trees. He was on a lip of an enormous valley; not climbing in a gentle curve like the vales of his childhood, but a sunken chasm, rimmed with an escarpment as abrupt as the one on which he stood.

On top of this, as far as the eye could see, ran an undulating plateau devoid of any mark of human habitation. It appeared to Ralph that some cataclysm had torn the bottom out of this world, and he was poised on the crust that remained. Compounding his sense of unreality, there hung over the whole scene a strange blue haze.

Ralph pulled himself back from the edge and subsided, dizzy. He must stay clear; one false step and he would plummet like a slate knocked from a cathedral steeple. Te Hakuwai had chosen well. No one would surprise him here. There must be only one way out, the track by which they had come. Wakened by his fright, he made his way back to the pool and refilled the water-bottle. The axe winked at him in the sunlight, the only artefact in all this vast wilderness.

It was cooler here than down on the coastal plain. With flowing water to clean his wounds and uninterrupted sleep, Ralph healed faster in the fresh air than he had in the poky, foetid hospital back in Sydney. He was reluctant to leave his refuge, but his store of food was down to three scant days' worth of ship's biscuit. He must go while there was still some left. Te Hakuwai might trap the vivid parrots flashing through the trees; Ralph lacked his skill.

The plan in which he had invested such hope lay in ruins. With a quick-witted friend who knew the roads, capable and cunning enough to smuggle him on board, he had the possibility of escape. Now he was days from the nearest vessel, with no idea of how to win his way aboard, even if he was lucky enough, and fit enough, to make his way back to Sydney without being caught. Such alternatives as he devised were flimsy and unconvincing, their force sapped by his crushing disappointment. All he could think of was to head back to the coast and take what chance he could.

He was sorry to leave his retreat. Here he had been alone, and safe. He took one last look at the sublime vista beyond, and turned his back on it, heading up the track.

In the mountains he travelled only by day, afraid of tumbling down some cliff in the darkness. He made little distance on his first stage, but pushed himself next day to the limits of his endurance, conscious of the need to reach settled land before his food ran out.

On his third evening he was forced down onto the road by the slope of the tree-clad hills. He inched down onto the sandy swathe as carefully as though he was stalking deer. Before him a toll-house commanded the way, squat and four-square, with a white door and deep-set shuttered window. He lurked in the shadows until darkness fell; then flitted past, diagonal strips of light from the shutters brushing his feet.

There were more lights as he crested the last hill, from farms and scattered hamlets, dotting the plain below. Momentarily his spirits lifted, after so long in the wild. But at these hearths he would find no welcome. He could not risk again the kind of entanglement that had ended so disastrously with Davies. He was like a stray dog, condemned to scavenge and steal. That night he descended the foothills to the river flats. He hid in a clump of trees, ate the last of his food, and slept.

When he woke he took stock. The descent had exhausted him; his clothes were in tatters. He tried to devise some plan. If he followed this road he would come to Parramatta: a good place to stay away from. A wide sweep to the south offered the safest course. He might find a boat in Botany Bay. The scheme lay leaden in his mind, with no gleam of hope.

He set off, trying to ignore his hunger, staying in sight of the river, which he hoped was the Nepean. After dusk he furtively approached a cottage, but was driven back by the barking of a dog, flinging itself furiously to the end of its chain. Ralph ducked behind a water-trough as a door opened. The farmer stood silhouetted against the light behind, the dark bar of a musket in one hand.

"Quiet!" the man snarled and stepped out into the shadow, head cocked. "Damned blackfellows again," he called back into the house. He fired off a ball in Ralph's direction. Ralph crept away before the farmer thought to let the dog loose.

During the night he came across the half-stripped carcass of a dead cow. He hacked off a chunk; too hungry to wait, and too scared to risk a fire, he tore at the meat raw. He went down to the river to refill his water-bottle. A dip in the river might dispel his fatigue.

His wet clothes were refreshing to begin with, but as the night air cooled they hung chill. He slept fitfully.

His skin burned to the touch. He set off walking, but found the weight of the axe and satchel intolerable and threw them away. He remembered reprimanding soldiers for shedding their kit on forced marches. The fierce sunlight hurt his eyes; he sheltered behind a tumble of rocks. Better to sleep by day and travel at night.

It was dusk when he awoke. Parched with thirst, he gulped the rest of the water. He could hear shouts, screams, gunshots; a pounding of hooves. He stood up. Another cry, much closer this time, sounded on his right. Bemused, he turned.

A rider burst over the crest of the hill. "Here's another!" he yelled, spurring his horse at the gaunt figure poised before him in the fading light. Ralph flung himself aside to dodge a clubbed musket. With a loud *"hulloa"* the rider hauled his mount around on its haunches. Ralph darted for shelter among the rocks. He crouched as the huntsman cast about, swearing, unwilling to venture the animal on uncertain ground. Then, at a yell from further away, he spurred down the slope.

The affray had lasted only minutes. Ralph, daring at length to break cover, was astonished at the rider's casual air. He might have been hunting rabbits, not men. Ralph was almost ready to dismiss the whole episode as a dream when he smelt a dying fire, and followed the waft of smoke to its source. His stomach clenched in apprehension, remembering those nightmare groves in Spain.

Chunks of charred meat littered the trampled embers. He tripped on a wooden spear. A dark-skinned man clung to its broken haft; the other hand clutched at the bloody hole in his chest. A half-grown boy, unscarred by tribal markings, sprawled, his head stove in. Beyond, Ralph glimpsed an old woman's skinny arms upflung in death.

In this frightful stillness he heard a faint mewing. Turning to the sound he stumbled across the legs of a young woman, face down. He lifted her to turn her over. The head lolled back, almost severed at the neck. Trembling, he set the body down, and jerked as he felt something move.

She had shielded her baby as she fell. It was a tiny thing, a dark scrap of skin and bone, frightened and squalling. Ralph picked it up, not knowing what to do: a squirming, naked little boy, whose fingers closed tightly on Ralph's skin.

He could not leave the child behind to starve, but how could he feed it? Already it was butting at his chest, like a hungry lamb. He was overwhelmed by his own helplessness, and a rush of fierce anger at the men who had murdered a family for the price of a cow. They would have killed him too, like vermin.

Only one way could the baby could be fed. He shied away from the idea, but the logic compelled him. He knelt again beside the mother's body, not yet cold. Awkwardly he wiped off what blood he could with his shirt-sleeve. How did one hold a baby to a dead breast? He managed as best he could, and felt again the flow of too-easy tears.

The baby ceased its suckling. Ralph had nothing to wrap it in. There might have been something in the rubble of the campsite, but Ralph could endure this charnel-house no longer. Cradling the child he lurched away, shaking with fever.

His mind wandered. The spirits of the dead wailed all around him, thin and sharp. The air was greasy with heat: the sky a grey paste, masking the horizon. Dust frisked in spirals as the wind gusted, turning to the south. The trees thrashed.

The air cooled. Ralph woke, weak but clear-headed. Beside him on the track lay the dead child, covered in a drift of leaves. He was still staring at it when the soldiers found him.

# 24

# *New South Wales, December 1816*

"Must be that bolter from Parramatta."

"How'd he fetch up here, then?"

"Hey, you! Who got you away?"

Ralph looked up slowly at the speaker, then back down to the dusty path.

"Happen he's deaf."

"Dumb, more like." A chuckle ran round the men. "I've seen them daft before, from being too long in the bush on their own."

"Up with you," said the first speaker, pulling Ralph to his feet. "Back to your mates."

Ralph's mind turned sluggishly to the iron gang, but the faces were indistinct. Too much had happened in between. He was haunted by the dead girl, her head lolling like a broken flower on its stem.

The party headed off, the corporal chivvying Ralph along.

"We'll never get back to camp at this rate," he grumbled.

"He can't go any faster," another supplied, reasonably. "He don't look up to much."

"We could stop at Bourke's," a third voice suggested. "My cousin in the 46th reckons they've got the best grog outside Chatham."

"That scrawny lot! They're off to Madras, I hear. Those hairy heathens will ginger them up, after four years of shooting kangaroos." The others sniggered.

The 46th ordered out! The news stirred Ralph from his apathy. That would mean Devereux gone, and one enemy less.

The party squeezed to one side of the track as a horseman passed.

"Afternoon, Father," shouted one of the soldiers, touching his fingers to the brim of his shako. The rider lifted his hat in reply and the chestnut trotted on, raising little puffs of dust, spicy with the dry scent of the bush.

Bourke's proved to be a slab-built shanty with a row of outbuildings beyond. Ralph slumped against a verandah-post while the corporal went inside. He came out, wiping his mouth on his sleeve. "Leave him with the horses."

At least the stable gave relief from the glare. They took him down to the last box and handcuffed him to the bars of the manger. He shifted about, seeking the least uncomfortable position, and closed his eyes.

"Is this the man, sir?"

"Yes, this is the one." The voice jolted Ralph out of his daze. Before him stood Devereux, in civilian clothes. "A little chipped at the edges, but indubitably he." He drew out a coin. "You may claim your reward at the bar. I shall be there directly."

The corporal's gaze dropped to his prisoner.

"Don't worry. He won't get away."

The redcoat tossed the coin in the air, pocketed it, and left. Surreptitiously Ralph tugged at his wrists. The movement caught Devereux's eye.

"You won't run this time," he remarked. "You will be pleased to hear I am not returning to India with the rest of the Regiment. I have sold out."

"Skulking off before the fighting starts?"

Ralph saw the kick coming and tried to dodge it, but the chain brought him up short.

"I'm a gentleman farmer now. I don't like sheep-stealers." There was a yard-broom leaning against the corner. Devereux wrenched out the handle and stepped forward. "It's time somebody taught you manners."

The priest, dowdy in his old-fashioned tricorne hat and dusty soutane, strode across the deserted yard. Light spilled yellow from the windows of the inn, along with snatches of drunken song. He frowned as he made out the words. Tomorrow was the Fourth Sunday of Advent: it saddened him that the soldiers—good Irishmen among them—could find no more fitting way to celebrate the birth of Christ.

The stable door creaked as he entered. Inside, the air was sharp with the smell of horses. He lit his lantern with care, as his father had taught him so long ago.

His mare trembled, nervous, not giving her usual whicker at seeing him. Something had disturbed her; alert for snakes, he inspected the row of boxes. In the last one a man crouched, wrists chained. The priest reached towards him, but the prisoner shied from his touch.

"I'm not going to hurt you. Let's have a look at you now." The soft brogue soothed as it would a frightened animal. He brought the lantern closer.

"Holy Mother of God!" The old anger stirred in him again. He had seen too many beatings back home, in the terrible aftermath of the Uprising.

"Didn't I see you this afternoon? What is your name?"

"Fletcher." The answer came in a dry whisper.

"Lean your head on my arm. Now, don't sit up, but we'll get a drink into you."

Ralph tried to move but was caught by the pain in his side. In an abrupt movement the priest stood and braced his weight against the manger bar. He was short, but broad and stocky. The wood splintered with a crack, and he eased the links over the stump.

Ralph could lie down now and there was water, wet and cool, at his lips. The matter-of-fact voice continued.

"Now this is going to hurt, because I think your rib is broken; but you'll feel better after." He was right; the strapping eased the fierce ache. He was fed some bread and cold meat: "Not too much at once, now."

"Why are you helping me?"

"What else would I do?" the man replied equably. "It is my business. I am a priest: Father Donavan, at your service."

"The priest on the horse," Ralph remembered aloud.

"Indeed."

Then, with a flash of suspicion: "I am no Papist."

"From the way you speak, I did not think you were."

A heavy tread sounded across the yard. Ralph stiffened. "He's coming back."

"Who?"

"Devereux—I crossed him once, in a matter too unsavoury to explain." He tried to sit up, and his face twisted. "Please—" he clutched at the dusty skirts of the soutane "—could you stay here, just for a little, until he goes away?"

"Was it he who beat you? Do you fear he will do the same again?"

"Worse." The flatness of Ralph's tone convinced the priest as much as his evident distress. Briskly Donavan strode back down the stable and hung the lantern on a hook. He flipped open his saddle-bag and opened a battered black book. As the footsteps neared he recited his breviary aloud.

*"Ad te levavi animam meum; Deus meus, in te confido, non erubescam;"* he began. *To Thee have I lifted up my soul; in Thee, O my God, I put my trust...*

To Ralph, tense in the hay-scented darkness, the Latin cadences were a magic spell, floating like incense on the warm air to keep evil away. The firm voice continued.

*"... neque irredeant me inimici mei: etenim universi, qui te expectant non confundentur..."*

*Let me not be ashamed; neither let my enemies laugh at me; for none of them that wait on Thee shall be confounded.*

The footsteps faltered. More cautiously they resumed. Ralph heard a rustling: Devereux on the other side of the wall, peering through. The steady majestic phrases rolled on. The hesitation lengthened into a pause; then, with a lighter, more furtive rhythm, the steps faded away. Ralph relaxed, with a sigh of fierce relief.

He woke to an argument. Outside his box a heavily-built, round-faced man with a high colour accosted the flustered corporal.

"Stand clear, man! I can't wait all day."

"With respect, Mr Redfern, sir, I can't hand him over. The prisoner is my responsibility."

"Should you not take better care of your responsibilities?" Under the weight of sarcasm the corporal's glance fell. Ralph's bruises had come out overnight, and the back of his shirt was striped where the weals had broken open. "The Governor may be interested to know how the prisoner came to be in this state."

"Lieutenant Devereux said he was trying to escape," the corporal muttered, doggedly.

"In that condition?" Redfern's voice rose, incredulous. "How far is it to Sydney?"

"Forty mile, sir."

"And you propose a two-day march, on foot? Your prisoner will perforate a lung. I trust that is not your intention."

The corporal glanced around. Of Devereux there was no sign. For all his dislike of civilian interference, the soldier was acutely uncomfortable. Surgeon Redfern, though an Emancipist, was a friend of the Governor. The corporal did not want to have to explain why he had been at the bar, drinking, while the prisoner was under his care.

He stood back with an ill grace. "You'd better watch him, sir. He's a runner."

"Don't presume to teach me my business, corporal. You can assure your Lieutenant that the prisoner will be kept secure. When he is fit for work, he will be returned."

Ralph was assigned to a carter carrying provisions to the new hospital in Sydney. Apparently the priest had ridden off the night before and fetched Redfern from his farm. And Redfern was close to Macquarie, a peppery autocrat who had declared it illegal for Government men to be punished outside due process of law.

Ralph gathered that many of the officers regarded this prescription as infringing upon their prerogatives. The driver of Ralph's cart, sniggering, regaled his mate with the tale of one unfortunate Emancipist, a little architect transported for forgery, who was horsewhipped through the barracks by an angry captain unhappy with his work. When the victim took the case to court, no one would testify.

The jolting cart swayed him into a painful doze. He strained to sift the words around him from his bizarre imaginings. He had heard—or had it run together in his mind?—that Devereux, finding one of his cattle speared, had instigated the massacre of which Ralph had so nearly become a victim.

Had Devereux ordered the heads of the dead natives boiled down, to be sent as souvenirs to England? That must be true because he could remember the pungent whiff of the driver's pipe, tobacco mixed with rosemary. But the heads belonged to Clancy's tale—or was it Te Hakuwai's?

Thin stone pillars ruled the sky into long blue rectangles. Ralph was back in Sydney, on the upper verandah of the new hospital. Compared to the old cramped kennel, this building was spacious, even elegant.

Something cold brushed his arm.

"Time to be bled," piped a pimply-faced orderly, brandishing a scalpel and a chipped tin bowl.

"Touch me with that and I'll cut your throat with it," Ralph growled, gaunt and unshaven. He flung the bowl clattering along the floorboards, and the scared boy scrambled after it.

A knot of men on his right turned at the din. One of them stared hard at Ralph.

"Well, if it isn't my old shipmate Fletcher!"

Ralph was astonished to recognize the long jaw and sharp nose of Thomasin, who had made such trouble for him on the voyage out. But this was a Thomasin changed from his furtive shipboard self. His angular frame had filled out, his clothes were well-cut; he wore a hat brushed till it shone. Only his eyes were the same; they flickered over Ralph, missing nothing.

"I have my Ticket-of-Leave now. I have been appointed confidential clerk to Molesworth and Company, where I am shortly to wed Miss Molesworth."

"Please accept my felicitations," said Ralph, dryly.

"I am engaged in business on my own account," Thomasin continued, lowering his voice, as self-important as if he were Rothschild arranging bank drafts for Wellington's army. "I purchase provisions unwanted here, and sell them through a friend of mine." He stooped lower, and whispered: "I can procure any medicines you need. Just send a message through the orderly." With a tight smile of farewell, he rejoined his friends.

So Thomasin had moved up in the world, as he had always intended. Ralph was more perplexed by his show of magnanimity. Had the bad feeling between them been so readily forgotten? Thus low had he fallen, to be patronised by a venal clerk!

At least he had learned that theft of food and medicines was rampant. *"Unwanted provisions"* indeed! Ralph would need to guard such rations as he received. After his outburst of the morning, the orderlies left him alone when they descended on the other patients, to bleed and purge them. There was, as far as Ralph could gather, no other treatment. The medicines provided for the convicts' use were being sold by the doctors to their private patents. The Medical Superintendent, the wealthy Emancipist D'Arcy Wentworth, did nothing to intervene. A charming fellow by all accounts, his aristocratic relations had arranged a posting as surgeon in Norfolk Island after youthful antics which came perilously close to highway-robbery. Now he was Surgeon-General for New South Wales. He had made a fortune from the contract to build the hospital, speculating in rum, but was too preoccupied with his business—and amatory—interests to concern himself with the shortcomings of the institution for which he was responsible.

At dusk the prisoners were herded inside and heavy wooden shutters fastened over the windows; after that they were left to themselves. A crack of light leaked in down the edge of a poorly-fitting shutter. The building was a gimcrack job, for all its fine proportions. Floors were uneven, joinery not square. The upper colonnade had shafts and capitals not of stone, as he had supposed, but of turned wood, some of them crooked.

Recoiling from the squalor of the ward, in which meals were cooked next to latrine buckets, Ralph appropriated the most remote corner, snarling at anyone who came near. He spent as much time as he could on the verandah, in the fresh air. From Thomasin, for reasons Ralph still did not understand, came a supply of better food.

Tomorrow would be Christmas. There should be snow, he thought, but well after sunset the room was still stiflingly hot, as the roof and walls gave back the day's heat.

A year ago he had been prosperous and free, among friends, planning his marriage. At least he had believed them to be his friends. He recalled the song Flavia had chosen:

*What makes you so far from all human nature*
*What makes you so far from all human kind…*

Had she betrayed him, or was she still waiting for him, like the girl in the song? Behind him the ward stank, and a drinking-game grew more raucous with each round.

"Can ye hear down there, Rosie?" one of the men shouted, banging on the boards.

"Sleep with Rosie and you'll get a Christmas present all right."

"What say ye to that, Rosie?"

There was a roar of laughter, followed by a thumping on the underside of the floor, and a muffled stream of abuse.

The women's ward was beneath; a bribe to the warders gained admission at night. Ralph was repelled by the notion of wretched women, raddled with disease, plying their trade in such disgusting surroundings.

Not, he thought bitterly, that he had the means to keep company with even such women as these. He reached for the stone bottle of rum which had come in Thomasin's last basket of provisions, and drained what was left. As he set it down, he realised the reason for the man's solicitude. It was Ralph who had caught him cheating at cards, and given him the nickname which had stuck to him for the rest of the voyage. He must fear that Ralph would spread the story, and it would get back to his prospective in-laws. The provisions were blackmail in advance, to keep him sweet until such time as Ralph was dispatched elsewhere and no longer threatened Thomasin's new-found respectability.

How could he have been so slow to work this out? Sickness was no excuse. He could not afford to wallow in sentiment about a life that was dead and gone. He needed all his wits about him to survive here and now.

Right on cue, like an extra at Drury Lane, Thomasin walked in, his face fixed in its mask of false *bonhomie*.

"Nobby! Come to join me for a hand of cards?"

Thomasin's smile vanished: his face hardened. "Don't think I've forgotten, Mr Recalcitrant. My mate in the Muster Office showed me your record. I have a good position, and soon a wife for my bed. In a week you'll be back in irons, for all your clever words, and off to the mines at Newcastle. The only woman you'll get is the five-fingered widow."

Thomasin shrank back as Ralph suddenly stood over him. "At least," Ralph said quietly, "when I look in a mirror I don't see a liar and a cheat. Compliments of the season to you."

Thomasin withdrew as quickly as dignity would allow. Ralph slouched on the narrow bed, elbows on his knees, his head hanging. He had scared the man, but it was a hollow victory. Thomasin's words burned like vitriol. So now *"recalcitrant"* had joined *"insolent"*, and *"grossly insubordinate"* on his record, along with his two failed attempts at escape and two convictions for theft. None of this was going to make his life any easier when he walked into the darkness of the mines.

Next morning he was surprised to see Father Donavan, nondescript in the light of day with his heavy square face and grey-streaked, greasy hair. He might have been any of a hundred Irish convicts or small farmers in Sydney's dusty streets.

Ralph was embarrassed. Te Hakuwai he had managed to impress with his Dutch courage; this common-looking Papist priest had seen too much of the truth.

The priest began: "You will be asking why I am here. You should know that Redfern tried to have Devereux charged."

Ralph's guarded expression quickened to interest.

"Devereux was an officer in the South Devons, was he not?"

Ralph nodded.

"Had he stayed in the Army, it might have been possible to bring a case under military law. But as it is, you would have to bring the action yourself—" Ralph gave a derisory grimace "—and none of the soldiers will testify."

God knows, thought Ralph, I should be used to this by now; but the injustice still smote him. "I'll settle the bastard myself!"

"It won't do you any good—"

Ralph's fragile control snapped. "Good!" he hissed. "What good has the law ever done me! Why should I expect anything from this pack of venal office-servers! You stick with the New Testament, Father; I'll stay with the Old: an eye for an eye, a tooth for a tooth!"

He was shaking with his own vehemence. The priest reached forward, but Ralph pulled away.

"You do Redfern and the Governor an injustice," Donavan said quietly. "Oh, there are land-hungry adventurers enough, ready to twist the law to their own advantage. But Macquarie is an honest man. He has made no fortune from his office. He has built roads, established towns, raised public buildings; indeed, this very hospital was his inspiration."

"Look at it!" retorted Ralph. "Fine outside; ramshackle within. Every room I stand in is papered with his regulations. If he has the power, why does he not enforce his own laws?"

"What country was ever founded as this has been?" the priest replied. "I wonder sometimes what we are bringing to birth. This place has few laws and no established customs. The Governor must make them up as he goes along. More to your point: he writes the laws, but others enforce them. He is no Napoleon, with secret police to compel compliance. One day the children of the men he has set free will enjoy the institutions he has devised."

"Meanwhile we suffer," Ralph interrupted fiercely.

"Meanwhile we suffer," echoed the other.

A week later, Ralph was transferred to the gaol for sentencing. The usual fifty lashes dealt out to escaped prisoners was remitted—at Donavan's intercession, Ralph suspected. He was grateful nonetheless.

Thomasin's prediction had been accurate: two years at Newcastle, in the coalmines. There would, commented the magistrate, be little chance of his running from there, and less to steal.

# 25

# England, Spring 1817

The hawthorn tree filled Marianne's window with its cascade of creamy blossoms. She heard the high voices of Hannah and Tobias, newly freed from their lessons, dodging among its drooping boughs. Benjamin lay asleep in the nursery, his small fist clenched around a floppy cloth kitten. Upstairs in his study Edmund was composing Sunday's sermon. As much as Marianne had enjoyed her time in London, she was deeply content to be home.

The most lasting consequence of her visit had been her chance meeting with young Flavia Stanton, which had burgeoned into friendship. At first Marianne had felt sorry for Flavia, motherless as she was. She had responded to the girl's generous spirit and thirst for new ideas. Marianne, gratified to be taken as a model, sensed that Flavia saw her as the older sister she had never had.

She set down Flavia's latest letter, untidily penned in an enthusiastic scrawl. Had she been wise to encourage an interest in reform? But Flavia was too intelligent to waste her mind on dressmakers' catalogues. Certainly she sounded happier and more confident now that she had opinions of her own and evidence to support them. Harriet and Bromley would keep her feet on the ground.

Marianne had heard hints that Robert was showing an interest in Harriet's *protégée*. Such attentions could be flattering. She herself remembered feeling a more than cousinly attraction for him when she was younger. He was handsome and assertive, with the polish that comes from wealth and taste. But she had grown out of this conceit when she met Edmund, gawky and painfully shy, a clergyman with nothing to offer but his deep faith and the force of his attachment.

In all the years she had known Bromley, he had never let slip an unguarded comment, or admitted he was wrong. Some women were drawn by such close and dominating natures. She suspected that for the orphaned Flavia, with her need for affection, losing her heart to such a man might be a mistake. There had been rumours of other women in Robert's life, but he had acknowledged none of them.

Only his mother held his loyalty; she took a fierce pride in his achievements. Marianne had always found her intimidating, with the airs, if not the title, of a duchess. How Dorothea Bromley hated the plain *'Mrs'*! She had been happy enough to accept Josiah's money and the luxury that it bought her, but had always treated him with a *hauteur* just short of contempt. Marianne reflected that Dorothea had always dismissed anyone, or any activity, which did not immediately serve her interest. It was the unashamedly plebeian Josiah who had taught nine-men's-morris to a visiting small girl; now Hannah and Tobias played it in their turn.

Marianne turned her attention to the letter.

*There has been a great rally here, presenting a petition for Reform which they claim has half-a-million signatures. The city is full of laid-off soldiers and sailors who cannot find work, and the Government fears an insurrection. Someone threw a stone through the window of the Prince Regent's carriage the other day. But you will already have read about this in the papers.*

*You asked how my cousin is faring. She has grown more testy of late, but still enjoys her Tuesday salons. Remember Mr Wentworth, the Antipodean gentleman she added to her collection? You may recall him as a rather handsome young man with a slight cast in one eye. This gives a disconcerting quality to his conversation, as you are never quite sure at whom he is looking! Bromley and he continued at daggers drawn last week.*

*Mr Wentworth is in favour of Reform, and asserts that "Australia", as he calls it, is a country with a great future. Bromley insists that the colony must continue as a place of punishment. "What possible respect can the lower classes have for law and order," he stated, "if the Government, upon declaring them felons, transports them to a life of opportunity among the promiscuous and corrupt?"*

*At this Wentworth pawed the ground, as it were, and grew dusky with indignation. (He has an Irishman's red hair, and the temper to go with it.) He considers himself entrusted with a mission to prove what native-born "Australians" can achieve. Your cousin, after he had gone, made dismissive remarks about "upstart young lawyers of bad breeding and worse manners".*

*Bromley has been spreading some gossip he has heard that Mr Wentworth's parents were not married. You know how strict he is about social proprieties. He calls him 'Master Fitz-Wentworth', which is most unkind. I sometimes wonder whether Harriet does not invite this brash young man simply to annoy Bromley. She can be quite malicious at times.*

Smiling now, Marianne set about her reply.

In a corner of Harriet's salon, Wentworth was holding court. Flavia had heard this story already, but it was an exciting tale and she moved closer to listen.

"So for days we worked our way westward," he was saying. "We toiled by day through the trackless bush—"

"*Bush* as in a garden?" interrupted Harriet crisply. She liked to form a clear notion of the subject under discussion.

"No, Ma'am; it is an Australian term for the indigenous flora—" he paused to think of an analogy. "Like furze or gorse, but drier and less green, without spines, and interspersed with native trees."

Harriet nodded, content, as he returned to his theme.

"Again and again we were brought up short by terrifying cliffs, dropping straight down for hundreds of feet. At night we could hear only the howling of native dogs, and the rustle of the natives following our track."

Everyone was looking at him expectantly. He caught Flavia's eye and winked.

"Then, just as we were about to give up hope, we reached the westward limit of the Blue Mountains, and the land fell away below us to the plains." He struck a pose.

> "*—nearer the beauteous landscape grew*
> *Op'ning like Canaan on rapt Israel's view.*"

Wentworth acknowledged his audience with an uplifted hand.

"Moses, descending from Sinai," Flavia observed dryly.

He snatched up a silver tray and held it at an angle, like the tablets of the law in Michelangelo's statue.

"Self-government, free press, and trial by jury!" he intoned. Flavia smiled. Wentworth might have a high opinion of himself, but he had an Irishman's knack of telling a good story.

"You didn't tell them what happened next," she said accusingly.

"About the three Government men who followed in our footsteps, and earned a hundred lashes for their presumption?" He gave a crow of laughter. "Poor old Sandy. He looked positively boot-faced when we returned. He didn't know whether to congratulate us for opening up thousands of acres of good grazing land, or clap us under a vow of silence so no one would be tempted to run away. It was months before he even published the news in the *Gazette*: an excellent example of the need for a free press."

"Surely *Old Sandy* is a disrespectful term for the Governor, who represents the King," she chided.

"I've called your precious Wilberforce *The Old Woman* before," he retorted. "And my friend Mr Campbell refers to the Reverend Marsden, that squat pillar of missionary effort, as *The Christian Mahomet of Botany Bay*."

Flavia was affronted. Marianne had the highest regard for Wilberforce, who had fought for so many years against the scourge of slavery. She excused herself and returned to the buffet, where she found Bromley at her shoulder.

"I see our young colonial is in full voice today," he observed. "If he assails mountains with the same energy he devotes to conquering drawing rooms, he must be an intrepid explorer indeed."

"Come, Mr Bromley," said Flavia, "I know you dislike his politics—"

"Lord Fitzwilliam and his Whiggish set—or should I say, *cast?*" Bromley discreetly touched a long finger to one eye.

"You are too unkind," said Flavia, but she could not forbear to smile. Bromley's wit was cruel; she would not like to be its target. But Wentworth was quick enough to hone his wit on others. "You should not mock a physical deformity over which he has no control."

"His tongue?" suggested Bromley.

"No," she said, trying to keep a straight face. "You know very well what I mean."

"I stand corrected, Miss Stanton. Perhaps he inherited it from his mother."

"You are incorrigible! But I must congratulate you," she said. "I hear you are to enter Parliament."

"Lord Bathurst has promised me a borough," he said easily.

Flavia felt a quickening of excitement. So Bromley had the interest of Lord Bathurst! The Colonial Secretary was an eminent patron indeed. She felt the lure of being close to power.

"Forget Wentworth's dreams of an Emancipist Utopia. Lord Bathurst is considering a scheme to breed flocks of merino sheep, suited to the climate of New Holland, and export fine wool to England. Mr Macarthur and the Reverend Marsden have already provided promising samples. This is where the future of New Holland lies, in large, prosperous holdings tended by well-disciplined convict labourers; not in Mr Wentworth's rousing of a rabble as ill-bred as himself. Why should those convicted in a court of law expect to enjoy in their place of punishment the rights they have abused? The notion is preposterous!"

"You feel strongly on this subject," she said diplomatically.

"Indeed I do," he replied. "You are a well-read young woman. I am sure you know enough about the French Revolution, and the Napoleonic tyranny that followed, to see the dangers of granting power to the mob. Government should be exercised by men of property, with experience of affairs and a stake in their country. Such has always been the English way."

"But what about the petition attacking Governor Macquarie?" Flavia suggested. "Surely as the appointed ruler of the colony, his authority should be respected?"

"You have been listening to that young firebrand," said Bromley coolly. "The misplaced humanitarianism of a John Company colonel is precisely of a nature to appeal to his rebellious notions. But surely even he would find the full range of the Governor's despotic powers too much to take. To admit felons to respectable society is an anti-British absurdity."

Flavia wilted under his disdain. She had thought the Governor's policies, when Wentworth explained them to her, benevolent and far-sighted. Was not forgiveness a basic tenet of Christianity? Should not felons be encouraged to become honest artisans? She kept her doubts to herself, unwilling to invite another rebuke.

"I see they have opened the new pianoforte," she said, to change the subject.

"Perhaps you will demonstrate its tone," Bromley replied with studied politeness.

Flavia, urged by Harriet to take a more active part in entertaining her guests, had practised all week. This time she knew she would play well.

The final notes died away to a flutter of applause.

"A fair rendition, if a trifle slow in the *Adagio*," said Bromley appraisingly. "Who is your music master?"

"I have taken no lessons since I arrived in London."

"You should do so. May I recommend M. Dupont? He trained as a court musician at Versailles. I shall send him to you."

Flavia was eager to learn from a teacher of such expertise. But should she accept Bromley's offer?

"It would be too much trouble for you."

"Not at all. Your talent should be encouraged. Music is a fitting accomplishment for a young lady."

Unlike politics, Flavia thought, smiling politely at her benefactor as he made his *adieux*. He appeared to have forgotten his earlier outburst. Perhaps he had money invested in Australia. Perhaps, she thought, remembering Marianne's words, he is unused to taking female opinions seriously.

Flavia found Harriet in her little parlour. Papered in an unfashionable dark green, cluttered with mementoes and framed silhouettes of friends long dead, it caught the afternoon sun.

Flavia hefted Hester aside and sat down. She wished Harriet would open a window. The room was close, smelling of dog, old cushions and an overpowering scent of lilies.

"Bromley has offered to pay for a music-master for me, a M. Dupont."

"Has he, indeed?" Harriet looked up with one of her keen glances. "You should be flattered. Bromley is considered discriminating."

Flavia suppressed a flash of annoyance. Perhaps Harriet had misheard. She was getting a little deaf these days.

"Would I not be putting myself under an obligation? It's not as if he is a relation."

"Do you wish to learn from this M. Dupont?"

"Most definitely."

"Then take your lessons. The only obligation you will incur is that of playing well, should Bromley wish to hear you. He is after all a friend of the family."

Flavia, relieved, jumped up and gave her cousin a grateful hug. "You are a great help to me," she said. "I have come so late to society that I am unsure what is acceptable and what is not."

Harriet regarded her with amused affection. "Let me tell you one of the secrets of a long life. Be wealthy, and you can afford to hold independent views. My acquaintance grew much more respectful of my opinions after I inherited dear Father's money."

Flavia's chuckle was interrupted by Wardell's knock. He entered with a silver tray.

"What is that?" Harriet demanded. "The hour is too late for the post."

"A letter for Miss Stanton's late father," replied Wardell, perturbed. "A most peculiar-looking foreign gentleman delivered it, a sailor or some such. He asked if this was the house of Mr Stanton, as he had a letter for him. I took it, thinking it to be for Mr Lucius. By the time I realised my error he was gone. Very quiet for such a big man. I must say I was relieved. There are some rough fellows on the streets these days."

The letter was grubby and water-stained, its edges furred against the glistening silver. It was directed to her father, in a firm hand she did not recognise. She turned it over. It was sealed with a plain wafer. The damp paper had an odd, unpleasant smell. She set it down with distaste.

"Bring it here, Wardell," Harriet commanded. She held it close to inspect it and her mouth turned down.

"Faugh! Even at my age, I know dead fish when I smell it. Where on earth did this come from?"

"I know Father wrote overseas; he once had a reply from Madras. We could open it and find out," suggested Flavia, doubtfully.

"No! Remember the trouble when you accepted that summons for Lucius? As heir to your father's estate, any correspondence is his to deal with. I will have it sent on." She snorted again. "Take it away, Wardell. It stinks! And bring water so we may wash our fingers."

As Flavia handed it over something rolled out: a hard little seed which had been caught in the folds. She picked it up to throw it in the fire.

"Wait!" Harriet ordered. "Perhaps it was some curiosity Charles requested for the garden. Plant it, and we will see what grows. At least his effort will not have been in vain. If it is of sufficient interest, we can send it to Kew."

Flavia pushed the seed into the earth of the nearest lily-pot. "You can add it to your mementoes," she said, smiling. Her mind turned to more pressing concerns. "If I am to learn from a French court musician, I had better practise my scales."

Bromley looked up, angry at the interruption.

"I told you I was not to be disturbed."

"I know, Sir, but Mr Stanton said—"

The servant was cut off as Lucius pushed past him. Water dripped from his cape onto the rug before the fire.

"I must see you," said Lucius, shortly, his usually pleasant expression grim.

Bromley looked at him sharply. "Can't it wait till morning?"

Lucius jerked his head towards the manservant, who left. Lucius pulled out a sealed pouch and slapped it down on the desk.

"Look at this."

"You could at least divest yourself of that cape and not ruin my carpet," said Bromley calmly, reaching over to the source of his visitor's agitation.

He drew out a letter, limp and travel-worn. As he saw the superscription, he stiffened. The carpet forgotten, he opened out the paper and read it.

He did not hand it back, but his eyes moved at once to Lucius. "When did you get this?"

"It arrived yesterday. I came immediately I read it."

"Who else knows about it?"

"It was sent on from Harriet's."

"Has your sister read it?" Bromley said swiftly.

"Why would she? It was not addressed to her," Lucius said cuttingly. "The seal was untouched." He leaned forward, colouring with indignation. "I couldn't care less how it got here. What will you do about it?"

Bromley smiled bleakly. "Nothing," he said with satisfaction.

"Nothing?" Lucius echoed. "Fairfax is in prison on the other side of the world and you won't lift a finger to save him?"

"Why should I? I sent him there."

"You *what?*"

"Why deny it? Take a chair, for heaven's sake; stop striking poses like the hero of a German novel. You forget: I sent him there, with your help."

Lucius looked stunned. His mouth opened in denial, but no sound came out. Abruptly he sat down.

"Let me explain. You may remember how, at my mother's ball, we played a practical joke on your friend Ralph. He was taken after you left to the Deptford hulks, and thence to New South Wales."

"But why?" Lucius's voice was barely a whisper.

"I had my reasons," Bromley stated in a voice that brooked no further inquiry. "So, I believe, did you. Was it not good riddance, to have him out of the way?"

With a start Lucius remembered how relieved he had been at Ralph's timely disappearance. Fairfax disliked the Lennoxes; he had made that clear enough. Lucius had feared Ralph would turn his father against them. And Flavia—Ralph had not run away with the German woman after all. He and Flavia would have been married by now.

Lucius was appalled. Ralph had trusted him, and he had betrayed him to imprisonment and disgrace. Fitful thoughts tumbled in his mind: to write to the authorities; confess to Harriet and ask her advice; tell Flavia.

"What can I do?" he cried, in an agony of indecision.

"Lower your voice, for a start," snapped Bromley. "You have given rise to enough talk already, bursting in here at dead of night. Luckily for you my man is discreet. Stop mewling like a chastised puppy."

"But I owe it to Flavia—" Lucius burst out.

"And what do you owe your wife? And your son?" Bromley interposed. "Poverty? Ruin? Where do you think the money came from for the comforts they so enjoy?"

He unlocked a drawer in the desk, lifted out a ring, and tossed it to Lucius, who caught it gingerly.

"There is the source of your good fortune." The flecks in the bloodstone of Ralph's signet glinted in the firelight.

With a derisive smile, Bromley scrawled a signature on a scrap of paper and pushed it over. It was identical to the one on the letter. Lucius set the ring down as if it burned and half-turned away.

"Think before you act, young man. Your generous instinct does you credit; but do you really want Fairfax to return? He is alive and under government care; he will eat better than many a pauper in England. You have only to listen to young Wentworth to hear how well transported men are treated under the present Governor." Bromley's tone was calm, reassuring.

"Besides," he went on, raising an eyebrow, "what if he *did* come back? His family are not noted for their forbearance. The repute of the Stantons stands or falls by your actions. What future would there be for your little boy if this story got out? What hope for your sister of a good marriage then?"

Lucius, troubled, still would not meet his eye, but Bromley sat confidently back. Stanton would agonise all night, and do what required least effort in the morning.

Bromley could count on Lucius being too wrapped up in his own dilemma to see the desperation behind the writer's words. Fairfax, with his quick tongue, had obviously not found convict life easy, and had already run foul of authority. *Sentenced to irons in a timber-camp*: Bromley recalled the phrase with satisfaction. Let his half-brother be denied *his* rights and see how he liked it.

"Forget the letter," he said. "Go home tomorrow. If anyone asks, say you came to London on an urgent matter of business—some stocks I had advised you to snap up promptly. I think you will find they bring a good return."

As he spoke, Bromley touched the corner of the paper to the flame in the grate. The pleading words flared up, then writhed and blackened, leaving behind a faint unpleasant odour. Delicately he prodded the charred fragments with a poker.

"You may stay here tonight," he said. "You will not speak of this again, to me or anyone else. Goodnight."

Wordlessly Lucius stood up and left.

That was Stanton taken care of, thought Bromley. A pity he had burned the letter, though. He would have relished reading it again.

# 26

## *New South Wales, Summer 1817*

Ralph set his foot on the anvil, his impassive face masking his bitterness. The thought of Te Hakuwai aboard ship mocked him, as the smith closed up the irons around Ralph's ankle and drove in the rivet with hammer-strokes that jarred Ralph's teeth.

Davies' baby would be born by now. It had better not die: not after what it had cost him. *Clang, clang, clang!* on the other leg. With casual expertise the freckled smith tightened up the linking chain. He looked a pleasant enough fellow; fettering men's limbs with as little thought as he would shoe a horse. The links clashed as Ralph shuffled away, hampered again by the hateful, familiar drag of the iron hobble.

He had missed the sailing to Newcastle, so was sent north with a gang bound for the Hawkesbury River, to complete his journey by boat. In other circumstances he might have enjoyed the scene. The broad river glittered in the heat, the tilled countryside green on its shores, Wiseman's Hotel set on the broad slope of the other side. Now he was indifferent to his surroundings.

He sat in silence, tying a strip of cloth around his chafed leg. When he had first arrived in New South Wales, he had regarded the convict system as a lottery. A few did spectacularly well, while the greater number saw out their time, and after a few years went on with their lives, more or less free.

What he only now understood was that with each slip downwards, a ratchet clicked. Each added sentence made it harder to claw your way back. Because Ralph had absconded from the timber gang, he still had the balance of that sentence to serve before the two years he had now been given in the mines. Two years! With each condition more intolerable than the last, he was like a debtor in the hands of moneylenders, damned by compound interest.

The escort lit up their pipes as they waited, and the convicts talked quietly among themselves.

"Miserable bastard, old Wiseman. They say he's got a curse on him."

"If every magistrate was cursed that ordered an unjust flogging, half the toffs in New South Wales would drop down dead." The speaker, a pert youth with a mop of copper curls, grinned at his own wit; there was a general laugh.

The corporal turned to silence his charges. He was distracted by a horseman galloping down the hill behind them, raising a cloud of dust. The convicts craned around; but the ferry, a bluff-bowed flat barge, had just pulled in. They were herded on board, their chains clattering against the wooden deck. Ralph, hard up against the gunwales, shoved to make room.

"Watch it!" complained his neighbour. "This ain't a skiff on the Serpentine."

"Close up in the bows!"

The ferry rocked to an unfamiliar motion. They were trying to lead a grey horse on board, but the animal was jibbing at the deck alive beneath her.

"We can't all fit, sir," urged the corporal. "We'll have to swim her across."

"Nonsense, man. Make room. I'm in a hurry."

Ralph's head whipped round at the voice.

"Well, well," drawled Devereux. His eyes took in Ralph's hospital pallor and the bloody rags round his ankles. "He can hold her," he ordered, indicating Ralph with his riding-crop. "He's good in stables."

Ralph schooled his features to immobility. Anger was a luxury he could no longer afford. And the corporal was right: a crowded ferry was no place for a frightened blood horse. But this was not for Ralph to say.

He snatched the reins under the snaffle-rings. Ralph was double-ironed, handcuffs and leg-irons both. Devereux grinned at his clumsy attempts to hold the mare steady as she flung up her head at the clinking chains and rolled her eyes.

The ferry pulled off low in the water, and crept over the surface of the river. Ralph was sweating and tense. He hoped the mare would not bite. She had already raked a hoof down his shin. He knew Devereux would charge him with negligence if she came to any harm. Should she slip on the greasy decking her knees would be bruised, or worse.

Halfway across, caught in an eddy of the current, the ferry lurched. The horse plunged. Ralph hauled his weight against her, but as the boat tilted she twisted on her haunches and lashed out with her off-hind hoof. Devereux was leaning against the gunwale, smoking a cigar. Caught off-balance, he was kicked over the side.

His head broke the surface in a swirl of bubbles. "Help!" he cried, flailing. "I can't swim!"

The boatmen cursed, straining. It was all they could do to keep the craft upright. Ralph fought to quiet the stamping horse. He clamped his hat over her eyes and she stilled, shivering.

Devereux clawed at the side of the boat, his nails scraping on the slippery wood.

"Give me a hand!" he screamed, keeping afloat by desperate effort.

A soldier in the bows flung a rope clumsily. It fell short. No one else moved. Ralph smiled at Devereux, and shrugged.

The white face whirled away in the current. Silent as a barge of mutes, the convicts watched him drown. Then the expanse of the river was empty except for a hat, twirling incongruously downstream.

The ferry jarred as it grounded on the other side. The red-headed lad brushed against Ralph as they disembarked. He whispered: "Anybody know who set that curse?"

Ralph felt a dreadful urge to laugh. He buried his face in the horse's mane while the other convicts quivered around him.

The corporal raged at them for clumsy oafs. As he had been holding the horse, Ralph was taken off for questioning. The little lieutenant examining him, obviously suspicious, hinted that Ralph had provoked the animal deliberately. Ralph countered, arguing that the mare was scared when she came on board, and showing the broken bruise on his shin as proof. Had his hands been free, he added blandly, he would of course have proffered help. The lieutenant threatened a formal enquiry.

At this, Ralph drew himself up to his full height and stared down on his inquisitor with derision. "Press me any further on this matter— *sir*—and I will make it known how I came to be in the hospital. I have witnesses—Assistant-Surgeon Redfern is one—and I assure you the tale will do nothing to enhance the late Lieutenant's reputation."

The officer glared up at him, unwilling to be bested.

The words floated unbidden to Ralph's lips. "After all, *de mortuis nihil nisi bonum:* isn't that right, *sir?*"

The man's hand clenched on the hilt of his sword.

"What did you say?" his escort queried, as soon as they were out of earshot.

"It's Latin: *Speak only good of those who are dead.*"

The soldier compressed his lips, and grunted. Ralph walked off with as much of a swagger as he could manage. For all their sharp looks, they could prove nothing against him; Devereux had died a victim of his own stupidity. Ralph had won a victory of sorts. But he knew he would pay for it. The clerk was probably that very minute adding a new epithet to Ralph's record at the lieutenant's dictation: "intransigent", perhaps, or "intractable". Give a dog a bad name, and hang him.

It was evening when they reached Newcastle. Darkness gathered in the great bay. A headland topped by a flagstaff reared abruptly above them. The sheer face of Nobby's Head lifted beyond a broad channel, as though a giant had sliced off a great chunk of land, and shoved it away in a fit of temper. On a rising plateau, tiny glimmering windows marked neat rows of white houses, their trim fences striving to fend off the immense wilderness beyond. A second flag stirred fitfully on a pole at the edge of the cliff.

Ralph had no time to stare. The escort had been rougher with him since Devereux's death. At a growled command, he was shoved forward on the rutted road to the gaol.

The heavy door clanged behind him. The cell was old and damp, with mortar flaking from the grimy stone. A branch of flowers, lit by the last rays of the sun, danced in the small, high window, glowing vivid in the sunset. He watched it until the square of light faded. If he reached up, he could just stretch his fingers through the bars.

Roused before dawn, he was marched down to the seashore. Waves rustled on the beach behind; before him stood a cliff, burrowed and worm-eaten, set with a gate. Stripped to his breeches, Ralph felt cold and exposed. The overseer strutted up; a thickset man whose head jutted forward. Tapping a cudgel against his palm, he circled Ralph, inspecting him carefully.

"My name's Pryor: *Mister* to you. I've heard about you, Fletcher: the funny bastard from Parramatta. You'll find nowt to laugh about here."

Ralph watched the cudgel as the man prowled. The overseer made as if to hit him; instinctively Ralph shielded his newly-healed rib, bracing for a blow, but Pryor sauntered off. "Get to work," he called back over his shoulder. "There are four rollcalls a day here, so you can forget about bolting."

Ralph entered the tunnel in the cliff. In the dank air, his nostrils flared. His only light was a candle, fixed to the brim of his leather hat. In fitful gleams he saw a receding perspective of props, shoring up the weight of the hill above.

A wooden barrow trundled towards him, piled high with coal and pushed by three men black as Negroes.

"Here! Lend a hand."

Ralph stepped forward and heaved with the others as they tilted the barrow forward. A black avalanche cascaded out, its edges slithering over Ralph's feet and sending up a cloud of dust that made him cough.

As the dust settled, a flickering light appeared in the distance. With a peculiar rattling jog, the four trundled the barrow back to the workings. Wooden wheels shrieked on wooden axles, every noise magnified, bouncing off the walls.

As he reached the end the roof pressed lower, forcing Ralph to stoop. Where the miners were digging into the coal-seam there was not room for a man to kneel. One lay on his back, his hat on the floor beside him, chopping upwards in short, expert strokes.

His companion, shovelling the coal into a sturdy wooden tub, looked up.

"What's your name?"

"Fletcher."

The outstretched miner twisted round in a rattle of falling coal. Teeth gleamed in a predatory smile. "Look what the cat dragged in! No word for an old pal?"

"Beckworth," Ralph said, not knowing whether to shake his hand or run. He eyed him warily.

"Can't say as I'm surprised to see you here," Beckworth continued. "You always were too uppity for your own good."

Ralph glanced at the man on the left.

"Don't worry: it's not Kennedy. We tried the same trick again and got caught. He got sent to Port Arthur and I came here, being a miner by trade. I don't suppose you've ever swung a pick in your life."

A low whistle warned them the overseer was coming. A shovel was thrust into Ralph's hand, and Beckworth slithered back into his working like a lizard into a crack.

Soon Ralph was as black as his companions, striped with paler runnels of sweat. The coal dust clung in his hair and gritted his skin; it went up his nose and made it run; it rimmed his eyes and made them sore. He could taste coal in his mouth, fouling his palate, thwarting all attempts to spit it out. Even the water when it came around, tasted of coal. He was too thirsty to waste the precious liquid by rinsing his mouth out first.

Today was Sunday. The others called it "payday". Ralph discovered why, standing to attention with the hundreds of other convicts as punishments were meted out. A runaway, defeated by the bush, had given himself up, starving. In his emaciated state he took his fifty lashes badly.

Ralph loathed the whole charade. To be compelled to dignify what was being done was almost as degrading as being flogged himself. He could never develop the indifference of the old hands. He felt sick, and fiercely angry; angry enough to overcome his disgust with Beckworth and question him after.

"Why was there no surgeon present? Isn't that in their damned rules?"

"Oh, but it is," Beckworth answered with genial contempt. "There's a medical officer to look after us, along with the Brevet-Major, the storekeeper, the superintendents, the gaoler, and the constable. But for less than a hundred lashes, he don't turn up."

Back in the bare hall of the barracks, Ralph was shown a patch of floor next to a lean gypsy scratching the boils on his neck. He stopped long enough to look Ralph over with black eyes hard as stones.

"So you're Fletcher. I'm Jarkman. He's Grimshaw." He jabbed a thumb at a teak-faced, broken-nosed old lag with a down-twisted mouth.

"I'm not bunking here," Ralph stated, his voice betraying his antagonism.

Bored and hungry, the convicts smirked at him expectantly.

"Reckons he's too swell for the likes of us," Grimshaw called over his shoulder. "Let's take a look."

They closed on him. Ralph struck out, but they flowed over him like rats. He was pinned face-down, struggling as they clawed at his clothes. Suddenly the weight on top of him eased. He twisted round to see Beckworth, cuffing off his attackers.

"That'll do," said Beckworth, elbowing the hulking Grimshaw aside with surprising strength. "Fletcher and me is old shipmates. Leave the cove alone."

Grimshaw's sinewy fists clenched. Then Jarkman marked the red-headed boy further down the room.

"That one's prettier," he said.

His assailants sauntered off. Ralph clambered to his feet as Beckworth gave a dry laugh.

"You should learn to look after yourself. Only a fool would throw away the kind of life you had and end up in a place like this. Anyone with two eyes could see what Devereux was after."

"Devereux is dead," Ralph said flatly. "He fell off the ferry. I saw him drown."

"Did you now?" said Beckworth appreciatively. "I heard as his horse kicked him, and you were holding it. Maybe we'll make something of you yet. If you can swallow your pride you can bunk in my corner. Steer clear of Jarkman and Grimshaw; they're a nasty pair of sods. They'll eat up young Kitty Carrots like mastiffs stripping a bone."

Beckworth might be a scoundrel, but at least he was a familiar face, and Ralph was too tired to argue. He settled into the narrow gap on the dusty floor and turned away. A whiskery chin tickled his ear.

"The look on your face when you twigged that Masters had stitched you up! Funniest thing I seen in a long time."

Beckworth chuckled, hawked and spat, and was snoring in two minutes. Ralph, goaded, could not sleep. He was wound up already after his encounter with Pryor. The threat of violence had been there; unrealised, it hung over him unresolved. A blow would have been easier.

He heard the sound of a struggle, a stifled cry, grunting. Repelled, he gathered himself to rise. Strong fingers clamped his arm.

Beckworth whispered out of the darkness. "Don't."

"Why not?"

"Because there's two of them and one of you." The grip tightened in emphasis, then relaxed.

Ralph rubbed his arm. He had held a grudge against Beckworth ever since suffering so cruelly in Sydney for the other man's crime. Now he was reluctantly grateful. Here in Hades he needed a guide, no matter how treacherous. He pressed his hands over his ears to shut out the sound, aware that but for Beckworth he would have been assigned to that end of the hut. He had just rid himself of the threat of Devereux. Jarkman and Grimshaw were more brutal and less restrained. Ralph knew he would kill rather than submit to such degradation, even if he had to swing for it.

As they filed down to the mine on Monday, Ralph questioned Beckworth reluctantly, driven to seek an answer. "Why did you stop them?"

"The hard word's gone out on you, my lad. If you're causing that much trouble you can do with some help. Besides, I've heard you're an iron man. You don't let the tyrants think they've won."

Ralph's mouth tightened in wry acknowledgement. An "iron man" was a prisoner who stayed silent under the lash. So he had a reputation. It was not quite what his father had in mind when he clapped him on the shoulder as he took ship for Spain, and told him to make his mark in the world. But it had proved useful all the same.

"Don't trust Pryor an inch," Beckworth warned him next morning. "He's so mean he'd skin a louse for its hide. He'll offer to turn a blind eye to you running, for food or your baccy. Next he'll turn you in, to win time on his ticket-of-leave."

All that day Pryor ignored him. Ralph was hungry by the time they lined up, tools on their shoulders, at the end of the shift. Pryor strode briskly down the line. As he passed Ralph he knocked him sideways into the loaded barrows by the base of the shaft. A torrent of coal poured onto the ground.

"You should be more careful where you set your feet, Fletcher. You'll eat when you've put that lot back. If there's anything left, that is. And don't expect to finish this shift and stroll back to your cosy barracks. You'll not see daylight again till Saturday afternoon."

Ralph's hand tightened on the haft. He looked down, so as not to be provoked into punching that sneering face. Seething, he drove the shovel chunking into the tumbled mass. Beckworth was right; he was a marked man, and Pryor was under instructions to make things hard for him. He remembered how he had resented Nelson and his starter, back at the timber camp. Now he thought of him with a kind of nostalgia. Nelson had been rough but simple, too stupid to play games.

As an experienced miner, Beckworth received an extra half-ration; from time to time he passed some of this on to Ralph, grateful for any additional food, and indeed for whatever would help him survive in this labyrinth.

"You done verses at school?" Beckworth queried. "Then learn this: more use than that other fancy stuff:

*If the mice move out, move out with them*
*If the rats run, your life is nearly done*
*When the roof begins to trickle*

*Father Time is sharpening his sickle*
*When your pony baulks, then death stalks*
*If your lamp goes out, don't muck about.*

Ralph had started as what Beckworth called a ripper, shovelling coal into the basket to be hoisted up the shaft; under Beckworth's tuition, he progressed to hewer. Cutting coal was only marginally less dull than shovelling it, and no less back-breaking; but it set Ralph a notch higher in the meagre hierarchy of the camp. They were, as his mentor candidly pointed out, like rats in a barrel: you clawed your way to the top, or fell to the bottom and got eaten.

Ostensibly Ralph had knuckled down under the routine, but the urge to escape raged inside him like a fire. He had twice escaped, and twice been recaptured. Every argument of logic and reason said he should settle like a bullock to the yoke and patiently wait out his time; display the subservience that would sweeten his gaolers' opinion of him.

Each week as they filed out, filthy and tired, from the mine, his eyes would be drawn to the vast curve of the horizon. Beckworth nudged him as scrubbed off the week's dirt in the waves of the beach, with a handful of sand. "I'm not the only one who's seen you looking out to sea," he said quietly. "Jarkman and his mate are keeping an eye on you." Ralph ignored him and wrung the seawater out of his tattered shirt. "If you're thinking of doing a runner, don't let anyone know. Everyone here has got one thing on his mind: how to get away. They'd split on you before you went a yard."

"All except you?" said Ralph, turning to him incredulously as he recalled how cruelly he had suffered from Beckworth's bad faith.

The miner threw back his head in an uninhibited laugh. "Me quickest of all," he said, his yellow teeth bared in amusement.

On the parade ground the convicts stood precisely ranked in the blazing sun, awaiting the arrival of their new Commandant, Major James Morisset. The only information they had gleaned was that he had been invalided out of the army, and had a hard reputation. The bugler sounded a flourish. Light flashed off the gold-braided cap and beautifully-cut uniform of the slightly-built officer trotting past. A bit of a dandy, thought Ralph. Then the rider's head turned. One side of the man's face was normal; the other a monstrous mask of misshapen flesh, with a dead eye and warped mouth.

Ralph tried not to show his revulsion. He felt a shiver of apprehension at the glittering perfection of Morisset's turnout, set against that hideous visage. A man so marred, yet so given to exactitude, would try to impose an impossible symmetry on the unfortunates under his command, to compensate for his ruin.

Ralph mourned the loss of light, yearned for the touch of the sun on his skin. Daylight he saw only in snatches. Beckworth was unconcerned by the darkness, the close air, the monotony; displaying in the confines of the mine the same mixture of rancour and indifference which Ralph had noted when he first met him. He envied the miner his composure. To Ralph this was a hostile world of jagged pit-props and sharp edges of rock that took the skin off your spine. When his candle flickered out, Ralph fought off panic, but Beckworth moved in the darkness as surely as a mole. He had no imagination. Ralph had never thought he would envy anyone so afflicted.

Beckworth's competence and imperturbability gave him standing among the other prisoners. Ralph they left alone.

"You know what's wrong with you?" Beckworth told him one night as they lay on the gallery floor in the stuffy darkness. "You think too much. While everyone else is slogging away, you've got these ideas burning away inside you, like a slow match in gunpowder. One day the whole lot will go up. Everyone gives you a wide berth, because you make trouble."

"That's ripe, coming from you," said Ralph bitterly.

"You still don't understand, do you?" replied Beckworth, like a teacher with a stubborn pupil. "If I get into strife, it's for a reason. I stole that corn and got caught. That was a gamble and I lost. But I might have won. I would have made a nice little bit of money. You now, you stirred up Masters for no reason at all."

"It was a matter of principle," Ralph returned fiercely.

"What's *principles* in a place like this?" retorted Beckworth contemptuously. "I can't spell 'em and I can't eat 'em. You're different, and our keepers don't like people who are different. If you had any sense at all you would knuckle under, but your mammy raised you to be honest, and you can't tell a lie to save yourself."

Ralph bit back a sharp reply. He had more in common with Te Hakuwai than with these men. For all he was a cannibal, he understood the concept of honour. Sweating, the sharp chips of coal sticking into his skin, Ralph tried to transcend his surroundings by picturing the wheeling stars. But the patterns escaped him, and he saw only the faint glimmer of the distant lamp against the glinting buttresses of his living tomb.

# 27

# New South Wales, Winter 1817

Outside, summer cooled to autumn, autumn to winter. Down the mine every day was the same; only the faces changed. Ralph felt condemned to a land of eternal night. Light in this place was rationed, like the inadequate food and rest doled out during the week. But even his few precious hours above ground on Sunday afternoon were a means to compel compliance.

The new Commandant was a stickler for oppressive detail, and Pryor happy to curry favour by interpreting his regulations with exemplary rigor. Not standing properly to attention, or neglecting to salute an officer, cost Ralph in an instant the scant free time on which he set such store. Instead he would be lumbered with extra shifts, or find himself at best in the wretched tedium of a solitary cell; at worst enduring another half-hour at the triangles.

Beckworth's nickname for the youngest of the new arrivals had stuck. Kitty Carrots was sorely changed from the pert youth with copper curls who had joked on the ferry. His hair was cropped to ginger stubble, his already pale skin pallid after months underground. Jarkman and Grimshaw treated him like a house-dog, flinging him extra food one day, beating him the next. He grew hard-faced and foul-mouthed, and carried tales.

After payday one Sunday they were mustered for Divine Service. Sullen and smarting, Ralph reflected sourly on Morisset's determination to harry his crew of reprobates into virtue. Pryor, searching Ralph's and Beckworth's end of the barracks, had triumphantly confiscated their few illicit means of enjoyment: a pair of dice, a well-worn pack of cards, four pipes and a pouch of tobacco. Informers were amply rewarded under the new regime, and Ralph had a fair idea who had spied these out.

A hellfire-and-brimstone sermon rounded off their compulsory moral instruction. Ralph had long since perfected the art of keeping a respectful expression while his thoughts wandered. There was something about "Sodom and Gomorrah", "filthy and unnatural", "snatched in a moment to face Judgement" but Ralph was watching a flock of cockatoos as they wheeled in a raucous skein, white with flashes of sulphur yellow.

Afterwards he went looking for Carrots. He had a score to settle with that young man for the loss of his cards. For once, his oafish protectors were not to be seen; lying low, Ralph suspected, given what he had heard of the sermon.

He tracked his quarry to the far corner of the yard, crouching between a shed and the corner of the wall. "Carrots! A word."

The youth looked up, alarmed. His face was streaked from crying.

"I'm not *Carrots*," he replied, wiping his nose on his sleeve. "My name is Patrick Maguire."

This unexpected reply jolted Ralph out of his anger. He knew the power of names to define and distort. He sat on his haunches next to the boy, who shrank away.

"Maguire—" Ralph's tone was gentler. "What's the matter?"

"The sailors started it," the boy muttered, "when we sailed from Cork. I know it's wrong, but Grimshaw and Jarkman won't leave off. The parson says God will punish me and make me sick. When I die I will burn in Hell, for all eternity." He looked at Ralph. His eyes, already too large in his thin face, were now huge with fear. "The affliction is upon me."

"Listen to me. If you go to the Commandant, they will be punished, but so will you. And what will happen if Grimshaw and Jarkman find out you dobbed them in? None of us can choose what is done to us."

The boy looked unconvinced. Ralph sighed. Maguire needed a Father Donavan to hear this abject confession, absolve him and provide a measure of relief. He had terrors enough in his current life, without the prospect of further horrors after he was dead.

Ralph searched for terms Maguire would understand. What would Donavan have said? "Can you remember your prayers?"

"I know my *Hail Mary*."

Ralph reached out to steady the boy with a touch on his arm. "Then pray for mercy. It's all you can do."

Ralph stood up and walked back towards the others. He had not gone six yards when he choked as something twisted across his throat.

"Keep your hands off Carrots!"

Ralph flung his weight into his attacker. He and Jarkman went down together, Ralph twisting away from the throttling kerchief. They rolled, scrabbling at each other on the ground, until Ralph jammed his fist into the gypsy's stomach. "Come near me and I swear I'll kill you!" he snarled. "I've done it before."

As his hands clawed at the gypsy's throat a powerful grip wrenched him to his feet. "*Ware hawk*," Beckworth whispered to Ralph, hoisting him abruptly over his hip and throwing him down, hard.

"Just practising my Cornish Hug, overseer."

Ralph lay gasping for breath until the grinning Pryor moved on. He grimaced as he stood. "What was that for?"

"Better than another Botany Bay Dozen for fighting. Jarkman thinks you're stealing his Kitty."

"Of course I'm not. Young Patrick has had the fear of the Lord put into him by that preacher's sermon. He's so scared he can barely move."

"A pity the parson didn't do something useful, like bring along his fat Missus and stow her in the barracks overnight," Beckworth observed. "Then he'd have nowt to complain of. I've told you before: don't get involved. And watch your back for the next few days. That's why there was a space in my corner. Jarkman and his mate took against the bob cull that was there before, and smashed his hand with an iron bar."

All next week, down the mine, Ralph jumped at every moving shadow. Here were so many ways to come to harm, and have it look like an accident. The picks were sharp, the heavy wagons awkward, heaped coal always liable to slip. Come Saturday, Grimshaw doled out the coarse dark bread, made from purple maize. Ralph bit into it and felt something move. It wriggled with cockroaches. He spat it out and worked the rest of the shift hungry. He preferred not to think about what they had done to the water, and left his bottle untouched. He was in a foul temper as he headed back to the barracks.

The soldier posted at the door lowered his musket as they approached.

"Nobody's allowed in. Carrots has killed hisself. Found him hanging, half an hour ago."

"His name isn't Carrots," Ralph said dully. "He is—*was*—Patrick Maguire."

The crowd stared curiously as the body was carried out. Ralph turned away from the twisted neck and swollen face. How desperate the boy must have been to take a step that would condemn him utterly in the terms of his religion, and deny him even a decent burial. As the evening went on other questions niggled: had Maguire killed himself, or had Jarkman decided he had become a liability, to be got out of the way?

Early next morning Jarkman and Grimshaw were taken off under guard. Jarkman lunged out at Ralph as he passed.

Beckworth clicked his tongue, "Manners, manners." He looked quietly pleased with himself. Had he or one of the other prisoners, appalled by the boy's death, shopped them? Or was Beckworth settling a score? Ralph remembered he had a grudge against these two already, for his mate's broken hand.

A darker thought occurred to him: had Beckworth set up the whole thing, killing Maguire to cast blame on the other two?

After all the others were asleep, Ralph felt a nudge.

Beckworth held up a bottle. "A toast," he whispered. "*To the dear departed.*"

As the others left, Beckworth and Ralph were drawn together by default. In Beckworth's taciturn reminiscences Ralph glimpsed another world.

"I first went down the mine when I was four," he said one night. "My dad had his bread and cheese in a box, and it was my job to keep off the rats. My mother carried baskets of coal up the ladders."

"Do women carry those?" Ralph interrupted, startled. It was barbaric that women should be expected to bear such burdens.

"My mother could carry two hundredweight," Beckworth went on in his hard voice. "She and my sister wore belts and chains, harnessed like dogs to a cart, crawling on their hands and knees. But it is work for ponies, not women. She had four dead babies."

Ralph recalled his own cosseted childhood, and the money his father had lavished on his frail mother.

"When I was thirteen, I ran away to join the army. I'd had enough of us all squeezed in two rooms, while Charley Fitzwilly, the fourth Earl Fitzwilliam to you, lorded it in his palace atop the Barnsley seam, with a room for every day of the year."

"Once Boney was beat I thought things would get better. But then you gentry in your fine houses passed the Corn Laws. The price of bread went up till a man had to steal it to eat. *Twelve rats starve while three rats thrive.*" He darted another of his sideways looks at Ralph. "I'll steal corn off any fat farmer."

Ralph sat silent. This deprivation of light and air, which so oppressed him, had been Beckworth's lot from when he was a child. Ralph saw his Fairfax-self in comfortable lodgings in Vienna, with coffee and chocolate-cake on the table beside him, welcoming the news of the Corn Laws in the London papers. Now he toiled in the guts of the earth so the civil officers could enjoy their free allowance of coal.

He had resolved to close off his past. But in the long hours of darkness he yearned for all he once took for granted, things as simple as hot water and a cake of soap. And as he drifted into an uneasy sleep, Flavia haunted him yet again, an enigma: her brown eyes warm, the glitter of diamond before the blow. His body still ached for her. But her betrayal cut across his memories as brutally as a hatch slammed across his fingers.

Summer brought little change in their surroundings. The seam they were following narrowed until it was almost impossible to work; the cliff wormed out over so many years came closer to collapse. Morisset ordered a new mine dug, dropping a shaft over a hundred feet to meet fresh seams of coal.

Ralph anticipated a change in routine, cheered by the prospect of time in the open air. But when the working-parties were being selected Pryor quickly disabused him.

"The officers still need their coal," he sneered. "Any fool can dig. You old hands stay here until we've broken through the new shaft. Counting on a holiday, were you? You won't get one while I'm here."

"Miserable bastard," muttered Beckworth as the overseer swaggered off. "I hear he's started a shop in the town. It would be worth breaking out to burn it down— hopefully with him inside."

Ralph took a swig from the water-bottle. "He can keep his new mine. We'll get to see it, soon enough."

"And I'll tell you what," said Beckworth with his wolfish grin, "it'll look just the same as the old one. Mines are like whores; where it matters, they're all the same."

From outside, the new mine was an unremarkable huddle of sheds. The best thing about it was the view, Ralph thought, looking over his shoulder at the sea, glittering silver to the horizon. Regretfully he turned to the dark opening ahead. Inside a framework of sturdy timbers, a thick cable ran to a large windlass turned by a gang of sweating convicts. Chained, their muscles taut with strain, they looked like galley-slaves.

Ralph leaned over the low rail. Before him the pit dropped away into nothing. Above it dangled a large wicker basket.

"We're not going down in that?" Ralph exclaimed.

"No," Beckworth replied with a sardonic grin, "you're going to fly. Of course you're going down in that."

Gingerly Ralph balanced in the basket, swaying in the cold air of the shaft, as it swung out over the abyss. As the cable unwound the walls rolled past him until he touched down with a thud.

He stepped out. He was at the junction of three tunnels. A fire burned; he felt the heat on his skin. As the light of the flames glinted on coal in the walls and roof, he wondered what would happen if it spread. The miners would be baked like bread in an oven.

Beckworth looked about critically, and paced out the distance from the base of the shaft to the coalface. "Might be handy to know, someday. The face is better too: more height to work."

Beckworth was sniffing about, curious as a cat. What on earth was he doing now, thought Ralph, tapping his feet, then stooping down and running his finger along the floor?

Beckworth sniffed. "Not so good," he murmured, almost to himself. "The air is stale already and the floor's sweating."

There were times when Ralph tired of Beckworth's pessimism. "At least it's a change."

"That's as may be," retorted the other dryly. "I don't want it to be permanent."

The convicts were kept separate from the boat crews. But hints from chance-heard comments grew, and were confirmed by a change in routine. Something was up. There were extra parades and drills for the soldiers, and half a dozen lucky men were drafted to the town to help finish the new guardhouse. They came back with the news that Governor Macquarie himself was expected for a visit in July.

This information set off ripples like a stone cast in water. The old mine attendant was found dead at the bottom of the shaft, where he had apparently fallen while drunk. The whisper was that he had overheard some of the Irish plotting to escape, and had been on his way to tell the sergeant.

Ralph too was agitated by these rumours. He would do anything to get away from this place. But how could he disguise himself? His skin was black with ingrained coal-dust: it set in his scars as they healed. Even his hair, close-cropped against lice, gave him away. The Irish had the resource of companionship with their own kind. His only acquaintance was Beckworth, who had already betrayed him.

One of the Irishmen fell sick with an inflammation of the lungs, and Ralph was sent to fill his place. The gang leader, a big red-haired man named O'Connor, refused to let him near the coalface, and set him to loading baskets. The others gave him hostile looks, muttering incomprehensibly among themselves.

When Pryor arrived to check their progress he snatched the shovel out of Ralph's hands. "You're here to cut coal, not make sandcastles!" he shouted. "You gentlemen convicts are all the same, too idle to shift your arses." He flung a pick at Ralph, who caught it by the shaft just before it hit him. "Get to work, or you'll sleep on your face for a week. Make way, the rest of you."

Pryor was too angry to notice how reluctantly the men fell back from the wall, but Ralph could feel the tension as he swung.

He checked just in time. Rather than biting into a solid face of coal, the point of the pick had knocked through hastily-packed rubble. Ralph's candle, as he leaned forward, glimmered on the scored face of a file and the rounded shoulder of a water-bottle: the cache for the Irishmen's escape.

He turned. A dozen eyes glinted like cats' in the light. Their watchfulness tightened into anxiety. Pryor was three steps away.

Ralph set the pick handle-down against the floor, leaned on it with folded arms, and smiled.

"Lazy bastard," bellowed Pryor, making to clout him with his stick. Ralph ducked and jabbed him on the nose. The overseer staggered back, his nose bleeding, and dropped his club. There was an animal roar from the Irish. They closed in a ring and urged Ralph on.

With a surge of satisfaction Ralph punched Pryor hard in the ribs. He grabbed for the cudgel on the ground. But the overseer, scared by the baying crowd around him, stamped down on Ralph's knuckles, snatched up his club, and clouted Ralph above the eye.

Ralph went down, half-blind with blood, while the overseer blew piercing blasts on his whistle, anxiously eyeing the now-silent ring of Irish. Now their secret was safe, O'Connor signalled them back to their tasks. The guards came clattering down the gallery, hauled Ralph to his feet and snapped on a pair of manacles.

"He set them onto me!" cried Pryor, shrilly.

"Nonsense—" began Ralph.

One of the soldiers hit him across the mouth. "If you're up for assaulting an overseer you'd better save your breath. Incitement to mutiny is a hanging offence."

Ralph licked his cut lip in silence.

In the cells of the new guardhouse, Ralph sucked the torn skin across his knuckles. He leaned against the cool, smoothly-dressed wall, his throbbing head in his aching hands. *A hanging offence*: he could die here. Thirty years ago mutineers in the Navy had been flogged around the fleet. Young Redfern had been given a death sentence merely for talking to them. Morisset reflexively crushed anything he interpreted as a threat to his authority; the number of hangings in the camp had gone up sharply, and there was no appeal.

Within the month Ralph could be gasping out his life on the gallows while the hangman hauled on his legs to break his neck. Ralph knew what a man looked like as he choked to death, from the eyes of that French guard at Badajoz. What had he said to Flavia? *Horsemen have strong hands.* So much for a young man's bravado. *Your turn next.* The sweat of fear soaked him.

He huddled in a corner while the little warmth in his body leaked into the cold stone. The pulse beating in his wrist could be snuffed out as simply as a candle-flame. He flexed his fingers, where the delicate mechanisms of nerve and sinew were already repairing the damage of the day before. He knew what happened to the bodies of executed convicts: he had seen the notices often enough: ... *there to be executed, and his body afterwards dissected and anatomized.* He veered away from the thought, but it opened like a void before him: utter annihilation, to die disgraced at the end of the world under a false name, his corpse hacked apart, unmarked and unmourned.

"Turnkey!"

Ralph started. A fair-haired young lieutenant, splendid in his best uniform, held a lantern high in the doorway.

"What's this bloody scarecrow doing here?"

"Came in yesterday, sir."

"The Governor's inspection's in an hour! You can't leave him here looking like that! Take him away and clean him up."

"But sir —"

"Do as I say, man!" the officer snapped. "Lord only knows where Old Sandy will poke about in his spanking-new guardhouse. You know how fussy he is about Government men." His parting words echoed down the passage. "Make it quick. And have the men fed by first light."

"Yes, sir, no, sir, do it yesterday, sir," the gaoler muttered. "What do they think I am? A nursemaid?" He prodded Ralph to rise. Bloody smears marred the light stone. The gaoler swore. "As if I didn't have enough to do! You'll have to wait."

He shoved Ralph ahead of him down the passage, out a rear door and across a yard to a wooden shed, where he flung open the door.

"You can cool your heels in here till they've gone." Ralph stumbled forward into the earth-scented darkness as the door behind him thumped shut.

From outside he heard a peculiar shuffling rustle. The door squeaked open. A man was framed briefly in the opening, dragging something heavy. The door closed behind him.

A candle flared. It was Beckworth, with the turnkey bound and gagged at his feet.

"I knew the Paddies were making a break," Beckworth whispered. "They were arguing whether to break you out, for not lagging them when you had the chance. So I said I'd save them the trouble if they took me too. I found this toad here—" he dug his foot into the recumbent body "—and persuaded him to tell me where you were stowed." A ring of keys jangled as he pulled them off the man's belt. "Here's one for the darbies."

Once Ralph's handcuffs were off, and their prisoner secured in the shed, they tried the keys for the blacksmith's shop next door. Inside it was still warm from the forge. Beckworth searched for a hammer and cold chisel; then, with a clang that made Ralph's ears ring, struck through first one rivet, then the other. The heavy links of his leg-irons slithered to the floor.

"For a fellow with so many long words, you've precious little to say."

"Don't think I'm ungrateful," Ralph returned haltingly, wielding the hammer on Beckworth's fetters in his turn. "I spent all night expecting to be hanged. You were the messenger bringing the reprieve. I won't forget."

"Don't count your promises until they come home to roost, as my old Dad used to say," Beckworth said lightly. "There's a bucket of water here; we'd better clean up."

They were almost finished when there was a brisk footfall outside.

"Todd? Is that you?" The voice was sharp with suspicion. Beckworth snatched up the hammer, but Ralph gestured him back behind the door, and gave a low groan. The lieutenant burst in, stopped short as he saw Ralph standing free and opened his mouth to call for help. But only a mumble came out as Beckworth clapped the grimy wash-rag across his face. Together they flung him to the floor.

"I'll take his clothes," Ralph whispered across the squirming form. "We'll go out as officer and servant."

They stripped their victim and lashed his ankles together. Ralph quickly donned the still-warm uniform, fumbling the buttons with his sore hand.

Beckworth loosened the officer's gag and hissed in his ear. "Where's your horse?"

"I shan't tell you," the officer squeaked, with as much dignity as he could manage in his drawers.

Beckworth reached up and turned Ralph's torn hand to the light. "Do you want to end up like this?"

"You wouldn't dare!"

"Why not?" Ralph cut in, fiercely. "Because you are a gentleman, and we are only *bloody scarecrows*?"

Incredulous, the young man realised that Ralph's accent was pure as his own. He glanced from one captor to the other, unsure whether to trust to Ralph's sympathy, or fear his revenge.

"I had no idea..." he faltered. He swallowed. "The bay with a white blaze, third stall from the right." He cast a final anguished look at them as the door opened into the faint light of dawn.

It was good to feel a horse underneath him.

At the gate a squad of soldiers was hastily forming up. A hatless officer dashed out of the brightly-lit guardhouse.

"There you are! Take a message to the Governor's brig. Twenty-four of the Irish have escaped. They're heading for Port Stephens, to capture a ship and turn pirate. Order the captain to double the guard."

Ralph threw up his hand in acknowledgement.

"Make way there!" Beckworth shouted.

Ralph trotted off down the rutted road towards the harbour. Once out of sight, they turned into a side-alley. Ralph stood in the stirrups and looked around. The darkness was fading into the grey light of dawn. People were beginning to stir. Soon all the town would be out. The hunt for the Irish would be concentrated on the coast, so Ralph and Beckworth turned inland.

They were walking the horse up a hill when they heard the sound of guns from the town below. Anxiously they looked back. Puffs of dirty white smoke billowed from the two brigs lying at anchor. A trim little barge, looking at that distance no larger than a toy, sped across to the wharf. A fluke of the wind brought a wisp of music from a military band.

Beckworth pulled at Ralph's arm. "Better get going."

"In a minute," Ralph replied, his eyes fixed on the remote procession below. The barge drew alongside the jetty. A flash of gold braid marked where the Governor stood. Ralph strained to hear again the piping of the band, but it was lost in the silence of the bush.

They travelled all day, stopping only to rest the horse. By late afternoon Ralph was dizzy with hunger. He squinted into the afternoon sun, and closed his eyes against the glare.

Beckworth, leading the horse, stopped.

"I can keep going."

"No you can't. You're done, and I'm bloody starving too."

Ralph dismounted, and the horse began nosing about for tufts of grass.

"How far to the nearest town?" asked Ralph.

"Town? You've got to be joking. But O'Connor reckons there's a sheep-farm in these parts, with a big house. I saw a thread of smoke from the valley yonder. I'll take the horse and bring something back."

"Very well," said Ralph, too tired to care. He cupped his hands to give Beckworth a leg-up and watched him ride off, jolting with an awkward pace. Really, thought Ralph, his seat was terrible.

He had no memory of falling asleep. When he awoke the moon rode high in the night sky. Of his companion there was no sign. Ralph chided himself again for his credulity; after all this time he should have learned not to trust Beckworth, of all people.

He stood up stiffly, and set off in the direction Beckworth had taken. He must find some food, and unless he was to gather berries and eat lizards like the natives he would have to steal from the nearest farm. No wonder so many runaways turned bushranger; their only hope of survival lay in preying on their own kind. No wonder too, thought Ralph grimly, most were caught.

He had been walking some ten minutes when his eye was caught by a movement ahead. Moonlight gleamed off the horse's bright coat. The reins lay slack on its neck. Where was Beckworth? He would hardly have gone off and left the horse behind, no matter how clumsy a rider he was. Ralph checked the saddlebags: they were empty. He mounted and carried on.

He had just come over the lip of a valley, and could see below him the cleared land of a farm, when he was hailed by a low whistle. Beckworth walked slowly out the scrub, rubbing his head.

"What on earth happened?" snapped Ralph.

"Fell off the damned thing, didn't I," muttered Beckworth. "Hit a branch in the dark. Whacked my head, and when I came to the horse had bolted. What are you laughing at?" he said morosely.

"I thought you had cleared out."

"I don't rat on my mates," Beckworth retorted.

They picked their way through the paddocks and stopped well back from the house. It was more substantial than Ralph had expected; stone, two-storeyed, with a verandah around three sides. They decided Ralph should go in alone to search for food; if challenged, he would claim to be an officer searching for the runaway Irish. His voice, bearing and clothes were right; in the darkness he might get away with it.

A brief yammering from the rear yard, quickly stilled, warned Ralph that there were dogs. He could not enter at the back. He dodged round a high, but unfinished, fence. The workmen had left a box of nails; he used one to prise open a shutter.

He found himself in an empty room still smelling strongly of plaster and new paint. Gingerly he opened the interior door. A long corridor ran to the back of the house. Placing his weight delicately as a cat, he edged through to the kitchen. On the scullery table was a tray set with a cold roast fowl, bread, pats of butter elegantly curled, and a flagon of wine. Ralph, ravenous, had wolfed half the supper down before he remembered he needed victuals for Beckworth as well. He found half a cheese and another loaf of bread. Pity about the wine, a fine dry Malaga. He gulped what was left, wrapped his finds in a napkin, fled swiftly down the hall, and jumped off the verandah.

He could hardly be drunk on one flagon of wine. But he could have sworn he heard a violin, thin and sweet, from the other side of the house: Mozart, sounds from another world. Ralph edged around the corner. One window glowed in the long dark wall.

Ralph had been starved of music for so long. The melody changed to something wilder, with a strong rhythm. He lifted himself on tiptoe and peered over the sill. The violinist checked in mid-phrase, as though sensing an interruption, and turned.

It was Masters.

# 28

# *New South Wales,*
# *August–November 1818*

Ralph dropped from the window as if stung. This was the last place in the world he should loiter. As he raced down the hill he heard shouts; dogs barking. He turned to look, stumbled on a length of wood, and fell. Beckworth yelled from ahead, galloping hell-for-leather towards him.

Ralph picked himself up and dashed for the fence. Where was the gap? He cast about desperately with the dogs closing in, and men behind them.

He flung the provisions over the palisade. "Run!" he yelled.

Jaws snapped on his wrist: tugged him to his knees. A second dog snarled, fangs inches from his face.

"Call off your dogs!" he shouted.

"It's an officer! Call them off!" At a sharp whistle, the dog released him, with a simmering growl. The men crowding around him fell back to let Masters through. He gestured a lantern forward.

Ralph turned his head aside, but his jaw was seized, and his face twisted to the light.

"This is no officer," Masters said. "Secure him." As Ralph was hauled to his feet he cursed his folly in lingering. He could have been through the fence and away by now. He hoped Beckworth had escaped.

Lashed to a chair in the library, Ralph tried to look nonchalant, but his eyes followed every movement as his host paced up and down, and finally stopped beside him.

"What were you doing here?"

Ralph glanced at the discarded violin. "Listening to the music," he replied, truthfully enough.

Masters' eyes narrowed. "Do not trifle with me. I have not forgotten who you are."

Ralph felt a surge of anger. "I have not forgotten, either, how you ran a blind man down and killed his dog."

He expected a blow, but got a look of derision.

"Only gentlemen waste sentiment on animals. Do not forget your place, convict." Masters leaned forward, and his face hardened. "Look at yourself. Whatever rank you held is long gone."

Ralph was suddenly aware of his lacerated knuckles and calloused palms. His bound hands flexed.

"You find your present situation intolerable," Masters observed. "Remember: no prisoner's condition is so bad that it cannot be made worse."

Masters' threat was oblique, but it was not idle. Ralph jibbed at yet another injustice. "Your achievements do you credit."

Masters slapped his face: a controlled blow that went on stinging.

"Do not provoke me, Fletcher. I have no love for those who spy on my affairs."

"I was not spying," Ralph flung back.

"Then what were you doing?"

"Running away." There was no point denying it.

"Where from? Newcastle?"

"Yes."

"With whom?"

A phrase flashed through Ralph's mind: *I don't rat on my mates.* He stayed silent, then winced as Masters gripped his bitten wrist.

"It was the convict Beckworth," Masters remarked. "I saw him. You waste your time defending such as he. He betrayed you before and would do it again. Every man has his price."

*What is the thing that matters?* Ralph remembered Te Hakuwai saying: *it is the people; the people; the people.*

"What is Beckworth, but a coarse brute?" Masters continued. "Surely you have education enough to see that."

Ralph remembered Beckworth's callous disregard, his coarse jokes, his dishonesty; the child that chased away the rats, the runaway who came back to free him, because he was his mate.

"He is a man," said Ralph.

"And what is a man?" Masters exclaimed. "A thinking animal, seeking power over his own kind. Look what happened in Europe over the last twenty years! How can you cling to the feeble myths of your childhood, in a place like this?"

"Because the world you propose is evil," Ralph replied, feeling acutely exposed. "Because there must be something better."

Masters gave a dry laugh. "An Antipodean Mephistopheles, in broadcloth and linen? Is that how you see me? I expected a more intelligent reply."

There must be something he could say, Ralph thought, to penetrate that cynical self-assurance. He recalled a tag from *King Lear*.

*"Goodness and wisdom in the vile seem vile,"* he quoted. *"Filths savour but themselves."*

He braced himself for violence, but was more disquieted by his captor's sudden stillness. Masters' smile died; his face was cold.

"What else is there inside that quick head of yours?" he said. "Perhaps one day we will find out."

This time there was no Te Hakuwai to spirit him away. When he was fit for work Ralph, loaded with an extra set of leg-irons, was sent upriver for four months, to the limeburners' camp. The rest slept in a hut; Ralph in the lee of the guardhouse, chained to a solid baulk of jarrah. Short of gnawing through his leg like a trapped fox, there was no possible way of escape.

Sometimes he dreamed of trying to run, but his limbs would not answer; of terror as the hooves thudded near. Always his nightmare drew him unwilling to the camp of bloodied corpses, silent except for the baby's thin wail. He would jolt awake, trying to shut the noise out of his ears. But the soft keening leaked through his fingers, resolving itself into the thrum of wind in the halyard of the flagstaff over his head.

There were no mates here, and no hierarchy of skill, however meagre, to give him pride. Kept hungry, they shuffled with barely strength enough to drag their chains, raking up vast heaps of shells, crushing and burning them, and loading the quicklime: a vile task as the gritty powder ate into any broken skin. Wounds ran to sores instead of healing, and water on them was agony.

No matter how long Ralph toiled there were always more mountains of shells. He was trapped in one of his mother's tales, where the hero was set one impossible task after another. Like *N'oun Doaré*, his name was *I do not know*. But here was no talking mare to fly him away, no king of the birds or the demons to wish his labours done; only his own strained and aching body: always hungry, always tired.

*There is no prisoner whose condition is so bad it cannot be made worse.*

Ralph had clung to the hope of justice until Hunter walked out on him; to confidence in his own resource until that failed him in the mountains. Down the mine he had survived on anger and pride. Now the next scant meal meant more to him than revenge. He was frightened to realise how little resilience he had left.

He must not let Masters know he had won. It would be so easy to sink into apathy like the others.

Only one day stood out from this time. Ralph was crushing shells for the furnace when a boat pulled in. They were forbidden any contact with those from the outside world, so Ralph paid no attention. Then he heard behind him a familiar dragging step, and turned.

Hunter looked just as Ralph remembered him; the same lean face and trim bearing; but in the play of the other's features Ralph saw puzzlement sharpen into shock.

"Please go on," Hunter said hurriedly to his companion. "I shall join you in a moment."

Ralph remembered vividly the pain of their last meeting. Hunter turned back, his face schooled to severity, but his eyes were troubled.

"Fletcher?" he queried, as if hoping for a denial.

"Yes." He did not think to add "sir"; nor did Hunter notice the omission.

"I am sorry to see you in this place."

Ralph shrugged. "I didn't take your advice." He had meant to jeer, but the words came out flat and toneless.

"Giving you trouble, sir?" Ralph flinched from the overseer's raised cudgel, and caught Hunter's frown.

"That will not be necessary," Hunter replied in a voice glacial with distaste. The overseer fell back with a look at Ralph that promised payment with interest later.

Ralph shifted under Hunter's scrutiny. "What happened to Davies?" he asked, to break the silence.

"He has his ticket-of-leave now," replied Hunter, a shade too heartily. "I shall put him up to head shepherd soon. He has two children."

"Two! Has it been that long!" Ralph tried to keep his voice even, but the bitterness broke through.

Hunter took a step forward. "Look, Fletcher," he said quickly, "Davies told me what you did for him. I could make enquiries—"

"It's too late!" Ralph cut in. "Can't you understand? Look at me. The only reason I wasn't hung as a bushranger is because Masters gets more satisfaction seeing me as I am. Can you believe, with my record, they will ever let me go?"

Ralph's words ended on a rising tide of anguish. He fought to control his breathing. He wished Hunter would go away; but he dared not turn away from him, conscious as he was of the festering tangle of half-healed scars splayed across his back.

"Take this, then." Deftly Hunter bound a clean handkerchief around Ralph's wrist, still raw where the quicklime had eaten into it. "Try to keep that wound clean. I would not treat a dog so."

Awkwardly Ralph untied the kerchief and handed it back. "Thank you, sir, but I can't keep it," he said gently. "They would say I had stolen it. Don't blame yourself," he added, giving an absolution only half untrue. "I'm too flash; I would have fallen foul of someone, sooner or later. Goodbye, sir."

Hunter walked on, his limp more marked, to where his companion waited curiously at the base of the cliff. Ralph raised his hammer and brought it down upon the heap of shells, one basketful of the thousands as yet ungathered on the beach.

# 29

## *England, December 1817*

Flavia pulled her furred hood closer. It was almost a year since she had come north to Fontclaire for the christening, and she had forgotten the bite of the December chill. Curious to see the improvements which Lucius had described so enthusiastically in his letter, she leaned forward, but the window clouded with the plumes of her breath. The glass squeaked as she scrubbed impatiently with her gloved palm. Peering through, she saw the ridge of Beacon Hill, grey-green against the opaque morning sky, and the Abbot's Tower standing clear of the faint mist which veiled the buttresses of her old home.

The carriage halted and Lucius handed her down, the horses behind him snorting little jets of steam.

"How was your journey?" he queried, then before she had time to reply, suggested "I'll show you my new coach-house and stables."

She followed him into a broad cobbled yard where he pointed out stalls and looseboxes on one side, and the harness-room and loft for fodder on the other. The coach-house with its wide doors, the fresh black paint gleaming, faced them across the end. Flavia tried to reconcile the new buildings with the lines of the old walled orchard she had loved.

"There! How do you like her?" Lucius stood back with a flourish, to reveal a dappled Arab mare with strong arched neck and delicate head, ears pricked at their approach. "I had to make your journey worthwhile," he said. "You have always wanted a riding-horse of your own."

Flavia hugged him in delight. "What a kind thought! She is the most beautiful creature!"

Marriage had made her brother more considerate; she reflected; not so long ago, provided he was well-mounted himself, he would barely have noticed if his sister was riding a donkey.

"It was not entirely my idea," he confessed, brushing down the damp patch her wet gloves had left on his shoulder. "Bromley found the mare for me. I know you consider him stiff, but he thinks highly of you. Her name is Zobeide. Remember *The Thousand-and-One Nights?*

Bromley! Flavia was even more surprised. It was flattering to be so singled out. She could not fault his taste. Zobeide nuzzled her hand, as sweet in disposition as she was perfect in looks. Reluctantly Flavia pulled herself away to return to the house, and meet her hostess.

"By the way," Lucius explained with some embarrassment, "Mother has your old room now, so we've given you the one next to the library. I hope you don't mind."

"Mother?"

"Mrs Lennox."

Flavia did mind. Those rooms had belonged to her mother Emily, and nothing would induce her to give that title to the Lennox woman. But it would be churlish to complain, after Lucius's magnificent gift. It had not occurred to her before that Fontclaire was no longer her home, but her brother's, and that choices she had once made were now the prerogative of his wife—or rather, she suspected, of his wife's mother.

Lucius walked her back to the main entrance, outlining the next stage in his plans, knocking down the ancient outbuildings. At the door she registered the unfamiliar sight of a tall footman, resplendent in green livery with gold facings.

"Flavia, this is Vickery, our footman."

Vickery fractionally inclined his tightly-curled head. His regular features moved in what might have been a smile as he held back the oak-planked door. Flavia felt like a stranger.

Caroline and her mother were waiting in the great hall by the fire. Thick new carpets covered the familiar pink-and-white-triangle tiles; elegant tables and chairs flanked a new sideboard.

"It was too cold to meet you outside," explained Mrs Lennox. "Little Charles has a delicate chest. Come to your aunt, Charles."

All Flavia could see of Lucius's son was a plump hand entwined in his mother's skirts. Caroline looked round and clicked her tongue.

"Don't hurry him," said Flavia quickly. She struck up a conversation with Caroline about the journey, and was shortly rewarded by a glimpse of a round blonde head.

"What a pretty child!" Flavia exclaimed, smiling. But Caroline frowned as the toddler dragged at her skirts; she twitched at the fabric but he clung tighter. With a sharp rip, a bunch of ribbon came away. Charles fell over, took a breath, and howled.

For an awkward moment Flavia wondered if she should pick him up. Caroline looked around for the nurse, and Mrs Lennox's mouth pursed. Then Lucius swept his son high in the air and jiggled him back into good humour, his pride in the boy transparent as Charles crowed with delight.

Dinner was resolutely formal. Flavia was relieved to excuse herself as soon as she politely could, and take Zobeide out to try her paces.

Cantering down the cool winter lanes, threaded with wisps of mist, her constraint eased. These hills and trees were the backdrop of her earliest memories. The coppice her father had planted in the year of Trafalgar was ready for cutting now. He had left a ride through the middle; she remembered bobbing through on her pony, when the saplings were no taller than she. Now they reached high above her head, straight and tall in their measured rows. Its orange beak bright against the shadows, a blackbird darted across her path. She slowed her mount to a walk, to savour the silence. She could hear only the snorting of Zobeide's breath, the muffled fall of hooves, and the faint rustling of the trees.

She had forgotten the exhilaration of being alone in the landscape as the light fades, and the hills bulk against the gathering dark. With a start she realised how close it was to night. She must turn back; Lucius would be concerned. She would save twenty minutes' riding by cutting across Dennison's hay-paddock. She turned off the lane.

Soon Dennison's barn reared to her right with its buttresses and slit windows, ancient and grey, as enduring as the surrounding hills, its huge arched doors warped and silvered with age. The White Monks had built it six hundred years ago, and her father had venerated it for its age. But as a child, Flavia had been terrified by Betsy Turner's whispered tales of murdered monks and strangled nuns. On this chill evening the squat unlit bulk had more of Betsy's dread about it than her father's antiquarian fervour. She was glad to leave it behind.

As she leaned down to secure a gate she heard a sudden noise. She checked the horse and looked about. A belt of trees ran into the shadows on her right; a haystack stood beside the path ahead; beyond the next fence she could see the road home, and the yellow glimmer of Fontclaire Priory in the distance.

She heard it again: a laugh. Were there poachers about? Reaching the haystack she pulled up short. It had been tricked out as a monstrous effigy; two round staring eyes daubed on the rick-sheet; a pumpkin stuck out as a nose. Long strips of white rag hung down as clerical bands, with "NO TITHES" roughly lettered on them. Again she heard a sniggering laugh.

Alarmed, she spurred forward, but three figures spilled from behind the stack and barred her way. Two held square bottles; one hefted a pitchfork. Cloth masks hid their faces.

"Say hullo to the Vicar, Miss." They capered about like goblins.

"Let me pass."

A hand snatched at the reins. She smelt gin. "Come on, miss, give us a kiss."

She dug her heel into the horse's flank and Zobeide surged forward, to be pulled to a whinnying halt as the man hauled on the bridle.

Flavia wanted to scream but her voice froze in her throat. The horse sidled. There was a shout and lights from further down the road.

"Let her go, you ox," hissed the third man. "That's Miss Stanton, who helped your cousin." He wrenched free the drunkard's fingers. "Do you want us to get caught?"

They vanished into the trees. Flavia cantered to meet her rescuers. She was surprised to see the tall figure of Bromley in the lead.

"Are you safe, Miss Stanton?"

She was grinning in relief. "Yes. They ran away when they heard you coming."

Bromley, frowning, rode up and inspected the haystack. As a parting gesture one of the men had flung his pitchfork into the stack, where it hung at a dejected angle. Bromley yanked it out.

"Remove all this," he ordered.

Flavia was shivering. Bromley's expression eased to solicitude.

"Here," he said. "Take my cloak."

"I won't t-trouble you," murmured Flavia, but she was grateful for it all the same.

Half-an-hour later Lucius returned from his own fruitless search, foul-tempered with worry.

"There you are!" he snapped. "What on earth possessed you to ride so far?"

Flavia looked up from her hot chocolate. "I'm sorry to have caused you concern," she said placatingly. "I forgot how late it was."

"I thought you had broken your neck in a ditch," he accused her, stripping off his gloves in jerky movements. "Goodness knows what would have happened if Bromley had not arrived when he did. It was a stupid thing to do."

Flavia had been thinking just that, but she bridled at her brother's tone. "You need not go on about it," she said tartly. "I am quite unharmed. I used to ride in the evenings before."

"That was different. Times were more settled then. This is not the first of these effigies hereabouts, and there have been rick-burnings as well. You must promise not to go out alone."

Flavia looked at him mulishly, unwilling to admit how frightened she had been.

"Did you see their faces?"

"They wore masks," she said quickly.

"I'll ask around the village tomorrow. Damned Radicals! They should be hung. Did you recognise any of their voices?"

"What would happen to them?" she asked, wondering whether to tell Lucius that one of them was Molly Simpson's cousin. She remembered him now: a clumsy day-labourer with a gaggle of ill-clad children.

"Three men went to the gallows last month for an attempted rebellion near Nottingham," Lucius replied. "These louts would go up before the Quarter Sessions on a charge of dangerous meetings and combinations. They would be transported at least."

Flavia stirred her chocolate to break the skin that had formed on the top. Certainly she had been alarmed, and men who set upon an innocent girl at dusk deserved to be punished. But she had come to no harm—in fact they had been about to release her as the rescue party arrived. To arrest Molly's cousin would deprive his family of their only breadwinner.

"I'm tired," she said. "Let's discuss it in the morning."

It felt odd to be at Fontclaire, yet not in her own room. Beneath the unfamiliar bed-curtains she lay awake, mulling over her confrontation. On the strength of her word, three men could be sent into exile, perhaps hung. She had never held such power before. She had remembered the identity of another of her assailants, the one who had spoken up for her: Dennison's son had that stocky frame, and he had been too well-spoken for a labourer. Farmers had to pay the tithe; a young farmer might well resent it. If they were convicted on her word— no, she could not do it. Dennison might be a hothead, but he was a decent young man, not long married. And she could not put Simpson's family out on the road in the heart of winter.

Next morning, she held to her story that she had not recognised anyone in the poor light. In retrospect it would make a good subject, suitably edited, for her next letter to Marianne. Bromley's sudden appearance out of the darkness had been quite Byronic.

She should thank him properly for his intervention, and found the opportunity when Vickery announced Bromley that afternoon.

"I trust you have come to no harm?"

"None at all, thanks to your timely arrival!" she returned. "Do you make a habit of rescuing maidens in distress?"

"Surely so capable a young lady could have extricated herself unaided. You told Lucius they were fleeing when I arrived. What had you done? Threatened to read them extracts from the *Political Register?*"

Unsure of just how sharp Bromley had intended his irony to be, she changed the subject. "What do they hold against the vicar? I remember him as a mild, inoffensive man."

"Some of the local youths have been inflamed by Orator Hunt," he said dismissively. "They have formed some alehouse association in the village, in imitation of the Hampden Clubs, where they drink and spout politics instead of earning an honest crust. It is the tithes they object to, not the vicar himself. This year's returns were better than last, so the rate has been set higher."

"But surely that is a tax on improvement."

"Tax or no, it is the way it has always been done," Bromley returned. "If mere tenants and day-labourers can decide for themselves how far their obedience extends, where will it end? However misplaced their notions, they have no right to harass a helpless girl. Should they come before my bench they will discover their mistake."

"Pray do not feel obliged to act on my account," said Flavia anxiously.

Bromley gave a dry laugh. "My dear Miss Stanton! I am a magistrate. When you have seen more of the world, you will know these agitators for what they are: mere nobodies, intoxicated by a sense of spurious importance. But I must go. I am relieved to see you in good spirits. Give your brother my compliments. I trust you will dine at Ash Park while you are here?"

"Thank you," said Flavia, conscious of the pressure of his hand. Perplexed, she watched him leave. She had sought his attention and been pleased to gain it. His compliments flattered her. But she was by no means in love with him; her meetings with Bromley had none of the urgency she had once felt with Ralph Fairfax.

She turned her mind to what Bromley had said. She must visit Old Sarah, who knew everything that was going on in the village. A hint in her ear that the agitators must lie low should solve the problem.

Down in the village, the older women smiled and bobbed a curtsey, but the younger ones gave her dark looks. When she saw Betsy Turner dodging out of the way Flavia grew angry as well as upset. Lengthening her stride, she caught up with the stout old serving-woman and touched her arm.

"Miss Flavia! What a surprise!" exclaimed Betsy, with patent artifice.

"What is going on, Betsy?" she demanded. "Why are you all avoiding me?"

Betsy's hands worked in the fringes of her shawl. "It's not you, Miss—I don't know how to say it, without upsetting you..." She sucked her lower lip and went on. "The folks have heard what happened last night and they're afraid their menfolk will be sent to gaol. We told them not to do it—" she stopped, realising she had given herself away, but ploughed on "—and we're so sorry they gave you a scare; but if you give evidence against them they'll all be transported."

"I know two of them already; Dick Simpson and Arthur Dennison," Flavia retorted. Betsy gave a start. "I'm on my way to Sarah's now to settle this. I don't want the men from the village punished any more than you do. If they promise to leave such tomfoolery alone, I will take it no further."

Betsy burst into tears. "I said you'd never be so hard," she sobbed, "but they're all stirred up, what with the corn so dear, and Mr Bromley so strict, and all the Longhallows servants losing their positions—"

"Longhallows?" Flavia echoed, her mind snapping to sudden attention.

"Didn't you hear?" said Betsy, dabbing at her eyes with a blue spotted handkerchief. She sniffed. "It happened while you were away. A terrible thing it was, too; all those decent folk who served Sir Ralph and his father before him, out on the road. The place is shut up now. And the tenants have been put off, with their farms turned over to sheep. There was bad feeling about it, I can tell you. Sir Ralph would never have done such a thing before; it must have been that foreign woman—begging your pardon," she added.

Flavia frowned. For Ralph to have humiliated her was bad enough; but to cast aside all his dependants: how could he have done such a thing?

"Are you sure?" she queried, unwilling to believe it.

"That's what Mr Frewin told them: *at Sir Ralph's express instruction*, he said."

How could Flavia have been so mistaken in Ralph? Had infatuation so blinded her judgement?

"I am sorry to hear it," she said. "Come: walk with me down to Sarah's and we will relieve one mischief, at least."

The cottage was even more dilapidated than before. The gate screeched as she pushed it; the garden was an overgrown tangle. A curtain twitched but there was no reply to her tap at the door.

"Sarah!" Flavia called crisply. "I know you are there: open the door."

There was a thump of furniture being shifted, and a low murmur of voices.

"Are you by yourself, Miss," Sarah's old voice quavered, "or are the constables with you?"

"The only constable with me is Betsy Turner, and if you don't open that door immediately I shall go back home and tell Mr Bromley to do what he likes!"

Ashamed of her outburst, Flavia mastered her temper. She thought ruefully that during her time in London, she had forgotten how set the countryfolk were in their fears. The door opened a crack, as Sarah checked there were no officers lurking in the bushes, then she gestured them inside.

Flavia compressed her nostrils against the smell of damp. Obviously Lucius had still done nothing about the cottage. She must speak to him again.

Her eye was caught by a movement in the poor light. A tousle-haired youth stood up from the chair beside the scant fire and slouched defiantly against the mantle.

"You were at the haystack," Flavia stated, his gesture triggering her memory.

"Aye, Luke Rusden, Miss," he admitted grudgingly, adding with an effort, "we weren't expecting nobody to come by. I'm sorry we gave you a fright."

"Now listen to what I have to say. If the three of you promise to stop these antics, I will take it no further. But you must give me your word."

"I only did it because of the hard times, Miss," Luke confessed. "If you get work, you can't live on what the farmers are paying. If we complain they put us off and take men cheaper from the Outdoor Relief. No wonder so many of the lads are turning poacher. But I'll paint no more hayricks." He reached out and shook her hand.

Flavia was heartened by her success. "Come up to Fontclaire tomorrow and I'll see you get wood for repairs and a spade. Meanwhile you can make a start clearing the path."

"Don't want to leave old Nan on her own." The boy grinned awkwardly at his grandmother, touched his forehead and ducked out the low doorway.

Sarah had sat immobile throughout the exchange. "Come sit by the fire, miss." Her voice was firm with satisfaction. "You'll be wanting a cup of tea."

# 30

## *England, early 1818*

A grey blanket of sky sagged down on the stable-yard. Flavia slapped her riding-crop against her ready-gloved hand. Harriet, hearing news of Zobeide, had sent a new emerald green riding-habit; Flavia rejoiced in the colour after so long in sombre mourning. Zobeide breathed warm down her neck, nudging her arm, keen to go. But the rain that had threatened all morning had now settled in, drumming on the roof and pooling between the cobbles. There would be no riding today.

Regretfully she handed the reins to the stable-boy. Even the walk back to the house would cake the hem of her new skirt in mud.

"There's a covered way out back to the scullery, Miss," the boy suggested, helpfully. "Past the servant's quarters."

She thanked him, following him past Zobeide's stall at the end, through a passage lined with saddles hung on pegs, to a narrow door. This opened onto a sheltered brick path, dank as she walked with the rain dripping steady off the eaves. Gratefully she ducked through the scullery, turning from old habit towards the kitchen, to warm her cold hands by the welcoming heat of the oven. But Mrs Wallace had gone, with the other retainers from her father's day, replaced by strangers like the new French cook and the supercilious Vickery, who owed her no loyalty.

Since the attack in Dennison's hayfield Lucius would not let her ride alone beyond the park. Excursions with her sister-in-law had not been a success. Flavia preferred to explore the hills and woods, while Caroline favoured a short canter along the high road, followed by an elaborate picnic.

With each passing week her discomfort grew as a guest in her old home. In her father's time, as *de facto* mistress of Fontclaire, Flavia had directed the servants and reviewed the household accounts. Now she was merely an observer, with Mrs Lennox's thinly-disguised hostility shutting her off from the offices she had once performed. Flavia would have found it easier to be supplanted had there been evidence of poor management. But the linen was starched crisp, the crystal gleamed, and the silver sparkled. Brusque Alicia Lennox might be, but she was undoubtedly capable.

All that was left of the worn, familiar furniture from her mother's time were a few pieces banished to the Abbot's Tower beyond the hall. Even the library, so long her haven, was now her brother's room of business, with brass-clawed chairs to match his pretentious desk and paintings of thoroughbreds on the wall. These days the estate accounts were locked away in an ironbound chest. Where the money had come from for all the changes Lucius had made, Flavia had no idea; Lucius said only that the investments Bromley had recommended had yielded excellent returns.

Long winter evenings with the Lennoxes offered only the yawning tedium of button-whist, local gossip and embroidery. The longer Flavia spent with them, the more their company grated. Caroline filled her day changing her dresses and reading *La Belle Assemblée*. Country life and its duties bored her. Her artlessness, too, was beginning to wear. She had more than once dropped comments to Flavia which would have been quite insulting, had they been deliberate. So far, Flavia had given her sister-in-law the benefit of the doubt.

Then there was the affair of the piano. On her arrival Flavia had found an elegant little pianoforte in the parlour, with scarce more volume than a harpsichord. She had resolved to maintain M. Dupont's daily regime of exercises and learning new *repertoire*, but on the second afternoon Mrs Lennox had sent a note: the noise was disturbing Caroline's rest. Next morning Flavia found workmen in the room, sweating and apologetic, measuring up for new curtains. Two days later Alicia stopped her at the door, explaining that a friend was coming to call: could Flavia postpone her practice until after four o'clock; unless, of course, she knew something lighter and more fashionable?

Flavia had swallowed her temper and spent the rest of the morning searching out her mother's old pianoforte, which she eventually found in the old schoolroom, up in the tower. She had it carried down to her bedroom. The keys twanged for want of tuning, and the case was clogged with cobwebs and dust. Flavia attacked it with a feather-duster, rags, and beeswax; a man came up from the town to repair and tune it.

Once he had finished the instrument answered very well. An unexpected delight had been finding a dusty pile of music in the schoolroom cupboard. There, in faded brown ink on the frontispiece of a Mozart sonata, her mother had written her name: *Emily Stanton.* Flavia touched her finger to the crumbling paper, warmed by a sense of contact with the mother she hardly knew. She opened out the music. As she finished playing, she saw that her nephew had strayed in to listen. She set Charles on her knee and let him plonk out some notes for himself. After that, they got on famously.

The weather cleared; eager for a change of scene, Flavia took Charles down to the village. She was pointing out the gingerbread-men in the window of the village baker when she heard her name. Turning, she recognised the stocky, fair-haired young man as Arthur Dennison, whom she had last seen in his father's hayfield, at dusk. He did not look like a revolutionary, clutching the brim of his new hat so tightly he was spoiling the nap. He had the air of having something important to say, but not knowing where to begin.

"Miss Stanton, may we offer you a seat in the gig?"

"That is most kind, Mr Dennison." Curious to see what this was about, she allowed herself to be handed up next to his mother, sturdily-built like her son, but with darker eyes, shrewd and observant. As Flavia settled Charles on her knee, he grabbed at the whip in its socket.

"Regular little coachman Mr Lucius has got there," said Mrs Dennison, easing her son's awkwardness. "But what we want to say is: thank you for not turning Arthur in."

Her son nodded. "We're much obliged to you, particularly now my wife's so ill. It would have killed her, me going to gaol."

"Ill? I'm sorry to hear it," Flavia exclaimed. "But you have not been married long."

"A year," said Dennison. "She has the consumption."

"Could you travel to a warmer climate?" Flavia suggested.

"My son is saving up to emigrate," said Mrs Dennison. "But the poor girl would not last the voyage."

"Leave the country for good? But your father has a fine farm; the best in these parts."

"My brother can take it," Dennison replied. "There's no future in it. The better your crop, the higher they set your tithes. Then your neighbour's mortgage is foreclosed, so you pay his share of the Poor Rate. And that's without the Game Laws." He leaned forward. "I can't kill the hares that eat my corn or the foxes that take my chickens, or even trim back the hedges that shelter them. Now you have only to be found at night with a net—not even a gun—to be transported! Sorry, Miss," he apologised, recalling his passenger, "but I've had enough."

"Don't listen to him," pleaded his mother. "I'm terrified he'll get into trouble. You should hear him and his father going at it, hammer and tongs."

"Father!" the young man snorted. "He'll not change. He's still broadcasting his turnips instead of sowing them in rows. I've been to Holkham. I've seen what can be done. I want a new country: new ways." He stared out over the horse's back.

Mrs Dennison looked at her son with mingled pride and fear. "If he keeps on like that he'll end up transported, or God save us, at the end of a rope!" She lowered her voice. "Couldn't you get Mr Lucius to encourage Arthur to change his mind?"

Charles had fallen asleep on Flavia's shoulder. She tucked her cloak around him. Lucius would never go to Coke's model farm to see how his estate could be improved, or anywhere else, for that matter. His money flowed into extensions to the house, new furniture, and dresses for Caroline. Flavia felt thwarted and powerless: she could have done so much had the decisions been hers.

Lucius had no sense of obligation towards his tenants, any more than did Caroline towards the sick and poor in the village. "The poor should know their place. Look what happened in France," Lucius had said, echoing Bromley. "And as the Reverend Malthus says, there are too many of them anyway." But Ralph had turned out no better, discharging his servants, laying off the tenants, and putting the arable land down in grass. How many families had lost their livelihood? There was more profit in sheep than corn.

Charles's blond head wobbled with the motion of the gig. She felt a rush of love for the child. How must Mrs Dennison feel, seeing her son in danger?

"I'm sorry," Flavia said heavily. "I would not raise your hopes in vain." She remembered her fruitless attempts to have Old Sarah's cottage repaired. "I would speak to him if it would do any good. But he does not listen to me."

Flavia's solace was the post. Harriet's letters were witty, Marianne's increasingly anxious in tone. In Manchester a summer of strikes had been followed in September by a huge parade from Stockport, dispersed without the anticipated violence only by the calm good sense of General Byng. "Byng is the hero of the hour," Marianne wrote, "but there is still great unrest among the hand-weavers. Once they strutted about with five-pound notes in their hatbands; now most have lost their work to the new machines and are sorely distressed. I fear there will be breaking of frames, and heads, before the year is over."

Flavia sucked the end of her quill. She had started a letter to Harriet, but after half a page, could think of nothing more to say. Then, in a sudden moment of insight, she snatched up another piece of paper.

*This house is no longer my home*
*I have no place in my brother's family*
*I would rather be back in London*

The black ink gleamed on the white paper, the words sharp with logic. Did she want to dwindle into a mere spinster aunt? What alternatives did she have? She could return to London to live with Harriet, but her cousin was old, and ill, for all she tried to hide it. At her death the house would revert under the terms of the entail to the nearest male heir. This would leave Lucius with two houses and Flavia with none. If she wanted a home of her own, she would have to marry.

For all the polish she had gained in the last two years, she dared not expose herself again to the grief that had engulfed her after Ralph's desertion. With him, love had grown as easily as a tree puts out leaves—until her jealousy had provoked him, and he had abandoned her. So much, she thought bitterly, for the marriage of true minds. She had met other men, at Harriet's afternoons and elsewhere, who had paid her attention; a gangling young doctor with freckles and a pleasant smile; a retired Major interested in antiquities, upright and intelligent. She had conversed easily with them, but at the first sign of closer interest, retreated behind scrupulous politeness.

She despised the annual cattle sale of the Season, where anxious mothers auctioned off their daughters to the highest bidder. She had not attended a ball since that disastrous evening with Dorothea Bromley. But in two years, or three, where would she live? At Fontclaire? It was irksome enough being a dependant of the Lennoxes for a few weeks. She could not endure the thought of being governed by Mrs Lennox, or worse, her daughter, for the rest of her life.

Could she bring herself to choose with her head rather than her heart, and make a marriage of convenience? If she wanted to be mistress in her own home, with a husband to provide for her and give her children, what other choice did she have? With patience, love might grow. She stared unseeing out the window at the grey overcast blurring the trees. A great sadness filled her. It was time to awaken from her youthful dreams. She sighed.

A blot had gathered on her paper. She picked up her note and fed it into the fire. She did not want the servants reading it, and reporting back to their mistress. Flavia reached again for her discarded letter and started a new paragraph.

*There is little to do here at this time of the year. I wish to return to London. Might you arrange stabling for my new mare? I shall send her down with a groom...*

"This is a great honour," Mrs Lennox observed. "Mr Bromley has invited us all to dine at Ash Park. He rarely entertains."

She glanced from Flavia to Caroline, pleased to have received an invitation to the wealthiest house of the neighbourhood, yet resentful that it was not on account of her daughter.

"Perhaps he has been distracted by the troubles in Manchester," Flavia suggested. "He owns a manufactory there."

Mrs Lennox regarded her sharply, as though suspecting her of some hidden meaning.

"Very like," added Lucius. He looked anxiously at his mother-in-law. Flavia wondered how many times he had apologised for his patron's tardiness in issuing invitations.

Lucius turned to his sister. "Bromley has a guest, a friend of Lord Bathurst," he said enthusiastically. "You will be able to talk politics to your heart's content."

"May I wear my new pearls?" asked Caroline expectantly.

Her mother's expression relaxed into an indulgent smile. "Certainly, my dear. You will be quite the prettiest woman there."

Even after so long, Flavia felt uncomfortable entering the domed entrance-hall of Ash Park on Bromley's arm. But she was no longer overwhelmed by the grandeur of the house. She had seen mansions more imposing in London. Her host, too, she found less daunting. When he put his mind to it, his manners were flawless.

"Miss Stanton, may I introduce Mr Bigge?"

A misnomer, thought Flavia, smiling down at the slight figure. The biggest thing about him was his nose.

"Mr Bigge has been staying with Lord Bathurst," Bromley went on, with a slight tinge of self-congratulation. "He has been appointed commissioner to head an inquiry into the affairs of New Holland."

Flavia had placed the little man as a provincial lawyer, with his mild air of well-tended bachelorhood. Now she noticed his calculating gaze and the brows elevated in disdain.

"When do you embark for the colony, sir?" she asked, to cover her mistake.

"In the New Year."

"Mr Bigge is an experienced traveller," Bromley said. "His previous appointment was Chief Justice of Trinidad."

And I had him down as a country attorney! Flavia thought.

At dinner, to her surprise, Flavia was seated next to the guest of honour. She was grateful for her afternoons at Harriet's, listening to Wentworth, which she drew on for topics of conversation. She could not help contrasting the spare, fastidiously neat Bigge with Wentworth's leonine head and uncouth energy.

Flavia welcomed the opportunity to speak to one so well informed. But though she ventured several of Wentworth's ideas about his homeland, the Commissioner was noncommittal in his replies. Flavia was unsure whether he disagreed, or simply refused to be drawn. Her mention of the Governor's policy of welcoming ex-prisoners back into society provoked a stronger reaction.

"I do not doubt Mr Wentworth's enthusiasm for such a scheme, circumstanced as he has been. However I am surprised that he would press upon a young lady a notion so manifestly inadvisable, indeed distasteful. What father would not be indignant at his daughters being exposed to such tainted society?"

Flavia bridled at his tone. She was sure he would disapprove of Cousin Harriet, open as she was to new ideas. She regretted Wentworth's absence: he was a more forceful advocate than Flavia could ever be. He loved his native land, and celebrated it with all its peculiarities. Bigge saw it only as a convenient prison. They might have been speaking of different worlds.

After this one foray into opinion, Bigge retreated into detachment. Bromley was amused by her attempts to prise open this oyster of reticence. Eventually he intervened.

"I warn you, sir, Miss Stanton will hold out for an answer. Of course no gentleman would welcome a felon at his table. But none of us will go running to the Whigs with your proposals."

Bigge gave only a dry smile. Flavia sought a new approach.

"Perhaps if Mr Bromley were to disclose his interest in New Holland, you might honour us with yours." Her eyes were on Bigge as she spoke, so she missed her host's appraising stare.

"Mine is a matter of profit," Bromley replied after a pause. "There is a growing demand for worsted fabric; English wools are too coarse. Finer wools, like the samples I have seen from Mr Macarthur's Spanish merinos, are much better suited to my new steam-powered looms."

Flavia had not considered that his prime interest might be financial. She had never realised that the difference between two breeds of sheep could be so important. This commercial acumen revealed a new side to Bromley.

Bigge sat back in his chair, his fingers steepled together. "From what I have read, and my experience of the plantation system in Trinidad, there is much to recommend your argument for a wool trade," he said to Bromley. "The climate of New Holland is suited to wool, as that of the Caribbean to sugar; and convicts can supply the labour which in the tropics is provided by slaves."

Flavia kept her questions to herself. Having drawn him out, she was unwilling to stop his flow.

"I welcome your frank avowal of interest," Bigge continued. "I have received representations from every conceivable body of opinion; how to reconcile them, only time and diligence will tell. The Home Office wishes to make New Holland a more severe place of punishment; the Treasury hopes to save money; the Benthamites are urging the introduction of model prisons—did you know that the Millbank Penitentiary has so far cost three hundred thousand pounds, and is not finished yet? The Quakers and Mr Wilberforce are disturbed by immoral conduct which we need not discuss here—" he glanced across at Bromley "—and the House of Lords has expressed its concern over the growth of crime."

He took a sip from his wineglass, savoured it unhurriedly, and went on.

"There is a further complication of which you may be unaware. There are over two hundred capital crimes in the Statutes, but in the last fifteen years there have been capital convictions under only thirty of these. Juries are increasingly reluctant to condemn men to death for transgressions of insufficient gravity. Criminals are now transported who would hitherto have been hanged."

His already supercilious expression altered as his eyebrows rose even higher; whether to condemn or condone this tendency Flavia could not tell. Mr Bigge was not a man who wore his heart on his sleeve.

"Transportation costs the Government some three hundred thousand pounds *per annum*. Can this sum be reduced? Should large sums be directed into schemes for elaborate buildings? When the gentlemen in iron ruffles—" (here he permitted himself a tight smile) "—arrive in the colony, the system should inspire them with a salutary terror, and act as a deterrent to crime."

Bigge glanced from Flavia to his host. "Excuse the length of my preamble. The short answer is that I am being sent to reconcile punishment with profit. The long answer you will, Providence permitting, read in some two or three years' time."

Bigge's formal mien relaxed a little. He carefully aligned his remaining forks and spoons as Flavia digested his answer. There was a sharp mind behind that unprepossessing exterior. While appearing strictly impartial, he had conveyed his opinion quite clearly. So Bigge disapproved of Macquarie's building projects. Flavia wondered what Wentworth would make of this. He took such pride in his family's descriptions of these edifices arising in faraway Sydney. To him they were a pledge of civilised institutions to come. The Commissioner did not share such romantic notions. He spoke with the confidence of unflinching rectitude. He would not treat felons unjustly, but he would always despise them. Conviction was to him a taint as lasting as the slavery he condoned in Trinidad.

Flavia found herself disliking Mr Bigge, for all his diligence. Worthy and industrious he might be, but he was also priggish and dry. She preferred Wentworth's fervour, despite his evident conceit and occasional boorishness. *"Australia"* was his passion. At least he felt some loyalty to the polyglot inhabitants of that remote gaol.

"It is your turn, Miss Stanton," said Bromley, regarding her closely. "The prospects of a distant colony are an unusual hobby for a young lady."

"My cousin collects curiosities," Flavia began. "At first I knew the country only for its strange animals. Then Mr Wentworth, whom even Mr Bromley will admit is a forceful speaker, excited my interest in New Holland as a society as odd in its origins, as in its flora and fauna."

Flavia found her thoughts shaping as she spoke. "Increasingly the colony has emerged as a topic for debate. Why should a place so distant rouse such strong feelings? In the light of Mr Bigge's lucid exposition, I wonder whether our interest in New Holland mirrors a deep concern with movements here in England. Consider the call for reform, the changes wrought by machines—" she gestured towards her host "—and the increase in crime."

She stopped abruptly, wondering whether she had said too much. Bromley regarded her with a half-smile. Bigge's expression she interpreted as grave approval.

"Perhaps my Lord Bathurst should send you in my place," he said courteously. "I had not expected so penetrating a discourse from so fair a witness. You are to be commended, sir," he said, turning to Bromley, "in finding such an Athene."

Flavia basked in the unfamiliar warmth of praise. I have it in me to say the right thing, she thought, and be noticed. Never before had Flavia enjoyed the frank approval of men so rich and powerful. Father would have been so proud. She felt quite giddy.

# 31

## *England, 1818*

With Bigge's words of congratulation ringing in her ears, Flavia had no shortage of subjects now for Harriet's letter. And encouraged as she was by the prospect of returning to London, she was less irritated by Caroline.

Flavia was also heartened by the prospect of riding out more often. Bromley had unexpectedly offered to escort her himself. She found him surprisingly good company, describing operas he had seen in Italy and asking after her musical studies. Increasingly these excursions took her along the bridle-path through Ash Park, which bordered an ornamental lake.

She had not considered where all this was leading until one windy morning when she reined in her mount at the edge of the water. She snatched unsuccessfully at the lock of hair which had escaped from beneath her bonnet; Bromley brought his horse alongside, caught the errant tress, and in easing it back under the brim, took her face in his hands and briefly kissed it. His hands were long and finely-shaped; his touch light. Her heart thudded in surprise. "You must excuse my taking advantage," he said. "I have wanted to do that for some time."

Flavia was confused. The caress had been cool and pleasant, unlike the urgency of Ralph's kiss.

"Mr Bromley—" she began.

"That is much too formal," he interrupted.

Her mount edged away, but he reached over and held the bridle. "Not so soon, my dear. I have something to say to you."

Flavia felt a sense of alarm.

"I would like you to be my wife."

His attentions over the last months fell into place. The thought of standing in so close a relationship with this man made him suddenly strange. He was rich, handsome and accomplished, yet the thought of committing herself sent her into a panic. She needed time to think.

"You have caught me by surprise, sir," she answered frankly. "I have not been altogether—" she nerved herself "—indifferent to your attentions. If you would give me a little time to decide…"

"A week?" Bromley suggested.

She looked at him, trying to decide if he was serious. "Mr Bromley—"

"Robert."

"Robert," she conceded reluctantly, feeling she had taken a first step towards capitulation, "no wonder you prosper, if you pursue your business with such vigour! Give me until Easter for my reply."

"I have waited this long; I can wait a little longer," he replied confidently. "Meanwhile I claim a right to exercise certain powers of persuasion." He kissed her again, lightly, on the lips. "There! Tell me you did not like that."

"Of course I cannot." She had never been courted like this before, with love played like a game.

"I shall, of course, make a formal representation to Lucius," Bromley continued. "But I considered you were the best judge of your own happiness, and should be approached first."

"Thank you," she said, flattered.

As Flavia rode ahead, Bromley smiled to himself.

She dreamed that night of the long-ago visit to the circus, with Ralph dishevelled and laughing outside the ruins of the bear-booth. She felt the old gnawing pain: Where are you? What went wrong? She strained to speak, but could not.

Flavia slipped out of the house early next morning. Lights shone in the servants' windows upstairs, but the downstairs windows were dark. She took the long-neglected path up Beacon Hill and climbed to the summit.

She sat on a stone as the light strengthened around her, so still that a thrush hopped right up to her feet. She reached down gently to brush the soft brown and cream feathers, but it fluttered away. A deep instinct led her back to this favourite spot of her childhood. She had spent too long hiding her pain from the world, as her father had done. Marrying Robert would mean a loss of innocence; she understood that. She would give her body to a man she did not love, in exchange for a home, children; the opportunity, perhaps, to influence the decisions of powerful men.

She knew there had been other women in Robert's past, but the knowledge provoked none of the jealousy she had suffered over Ralph. She would not endure such turmoil again.

Unthinkingly she glanced across to Longhallows, but the low sun had not yet touched it, and the woods between were still cocooned in mist. She sighed and turned away. What alternative did she have? Dwindling into a maiden aunt, a despised dependant in her brother's house? She would walk clear-eyed into this marriage. Love would come from her children. They would be fair-haired, not dark, like the smiling young man who had come striding up the hill. The world would envy her choice, so why did she feel as though she was smothering something deep inside her?

She could not waste the rest of her life mourning a youthful infatuation. She knew of marriages of convenience that had proven very happy, and love-matches that had turned sour. But it was her life she was considering, not someone else's; marriage to a man she had only just begun to know. Would it be a challenge, or a dreadful mistake?

"Lucius, I must speak with you."

"Is something wrong?"

She gave a little laugh. "Quite the contrary. I have just received a proposal of marriage."

He started. "A proposal? From whom?"

"A suitor I would never have expected: Bromley."

A variety of expressions chased one another across his face. "But that's great news!" he added heartily, after a faint hesitation.

"I don't know whether it is great news," she said. "I don't know whether to say yes or no."

Flavia sat down heavily, her hands curled in her lap. Lucius was troubled. He owed it to his sister to tell her the truth about Ralph: she would have had no doubts answering him. But Ralph was gone, and this was a most advantageous match.

"How do you feel about him? Do you love him?"

"I find him—interesting." She said, colouring.

Lucius smiled. So his prissy little sister was not entirely indifferent to the lures of the flesh. "Do you not love him?"

"No."

"Does 'No, I don't love him' mean 'Yes, I do?'"

"I can't tell!" she burst out. "I've been thinking in circles all night."

Lucius chewed his lip. Flavia's marriage would be a coup. It would secure his own position in society. The more he thought about it, the better it looked. But Flavia would need careful handling in this turbulent mood.

"You would be happier with an establishment of your own," Lucius suggested gently. "As Bromley's wife you would have scope for your abilities."

It was unlike Lucius to be so perceptive, she thought. Flavia recalled her success at Bromley's dinner. There would be many more evenings like that in the future, where her opinions would be taken seriously.

"I never thought a proposal would confuse me," she admitted. "I thought I would know immediately what answer to give."

"My marriage was not straightforward," Lucius confessed. "I was afraid to tell you then, because I didn't know how Father would take it, but Caroline was with child. We too had our difficulties, but they resolved themselves eventually."

Now it was Flavia's turn to look surprised. This explained her brother's odd behaviour at the time. So other people took rash decisions which turned out well. She might have children as delightful as young Charles.

"You would make a good mother," said Lucius, echoing her thoughts. "I see how well you get on with my little fellow. You deserve to be happy, Flavia."

She was touched by this sincerity, and blinked, close to tears. "Thank you. You have been a great help."

"You'll say yes?" he enquired, hopefully.

"I think so," she answered, with a rueful smile. "But I won't tell him yet. It will be a new experience for Bromley to be kept waiting!"

Lucius was pleased. Obviously, Flavia was more attracted to Bromley than she would admit. He tilted back his chair. It had been a good idea to tell her the truth about his own marriage. Somehow that had swung the balance. He congratulated himself on his honesty.

Bromley turned the sapphire to the light. It was true, he thought, that it had been Ralph who first drew his attention to Flavia. Then she had been only a gawky girl. But she had grown and developed polish during her time with that old harpy in London. She had brains, and some tact; she had handled the dinner with Bigge with unexpected aplomb.

His mother had pleaded with him not to take the ring from her. She had begged, stormed, and in the end, wept. Dorothea was used to getting her own way. But it was she who had driven him from boyhood to seize his rightful place, and establish their dynasty. This marriage would achieve that. Now his mother understood, however unwillingly, that he and his heirs were the future of their family, and she its past.

Flavia would support his new career: Mrs Robert Bromley, the political hostess, and one day, Lady Bromley. He sensed her ambition. Once engaged in the world of affairs she would forget this bookish nonsense about Reform, just as she had forgotten Fairfax.

All the same, he wished she had answered him immediately; it was galling to wait like some yokel suitor at the door, cap in hand. In a more sophisticated woman, the delay would have been deliberate. The thought that she might say no made him want her all the more. His pride was at stake.

Not that he was seriously worried. He had dispatched his only rival years ago. She would accept his offer. It was only a matter of time.

"I hear that you are destined for great things," Harriet observed on Flavia's return to London.

"What do you mean?"

Harriet's eyes glittered with malicious humour.

*"Fate hath but very small distinction set*
*Betwixt the Counter and the Coronet."*

Flavia smiled. "Come, Cousin; Bromley is only a humble Esquire. I can hardly be accused of vaulting ambition."

"Esquire, perhaps, but hardly humble," she retorted. "Anyway," she went on in her direct fashion, "do you propose to accept?"

"I am almost at the point of saying yes."

"Almost? What reservations do you have?"

Flavia looked across at the old woman. "You know them."

"If Ralph had wanted you, he would have come back by now," Harriet retorted. "You can't waste the rest of your youth mourning for him, as I did for his father."

"I know that with my mind. It's just that I feel this—reluctance."

"Twenty thousand pounds a year will overcome a fair measure of reluctance," Harriet asserted. "You will be able to attend all the concerts you wish, travel; hold a salon of your own." You might even find love again, she thought, but that is a matter you will have to decide for yourself. If I told you that now, you would be scandalised.

"Then you should send Bromley an invitation," said Flavia. "For Easter Sunday."

Flavia gave her consent in the morning-room, vivid with spring flowers. Bromley's handsome face smiled with triumph as he slipped onto her finger a long sapphire of the deepest blue, tapering at the ends, rimmed with a double row of diamonds. She felt its weight of it as she moved her hand, marvelling at the blaze of colour.

"It is a family piece." His voice was rich with satisfaction. "The stone came from India."

What stories could it tell? She felt almost guilty at its worth. Her new life certainly promised to be very different from the old.

Bromley took her in his arms. He was taller than Ralph; she tilted her head back. The sun was in her eyes and she closed them. This time he kissed her harder.

As the weeks passed, Flavia's sense of strangeness began to ease. She acknowledged that by accepting Robert's expensive gifts, she incurred an obligation; in a marriage such as hers, happiness did not simply happen; it must be worked for. Bromley's behaviour was impeccable; it was up to her to do her part.

As the springtime evenings lengthened, she had to admit that the obligation was not onerous: opera in Bromley's box at the Haymarket; excursions in his curricle; shopping with mysteriously increased credit. The evening she most enjoyed was a concert by a woman pianist, Lucy Anderson, playing pieces by two German composers, Hummel and Beethoven. There was something new and vital about Herr Beethoven's sonatas. The incisive melodies stayed in her head for days, and she found herself tapping out their insistent rhythms on the edge of the parlour table.

"If you wish to practise, do it elsewhere," said Harriet with acerbity.

"I'm sorry, Cousin," Flavia said guiltily. Poor Harriet had looked unwell of late, and was more than usually tetchy. "I did not mean to disturb you."

"Mrs Anderson played here once," Harriet went on in a gentler tone. "Perhaps after your marriage you may arrange a private concert. You will be able to afford such luxuries."

"Could I?" This had never occurred to Flavia. She would dearly love to meet the pianist. She had been impressed by the example of a woman earning a living by a display of such skill. She must ask M. Dupont for the music.

"Beethoven?" More wrinkles grooved Dupont's creased face. "I give you Lully, Haydn, the divine Mozart, and you want these noisy modern *explosions*. Too masculine for a young lady. Too long; too obscure."

Flavia was used to his outbursts. "Please, Monsieur," she pleaded. "Is the music available here?"

"I may have to send to Leipzig for it," he sniffed, reluctant. "As though I was not burdened with cares enough!"

Poor M. Dupont, with his powdered wig and satin knee-breeches; his world had died twenty years ago, under the guillotine.

"What has happened?" she enquired.

He flourished his left hand, whose third finger was cocooned in white bandage, like a very small mummy.

"That fool Gaston shut the carriage-door on my finger. I am engaged to play next week. Never before have I cancelled a recital."

Flavia was about to express her sympathy, when an audacious idea struck her.

"Do not cancel the concert," she said.

"What do you mean, *Mam'selle*? I cannot play with one hand alone."

Flavia smiled at his perplexity. "I will go in your place," she said. "Say I am your niece."

"It would not be suitable!" exclaimed the teacher.

"Why not? If Mrs Anderson can play at a public concert, then why can I not appear for three-quarters on an hour at a private recital? You have said yourself my touch is much improved. Surely we can find a programme which I can execute to your satisfaction. Please, Monsieur."

Dupont looked disapprovingly at his pupil, then down at the keyboard; then looked up again with a smile which revealed the charm he must have had as a young man. "I should say *absolument, non*," he said, "but I remember what it is to be young, although you may not believe it. I shall agree, before reason reasserts itself. But I will require you to work hard!" he said sternly. "If you are to appear as my niece, you must give a good account of yourself."

Flavia flung herself into the work with an intensity she could not explain. Previously she had shied from playing in public, but upon this madcap project she and M. Dupont laboured with the fervour of conspirators. At nine o'clock on the appointed night, dressed in a plain blue gown, she walked through the tradesmen's entrance of a strange house. On entering a pale green drawing room, she was introduced by a pleasant, plump woman as "Mademoiselle Ladomerska, who has kindly agreed to replace her uncle at short notice."

Flavia curtsied to the blur of faces. M. Dupont had taken great care instructing her in her curtsey, assuring her it was up to the strictest standards of Versailles. She nodded briefly to her "uncle" in the doorway beyond, and sat down at the piano, a new Broadwood, a magnificent instrument, far superior to her own. Captivated by the opportunities it presented, she confidently performed her programme, stood, recited the little speech she had memorised in French, and retired to warm applause.

Dupont whisked her off, deflecting requests for an encore, to where an anxious Gaston waited with the carriage. As they trotted homewards her teacher withdrew a purse of coins from his pocket. He pressed the money into her hand.

"But Monsieur!" she protested. "I cannot possibly accept it. The money is yours. I did it for my own satisfaction."

Dupont shook his head. "You have earned the fee: take it. My reward has been in your delight at the talent you did not know you possessed, and my pride in your performance. I have few enough students who can shape the soul of the music."

Flavia counted the coins in her hand: five guineas. Five guineas for an evening's work; a quarter of what she had spent on her last visit to the dressmaker, but for the first time in her life, money she had earned herself, by the exercise of her own skill.

"Thank you," she said with feeling, and gave the old man a quick peck on the cheek. She knew what she would do with her windfall: buy those Beethoven sonatas she had set her heart on.

Her subterfuge might have gone undetected if, two weeks later, she and Bromley had not met her erstwhile hostess on the steps of St Paul's. Bromley tipped his hat to her, and was about to effect an introduction when the lady intervened.

"Miss Ladomerska and I have already met."

Bromley, taken aback, looked from one to the other.

"How kind of you to show her the sights of London," the woman went on. "Though I had no idea you spoke Polish, Mr Bromley. Or perhaps you communicate in French?"

He looked so astounded that Flavia had to laugh.

"I have a confession to make," she said. "*La Ladomerska* was an imposter. I urged the whole project upon my music-master, who had injured his hand."

"This is capital!" the woman exclaimed, smiling. "Your playing was even commended afterwards by Countess Lieven. 'Such purity of style,' she said, 'I have not heard since I left Warsaw.'" She turned again to Bromley. "But who is this young Euterpe?"

"Allow me to introduce my fiancée, Miss Stanton," he replied, stiffly.

"I shall always remember you as *la Ladomerska*, my dear," said the woman cheerfully. "Wait till I tell my husband! Thank you again," she added, with a farewell wave to Flavia. "Your performance was most enjoyable."

Bromley walked her back to the curricle in silence. Flavia could tell by his set expression that he was angry. But she refused to give an apology. She was proud of what she had done.

Curtly he dispatched the groom on an errand, and took the reins himself, turning the team out into the road with a sharp crack of the whip. "I hope you are satisfied with making a fool of me," he said.

"It had nothing to do with you. It was a private matter."

"Private!" he retorted. "The story will be all over London by next week: my fiancée playing for money!"

Flavia was stung by his reaction. "I cannot understand why you feel so strongly about it," she said.

"I had not thought it necessary to explain to you," he returned coldly, "that as my wife you will have a position in society to maintain. To play privately for friends is an acceptable accomplishment. To play to strangers for money is an insult on my competence."

Flavia was stung by his dismissal of her music as merely *"an acceptable accomplishment."* But Bromley had not finished. "You might also consider," he went on, "the propriety of an engaged woman gadding about London without a chaperone."

Flavia could not let this pass. "I went straight to the house in a private carriage, played for less than an hour, and returned straight home, accompanied all the while by M. Dupont."

"An elderly French libertine! At night! I can guess what the ladies at Almack's would make of that."

"You go too far!" she flashed out. "Set me down."

She glared at Bromley, who made no attempt to slow the horses' pace. Silence smouldered between them; she stared at the brick facades of the buildings as they passed. She felt like snatching the reins herself, but so undignified an act would only humiliate her further.

At length he spoke, in a gentler tone. "My concern was for your good name. You are too young to understand how important it is to conform to the usages of society."

Reluctantly Flavia turned to face him. He was trying to bridge the gap; so should she.

"Had I known it would perturb you, I would have consulted you first. You will not punish poor M. Dupont, will you?" she went on, anxiously.

"No, my dear," replied Bromley, mollified by her display of contrition. "If his lessons are bearing such fruit," he added magnanimously, "perhaps you should perform more often at your cousin's *salons?*"

Much as Flavia appreciated his attempt at generosity, she still felt cheated. She could not discern why until a package was delivered to her the next day. In it was a delicate bracelet of rubies and pearls, with a note: *"A tribute to your skill."*

Flavia drew out the bracelet and clasped it round her wrist. It was an exquisite piece, and a graceful gesture. How could she carp at such a gift? But it did not warm her heart like the paltry five guineas she had earned herself.

# 32

## New South Wales, late 1818

The chain clattered against the log as the sergeant yanked it free. Ralph stood uncertainly, the Union Jack above him snapping in the spring breeze.

"Your time at Limeburners' Creek is up. Report to the gate."

As he joined the line Ralph, who had not laughed in months, found himself smiling at half a dozen men, capering about like demented scarecrows. They had just been ordered to Sydney to work on the new convict barracks. After Limeburners' Creek, Sydney Town was the Promised Land. Ralph did not expect so startling an improvement in his lot; he had learned how subtly influence could be brought to bear. He still had over a year of his sentence to serve in the mines.

The last four months had shaken him. Stripped to the skin, half-starved, and too weary even to think of escape, he knew himself to be no better than the compliant old lags he had so despised. He must not become reconciled to his lot. Beckworth, who had had to fight all his life, was far better equipped to survive in the camps than Ralph. Beckworth had no expectations, so was never disappointed.

Ralph hoped his companion had got clean away. But as he walked through the barrack-room door back at Newcastle, there was Beckworth, propped against the wall, eyes closed, smoking a pipe.

Ralph tapped him on the shoulder. He jumped.

"Jesus! Where've you been, then? You're as scrawny as an old man gum."

Ralph gestured briefly with his blistered hands. "Burning lime."

"I fell off that useless nag again, and got sent straight back here." He looked at Ralph expectantly. "Give them a run for their money, did you?"

Ralph said nothing.

"It gives us all a bit of hope, seeing how you make the tyrants sweat. They despise us; they always have. It was no different when I was in the army. But you've got brains. You make fun of them, and that hurts them more than anything else."

"*Safe from the bar, the pulpit and the throne,*" Ralph murmured, *'But touched and shamed by ridicule alone.*"

"Eh?" Beckworth went on. "Half Sydney was sniggering over those dogs; and you tweaked them Parramatta beaks in their own courtroom. I couldn't do that," he added in a rare moment of humility. "I haven't got the style."

Wryly Ralph considered this unexpected tribute. At the time his actions had been gestures of purely private retaliation. "I used to think I was achieving something. Now I'm not so sure. Be as clever as you will, it all ends at the triangles." His eyes dropped before Beckworth's scrutiny.

"You didn't even try to run! You're scared!"

"Try running double-slanged, chained to a log! I'm tired."

"Crawl away into your little corner then, and feel sorry for yourself," Beckworth jeered.

"It's easy for you," Ralph flashed back. "You don't have Masters on your back!"

Beckworth's expression set into its old sneer. "Tell you one thing: if I had, I wouldn't let the bastard get me down. That's the trouble with you gentry: they breed you for looks, not guts." He strode off.

Ralph stared after him in angry incomprehension. He had thought Beckworth was a friend, but what did he expect of him? Ralph had been prepared to defend him against Masters, in the face of violence; why would he turn on him now?

Masters terrified him; he could not deny it. He knew he would never be forgiven for humiliating the man in public. His malice would follow Ralph wherever he went. He would never be allowed to leave the punishment camps.

Ralph could not understand Beckworth. They had been thrown together by circumstance; they shared nothing but their chains. Paradoxically, Ralph was closer in background to Masters, with his ear for music and library of French novels.

Once more they filed into the familiar darkness of the mine. Ralph sighed as he shouldered his pick. Coal, shells, quicklime: what difference did it make? There was always more to dig; more to carry. He whistled under his breath. It eased the monotony a little.

"You and Beckie fallen out, then?"

Ralph ignored the speaker, but the man propped one shoulder against the wall and went on. "He always was a sour-tempered bastard."

Ralph was curious despite himself. "You knew him before?"

"In the Peninsula. Sappers with the Engineers." The man pecked out sentences like a pigeon picking up crumbs. "Thought you did too. That tune."

Ralph looked up. "The one you was whistling," repeated the other. "Even the Frenchies were singing it."

Ralph could hear the wheels of the returning barrow shrieking on its wooden axles. "Yes," he said to end the exchange, and chopped into the unending wall of coal.

That night, as he tried to sleep, the words came back into his mind. There was something he had missed. Then he had it: that melody. It was the one Masters had played.

Ralph felt a sense of dread, like the cold flow of air from an ill-fitting window-frame. What connection could this gentleman pastoralist have with Wellington's army, years before in Spain? Ralph would not have been surprised if he had been an officer; he had an air of command. But so did all Exclusives in a convict colony like New South Wales.

Masters' assurance went deeper than that. He had a detachment, almost a contempt for his class, which had run like an undercurrent though his exchange with Ralph. And he had welcomed the opportunity to practise his cunning, as a dog will chase a fly when there are no rats about.

Yet he had addressed Ralph almost as an equal. Had he recognised in the runaway some quality he shared? Was he a cashiered officer, perhaps? Ralph raked through his memory for old scandals, but none of the faces fitted. Seducing the Colonel's wife or cheating at cards were hardly Masters' style. A civilian contractor? He must have got his money from somewhere.

The strain echoed in Ralph's head, but he was too tired to stay awake for long.

Sullenly Ralph resumed the routine of the mine, like a bullock fighting the yoke. Which was worse, a future of futile struggle and sharp correction, or what Beckworth had accused him of: lapsing docile into submission?

Still Beckworth avoided him. Ralph's initial regret at losing his company hardened into resentment. It was all very well for Beckworth;

he had been ready enough to follow Masters' prompting at Ralph's trial, cheerfully perjuring himself to save his own skin.

Nothing had changed. All week Ralph hacked and hauled underground; come Sunday, they lined up, sullen under a faded sky, as Pryor flourished the punishment list. A breeze, cool after the mild spring weather, had sprung up from the southwest. Pryor's voice strained as he pitched it higher, trying to be heard above the wind in the trees. Ralph glanced up: the sky was darkening rapidly. Then the thunderstorm hit them, with a flash and a great crack, and sudden driving rain.

Pelted by the fat drops, the overseer dashed for shelter. The men ran for the barracks. All day and night it poured. Water trickled through the thatch; the shed was lit by vivid flashes of lightning, and thunder ripped overhead.

Next morning the storm passed as swiftly as it had arrived, and the prisoners were mustered again amidst the puddles. Ralph was surprised to see Beckworth arguing vehemently with the sergeant of the guard, who waved him away.

Beckworth turned to Ralph, dour-faced. "I don't like the look of this weather," he said, with none of his usual cynicism. "I told that shake-bag lobster not to send the men down the new workings, but his ears are as thick as his shell. See if he'll listen to you."

"Why should he?" Ralph said stiffly.

"Someone will die if he doesn't," retorted the other grimly. "That new gallery is fine when it's dry, but it lies under the hollow and water has been gathering there for the last two days. He just might take it from you."

Ralph had never considered the lie of the galleries in relation to the hills above. Now he saw in imagination those torrents of water squeezing through rifts in the soil, saturating the supporting timbers. Still he resented Beckworth's high-handedness: having ignored him all week, he now expected Ralph to get into more trouble over what was, after all, only an instinct.

"He won't like this," muttered Ralph, but he went over anyway, to argue uselessly in his turn.

"What did he say?" Beckworth asked as he returned.

"That he'll see me on payday," said Ralph tersely. "And that you and I can go down first, for our cheek."

Beckworth caught Ralph's bleak look. "At least you tried," he said.

"A note for you, sir."

Masters flicked the wafer with his thumb and opened the paper. The writing was clumsy; the penstrokes uneven.

*"Dear Sir,"* the missive ran. *"You know as how you wanted information on the prisoner Fletcher. I have it from a reliable Man that he knew the prisoner Beckworth in the Army in Spain.*

*"Also I hear that a Gentleman from Sydney met Commandant Morisset here yesterday. This Mr Hunter wants an enquiry into Fletcher's case and says he should be released.*

*"There is no chance of that as Fletcher is a great Nuisance and has been sentenced for absconding, sheep-stealing and attacking an Officer since he came to the Colony, but I thought you should know.*

*"Trusting you find this useful on the same terms as before,*
*Yr Obedient Servant,*
*Js Pryor, Overseer."*

Masters stood for a moment, then screwed the paper up and flicked it into the fire. He rang a bell.

"Saddle my horse," he ordered. As the door shut, he unlocked a drawer and drew out a long flat box. With swift, precise movements he began loading a pistol.

Beckworth confronted Pryor at the top of the shaft. "I'll not go back down!"

"Yes you bloody will." This time Pryor was taking no chances. His whistle shrilled out and two soldiers came running. "These two refuse to work!"

With a click the redcoats fastened their bayonets.

"I tell you, it's not safe!" Beckworth shouted.

"Looks all right to me," said the sergeant. "I've had enough of you two. Down the mine *now*, or you're both on a charge of malingering. Then we'll see how safe you find it."

Beckworth and Ralph exchanged glances. If they were to be arrested they would at least stay above ground. Ralph was less concerned by what might happen on payday than by his companion's fey mood. He had never seen Beckworth like this before.

"Move!"

Ralph recoiled from the levelled musket. He tugged Beckworth's arm. "Give it away. Anything's better than a bayonet in the gut. Maybe it's not as bad down there as you think."

As they rode the rope down, Beckworth reached out and ran his finger over the exposed surface of the wall. It came away slick. He wiped it down Ralph's forearm.

"You could glaze pots with that," he said bitterly.

The gallery was dank and the air had a mouldy smell. The rest of the working-party had fallen quiet. Beckworth was known as a hard man; Ralph as a rebel. There must be something to it if these two were worried. Even Pryor abandoned his usual chivvying at the coalface and kept well back.

The ground in the new workings was greasy underfoot. Twice Ralph almost slipped, and recovered himself with a jingle of chains. There was a muttered undercurrent among the men.

"Silence!" snapped the overseer. "The next man who opens his mouth, I'll have his hide every Saturday for a month!"

The hours crawled past. Surely it must the end of the shift? Beckworth looked up expectantly: he could read off hours underground as if they were blazoned on a clock-face. Ralph lifted his finger to his lips. Pryor had recovered his nerve. Any further attempt to force his hand would only make him more stubborn.

Ralph had just tipped out his barrow and was heading back for the coal-face when something moved at the edge of his vision. He turned. A thin trickle of water oozed from a crack as fine as a razor-slash. As he bent closer it spread into a runnel, pulsing out from a widening split. A tremor ran through the pit-props like a sigh. The whole wall was bleeding water. He jumped back.

"Get out!' he shouted. "The wall's going!"

As he turned to run, it leaped out to engulf him. He choked on a cloud of coal-dust. A crushing weight pitched him into darkness.

Ralph opened his eyes. He could see only phantom spots dancing inside his skull. He turned his face and felt the rasp of pit-sawn timber across his cheek. He had been caught under one of the baulks as the ceiling caved in: buried alive. The fear inside swelled to blend with the blackness beyond. He blinked grit from his eyes, but it made no difference; he was sightless, lying in mud. Soon the mountain above would press his face down into it and he would choke.

He clung to a thread of reason. He could move his legs; if he could haul backwards, pull himself clear, there might be a sound part of the mine where he could shelter until they were dug out—if anyone came to dig them out…

Shifting one leg set off a little avalanche of pebbles. They tumbled down and the dust made him cough. With exquisite care he brought up his knees, braced his left hand, and tugged.

Pain ripped down his right arm: broken, and trapped above the elbow. Gasping, he laid his head back in the cold ooze. This was the end, dying blind, what he had been running away from ever since the torture-chamber at Badajoz.

He recalled exactly the few moments he had spent there: the glare of the brazier, the twigs snapping in a stream of sparks; Juan's terrified defiance of the French officer in the shadows; incongruous, a violin inlaid with mother-of-pearl, on the table by the door. Then it struck him: with the French novels, and the Spanish song that tugged at his memory. He had seen that violin in Masters' library.

It was impossible! Masters and the French officer could not be the same. Ralph had glimpsed him only briefly before he dropped his eyes, terrified of inviting scrutiny. Then the guard had dragged him out. But take away the uniform and moustaches, and the build was right. The Frenchman's side-whiskers had gone; his hair grizzled in the years between.

His mind raced. It was ridiculous that such a man would have chosen to come here. But was it? Anyone who had done what he did in Spain would be the target of a score of vendettas. Talleyrand was not the only Frenchman who saw which way the wind was blowing after Moscow.

If the Frenchman's English were as good as his Spanish, the choice made sense. A renegade aristocrat, perhaps? That would explain his effortless assumption of Pure Merino manners, and his subtle contempt for those around him. From his treatment of Ralph, it was obvious that his callousness went back a long way. Where had he learned to inflict pain? In Spain, or earlier? Ralph remembered his mother's disjointed tales of the atrocities she had seen as a girl. Had Masters honed his skills in the Vendée, one of the ambitious young Jacobins who followed Westermann? Had he, under whatever name he bore at the time, been one of those who so casually stripped Ralph's grandparents, roped them together, and condemned them to 'vertical deportation' in the waters of the Loire?

New South Wales offered wealth as well as anonymity. A gentleman of capital with few scruples could do well here. In time, when the heat of revenge had cooled, he could return to the Old World, a rich man with a new identity.

Ralph writhed under the irony of his situation. He had made an enemy of the one man in New South Wales with every reason to want him dead, and had identified him too late.

There was another little slide of dirt. Ralph shook his head to clear his face. He spat grit. His pocket of air was growing stale.

Then, with a lurch of hope that turned his heart over, he felt a tug on his ankle. He kicked to show he was still alive. Through the rubble he felt someone digging.

"Go easy there! My arm's caught."

"Well, crook my elbow," came Beckworth's flat voice. "I should have known it was you."

# 33

# *New South Wales, late 1818*

Surely, quickly, despite the darkness, Beckworth dug Ralph's head and body free.

"You've done this before."

"Riding is not my only talent. I'll find something to shore up that baulk. Move and you'll bring the whole lot down."

"Don't worry," Ralph replied dryly. "I'm not going anywhere."

The pain in his right arm settled to a dull ache, tolerable as long as he did not move. He lay still, daring to hope that he might survive after all, while the mud dried tight on his skin.

Suddenly his surroundings sprang into form. After the total darkness, the lantern was dazzlingly bright. Ralph lay in his own shadow, which angled as Beckworth squatted beside him.

"You were lucky with that beam," he said appraisingly. "A few inches higher and it would have caught your head. I'll dig underneath and try to lever it away. Pull back when I tell you."

Grunting with exertion, Beckworth forced a rock beneath the beam to take the weight, then braced his pick on a stone.

*"Now!"*

Ralph grasped his useless arm with his other hand, and flung himself back. His arm shrieked at him as he wrenched it free. He hugged it, breathing in long ragged gasps.

Beckworth peered, dabbing at the darker streaks on the clay. "It's broken but the bone's not through the skin. Wait."

He went off again and returned swinging Pryor's whistle on its lanyard. Splitting a plank off the cart into slivers, he bound them into a rough splint with the cord.

"Did Pryor get away?"

"Yes, more's the pity. Took off quicker than the Sunday rooster. God knows what happened to the rest." He looked around. "We'd better start digging out." The mine groaned around them. "This lot could go at any minute."

Beckworth chipped delicately at the slumped coal and fallen rock. With his good hand, Ralph carefully eased the debris behind them. They crept forward, scooping out their fragile cranny, Ralph keenly aware of the weight of the hill above. Then, with a surge of relief, they crawled through a hole in the rubble. Here the props still held. The tunnel receded, reassuringly square, down the gallery to where they could feel air on their faces from the draught coming down the shaft.

"I'll shin up the rope and let down the basket," Beckworth said.

"No. As far as they know, we're dead. We can hide here till dark and get away."

"Thought you'd had enough of running," Beckworth grunted. "What made you change your mind?"

Ralph shied from entrusting Beckworth with his true reason: evading Masters.

"I'll not be cut to pieces again by that bastard Pryor. I'd rather go bush."

"What about the door?"

"There's that stock of tools by the windlass," Ralph replied. "We can force it. And we'd better take some supplies from the Government Store. We don't want to be caught hungry, like last time."

Beckworth squinted keenly at him over the guttering candle. "You're a rum 'un," he remarked. "A week ago you were ready to throw in the towel, and now you're off and running."

"You don't have to come if you don't want to," retorted Ralph.

"No need to get your back up," replied Beckworth equably. "It's just that you're up and down like the piston on a pumping engine." He paused. "There's always a sentry on the Store. Why not visit that little shop of Pryor's? He owes us a good turn." The faint light caught his teeth as he grinned.

The candle flickered and died. Within the darkness there were degrees of shadow, faint refractions from the shaft. Twice they heard voices calling from above, but made no reply. No one came down to investigate. Ralph guessed Pryor had exaggerated the extent of the collapse, and the searchers feared another fall.

Beckworth's whisper tickled Ralph's ear. "They're not raising a sweat to get us back. Issuing a tot to celebrate, more like."

Still as he was, Ralph felt the cold seep into him. The mine creaked, but his arm ached too much for him to dwell on other dangers. He shifted from one position to another, seeking the least uncomfortable.

He felt Beckworth stand beside him. "Night-time now: let's go."

Ralph followed, feeling his way forward in the gloom with his good hand. The flow of air was suddenly colder and more urgent. Beckworth looked up and tugged at the rope.

"Good. They've left the brake on."

He grasped the rope and hauled himself up hand over hand, bracing his feet against the side of the shaft. Ralph heard a click from above as the brake was released, and the basket jiggled down towards him. Clumsily he clambered in.

At the top they found a crowbar. The heavy lock resisted their efforts until Beckworth lost his temper and splintered the jamb. It shattered with a loud crack. He prised open the door, and they were out.

Ralph sucked in great gulps of the clean night air. He was cold and hungry and in pain, but alive. Overhead the moon, near full, rode blank above patches of cloud. They dodged through the outbuildings and down a lane, keeping to the shadows. Ralph glanced back anxiously at the officers' cottages, but there was no sign of pursuit. Again, he wondered how far to trust Beckworth. He must stay out of Masters' way. With luck, Masters believed him dead.

Pryor's shop, little more than a shed, was silent and dark. With the skill of long practice, Beckworth forced the window. They stuffed a canvas bag with ships' biscuit. Beckworth checked the cashbox but it was empty. He reached further under the counter and pulled out a square bottle of rum.

"I knew he'd have it somewhere, whether Morisset likes it or not," Beckworth whispered. "You go first."

Ralph eased himself over the window-sill onto the ground. He dodged by instinct as a cudgel whistled past his head. Directly before him stood Pryor, smirking.

"I knew if you was alive you'd sneak out at night, like a rat from its hole." Behind him, Beckworth slipped out the window. His gaze fixed on Ralph, the overseer stepped forward, cudgel raised. Ralph charged him, punching him hard in the belly with his good arm. As Pryor doubled over, Beckworth swept his feet from under him with the crowbar, clipping him over the head for good measure as he fell. Pryor lay still.

"Is he dead?" asked Ralph.

"I bloody hope so," returned Beckworth with feeling. "But we'd best get well away. It'll be the rope's end for us for sure, after this."

He snatched up the bag, and they ran into the tangled shadow of the trees.

A wet towel pressed to his head, Pryor faced his unwelcome visitor. "You had them, and let them go?"

"They took me by surprise," said the overseer sulkily.

"Keep your excuses for Morisset. Does he know of this yet?" Pryor's eyes dropped. "I knew you would lack the courage to tell him. You'll lose your ticket-of-leave for this."

Pryor looked up, alarmed. Masters went on. "Perhaps he'll send you to the iron-gang in their place. I'm sure your companions will remember your past kindness."

Scared, Pryor let the towel drop. A lump stood purple above his eye. "The Commandant thinks they're dead," he muttered.

"Your only hope is to find them before anyone else does. They might meet with an accident."

Pryor's face lifted. "There's that old blackfellow hangs around the camp. They'd never get away from him. I'll get him first thing tomorrow."

"Get him now. There's moonlight to see by. We'll follow them all night if need be. They can't have gone far. Perhaps the Commandant need never know of your stupidity."

As the moon rose higher, the fugitives made a reasonable pace, taking their bearings from the Southern Cross. Then the milky light faded as it came on to rain, and the stars were veiled by cloud. They tried judging their direction by the sound of running water ahead, but now the trees all round them pattered and rattled, and fingers of cold water drew away their little warmth. Ralph, hunched over, stumbled in Beckworth's tracks. His irons snagged repeatedly, tripping him, jarring his injured arm. Each time he pulled himself up more slowly, until at last he lay exhausted.

He's gone ahead and left me, Ralph thought. He doesn't want a cripple holding him up.

"There you are," came Beckworth's voice from above.

"Give me a hand up," Ralph said as briskly as he could manage. He was so cold; all he wanted to do was lie down and sleep...

He felt Beckworth's hand on his forehead. "You've got a fever. We'll have to rest."

"I can't have," Ralph protested. "I'm frozen."

Beckworth heaved him up, Ralph's left arm around his neck. "Time we took a breather anyway."

In an awkward tangle of chains they made for a huge gum, standing alone. The trunk was hollowed out with age, and big enough to shelter them both. Inside it was dry, the floor soft with rotten wood. Beckworth ferreted in the bag for the rum.

"Here: eat some biscuit and wash it down with this. Put some fire in your belly."

Ralph gulped down the raw spirit. "You'd best leave me behind."

"Nah," said Beckworth through a mouthful of biscuit. "You'd not last on your own."

"They'll catch you too if you don't!" Ralph burst out.

"They'll catch me anyway," Beckworth replied reasonably, "unless we're lucky, and I'll be no more lucky on my own than the two of us together."

"Why did you run, then?"

"Sick of the place, same as you."

Ralph lay still, digesting the implications of the exchange. "Thanks," he said. Masters was wrong. There were bonds stronger than the chain and the lash. "What will you do if you get away?" Ralph queried.

"Open a little pub, I suppose. It's not a bad country, once you're free."

"You would stay here?" Ralph was surprised. "I'd go home."

"Back to being a swell?"

Ralph brushed the taunt aside. "I'd get the bastard who sent me here."

For the first time Beckworth was frankly curious. "You've never slipped a whisper where you came from. Got a wife? Kids?"

Ralph shook his head. "There was a girl in I wanted to marry, but she—lagged me," he said, using words the other would understand. Flavia would have been the mother of his children. Not now.

"I had a girl in Spain," said Beckworth. "Jacinta, her name was. I never could get my tongue around it, so I called her Jack. She had a little boy she swore was mine. He'd be quite a lad by now."

Ralph cut across this casual reminiscence. "Were you at Badajoz?" he asked urgently.

"Yes, I was," said Beckworth.

"So was I—but not in the Seventh," he added, forestalling Beckworth's unspoken question.

His companion looked puzzled. Ralph paused for a moment. If Beckworth went to Masters with this information, Ralph was as good as dead. But he was as good as dead already, and someone must expose Masters for what he was.

"I'm going to tell you something —but it's dangerous. If I don't make it to Sydney will you tell Hunter for me?"

"That navy cove with the limp, who was at the trial? Would you trust me?"

Ralph let out his breath. "Yes."

"Some people never learn," Beckworth said, but he sounded pleased all the same. "I'll take your message."

"Tell him Masters was a French officer at Badajoz," Ralph said, committing himself. "In the secret police."

He had Beckworth's total attention now. "Are you sure?"

"I saw him there," Ralph said flatly.

"Not as a private soldier, I'll bet," said Beckworth shrewdly. "And you want me to go to Hunter? He did nowt for you before."

Ralph leaned back wearily against the tree-trunk. The stringy fibres crumbled under his weight. "I know. But no one else would even begin to believe me."

Fatigue dragged at his eyes. He was falling asleep as he sat. His head drooped.

Beckworth shook Ralph awake. "We'll get nowhere like this," he said. "Come daylight they'll have the dogs on us, or a tracker, and catch us sleeping like babes. There's a farmer upriver supplies the officers' mess. He's got a boat. I'll go ahead and nab it. We'll make better speed on the water, and they'll lose our trail."

Reluctantly Ralph forced himself to concentrate. "Where shall I meet you?"

"Keep straight ahead: the riverbank's some two mile along. There's an archway in the rock; you can't miss it. I'll see you there."

Ralph rubbed his shoulder, trying to dispel the throbbing in his arm.

Beckworth checked as he hefted the bag. "Are you up to it?"

"I'll be right," said Ralph. "It's you I'm worried about. Got to keep you off the horses."

Beckworth gave a dry bark. "I'll wait for you till dawn," he said. He ducked out the irregular opening and strode off.

Ralph watched until Beckworth vanished into the darkness. He hauled himself through the opening and set off down the narrow path.

The bush whispered around him. He was utterly alone. Get moving, he chided himself. You can't go back to Newcastle: not with Masters after your head. The rain had stopped now. For a while the moon sailed free, throwing tabby-stripes of shadow through the trees. Then the sky faded to an indeterminate grey. He found it harder to pick the way; the trees all looked the same. It had been hard enough following Beckworth when they were together; now he feared he was lost. Was that the sound of the river? Or had he taken a wrong turn, and was heading away?

Ralph paused, uncertain. He turned to retrace his steps, seeking the reassurance of a familiar landmark, keeping the breeze on his left cheek, and praying it would not shift. At least he trusted Beckworth to make the rendezvous; he was no longer a fellow-convict, but a friend. Thank God! There was the clearing where they had separated: he recognised the towering tree, with the gap at its base.

A twig snapped. As his head turned, hard fingers closed over his mouth. A shock of steel chilled his throat.

"Got him, sir!" Pryor's voice hissed in his ear.

Fiercely Ralph bit the restraining hand. He tore himself away. The blade ripped his shoulder and Pryor's weight brought him down. He fell on his bad arm and cried out. A hand tightened on his throat. Trees slewed above him as he twisted his head away from the knife-point under his jaw.

"Stop!" Master's voice cut like a whiplash. "I want him alive."

"Aye, sir," Pryor grunted resentfully. The crushing fingers eased.

Ralph swallowed. He gathered himself to pull away, but Pryor pinned him down. A handcuff snicked around his wrist, chaining him to his captor.

"Get up."

He was yanked to his feet. Suddenly cold, he tried to suppress a shiver. The knife flashed again.

"Run again and I'll hamstring you. Right?"

Ralph could feel his pulse thudding. He was only just beginning to realise the enormity of this disaster.

"Where's your mate?"

"I don't know."

"I don't believe you," said Pryor unpleasantly.

"We quarrelled," Ralph muttered. "He said I was holding him up." He looked down with what he hoped would pass as embarrassment. He could sense Masters' gaze; then Masters turned back down the track. Ralph heard his low voice followed by a guttural reply.

"They parted at this clearing; that much is true at least," said Masters. "I have sent Jacky back with the horses. We take Fletcher with us."

"What about Beckworth?" queried Pryor.

"You'll get your chance. For all you know, he's hiding behind the nearest tree. You can have him once Fletcher tells us where he is."

"You'll get nothing out of me!" Ralph flung at him.

Masters gave a dry laugh. "The whereabouts of your untutored friend will do for a start. There are other matters as well."

Like who I am, thought Ralph, and why I was in the castle at Badajoz? Beckworth must get away, for both their sakes. Perhaps he was still within earshot. Ralph gathered his breath for a warning shout, but a blow from Pryor winded him. He was still fighting for breath when Pryor tightened the gag.

They did not turn back towards the camp, but continued towards the river. Now Ralph could hear it clearly, rushing, swollen by the rain. They turned upstream. The land to their left was partly cleared, and Ralph wondered why they did not use it; why this procession in the dark? Then it struck him: Masters did not want to be seen. His silhouette dodged black before him, the Dancer of Death, the *Ankou*.

Ralph had known fear before, but this was different. He knew what Masters could do, free from any consideration of law. And Ralph had so little strength left. He tried to wrench his mind away from what must lie ahead.

They turned onto a path leading to a jetty with a long wooden shed. Ralph pulled up.

"Keep moving," snarled Pryor, yanking at the chain.

Ralph hesitated a moment. There was no alternative. He walked on.

The door scraped open. He was shoved inside; the gag tugged free. It was dry in here, and warmer. Through his feet he felt the river, straining against the piles. A cold draught seeped around the edges of a trapdoor in the floor. He brushed against bones. Ahead of him, squat and ugly, sat a massive chopping-block, hacked and stained.

Shadows cowled the roof as Masters trimmed a lamp. There was a rough iron brazier in the corner; he kindled it carefully.

"There always was something about you that caught my eye. Your name is not Fletcher: that is obvious. Who are you?"

"You have made a mistake," said Ralph doggedly. Fletcher was his only protection.

"You have seen me before. You remember: I can tell."

Masters leaned forward, Ralph's skin crawled. He twisted in Pryor's grip, clutching at a last faint hope.

"Do you know what this man is? Take me back to camp and I'll tell the Commandant! He'll give you a reward!"

Pryor unlocked the cuff from his wrist with deliberation. He rattled the coins in his pocket. "I've got my reward already." He snapped the shackle shut on a projecting staple.

"But he's a torturer!" Ralph burst out.

"I don't care if he's Beelzebub. He can do anything to you that he likes," said Pryor with venom, reaching over and slicing apart the makeshift splint. Ralph's breath rasped over the crackling of the fire.

Pryor briefly touched his hat-brim. "Let me know when you want me, sir."

The light fluttered as he shut the door.

"I have no time to waste," said Masters. "I will have an answer."

Bone grated on bone. Ralph screamed.

# 34

## *New South Wales, late 1818*

Oars creaked against the rowlocks as the heavy-laden cutter pulled out from the shore.

"Keep her head on the ship," the mate growled to the skinny boy at the tiller. Overhead the ragged remains of yesterday's storm-clouds straggled across the sky.

"Sorry, Mr Hales, but there's a dead tree ahead."

Hales followed the boy's outstretched arm. A deal of flotsam had washed down the river in the storm; there had been a drowned sheep on the beach where they landed for water. The lad had eyes like a hawk, to pick out a half-submerged tree against the glare of the morning sun.

"Very well, boy."

We should have taken that sheep, mused Hales. We're short of fresh meat.

"Mr Hales! In the tree! Look!"

The rhythm of the oars lapsed as the sailors craned to stare. Hales peered into the sun-glitter. It might be something useful.

"Pull her over, then."

The tree wallowed in the water as they approached. Caught in the branches was the body of a man. His legs trailed in the water; one chained hand stretched above his head, the links wedged in the end of a shattered bough. The other arm hung at an awkward angle.

"Runaway convict," muttered one of the sailors. "Poor bastard didn't make it."

"Had a hard time, by the looks," another remarked. "No wonder he bolted. Must have tried to swim the river and drowned."

"Back to the ship," ordered Hales. There was no profit in a corpse.

The second sailor turned in his seat, resting his oar. "I had a brother at Coal River, Mr Hales. Can't we take this fellow back to the ship and bury him properly? We can't leave him for the sharks."

Hales cursed the soft hearts of sailors. Lomas was a good hand.
"Bring her alongside, boy."

The tree bobbed as the boat nosed alongside, Lomas balancing in
the bow, reaching out with the boathook to draw the chain free. The
boat lurched as they hauled the body over the transom with a clatter of
iron links.

Hales frowned. Everything about this runaway was wrong. His
broken arm was black with bruising, and a wound gaped across his
shoulder. Seared along the gash were ugly strips of raw blistered flesh. A
thin trickle of watery crimson ran down the still face. Hales leaned forward
and saw the broken swelling beneath the cropped wet hair. Someone had
given him a right drubbing, set a hot iron to him by the looks, then cracked
the poor bugger over the head and tossed him into the river to drown.

"Throw him back," he ordered curtly.

"But—" began Lomas.

The boy, who had laid his head on the gaunt ribs, sat up suddenly.
"He's alive."

This was the last thing Hales needed, to be landed with all the
complications of a runaway convict, and one nearly dead at that. But the
men were watching him, and he had been too long at sea to leave a man
to drown.

"Damn and blast you all for a pack of old women!" he swore, to
relieve his feelings. "Bring him aboard then. But I warn you, the Captain
won't like it."

The Captain did not. Lomas had pumped some of the water out of
their find, who lay seeping blood onto the brigantine's freshly-scrubbed
deck.

"What am I to do with him? Spare a hand as nursemaid? I'll have
Government officers crawling all over the ship as soon as I make
Sydney Cove, and letters to write, all for some scarecrow fit only to feed
the fish! Where's that boy?"

But the boy had slipped away to fetch the ship's sole passenger,
tugging him by the skirts of his coat through the crowd of sailors.

"Back to your work! Hoist that gaffsail! Lively there!" The captain
roared. He turned. "Sorry, Father; I didn't see you."

"Your boy says I may be of help," said Father Donavan quietly.
"What's this about?"

"The men fished up this runaway. He's no use to me. I've no time
to turn about; I'll lose three days sailing if I miss these winds."

The priest stooped. Not Fletcher, surely? He laid his hand to the man's ribs. The heartbeat fluttered under the clammy skin.

Donavan looked up. "I'll take him."

"What?" The captain stopped, nonplussed.

"Drop us ashore, and I'll take him for you. I can nurse him for a day or so—and bury him too, if needs be," he added, sombrely. "Strike off those chains!" he snapped at Hales. "It's not decent he should be tied up like a dog drowned in a sack."

Hales hurried back with a hammer and chisel. Donavan, face set, kicked the fetters over the side. The mate was startled by his anger. The priest looked fit to knock someone down if they got in his way.

"Don't stand there staring like loons! Fetch me a blanket."

Lomas dashed off.

"Here, Father," he said shyly. "He can have mine."

With surprising gentleness for so clumsy-looking a man, Donavan wrapped the body in the cheap grey blanket. He stood braced against the deckhouse with the fugitive cradled in his arms.

"Who's rowing me ashore then?" The words rang out like a challenge. "I'll take up no more of your time."

The hands whispered among themselves. The captain had not expected to be taken so literally. "Sorry, Father...I didn't mean right this minute ...I can set you down tomorrow at Broken Bay, if that suits."

"God bless you for your charity, Captain," said the priest, making it sound like a threat. "That will answer very well." He settled his burden again in his arms. "Make way there." He headed aft to his cabin.

Towards evening a gale blew up and they stood out to sea. Under shortened sail, the brigantine heaved and tossed. Desperately the priest fought for Ralph's life, coaxing a tinge of colour back into his pale skin, wrinkled from hours in the water; checking the slow, irregular pulse; setting the mangled arm as best he could; even stitching the gaping shoulder wound with a sailor's needle and thread.

Lomas knocked at the door of the tiny cabin with two more blankets, contributed by his mates; and the boy scurried across from the galley for as long as the fires were lit, ferrying a supply of hot bricks. When all the fires were doused, they ran for another day and night before the heavy seas. Donavan lashed a chair to the frame of his bunk and sat there for hours, cradling the almost-lifeless form; trying to keep him warm, or spooning sugar-and-water into the lacerated mouth. It was as though he were keeping Ralph's body tenuously alive by sheer power of will until the spirit should return to it. Even the captain was impressed by Donavan's fierce effort, donating to his unwanted passenger a pair of old trousers and a sailor's blouse.

The object of this concern lay silent, giving no sign of recognition, his only reaction being to turn away from the light. The ship's company tapped their heads significantly and said he was mazed from that crack on the skull. Donavan was less sure. Occasionally he caught Ralph's eyes on him as he turned, but each time he would look away.

Once landed, Donavan hid Ralph in an abandoned shack, walked to the nearest settlement and hired a horse: travelling all night, he had Ralph in his rooms in Sydney by the next morning.

By then Ralph was shivering in the first stages of pneumonia. He winced at each breath. On the hurried journey through the bush he had trembled with cold; now he gasped as his body burned. As the fever grew he broke his silence, babbling in nightmare, threshing about so that Donavan tied him to the bed to prevent him hurting himself. The restraint seemed to distress him further, so that finally the priest made up a bed on the floor and set Ralph on that. It was a week before the crisis broke. The threshing body stilled, and the sweat on the burning forehead cooled. The patient slept: whether in health or death Donavan did not know. He had fallen asleep over his breviary.

"What day is it?"

Donavan started awake. Ralph was regarding him, the hectic flush gone from his cheek and his eyes shadowed but sane.

"Wednesday."

Ralph frowned down at his splinted arm. He tried to sit up, but caught his breath. His face tightened. "How long have I been here?"

"You were fished out of the sea nearly two weeks ago. First you had a great crack on the head and then the lung-fever."

Ralph's eyes sought the priest's in an unspoken question.

"There was none to hear but me."

"You know what happened, then?"

"I imagine so," he said, levelly. "I have heard worse in confession."

"You shouldn't have bothered to keep me alive."

"Where there's life, there's hope."

Ralph coughed. He tasted blood stale at the back of his throat. His shoulder was raw to the slightest movement, and his arm felt as though someone had driven a stake through it. The fingers lying slack on the coverlet were yellow as old ivory.

When he had first hit the water the icy shock biting into his wounds had brought him round, flailing maimed and desperate against the weight of metal. His sound hand had snatched at the tangle of branches bearing down on him; in a last, instinctive spasm he had heaved his body clear of the water, wedged the chain in a split bough, and fainted.

He had a memory—whether real or delirious he could not tell—of a vast expanse of water at night. Arched above, constellations of stars wheeled in a silence broken only by the slapping of the waves.

"Why did you meddle? I would have been better dead," he said bitterly.

"I did what was right," said the priest with galling assurance.

"Right?" Ralph jeered. "*Render unto Caesar the things that are Caesar's.* How square your conscience with harbouring an escaped prisoner?"

"Were you simply an escaped prisoner I would hold it my duty to return you, as I did before. But you were not an escaper: you were left for dead. And," he added quietly, "there is no mandate, under any law, for what was done to you."

Ralph's pale face flushed. "Never argue theology with a priest," he muttered to the wall.

Later, Ralph felt a twinge of shame for his churlishness. But as day succeeded day without any apparent improvement he resented his dependence. He was humiliated by the ministrations which the priest performed with uncomplaining competence. He flinched at every touch, and the changing of his dressings reduced him to tears. The gash on his shoulder would not heal, but throbbed red and angry. When Donavan told him he would have to open it again to drain it Ralph raged at him for an interfering Papist bastard. Donavan heard him out and clouted him on the jaw.

The pain had eased when Ralph came round, but he was too angry to give his rough surgeon the satisfaction of telling him so.

"Why go to all this trouble? You can't bear to let me die; it would upset your order of things. I prayed, dear God I prayed, to endure, in the end to die. Nobody heard."

The priest chose his words carefully. "I do not claim to understand the mind of God, any more than Job did. Christ upheld his trust in God, though He too was unjustly accused, flogged, and tortured."

"But Christ died at last in despair," Ralph retorted. "*My God, my God, why hast Thou forsaken me?*"

"Perhaps until one has given all," the priest suggested gently, "one cannot begin to be redeemed."

Ralph gave a bitter laugh. "After what I did?"

"Do not despair; many have done worse. You must consider your immortal soul."

"Immortal soul!" Ralph paused. "*Dead meat*, Masters called me; he was right. Fletcher is dead."

"What about Fairfax?" said the priest, levelly.

"No!" Ralph was hoarse with anguish. "If you know who I am, you know you are wasting your time. My name was all I had."

The priest went on remorselessly. "You can't pretend it didn't happen. You must come to terms with it, sooner or later."

"You're too late, Father. Masters got there first. The flag is struck; the citadel surrendered. He knew me better than you do. He said I would break, and I did."

Donavan's heavy face was troubled. "I must go now," he said. "Try to sleep." He set down a glass of water and stumped across the room. The door clicked shut.

Painfully Ralph dragged the bandage from his wrist. The veins stood out livid against the sallow skin. He smashed the glass and drew across the long, wicked shard. The sheet splashed crimson. Ralph cried out as a powerful grip seized his hand, twisted it back, and prised open his fingers. Ralph was flung aside as the bloodied sliver tinkled on the floor.

"How dare you do that!" Donavan's square peasant face was suffused with rage. "Your life is not yours to take! You cannot throw it away, like a tool that breaks in your hand!"

"I don't want to live!" Ralph spat out each word.

"I don't care! I'll not stand by and see you destroy yourself!"

He crouched over Ralph, his freckled fists working: Ralph cringed. Donavan saw the movement and gave a violent explosion of breath. His fury died like a doused torch.

He dropped to his knees, snatched up the corner of the sheet and pressed it to the pulsing gash until the patch of sodden crimson ceased to spread. Quickly he bound the wound tight.

Donavan turned to Ralph's other hand. The palm and fingers were cut; he had not meant to be so rough. Fiercely he prayed for patience. He felt the head roll slack: Ralph had fainted. Carefully Donavan picked the splinters from the young man's hand.

Ralph woke before the priest returned. He felt ashamed of his attempt to kill himself, as if it were some gross obscenity with which he had defiled the priest's home. He knew that was how Donavan would see it. This obstinate, God-driven man had earned some consideration, even from such a graceless patient as himself.

Ralph heard the characteristic rhythm of the priest's mare slow from a trot to a walk; there was silence for some minutes; then a heavy tread on the stair. Ralph gave a wry smile as Donavan's eyes moved to the new bandages.

"It's all right, Father," he said quietly. "I won't do that again, not while I'm here. I give you my word." *Fortiter ad finem.* With anguish he remembered that his honour was as shattered as his useless arm. "For what it's worth."

The priest touched his shoulder briefly. He looked relieved. "I'll take it."

He moved over to the table, and chopped up a piece of liver, preparing their supper. Ralph was fiercely hungry. It was a scant meal and Ralph ate most of it, but his body craved more. Donavan had little enough money; he could not afford to shelter Ralph indefinitely. All the same, he was unprepared for the priest's next remark.

"You will have to move from here," he said bluntly.

Ralph felt a rush of panic. Beyond this simply-furnished room he was still a convict unlawfully at large, with the gallows waiting — if Masters did not get to him first. His throat was suddenly dry. "Why?"

"Someone has been asking after me at the apothecary's. It sounds like the first mate, Hales. He has been tracing my movements and he will soon find where I live. He was unhappy about the whole business from the start. I fear he will go to the authorities."

*Not back to Masters!* The words hammered inside his head. "Please don't send me back!"

"I was not going to." Donavan sighed. "There must be some way we can get you out of the colony, though I don't know how. Can you think of anyone who might help?"

Ralph tried to rein in his racing thoughts. What friends had he made in his time as a convict? There had been Macey, the cashiered sergeant on the ship, so long ago, now: he was dead. And Beckworth too, killed for sure once Pryor reached the rendezvous. Hunter, whose innate obedience to authority had always outweighed a tenuous bond of sympathy: he would not shelter a convict on the run.

For that Ralph needed someone beyond English law. Only one man had offered him freedom unbidden. It was an outside chance, but he had to take it.

"His Reverence may have mercy on us yet," said Ralph, thinking aloud.

"What?"

"Your fellow in the cure of souls. The flogging parson." Ralph had to smile at the other's astonishment. "Send privately to the home of the Reverend Samuel Marsden at Parramatta and ask after the chief Te Hakuwai. If he has returned to Sydney that is where he will be."

The matter of Ralph's recovery took on a new urgency. He no longer fought Donavan's ministrations. The changing of dressings he endured; he rested when he was told. His body, when first he stood up, felt empty and out of balance, but he forced his first tottering steps. He flexed the fingers of his right hand, willing new life into the broken bone and torn muscles of his arm.

It was bad luck to think what he might do once he escaped; he had been thwarted too often in the past. But of one thing he was sure: he would exact revenge for every humiliation, every blow.

Donavan rode off early one morning and returned late. Ralph, now acutely suspicious of every sound, heard him trudge up the stairs.

The priest looked tired. "I saw your cannibal friend," he said shortly. "At first he looked more like to eat me than talk to me, but after I gave him your message he soothed down a little. He's been to London and is on his way home."

"When does he sail for New Zealand?" Ralph asked eagerly.

"The ship leaves in two days, sealing in the Southern Island. He'll smuggle you aboard as one of the crew. I must say he seemed very confident about it. He said to make sure that this time you don't miss the tide."

Here it was, after all this time: the promise of escape. Ralph felt curiously unmoved.

Since he arrived, Donavan had been uncharacteristically testy.

"Where's your horse?" Ralph realised he had missed her light step.

"It has nothing to do with you," said the priest, uncomfortably.

"Yes, it does," said Ralph with certainty. "You're a bad liar."

"It will add three days to your life."

Ralph was suddenly still.

"I think you have little desire to go back to Newcastle, for all your prating of death. I'd like to say it was easy, but it wasn't. If Hales wasn't a friend of Pryor—"

"Pryor!"

"Don't fret yourself, I couldn't do that to you, in all charity. Hales was nosing around again, and Pryor has got to hear of it. He knows now you were pulled from the water alive. Hales has promised me three days' silence. I hope he will not use the mare ill."

"He'll sell her for what he can get for her." It was the only consolation Ralph could offer. He bitterly regretted the sorrow on the other's face. "This is all my fault."

Donavan looked at him keenly. "I'll have a promise out of you while you're feeling contrite; in exchange for my mare. Will you give it?"

He could not deny such a challenge. "Yes."

"You won't come again at that foolishness you tried the other day? Neither here nor later?"

Ralph sighed. "No."

The priest stood up with a look of business. "Thanks be to God, we've kept you alive; let's see what we can do about getting you home."

To Ralph, after so long indoors, the dark streets of Sydney were threatening and exposed. They made their way by back alleys down to the Rocks. Ralph's heart thudded when they were challenged by a watchman with his lamp hanging from a pole; but he wanted only to ask the priest about a baptism. Ralph hung back in the warm shadows, under the powdery-scented blossoms of a wattle tree. It was strange to think that for the people of Sydney it was the start of summer, when so much of his life had come to an end.

They continued on their way. Ralph saw with a chill the arched gateway of the gaol. He skirted the wall on the other side of the street.

Though they had been walking barely half an hour, Ralph was almost spent. They clambered up a steep alleyway around which cottages clung like barnacles. Donavan unlocked a door. Ralph sniffed the stale air suspiciously.

"Seamus won't turn you in," Donavan reassured him. "I knew him back in Wexford. He leaves me the key when he's away."

Ralph went over to the window. Below him slept Sydney Cove, etched with the sticks of masts and spars, with the long harbour beyond, dark and glittering.

"Sit you down," said the priest. "You must eat. You can climb out over the roof of the house below, if that's what you are worried about."

Ralph was stirred by a terrible impatience. Despite his tiredness, his nerves were taut. He felt irritable and tense.

"Why did you do it?" he challenged the priest. "Take me in? What would drive a Roman priest to succour a renegade Englishman?"

The priest munched on a piece of bread and cheese as he considered his reply. "There is no sinner here worse than I, my fierce young gentleman," he said. "I too was angry in my youth, at the great sufferings of Mother Ireland, so come the '98 I preached revolt. My parishioners rose up, and their leader was hanged."

"Well?"

"His name was Terence Donavan. He was my brother. You betrayed your friend. I committed the crime of Cain."

The priest pushed aside his plate and pulled out his stubby pipe. "You are angry because you consider yourself the victim of a great injustice."

He tamped down the tobacco with his thumb, held a match to the bowl, and sucked vigorously. Two deep puffs, and the tobacco had caught sufficiently to go on burning as he talked.

"You cannot fool me, for I once felt the same myself. But my bitterness was for all of Ireland, much greater than yours. I accomplished my revenge, five soldiers killed, but it was slaked in blood; the blood of my brother and my people." He looked through the wisp from his pipe as though seeing the smoke of burning cottages. "I learned then that you cannot serve both God and hate. You remind me of Terence," he added.

Ralph fought the lure of the other's rhetoric. "I'm grateful for what you have done for me. But don't try to haunt me with your brother's ghost. Hatred is all I have."

"Life is all you have, young man," Donavan corrected him. He hauled his stocky body out of the cane chair and it squeaked, relieved of his weight. "My mother said that when God wishes to punish us most severely, He grants us what we pray for."

"I have tried to pray," cried Ralph. "But all I can say is: *Why?*"

The priest looked up from making a bed. "Remember that those who hunger and thirst after justice are blessed. There is grace in your path, though you cannot see it."

It was a long time before Ralph could sleep. What did the priest's words mean? In this world only the strong survived. Te Hakuwai had the right idea: *utu*, revenge; redressing the balance. Yet still Ralph was troubled. He stared past the priest in the chair, reading his breviary, out the uncurtained window, to the blue-black of the fierce, beautiful harbour beyond.

Lapped in a musty sail behind a spare hatch-cover, Ralph heard the dull thuds as the inspecting officers poked into crevices and sounded lockers. He could feel the ship's movement already urgent through the decking, as she strained at the tide to be away.

After a time marked only by the beating of his heart he heard overhead a scuffle of feet; then oars knocking against the side as the longboat pulled away. The anchor was weighed; the ship's motion changed. Once they were clear of land, Te Hakuwai disinterred him from his makeshift shroud. The captain had lost three men to fever and was glad enough of an extra hand, even one with runaway convict stamped all over him. Besides, the New Zealander had secured the man's passage with a cargo that would fetch a good price anywhere: shrunken heads.

The captain entered him on the books as *Jack Nastyface* and enquired no further. Even if the fellow died he would make a profit.

# 35
# *England, Spring 1819*

Happy to be back in London, Flavia sat out in the back garden, soaking up the evening warmth. Against the wall espaliered roses ventured their first tender buds; two busy starlings chirked as they ferried twigs to the crevice where they were building a nest.

She folded her latest letter from Marianne. There had been trouble in Manchester at the beginning of the year, when Loyalists forced the Radical Orator Hunt from the theatre where he was booked to speak. The dank spring had done nothing to ease the widespread discontent. Now Marianne wrote that a string of scandals had further incensed the people against the authorities.

Harriet relished a good scandal. Flavia went to pass on the news. She knocked on the bedroom door, but there was no reply.

"Has Miss Harriet retired yet?" she asked Wardell as he passed.

"No, Miss; she was resting in the parlour and asked not to be disturbed."

The parlour door was shut, with Hester curled asleep outside. The dog awoke at Flavia's approach and scratched at the panels, whining gently. Flavia eased open the door and went in.

The room was in darkness, lit only by the afterglow of the fading day. Harriet lay on the sofa, glasses askew, hands folded over a book. With a fond smile, Flavia tiptoed over and drew up the rug which had slipped to one side. Her hand touched Harriet's. It was as chill as stone.

The dog whimpered, then whined more insistently. A servant looked in. "You had better fetch Wardell," said Flavia calmly.

She was sorry the dog had alerted the others. She would have liked to sit in silence with Harriet one last time.

It was comforting to be cosseted. Before she quite knew what had happened, she was whisked off to Bromley's town house under his mother's care while he undertook the necessary arrangements. Lucius came down for the funeral, doing his best to look sad at the reversion into his hands of a prime London town house.

Harriet had left Flavia her jewels. Inside the tortoise-shell-and-ivory box was a note:

*My dearest Flavia*

> *This is the jewellery of an Indian bride. Papa said it belonged to her alone, to hold or sell at need, or pass to her children.*
> *You are the nearest I have to a daughter. Take these jewels with my love. Remember that they are there to use, should your circumstances require it. Whatever you do with them, you do with my blessing.*
> *Yours in deep affection*

*Harriet*

Despite her tears, Flavia smiled as she shut the jewels away, grateful to have them as a memento. One piece, stirring painful memories, she would not keep: the diamond *aigrette* that she had worn that night she quarrelled with Ralph. She had it sold, and distributed the money among the servants.

Other than that she took only Hester and Harriet's pots of lilies. To care for these was the only service Flavia could now perform for her cousin. The important things which Harriet had bequeathed to her were qualities of heart and mind.

Flavia wanted to go into full mourning. Harriet, she said, had been like a mother. Lucius pointed out that she had obligations to the living as well as the dead. It was hardly fair to Bromley to postpone his marriage for a year because of the death of an old woman who was, after all, only a second cousin of her father's.

Reluctantly she conceded he was right. Bromley had waited once; he could not be expected to do so again. In deference to her feelings he would postpone the wedding until September. Flavia assented, suppressing her relief at having an excuse for delay. Meanwhile, where was she to live? Lucius wanted Harriet's house for the rest of the Season, and Flavia had no desire to submit herself again to Mrs Lennox's régime at Fontclaire.

Staying with Robert's mother was only a temporary expedient. Flavia found Dorothea Bromley daunting. Her attention was fixed on her son, and Flavia suspected that she resented the prospect of sharing his life with another woman. Her prospective mother-in-law was always exquisitely turned out, and every comment chillingly polite, but she invited no confidences. Flavia mourned the openness she had enjoyed with Harriet. The house, too, was run according to strict protocol, with the servants trained to turn their faces to the blue-brocaded wall as Mrs Bromley passed. Flavia reassured herself that once this was her home, she would order things differently.

The solution arrived in the mail, with a letter from Marianne. Would Flavia come to Manchester and stay with her? She could be married from there, if Bromley agreed. Flavia was grateful for this gesture of friendship; so grateful she burst into tears. Bromley was pleased. He would be able to visit her while he was there on business, and it would introduce her to a city where she would spend much of her married life.

Her tears made little dark splotches on his superfine coat; his touch was cool on her cheek. He said her nerves were overwrought, and that she would feel better for a change of scene. He would arrange for her to leave within the week.

This time there was no squashing in a hired post-chaise; she travelled in Bromley's carriage, with Lucius as chaperone. Nor did they eat greasy chops at public inns. Lucius reminded her of these as they sat down to their excellent dinner on fine china in a private room.

As they neared Manchester the flow of traffic thickened. Coaches, carts, and heavy wagons rumbled towards a grey cloud on the horizon. Gradually this resolved into a forest of chimneys spewing a pall of smoke. The tang of cinders bit the back of her throat. She heard a low thrum, like a buzzing hive of enormous bees.

Lining the road were huge plain brick buildings, four and five storeys high, slotted with rows of identical windows. Flavia started at a sudden hiss of steam, drifting clammy and white across their path. Beyond a roof, a great beam rose and fell like a giant's hammer. The carriage clattered across a narrow bridge. From a pipe high up a wall, dirty water flowed gushing into the river below.

Some of the towering manufactories were silent, their windows blank. Shabby, grim-faced men gathered in knots at the side of the road, darting surly looks at the glossy carriage as it passed. Flavia craned to read the handbills plastered on the walls, but could make out only: *MEETING*; *REFORM*; *EMIGRATION*. Lucius tweaked down the blind.

When he drew it up, Flavia was relieved to see they had left the huge factories behind and were driving through a neighbourhood green with trees, well-tended lawns and hedges laden with blossom.

They arrived at Marianne's address, a comfortable two-storeyed brick house with a large garden, backing onto a lane. From beneath the scrolled fanlight came an echo of noise from the corridor. Stepping around the scatter of wooden blocks on the hall floor, Flavia realised that never before had she lived in a household with several children. What were their names again? Hannah, Tobias and Benjamin.

Just what this might imply, she discovered when dressing for dinner. Her bedroom was on the ground floor, at the back, with a view of the garden pond. She had noticed the window was open, and thought no more of it, until she reached for her glove and saw it move. She lifted it carefully. As it croaked at her there were smothered giggles from outside. Inside the glove was a frog. She tipped the creature onto her hand, where it sat splayed on its little cold feet, blinking and swallowing.

Ralph was the last person who had played a practical joke on her. Bromley's wit always had an edge; he would never laugh at anything so insignificant as a frog. For a wild moment she thought of smuggling it into the dining-room and letting it loose under the table. But Bromley was to join them for dinner. She would soon be a married woman and beyond such tricks. Regretfully she tipped it out the window. Let young Tobias return it to the pond.

The Reverend Edmund Backhouse was one of those disconcerting people who speak only when they have something serious to say. At the table Flavia sat with head discreetly bowed as their lean-faced host recited a lengthy grace. The light of the triple oil-lamp glinted off his pebble-glasses.

As the prayer ended she turned to Bromley. His fair hair gleamed in the light. "Who were those men gathered on the street?"

"Do not concern yourself with them," Bromley replied. "They are handloom weavers angry at losing work. They will come to their senses soon enough."

Marianne leaned forward. "It is not as simple as that, Robert. Their earnings now are half what they used to be. With the Corn Laws pushing up the price of bread, they cannot eat. The Prince Regent has ignored their petition. It is hardly surprising that they are turning to the Radicals."

"Pray what will they achieve by that?" said Bromley dismissively. "Parliamentary reform cannot cure their distress. Can they eat secret ballots, or pay the rent with broader suffrage?"

Edmund intervened with calm authority. "They are the house of Israel, in the vision of Ezekiel: *Our bones are dried, and our hope is lost: we are cut off for our parts.* Reform would at least give these people a voice. How can efficacious policies be devised for a city like Manchester, with over one hundred thousand inhabitants, when it lacks a single member of Parliament? Yet the rotten boroughs, with their handfuls of voters, endure."

Bromley set down his soup-spoon. "Rotten boroughs have worked well enough in the past. The Duke of Wellington himself defends them. Why should their owners be dispossessed of what is, after all, their property?"

"But is it not unjust," queried Marianne, "for a peer like Newcastle to own nine constituencies, and evict those tenants who vote against him?"

"Why not?" returned Bromley. "I would. He gives them work and the roofs over their heads. They owe him loyalty." He glanced challengingly round the table. "I agree with the Iron Duke: *Beginning Reform is beginning Revolution.*"

Flavia stirred uncomfortably. She was moved by her hosts' appeal to justice; but Robert was entering Parliament through a pocket borough. He would construe a public attack as disloyalty. The others looked at her expectantly.

"I believe the great Pitt himself entered Parliament through such a borough," she said tentatively.

Smiling, Bromley resumed his soup.

After dinner Bromley walked Flavia around the garden. "Your support this evening was most pleasing, my dear," he said, drawing her arm into his. She wanted to confide her doubts, but Bromley would not understand them. He was always so sure in his opinions.

"Bye the bye," he added, "I heard news in London of your acquaintance Wentworth."

"Is he not still in Paris, writing his book? Has he returned?"

"Doubtless he wishes he had not. Some family history has come to light which will dent the assurance of even that cocksure young man."

"You cannot tell me that much," she said reluctantly, "and not the rest."

His lips curled in a smile. "Seeing as you ask, he has been revealed as the bastard son of a convict mother."

"But that was only gossip, surely!"

"No: proven beyond doubt. Furthermore, his father was twice bought to trial in his youth on charges of highway-robbery, and was lucky to escape the rope. No wonder he was so keen to practise his profession at the other end of the world."

"But where did these libels come from?" she exclaimed. "His family is much respected."

"He cannot disprove an open letter to Lord Sidmouth, from Mr Bennet, the Member of Parliament. Wentworth threatened to call Bennet out, until his father's own agent vouched for the truth of the story. I would not give twopence for his prospects now. So much for his understanding with Miss Macarthur. Who would wish his daughter disgraced by such a connection?"

"What crime is there in believing one's mother honest, and one's father honourable?" Flavia returned.

She was surprised by the force of his reply.

"He is arrogant and opinionated. He was riding for a fall. This may teach him humility."

Wentworth? She hardly thought so, recalling the bubbling self-esteem which had so enlivened Harriet's *salons*. She remembered those afternoons with affection, and a pang of loss.

Marianne was unceasingly busy, supervising the household and children, taking food and clothing to needy families round the parish and running the Sunday School. Flavia wondered how she had found the time to write those long letters. Though Flavia helped as best she could, she was conscious of imposing, particularly when she considered the added burden of the wedding to come. Flavia raised the subject as they sorted baby clothes for one of Marianne's charities.

"Thank you for taking me in," she said shyly. "You have so much to do already."

Marianne smiled. "Some days are vexing, when the children are ill in turn, and it rains for a week. But I am blessed in my husband and family, and the knowledge that what I do is worthwhile."

"That was the problem at Fontclaire," Flavia confided. "Nothing I did mattered. That was one reason I accepted Robert's offer. I hope you do not consider me mercenary. I wonder sometimes if I made the right decision."

Marianne studied her companion's troubled face. "I suspected as much from your letters," she said quietly. "I proposed that you stay with us so you would not enter the family as a stranger. Robert is not an easy person to know; it will be hard for him to consider a wife in his arrangements, after years alone."

"Your circumstances, without a mother to guide you, have not been easy; and an unmarried woman's lot can be lonely. I can understand your choosing as you did." She looked at Flavia keenly. "Am I right in supposing a previous attachment?"

Flavia coloured. "Yes. With a neighbour. He ran off with someone else."

"Excuse me for seeming to pry. But a disappointment can make it harder to commit yourself again. Do you hold any hope of his returning to you?"

"Hardly," replied Flavia bitterly. "He has been gone from the country three years, and I have had no word."

"In that case, my dear, you are wiser to follow the path you have chosen. Trust to Providence, and the children who will bless your union, to strengthen your affection. I cannot remember Robert ever singling out another girl as he has you. You have the good sense not to expect from him demonstrations foreign to his nature; and too active a mind to do nothing during the absences which his business affairs will demand. Perhaps you could help me with the Sunday School? This is a good work: so many of the working men cannot read or write, and have no hope of education."

Flavia was struck by Marianne's perception. This was one of the things she had been seeking: a sense of purpose.

"Why not?" she said, her face easing into a smile. "It's time I did something useful."

"Sunday School?" queried Bromley with a mocking smile. "Does time hang so heavy on your hands?"

Flavia bridled. "I must have something to fill my days, and there are few concerts here."

"I shall take you to Italy once we are married. There you will find concerts enough. Rome? Paris?" His smile became more marked as she registered what he was saying. "But take care not to educate your charges beyond their station. As Dr Paley says, *The lot of the poor is one of invaluable blessings.*"

Was he making fun of her? She could not see how labourers would be encouraged to disaffection simply by learning to read. And had he meant what he said about travelling in Europe?

"Shall we truly visit Rome?" she asked, excited. She remembered poring over her father's engravings of the piazza of St Peter's, depicting the raising of the obelisk in intricate detail. It was hard to believe that soon she would see it for herself.

The following Sunday Marianne invited her to hear the preacher at Stockport, the Reverend Harrison.

"Don't look so alarmed!" she said to Flavia. "We are not trying to make a Nonconformist of you! I want you to hear what he has to say about Sunday Schools."

Swallowing her misgivings at the prospect of a lengthy sermon, Flavia accompanied Marianne to the simple yellow brick church. They squeezed into a pew as the aisle beside them filled with women in faded cotton prints and men in worn jackets, out at the elbows, their faces staring forward, fixed in expectation.

Harrison's voice rang out above the throng.

"What is the aim of educating the working classes?" he proclaimed. "Reform will come, whether our masters will or no; we must have faith in the intelligence of our working people. We are educating them for the responsible use of power."

She felt his words running through the crowd like an electric current, fusing them as one. They echoed in her mind all the way home. *Reform will come…The responsible use of power.* She was filled by a sense of purpose. Her two hours teaching each Sunday were little enough in themselves, but at last she was doing something to change people's lives.

# 36

## *England, mid-1819*

Despite her efforts, Flavia could not warm to this grimy city. Whenever the wind blew from the town, the air was sour with factory soot. Marianne scarcely noticed it, but Flavia felt grit prickle between her fingers and the pianoforte keys as she played. Even the daffodils were barred with dark rings inside their yellow cups. Her visits to the city merely reinforced her original impression of ugliness, bustle and noise. The new buildings were too much in the same style to be interesting; there was none of the grandeur and variety of London to offset the rawness of this overgrown factory town.

Flavia had not realised how much she had come to rely on Harriet's steady unstated affection, her clear thinking and sharp wit. Marianne's friends, though pleasant, were preoccupied by their children and domestic concerns. For all that it was worthwhile teaching gawky apprentices to read, Flavia yearned for a stimulating conversation.

She had committed herself to living here indefinitely. The weather did not help; a dank spring passed sullenly to a wet summer. As the grain rotted in the fields, hunger grew.

At last her Beethoven sonatas arrived. Eagerly she tore open the parcel. These books were hers, bought with money she had earned herself. She took them immediately to the pianoforte in the drawing room. Scarcely had she reached the third page when Tobias burst in, chasing his sister. Just as Flavia settled again to the music the housekeeper bustled up, complaining that Hester was loose in the fowl-run. Flavia, reluctantly wrenching her mind from the sublime, spent the next ten minutes with the gardener's boy chasing the dog, guilty, triumphant and elusive, amidst squawking explosions of indignant hens.

Angrily she rinsed the fowl-dirt and dog-hairs off her hands, changed her gown, and returned to the drawing room, only to find Hannah slumped on the piano-stool with her face flushed and eyes red.

"Mother says I must practise my pieces *right this minute,* or I can't wear my new sash," she intoned dolefully.

Flavia snatched up her music, doomed to remain for ever unheard, and retired fuming to the garden. Of course the children should be allowed into the drawing room; it was their home after all. She had brought Hester with her; the dog was her responsibility. Naturally she must take second place in Marianne's domestic arrangements. But she was still angry.

"May I keep you company?" enquired Bromley. "Or will I be bitten?"

Flavia forced a smile.

"Do excuse me. I have been trying to play this last hour, and have been thwarted by one interruption after another. At home the piano was mine whenever I wished," she admitted.

"I have already planned a music-room for your exclusive use, once we are married. I ordered two pianos from Broadwood last week. Meanwhile, shall we dispel those black humours with a turn around the garden?"

Bromley was in a particularly buoyant mood during his visit, but gave no hint as to why. The only answer he gave to her queries was: "You will discover, in good time."

"Marianne," said Flavia, as they sat sewing that evening, "do you know what Robert has up his sleeve? I have never seen him look so pleased with himself."

Marianne sat for a moment, thoughtful. "There was a man in the curricle with him when he arrived. They were discussing property. Perhaps he is buying another house."

Flavia remembered his talk of a music-room. "But he already has Ash Park, and his townhouse in London," Flavia objected. "Surely he is satisfied with that."

"On the subject of what is due to his family, Robert is never satisfied," Marianne replied, smiling. "But I heard the fellow's name: Frewin."

"Frewin?" echoed Flavia blankly. "But he is the agent for——" she stopped.

"Do you know him? Look! You've pricked your finger. I should not have distracted you. Let me fetch a court-plaster."

Flavia remembered Ralph's anger when Frewin sold Bromley the bronzes. Ralph would never sell him Longhallows. Marianne must be mistaken.

She forced her attention back to what Marianne was saying. "I have told the children to play upstairs tomorrow, so you may use the piano undisturbed."

"You are most kind," said Flavia.

This music was powerful, thrilling, superb. She sat back, satisfied. There was a tentative knock on the door.

"Begging your pardon, Miss," said the housekeeper doubtfully, "there's a boy here to see you. Cheeky young scamp."

Flavia had been expecting news from Molly. "His name would not be Sam, by any chance?"

"So it is! I told him be to be off, but he said he had a message for you."

"Show him in," she said. "Or if you prefer, I will see him in the kitchen."

"Oh no, Miss," the housekeeper replied, shocked. "You can't go sitting among the servants! What would Mrs Backhouse say? Please use my parlour."

Sam was taller now, about fifteen, Flavia guessed, quite the young man in his green velveteen coat. He grinned and bowed low, flourishing a tall glossy sealskin hat, which he set down carefully on the seat beside him. Elaborately he peeled off his gloves, which had the ends of the fingers missing. It was all done with such aplomb that Flavia smiled.

"Come on, Miss," he said reproachfully, "I'm an uncle now. Aren't my manners proper?"

"Your manners are exceeding proper," she assured him. "Will you take tea?"

"That would be most appreciated," he replied. He leaned forward conspiratorially. "Molly wants to see you."

"She is well?" He nodded. "And the child?"

"Happy as a grig. They've got a room with a lady in town, who looks after Maria while Molly's at work."

"And what about you, Sam?" Flavia queried as the buxom maid, with a disapproving frown, edged the tea-tray around the door. Sam's eyes dwelled on her appraisingly. The girl plumped the tray down so hard the cups rattled, and flounced off.

Whatever would Robert make of the scene? The incongruity was too much, and Flavia had to sneeze into her handkerchief.

"I got a new position," Sam said. "I was at a place in Ducie Street, but it was seven in the mornings till nine at night, with Sundays off. The b—" he recovered himself "—bosses was putting the clock forward in the morning and setting it back in the evening. And if the machines broke down, we had to make up the lost time, with no extra pay."

"But that's dishonest!" Flavia exclaimed.

"That's what they do, Miss," said Sam. "And there was kids there much younger than me. Some of them was so small they had to carry them to work 'cos they was asleep."

"How old?" Flavia queried, indignantly.

"Oh, six or seven. Piecers and scavengers. Their fingers are small, see, to get between the machines."

Flavia thought of children the age of Marianne's Hannah, toiling inside those massive buildings.

"But that's terrible!" she exclaimed. "Are there no laws against it?"

Sam said nothing, but shot her a look far beyond his years.

"I'm sorry," said Flavia, recovering herself. "I interrupted you."

"I ran away," Sam resumed, "and joined Michelangelo's Peep Show. Mick's not really Eye-talian," he confided, "but we dosses down in Angel's Meadow when we're in Manchester, and it has a better ring than O'Leary. I call the people in. Mick works the show, and his Missus takes the rhino: the money, that is."

Flavia tried to envisage this entourage, but could recall only the circus that Ralph had taken her to, so long ago.

"And do you enjoy the life?" she asked, almost wistfully.

"Oh, it's capital!" he replied, eyes aglow. "We do the winter fairs in London and move up north in the spring. Then we follow the big fairs round the towns and come back in October. We see such places!"

Flavia felt a stab of envy. This boy, barely more than a pauper, could go wherever he liked, and do what he wanted. Then she noticed Sam's grubby fingernails against the delicate porcelain. She set down her cup and saucer with a click.

"Thank you for coming, Sam. I am currently engaged, but if you can tell me where Molly is lodging I will endeavour to visit." She paused, aware of how stiff she sounded. "I am happy you are doing so well."

"Marianne," she asked later, "may I invite Molly Simpson here? I would like to see her and the child again, before I am married."

Marianne set down the dress she was hemming.

"She is scarcely a suitable acquaintance. She is in good health and gainfully employed; you should leave it at that."

Flavia felt the sinking sense of committing a *faux pas*. "Please excuse me. I should not have asked. But as Harriet was prepared to accept the girl under my patronage, I thought you might too."

"I know you hold your cousin's memory in high regard," Marianne returned. "But her unorthodox opinions made her an unsuitable influence for a motherless girl."

Flavia flared up at this slur on her cousin. "I have heard you urge pity for girls in Molly's plight!" she exclaimed.

"I do them what good I can, in body and soul. But I do not extend to them the familiarity which should follow respect. There is vice enough on the street, without appearing to condone it."

Flavia's cheeks flamed. She had assumed that because Marianne was her friend, and had encouraged her interest in the condition of the poor, that their moral judgements would be the same. Now she wished she had never spoken.

Dressing that evening for dinner, her eye fell on the boxes holding Bromley's gifts. The ring was inherited, but what about the other pieces? She knew nothing of how his factories were run. Had the money for that bracelet come from the labours of little children?

When Bromley first suggested they attend the Yeomanry Ball, Flavia demurred.

"I don't like balls," she said.

"Why not?" he pressed.

"There is always such a crush." She knew how feeble this sounded. But she could hardly tell the man she was about to marry that she had never attended another ball since quarrelling so disastrously with the man she loved.

"Nonsense," he replied briskly. "That is the charm of a ball. One never knows whom one might meet."

She looked up at the faint inflection in the last sentence. But he was smiling down at her. "It will lift your spirits. Besides, you must allow me to show you off to some of my colleagues. My cousin will be your chaperone; she deserves an evening out. I doubt her dull dog of a husband has taken her to a ball in years."

The room blazed with candles. Long mirrors reflected the colours of women's gowns, intermingled with the blue and white uniforms of the Manchester and Salford Yeomanry, the blue, silver-frogged jackets of the Hussars, and the red coats of regular officers. A band played, but from the volume of conversation, already rising to a roar, Flavia suspected there was more drinking than dancing being done.

She was aware of Robert's eyes on her. As his wife she would attend many such functions in the future. Like the dinner with Bigge, this was another test. She swallowed, feeling around her throat the unaccustomed constriction of his latest gift, a sapphire necklace, matching the long ring heavy on her finger. Bromley found them seats, and excused himself for a moment. The room was crowded and hot; Marianne plied her fan. Through the partition behind them, Flavia heard a booming voice.

"*What's wrong with seven shillings a week?* I says to this fellow. *But they're eating weeds,* he pipes. *So the sons of bitches have eaten up all the nettles for ten miles round,* I told him, *but don't tell me how to run my business. How else could I sell you goods so cheap?*" There was a rumble of laughter. Flavia, used to the polished manners of London drawing rooms, was taken aback.

Bromley returned. "There are people here I want you to meet."

They must be important, thought Flavia. I must remember their names. He ushered Flavia and Marianne through the press. Flavia saw a blur of faces as he made the introductions: Norris, Dodds, Reverend Ethelstan, Captain Birley. They looked at her across the table with hard, evaluating stares, and immediately returned to their conversation. The youngest man, with a regular, almost pretty, face, spoke first.

"There were thousands at the meetings in Birmingham and London. What shall we do if Hunt returns?"

"We can send him a welcoming committee, Mr Hutton, as we did in January," said the captain with a smirk.

"We could close the Theatre Royal," said Ethelstan. "That kept him quiet the last time."

"But what if he does not ask for it?" put in Norris, nervously. "My guess is that having been thwarted once, he will hold his next meeting in the open air."

"Then they'll hear nowt," stated Dodds.

"They don't call him 'Orator' Hunt for nothing," Birley retorted. "They'll hear him all right, and you'll have a riot on your hands. I say meet force with force."

Flavia longed to know what force they were talking about, but dared not interrupt.

"It's all the fault of the Radical press," Norris complained. "Cobbett was bad enough, till he ran off to America. Now every gang of apprentices who can scrape up sevenpence is buying the *Observer*, to stir them up again."

"I reckon it's these Sunday Schools," Dodds grumbled. "They gave no trouble when they couldn't read."

Flavia took breath, then started as Marianne nudged her ankle.

"Are you all right, my dear?" Bromley enquired.

"Perfectly," Flavia responded. "Please continue, gentlemen. I am new to Manchester."

Dodds cast his heavy gaze upon her, obviously disapproving of a woman taking an interest in such matters. The more urbane Norris turned to her.

"I do not wish to alarm you, Ma'am, but there has been talk of seditious groups drilling with pikes."

"Surely this is exaggerated?" Marianne put in. "I go among these people all the time, and have seen in them no disposition to violence."

"Then who shot at Constable Birch last week, when he was bringing that Radical Harrison in from Stockport?"

Harrison arrested! Flavia's eyes met Marianne's.

"Come, gentlemen," Bromley interposed, "you are alarming the ladies. We will leave you to your deliberations. Flavia, an old friend of your father's is here, and wishes to meet you. Did I not tell you that was part of the charm of a ball?"

As they rose from the table, the conversation switched to cotton, nankeen, and the fall in price of four and seven-eighths calico.

"Are they all so fierce?" she asked Bromley lightly.

"Your frivolity is misplaced," he replied. "Those are powerful men: Norris and Ethelstan are magistrates; Hutton their chairman; Birley a captain in the Yeomanry. Dodds could buy and sell your brother five times over, for all his lack of education. Up here they do not play at Reform."

Flavia read the warning. In London she could amuse herself with fashionable notions; in Manchester she would have her husband's reputation to uphold. To her relief, the next person he introduced her to was a confident man in his late forties, with an alert military air: General Sir John Byng.

"So you are Charles Stanton's daughter." He smiled at Flavia, and glanced across the room to where Hutton stabbed the air with his finger. "Our giant-killers don't quite trust me, you know—an unregenerate Whig who refuses to order in the Hussars, flourishing their sabres. If I didn't keep dispersing these dismal gatherings, they would send me home on half-pay! Did you not have a brother? I remember him pestering me once, years ago, to find him a place in the Army."

"That's Lucius. He is married now, with a little boy."

"Good thing I didn't whisk him off to Spain, eh? He might never have come back. But there was a neighbour of yours with me in the Peninsula—promising young fellow—Fairfax. What happened to him?"

Bromley interposed smoothly. "I understand he is travelling overseas."

Flavia turned the conversation to other channels. "Tell me, sir, how do you break up those marches without anyone being hurt?"

"Sympathy, my dear!" he replied with a smile. "How could I command the King's Dragoon Guards, victors over Napoleon's *Grande Armée*, to charge beggars in blankets? These were no Jacobins. They wanted an ear for their grievances. It was the same in Stockport last September. Why call out the troopers? A small force of constables was enough. With a little kindness, they dispersed in peace."

"You make it sound very simple," said Flavia.

Byng gave her a sharp look. "You are a perceptive young woman. Most girls of my acquaintance fall into raptures of congratulation. But you are right. There is more to it than the charm of my address; we are informed of all that passes in their councils. And there is a degree of experience required. Keep calm, don't let them panic. As the Duke says, anyone can march in ten thousand men, but it takes a real general to get them out again!"

Flavia found his cheerfulness refreshing after the magistrates' gloom.

"We shall sleep more soundly knowing you are here to protect us," she said with a smile.

"You must honour us with a visit, sir, when next you come to our part of the country," Bromley added. "The hunting is excellent."

"With pleasure!" replied the general, heartily. "Chasing foxes will make a welcome change from shepherding mobs!"

The music resumed and Bromley led her out on the floor. He danced well; she felt the pressure of his hand on her waist. She wondered again what it would be like being married to this man. In the eyes of the people here, she was already the future Mrs Bromley. Soon Flavia Stanton would be gone forever.

"What are you thinking about?"

"I must practise signing my new name."

He smiled as they swung into a waltz. His grasp tightened; she felt a forgotten pain, as if she had knocked an old bruise. She had danced with Ralph to this melody.

She forced down her misgivings. There was no point dwelling on the past. From this marriage she would gain a home, children, travel, and the opportunity to pursue her interests. Youthful dreams were the price she had to pay.

In the carriage going home, Flavia yawned. A piece of almond from the white soup had stuck in her teeth. She worried at it surreptitiously with her tongue. It was very late, or very early. Marianne's head bobbed on the cushions opposite. Unused to such hours, she was already asleep.

"Robert, could you show me round one of your factories?"

"What on earth for?"

Flavia could hardly tell him she wished to inspect the workers' conditions.

"As your wife, I should not be ignorant of your affairs."

"Business is not the province of a wife. You will have plenty to occupy you at home, I assure you."

Flavia registered the snub. But it pained her to think that the money for her support might be wrung from exhausted children. It was impossible to approach Bromley on such subjects: he withdrew, aloof. Perhaps she could draw him out indirectly.

"What do you think of the new Cotton Factories Registration Bill?"

"Good God!" he exclaimed. "At three o'clock in the morning?"

Flavia would not be frightened off. She could not spend the rest of her life avoiding topics she felt strongly about. "I meant to ask you before," she said, "but I didn't get the chance."

"If you really want to know," Bromley said coldly, "I agree entirely with Mr Peel."

"What did he say?"

"Ask my cousin in the morning. She is sure to have it written down somewhere."

He drew himself back into his corner and twitched down the blind.

"Here it is," called Marianne, on her knees beside a pile of newspapers. *"No children are to be employed under nine,"* she read. *"Children from nine to thirteen are to work no more than twelve hours a day. Mr Peel, of the well-known family of cotton manufacturers, has attacked the Bill, saying that it restricts free labour, supersedes parental authority, and establishes inquisitorial inspection over manufacturers."*

Flavia remembered the men she had heard at the ball. "It is a relief to know there will be some oversight for those poor children."

Marianne, who had been scanning the rest of the page, looked up. "I fear this will make little difference. As there is no provision for inspectors, this is merely a paper law with no teeth. The good employers may enforce its provisions, but they take care of their workers anyway; the rest will merely continue as they are. But enough of that. The samples arrived this morning for your wedding dress. It is time for you to choose."

# 37

# *England, July–August 1819*

Arm outstretched like a Greek statue, Flavia stood unmoving, as the mantua-maker shuffled around her on her knees, deftly twisting and pinning the heavy silk.

"Had I known how much bother this would be," said Flavia with feeling, "I would never have agreed to it!"

"My dear," Marianne smiled, tweaking a fall of fabric, "I was just as anxious. I felt my wedding would roll on like the Juggernaut, whether I was there or not!"

Reassured, Flavia let fall her arm, careful of the sharp pins. So this nervousness was to be expected, not a sign that she had made a mistake. Dresses, gloves, new satin slippers: she ran down the list in her mind. She had not yet visited Molly. She was determined to do it before the wedding; it would be impossible after. Next week was taken up helping Marianne with the final details, but she would be free the following Monday. She must send a note to the address Sam had given.

Marianne's voice came from behind. "I meant to tell you. There is to be another big Radical gathering here in Manchester."

"When?" The woman was working on the bodice now. Flavia could not turn without impaling herself on a dozen pins.

"Next Monday, the ninth of August, near St Peter's Church. I wonder what our acquaintances of the other evening will make of it?"

"Pray for rain, I imagine," said Flavia. "I would love to go," she said wistfully, "just to see it." She remembered the thrill of Harrison's sermon. Great events were in the making, and she longed to take some part in them.

Marianne shook her head. "Robert would never approve."

Bromley raised the subject first.

"It pains me to speak of this, but it has come to my notice that you attended a meeting addressed by that Radical Harrison. Is this true?"

"Marianne and I heard a sermon," she replied. "I was unaware I needed permission to attend church."

His mouth compressed. "I made it plain that you should not dabble in Radical politics. As Mrs Robert Bromley, your every step will be watched and commented on."

Flavia stared at the fireplace, her jaw set. She resented this assumption of control over every aspect of her life. She had given way over her piano-playing, swallowed her true opinion of the rotten boroughs, and suppressed her qualms over his workers. She had undertaken to be his wife, not his daughter. She had never stopped to think before how much older he was.

The voice above her went on. "Monday's meeting has been declared illegal. You must give me your word to take no further part in these activities."

I care passionately about what is happening here, she thought, and he all he sees is a childish whim. She sniffed, humiliated.

"Flavia!" his tone was gentler this time. "I did not wish to upset you." She felt his hands on her shoulders. "A crowd can quickly become a mob. You have no conception of the dangers to which you expose yourself." His fingers gripped in a half-shake, half caress.

She took a deep breath and forced back the tears. She was touchy and nervous with the wedding coming up.

He relaxed his grip and smiled. "Your promise, please. It is so short a time until the wedding."

Now that he was asking, rather than ordering her, she felt more disposed to comply.

"Very well," she conceded.

He followed up his advantage with a long, pressing kiss. The door opened as Marianne returned. Flavia pulled away, embarrassed.

Next day, as they threaded ribbons into the girls' wedding bonnets, Marianne looked up. "I hear next week's meeting has been outlawed."

"I know," Flavia replied. "Robert told me."

Surprised, Marianne went on. "They intend to hold it on the sixteenth, whatever the magistrates say."

Flavia laughed. "Robert made me promise not to go," she explained. "But I have an engagement that day anyway." She did not tell Marianne it was to see Molly.

Molly had changed less than Flavia had expected; still pretty, but with a wariness in her expression that she had lacked before.

From outside came the hum of a large crowd, gathering on the open ground beyond the church. Flavia had passed throngs of them on her way; workmen in groups wearing sashes, some hoisting brightly-painted banners painted with slogans—*Suffrage Universal, Vote by Ballot*—some bearing garlands of leaves; families with women and children in their best clothes, hefting baskets of food. It might have been a picnic.

Flavia had come alone, telling Marianne she was visiting a friend and would be back in the afternoon. She would not linger with Molly; they had little to say. But it pleased Flavia to tie up the loose ends of one part of her life before she began another.

"Are you happy in your employment, Molly?"

"I'm a reeler down at Lockley's Mill," the young woman replied. "Long hours, but the work's regular."

"Will you stay here?" Flavia asked curiously, trying to imagine what it was like to be a mill-girl with an illegitimate child to support.

"No one's asked me to marry them, Miss, if that's what you mean," said Molly, smiling. "I'm putting some money in the Savings Bank," she said proudly. "I'd like to go overseas, and make a new start."

"A friend has just written a book about New South Wales," Flavia said on impulse. "They need young women there. Your child would not be held against you."

"You really think so? But I wouldn't want to marry a convict!"

"Not everybody there is a convict. There is sun, and the air is clean, and the Government helps new settlers with labourers and grain."

Molly's guarded expression eased into momentary hope. Poor Molly, thought Flavia; her lot cannot be easy. There was a timid knock at the door and Molly's landlady came in, leading Maria by the hand. The frail, solemn baby Flavia remembered had grown into a graceful child with her mother's dark, curling hair, but brown eyes more deeply set. Flavia offered the little doll she had brought. Maria turned in query to her mother and reached out with slender arms. She whispered her thanks with a shy smile.

"You have done very well," Flavia said.

She meant the compliment sincerely. All this beauty and promise was Molly's achievement, moulded by her own effort out of disgrace. It was time to go. She stood up, and made her farewells.

Molly, with the child on her hip, led Flavia down to the street. As she opened the door the distant murmur grew. Flavia was about to leave when Molly said hesitantly, "I'm taking Maria to see the parade. You wouldn't like to come too?"

Flavia caught the distant notes of a band. She remembered Sam, and his delight in the fair. Robert could hardly complain if she took one brief look from a distance. She would walk to the end of the road, just for a glimpse.

"Very well," she said, smiling. "A few minutes won't make much difference."

They passed houses and shops, quiet and shuttered as though it were Sunday. From behind a high wall they heard jingling harness, a loud guffaw, and a tinkle of breaking glass.

"Not much work being done in Pickford's today," Molly observed.

The high wooden doors squealed open as they drew level. A squad of horsemen trotted out, wearing the blue-and-white Yeomanry uniforms which Flavia had seen at the ball. She recognised Birley as he turned in the saddle. The horses were nervous; the bits jingled as they tossed their heads.

The troop made a stirring sight, thirty-odd riders in bright uniforms and high shakoes, white sheepskin saddle-covers setting off the gleaming coats of the horses. But there was a half-drunk excitement about them that reminded Flavia of the men who had stopped her that night by the haystack.

Flavia coughed in the cloud of dust. "Shall we turn back?" she suggested, a note of anxiety in her voice.

"We're nearly there, Miss: honest."

Molly wriggled, pointing at the vanishing troop of horsemen.

"Let me carry her," Flavia offered. She scooped the child up. Maria was heavier than Charles. Lithe fingers grabbed at Flavia's gold chain.

"Maria, don't! You'll break it."

"Don't worry, my nephew has pulled it often enough."

The babble of the crowd was closer now. Flavia hitched the child on her hip. Molly touched her arm and pointed. Flavia saw the gap at the end of the street, and a glimmer of haze from the open space beyond.

They stepped out into the road. Halfway across the doll slipped from the girl's grasp. She stiffened and began to cry. Awkwardly Flavia hoisted the struggling child towards her mother. At a shout from behind, Flavia half-turned. She glimpsed a chestnut blur; a staring eye; a flash of blue-and-white. Then the pumping block of muscle hit them like a wall. The ground spun up to meet her. She heard a scream, cut off.

Flavia pulled herself up shakily, taking her weight on grazed palms. Barely a yard away Maria lay still, her head against the red-stained granite kerb. Flavia felt for a heartbeat, but her fingers were numb. She snatched a shard of broken mirror from her reticule and held it to the child's lips. A scatter of dust-motes drifted across its trembling surface: no cloud of breath.

I saw her born, she thought dully; now I have seen her die.

She turned to Molly. She too had been thrown, but not so far. She lay a foot from the rim of stone, the pulse still beating on her wrist.

She must move the child's body and get Molly to a surgeon. But her hands were shaking, her fingers useless as sticks. Why didn't he stop? Why did he not turn back, to see what he had done? Sensible Flavia, she railed at herself, you who always know what to do, kneeling tearless in the middle of the street.

A touch: a woman was bending over her. Beyond, a group of workmen had bunched to a stop around a banner. With Flavia half-dazed and the woman's thick dialect, she could not understand what she was saying, only the final "Tha coom wi' me, lass."

"The trooper ran us down," Flavia whispered. "Please take my friend back to her house..."

The banner dipped as the men propped it against the wall. The woman helped Flavia to her feet and the sad little procession followed her down the road. They had to bang the knocker twice before the landlady would open up to the strangers outside.

They laid the child on the table, and tried to bring her round; fanning her, burning feathers; waving smelling salts. The thin arms, with their fine downy hairs, lay still. One of the men leaned forward and drew the lids down over the brown eyes, fixed now and lifeless.

Flavia turned in desperation to Molly. Her hair was matted with blood. Flavia turned to the white-faced landlady. "Is there a surgeon hereabouts?"

"There's Mr Maxwell down at corner."

"I will pay. Tell me the number of the house, and I will fetch him."

With a doubtful look, the woman complied. Flavia ran downstairs. Guilt gnawed her, and bitter regret. If only the horseman had not been in such haste. If only Maria had not cried so they stopped in the middle of the street. If only Flavia had ignored her outburst and borne her safe to the other side.

If only the surgeon were at home... He was not. He had gone down to the meeting; she might catch him yet. What did he look like? Oh, thickset, gingery hair, half-glasses; a black coat.

She broke into a half-run, regardless of the startled looks of passers-by. Now, her breath catching in her throat, she could see beyond the end of the street a vast mass, dotted with upraised banners hanging limp.

She stopped, scanning the huge crowd. There came the high, clear tone of a man speaking, too far away to make out the words. She stretched on tiptoe, peering over the shoulder of the sweating workman whose knitted grey cap blocked her view.

Never had she seen so many people together. There must have been thousands crushed onto St Peter's Field, lapping like a tide against the walls of the houses. Raised above the sea of heads was a long platform, its banners topped with garlands.

She would never find one among so many. Her anxiety for Molly swelled into a sob. She turned back.

She was almost at the corner of the street when the heads about her turned. Another speaker, shrill with distance, cut across the first. The crowd stirred. There were boos and catcalls; some ragged cheers; the ringing tone of a bugle. A tremor ran through the air, like a collective drawing of breath.

Flavia felt a drumming through the ground. The vast press surged back, squeezing her against the high brick wall behind.

"They are riding us down!" a man cried, unbelieving. A black horse reared above the sea of heads, hooves flailing. A girl screamed. The rider raised his sabre. It swept down in a flashing arc.

The rumour of the crowd swelled into a roar as squads of horsemen, both Yeomanry and Hussars, bore down on the hustings. Steel clashed as an officer knocked up a Hussar's sword.

"Stop!" he shouted. "They cannot get away!"

Again the horsemen cannoned into the crowd. Desperately the people turned to run, but their numbers clogged every exit. Flavia stared in horror as an old woman tripped and the terrified mob flowed over her like a wave.

Fearful of being crushed, Flavia pulled herself up by a rail and clambered onto a ledge. The people struggled past, bloody and scared. She fought not to be swept up in their current. Her purse was gone, her shawl torn away.

As suddenly as it had begun, the *mêlée* was over. Flavia climbed down, shaken and uncomprehending, and walked out onto the trampled field, littered with the jetsam of the fleeing crowd: shoes, a crushed bonnet, a tumbled wicker basket spilling apples. A faint breeze stirred the dust. A woman stood with her head in bloody hands, her bodice an unflattering shade of red, streaking unevenly into the white skirt. The red was blood. A man held the drooping woman up, his arm around her shoulders. "They were using the edge!" he shouted. "The bastards were using the edge!" Further on, she recognised one of the apprentices from her Sunday School sprawled like a piece of discarded rubbish.

Beside the abandoned hustings, with its hacked flagstaff and slashed garlands, Flavia saw two men, gentlemen by their dress. They looked up as she approached, their faces strained.

"Where can I find a surgeon? We were knocked down. My friend is insensible—her little girl is dead."

The men looked at her closely. She realised how odd she must appear, with her hair half-down and clothes askew. "It was one of the Yeomanry, a straggler," she added in corroboration. "I think he was drunk."

"They must all have been drunk," one man said under his breath. "Look, Miss..."

"Stanton."

"You had best go home. This is no place for a young lady. Can you find your way? You look unwell."

Flavia felt a lurch of disappointment. As she turned away, the men resumed their conversation.

"— though what the Deuce Hulton thought he was doing, reading the Riot Act to a crowd that size—"

"Perhaps he thought the troops were in danger."

"From women and children?" They moved away to a flotsam of bodies against the edge of the platform, driven hard against it and suffocated by the press.

Flies buzzed over the streaks and puddles of blood. A banner stirred as she passed; a boy about Sam's age crawled out from beneath its folds. He tried unsteadily to stand.

"Here: let me help you." Flavia set her arm under his elbow and hoisted him upright.

"Got you too, eh, Miss?" remarked the boy almost cheerfully, squinting at the bruise darkening on her forehead. "Gave that Hussar as good as I got, anyroads. Caught him a butt in the belly with my pole."

The boy could not stop talking. She guided him across the littered ground. Why were those men staring at them and doing nothing to help?

"This lad answers the description. I'm arresting you, boy. And you had better come along as well, young lady."

# 38

# England, August 1819

Flavia's head ached. The setting sun, glaring over the wall of the prison-yard, pained her eyes. She was still here after five hours, because nobody would believe her story. Her stomach ground uncomfortably. She had never been so hungry, but without her purse she could buy no food. Impatiently she turned away. What had happened to Molly while she was stuck here?

She had argued fruitlessly with gaolers unconvinced either by the truth or her tears. Now she was incensed by the arrogance of these jacks-in-office. Would they take her seriously if she mentioned Robert's name?

Her pride shrank from it. She had got herself into this predicament; she would get herself out. She could not help contrasting her current plight with the respect she had previously taken for granted. Did the authorities brush aside any young woman unprotected by a husband or father? Was this what Molly had endured for years?

At least she still had her watch. She opened it, cupping it in her hand, aware there must be pickpockets around her. Almost seven o'clock.

An older man pushed through the crowd, better-dressed than those she had yet seen, his head stooped forward apologetically. He doffed his hat. At last, Flavia thought, they have realised their mistake.

"My dear Miss Stanton! Please excuse our lamentable error—so busy today—"

He bobbed along beside her as she strode out of the yard, more angered by his obsequiousness than she had been with his colleagues' neglect. She said nothing, not even when she saw Bromley waiting.

His expression, as he handed her into his carriage, was forbidding. The journey began in prickling silence. Flavia knew he was waiting for an explanation, but she could not bring herself to speak.

"I trust you have sustained no injury," he said at length, coldly.

So much for sympathy, she thought bitterly. I might have been a pedigree dog that ran onto the street, and caused a nuisance.

"A few bruises, nothing more." His stony expression did not change. She continued, with the detachment of one performing a scientific experiment. "We were ridden down by a drunken militiaman as we crossed the road. The child I was carrying was killed."

"I told you to have nothing to do with this unlawful assembly."

"Don't you understand?" exclaimed Flavia, turning towards him. "A little girl—a life snuffed out—like that!" She snapped her fingers. "A child I saw born!"

"You cannot expect me to mourn some mill-girl's bastard," he said dismissively. "You are far too familiar with servants. I am deeply disappointed in you, Flavia. You gave me your word, and you broke it."

Flavia's eyes dropped to the stiff shoulders in their beautifully-cut superfine cloth. "Are you calling me a liar? I said I would not take part in the march, and I did not."

"How can I believe you?" he retorted. "Sneaking out of the house on your own; renewing a most unsuitable association; taking part in a street brawl; then getting yourself arrested! Have you any idea of my humiliation, having to extricate my future wife from a common gaol? Have you no feeling at all for what is due to my position?"

"Have you no feeling for anything else?" she flashed back. She felt the stirring of a new emotion: dislike.

"I will hear no more of this," he stated. "Henceforth you will leave my cousin's house only with my express permission. I will not have my wedding degraded by further scandal."

I explain what happened, Flavia thought, and he accuses me of lying. I could have had my face sliced open like that poor woman, and he would register only the disgrace. Molly may be dead, but he will not lift a finger to find out. She stared out at the brick facades blank under the fading evening, gripped by the crawling certainty that she had made a terrible mistake.

That night she reached a decision. She would not marry this man, so harsh and unfeeling, for whom Maria's death was a mere embarrassment, and her own distress irrelevant. As Robert's wife she would be forever hammered into his mould. Every gesture of independence would be suppressed, and her friendships dictated entirely by his ambition. Handsome, wealthy, charming when it suited him, she realised that what she had seen was only a facade. At heart he was cold and domineering. At least she had discovered his true nature before she was irrevocably bound to him. She could marry without love, but not without respect.

She recalled that day on the Thames, with Ralph; his concern when she quailed from the grim walls of the Tower. Only a little thing, but he had sought to comfort and reassure. Bromley had not even asked if she was hungry.

What had happened to Ralph? The ache of loss reverberated like an echo. He had been angry and humiliated by her accusations: even so, his disappearance made no sense. A strange notion seized her: that Ralph had died that night, and they had kept it from her.

You are distressed by Maria's death, and your fears for Molly, she told herself. This guilt has raised old ghosts. You behaved like a foolish girl, and the man you loved deserted you. But a niggling sense of wrong remained, like the lingering smell of something rotten from beneath a cupboard which has been scrubbed again and again.

Feeling as she now did about Robert, marriage to him was out of the question. There would be a terrible row, and scandal to follow. She must leave Marianne's house, of course, and Lucius would leave her in no doubt of his disappointment. She would be poor and alone; no more gems and fine clothes, and dinners with the powerful.

But once the decision was made she felt an immediate release. All these things she would willingly accept as the price of her freedom. How would she support herself? She could not return to Fontclaire; she must find a room somewhere. She had Harriet's jewellery to sell. Perhaps she could earn a living from piano recitals, or giving lessons.

Her mind veered back to Molly. Had the surgeon got her message? Again she saw Maria lying rigid, her gaze fixed, never again to see the dawn. Flavia wept.

Next morning, calm in her new resolve, she confessed to Marianne what had happened.

"How distressing!" Marianne exclaimed. "Robert can be hard at times ..." Her voice tailed off. "We have some good news at least," she continued. "We had a message that Molly Simpson has recovered. She said to thank you for trying to help."

"Thank me!" said Flavia bitterly. "Had I had not been carrying Maria, she would still be alive."

"Don't take this death upon yourself," Marianne urged. "You cannot unmake the past with regret. To visit the Simpson girl was unwise, but the fault lies with that drunken trooper."

"He was one of Birley's men. I had thought of asking Bromley to use his influence to bring a case against him. Upon reflection I would be wasting my time."

"You cannot condemn Robert entirely without giving him a chance to prove himself. He was angry yesterday because he believed you had broken your promise. Perhaps now his temper has cooled he will be more open to persuasion."

"Perhaps." Flavia had said nothing to Marianne about her intention to call off the wedding. She must tell Bromley first: she owed him that at least.

Marianne passed over the morning paper. "Here is a report on the whole dreadful business. They are calling the Captain 'Hurley-Burley' now."

Flavia gave a wan smile.

"And they explain, too, why General Byng was not consulted. He was at his headquarters in Pontefract. He had been told he would not be needed."

"Another 'if only'," said Flavia grimly.

Flavia assembled the gifts Bromley had given her. Tomorrow she would hand them all back. If only it were that easy to walk out of an engagement! 'Jilt' would be the kindest thing said about her. But she did not care. The sooner she left this stifling provincial town with its leaden respectability, the better.

She wrote a note, and rang the bell for a servant.

"Deliver this to Mr Bromley. And wait for a reply."

*Three o'clock tomorrow.* She stared at the note, trying to discern from the writing what sort of mood he was in. At least he had agreed, however tersely, to the interview. It loomed before her all the next morning, like a visit to the dentist for an aching tooth. Repeatedly she rehearsed her arguments. She sorted and re-sorted her little pile of boxes. She tried to reassure herself: by this evening it will all be over. Surely he must understand now that we have no common ground on which to build a marriage.

Time to go. Flavia gave a shaky sigh to dispel her nervousness and knocked on Marianne's door.

"I have asked Bromley to call," she explained.

Marianne had been tying the ribbons of her bonnet. "Shall I join you?" she asked anxiously, taking in the shadows under Flavia's eyes, and the carefully-wrapped parcels in her hands.

"Thank you, but no. You have an engagement already this afternoon. I must see him privately."

"Can you face this, after the shock of yesterday?" Flavia nodded. "I shall instruct the servants to stay away."

"Thank you." What a pity, Flavia reflected, that Bromley had so little of his cousin's consideration.

The drawing room was unusually quiet. As the windows had not been opened, the air was heavy. Faintly from outside she could hear the call of a bird. She scrutinized yet again the step she was about to take. Had the shock of Maria's death distorted her judgement? How would she manage? Had Bromley changed, or had she come to know him better?

She looked around with a start. While she had been musing, he had entered the room, quiet as a cat.

"You said you had an urgent matter to discuss," he said sharply. "I trust you have no further disclosures to make."

"I have done nothing to be ashamed of," she returned. "But I must know where you stand." Nothing in his expression made this easier. "Do you still believe I lied to you about taking part in the march?"

"You are very cool about it," he said with a little snort of disbelief. "But as you insist, yes, I do."

"And you expect me to apologise for my behaviour?"

"Most certainly. Thank goodness you can see that, at least."

"Will you find the man who ran me down, and have him brought to trial?"

He made an abrupt gesture, unusual in so controlled a man. "What new folly is this? Has my cousin put you up to it? I can see now it was mistake letting you come here. I should never have allowed it."

He turned away as he spoke and strode across the room, tapping his thumb on the ledge of the mantelpiece with the air of a man at the limit of his patience.

This exaggerated forbearance goaded Flavia to anger. "Good God!" she cried. "It has nothing to do with Marianne. Must I ask your permission to think?"

"Think? What use it is in a woman to think! Napoleon was right about that at least: *What a mad idea to demand equality for women! Women are nothing but machines for producing children.* Except in your own case," he went on, cuttingly, "your meddling kills children rather than produces them."

Flavia flinched. She gestured at the boxes on the table. "If that is truly how you feel, our engagement must end."

He straightened up; looked from her to the boxes, then back again.

She swallowed. "I am sorry. The mistake was mine. I should never have agreed to this marriage in the first place. We are too unlike."

She twisted the ring off her finger to set it on the top of the pile, but her hand shook, and the jewel rolled to the floor in a blaze of blue fire. She stooped to pick it up.

Bromley, breathing heavily, seized her wrist and pulled her up to face him.

"Do I understand you aright? You walk in here, two weeks before our wedding, and calmly inform me you've changed your mind?"

He might have been acting before; now his rage was real. She could feel it in the force of his grip.

"I am sorry if it offends you, but yes. Please let me go." She tried to pull away, but he wrenched her closer.

"Not so fast, my girl. You were keen enough before. Why this change of heart?"

"Must you haggle like a shopkeeper? You won't believe me, and you don't care! Scores of people were hurt and killed. I was run down and arrested! Does that not matter to you? Have you no sense of justice? Or is the law something for you to manipulate for your own ends?"

"What are you saying?" he said, hoarsely. His tone frightened her.

Her wrist burned. "Please let me go. Marianne is expecting me."

"Marianne is out for the afternoon," he said flatly.

Flavia was silent. With his free hand Bromley snatched up the ring. She glanced at the door, but he blocked her way.

"So the name of Bromley is not good enough. Have you taken some other lover, who can offer you the rank I cannot? You were less particular with Fairfax, as I remember."

"Don't be ridiculous. Ralph has nothing to do with it."

"Has he not? Still *Ralph* after all this time?" He shook her. "I'll wager you did not stiffen so, when he touched you. You were in love with him, weren't you?"

"Yes!" She flung the answer at him. Her heart hammered.

"He's gone for good! You won't see him again!"

Repelled, she tried to turn away, but he pulled her roughly to him, his fingers digging into her shoulders.

"I will not be made a laughing-stock." Her finger hurt as he strained it back and wrenched the ring over her knuckle. "You gave your word to marry me, and marry me you shall."

Flavia struggled against him, but this only inflamed him further. "Our wedding will proceed. You will be mother to my children, and mistress in my home."

"You cannot force me! I will never agree!"

He slapped her; her head snapped aside, cheek stinging. "I will give you no alternative."

His weight bore her downwards. The floor was hard beneath her back. She opened her mouth to cry out; his hand pressed it shut. She struggled and tried to twist free, but she was trapped, pinned down. He loomed above her, blocking out the light. His mouth closed over hers.

# 39

## *England, August 1819*

He had gone. Sobbing, she pulled herself shakily upright, and blundered to her bedroom, turning the key, locking the door. She leaned against it, shuddering in a terrible guilt. She tugged shut the curtains, trying too late to hide. She tore off her clothes and washed with jerky strokes. Her body was not hers any more, but bruised and fouled. The cold water made her shivering worse.

What had he done to her? It hurt to walk. No one must know what had happened. She must wash her clothes.

She should have kept some of the water in the jug, but she had used it all, trying to scrub away every scent and trace. And there was only a scrap of soap, slippery and useless. She could not go outside to the laundry, and dared not call a maid. Tears spilled over the back of her hands: she could not see what she was doing. Desperately she shoved the stained and bloody gown down the back of her dressing table. Tugging at the ring only swelled her knuckle more. Her night-dress mocked her with its virginal white. She crept into bed.

The afternoon hung motionless outside the window. She heard noises from outside, a dog barking, a child calling. Stupefied by shock, she lay unheeding.

The light faded. A knock at the door. She stared at the criss-cross weave of the sheet.

"Flavia? Are you there?" Marianne's voice.

"I'm resting." Nothing would ever be the same again.

A keener tone, with a note of concern, "Are you unwell?"

"A headache," she called, trying to keep her voice steady. That lie would do as well as any other.

"May I come in? Your door is locked."

Flavia rose reluctantly and opened it, then returned quickly to the bed, swiftly pulling the coverlet up over her bruised shoulders. She turned away.

"My dear! What is the matter? You are white as a ghost!"

Fingertips touched her forehead.

"I hope it is not that knock you took—shall I send for the doctor?" Marianne half-rose from the edge of the bed. "You poor girl! You're trembling—"

"Don't bother him," she gulped. Tears welled up again at Marianne's sympathy. She must not let them fall. "It's yesterday. I'll be better in the morning." Flavia dared not catch her eye.

Marianne sounded unconvinced. "If you are sure... do you want a sleeping-draught?"

Flavia nodded, snatching at the promise of oblivion. She heard the rustle of Marianne's skirts as she left, and her return. Flavia levered herself carefully upright, clutching her nightgown tight at her throat. Her teeth chattered against the edge of the glass, but she swallowed most of the syrup, heavy with the taste of laudanum.

When she awoke it was full morning. Marianne sat upright by the bed, her face stern. Behind her on the table Flavia glimpsed the crumpled gown she had so desperately discarded the day before.

"Please explain to me," Marianne demanded, "what this is about? You were welcomed as a guest under our roof! How could you so betray our hospitality?"

Flavia was too astounded to reply.

"Had you no thought of how I would feel, knowing my home has been used as a house of assignation! I am appalled that Robert would consent to such a thing! That you should be so lost—"

"I didn't want to," Flavia whispered.

"Please, Flavia: no lying excuses."

"I didn't want to," she repeated, raising her voice with an effort. "I told him I would not marry him. I never thought..." A great wave of humiliation broke over her.

Marianne frowned at her.

"I gave everything back. The ring too. But he forced it back on." She spat on her knuckle to twist the ring free and held it out, her hand uncertain.

Marianne took it, startled. She set it down. "What are you trying to say?"

"He said he would not be made to look a fool. He said—oh, what does it matter. It's too late anyway." She broke off.

There was a moment of silence.

"But I *won't* marry him," Flavia added, almost to herself.

Marianne leaned forward. "Are you trying to tell me," she said in an altered tone, "that Robert..?" She paused.

Flavia turned towards her with a sigh. "Choose whatever words you like," she said tiredly. "They are all ugly." Her lip quivered.

Marianne saw the bruise on her cheek, the dark smudges on her collarbone. Her hand came up to her mouth. "Oh, no."

The clothes were burned. Flavia lay in her darkened room, her mind like a music-box out of tune, endlessly replaying every intimate detail. These things did not happen to girls of good family. She had heard vague warnings of men "taking advantage", but she had never anticipated this: humiliating, painful, obscene.

So this was what they meant by *violation;* this gross intrusion into her inmost self, defiling everything. The sight of her body filled her with shame; she felt his eyes on her again, and the weight of his body pressing her down. She shuddered.

Word went out that she was ill with a fever. Bromley tried to call but Flavia refused to see him. Initially Marianne shared her indignation. But as the date of the wedding grew closer, while Flavia held inflexible, Marianne began to waver. When Flavia ripped up a third letter from Bromley, unread, Marianne voiced her doubts.

"Are you sure of what you are doing? At first I agreed you should sever all connection with him. But what options do you have? Perhaps you should let the wedding stand." Flavia made an impatient movement, but Marianne reached out to stay her hand. "I have discussed this with Edmund. As much as we deplore Robert's conduct, you must grant that his intentions in the long term are honourable. It is not as though he means to abandon you."

Flavia felt the ground slipping from under her feet. Bromley's words echoed: *"I will give you no alternative."*

"It is a reprehensible thing he has done, Flavia, but he regrets it deeply."

"Have you been speaking to him?"

"Edmund held that some contact must be made for the sake of your future. Continue with the marriage and there will be no stain on your reputation."

"*My* reputation! He was at fault!"

"My poor girl! What other match can you make now?"

So Bromley had subverted even Marianne. Now Flavia had no one to turn to. What could she do?

"I'll go back to the country."

"With your brother? Can you see his family cutting themselves off from society for your sake?"

"I won't tell them," she said doggedly.

Marianne threw up her hands in exasperation. "These things always leak out. Servants talk. And the wedding date is so close! All the invitations are returned."

She resumed her argument. "I know the topic distresses you. But have you considered that he may simply have been carried away by the strength of his feelings?"

Flavia gave an ugly laugh. Jealousy, anger, aggrieved pride: these were Bromley's true feelings, hidden from his cousin all her life. She would not acknowledge them now.

"And there is another thing I beg you to consider. What if you should bear his child?"

Flavia had lain awake agonising over this very possibility. A loathed incubus might already be lodged inside her, growing. Perhaps it would die. Perhaps (she recalled conversations half-overheard) she could visit old Sarah.

But the memory of little Maria haunted her. At least a child would be something that belonged to her. But how could she support it, or herself? It was hopeless.

Flavia sat alone in the breakfast-room. The windows faced east and Marianne, worried by her pallor, had settled her there to catch the morning sun. Flavia was leafing through the morning papers, but there was little in them to lift her spirits. They had dubbed the St Peter's Field massacre "Peterloo": eleven killed, they said; four hundred injured. From what Flavia had seen, this estimate was much too low. How many of the wounded would alert the authorities by lodging complaints or seeking help? The Exchange was closed; soldiers patrolled the streets. The correspondent for the "The Times" had been arrested. The Prince Regent had offered the Manchester magistrates his congratulations. A meeting of public protest had been cancelled because of the military precautions taken against it. It was rumoured that Hunt, too, would be arrested.

Flavia remembered the mood of the rally; cheerful, almost festive. She laid the paper down. The ruin of so many hopes only weighed further on her spirits.

Heavy footsteps rang down the passage; the door flew open. At the sight of Bromley Flavia sprang to her feet, poised like a deer for flight.

"Don't you understand?" he shouted at her. "You must marry me now!"

Her anger flared. "Never!"

"You have no money. Your brother will not keep you!"

"Have you seen to that already?"

"What will you do?"

"I'll think of something."

"Don't think you've won, Flavia. I'll have you yet. I always get what I want, in the end."

Flavia confronted him. "That's all I am to you, isn't it? Something you want! If I married you, I would be merely another possession. What lack do you have that I could fill? You are sufficient to yourself. You don't need a wife: you need a mirror."

Bromley took a step towards her. Flavia shrank back. To her relief, Edmund appeared in the doorway.

"The wedding stands," Bromley said tightly. "You have the week to come to your senses."

He turned on his heel. Flavia sat down abruptly.

Returning to her room, the first thing she saw was the hateful ring, back on her dressing-table. She could barely bring herself to touch it. Harriet had told her once that in India sapphires were thought unlucky because they were under the influence of Saturn. What joy had this one brought to her? She marched upstairs to Edmund's study and flung it bouncing on the desk. "Send this back. If I see it again, I swear I will smash it with a hammer."

Without waiting for a reply, she walked out.

Seven days. Flavia was at her wit's end. She had nowhere to turn. Lucius would take Bromley's side; he had worshipped too long at that shrine to overthrow his idol now. Insistent, Marianne and her husband urged her to forgive Bromley and take up his offer, as her only remedy for disgrace. With no money and no friends, she could not fight him and them together.

A tap at the door interrupted her thoughts: Marianne.

"There is someone in the parlour to see you."

"I am not at home to visitors."

"I thought you might make an exception. It is Molly Simpson."

Flavia rose, perturbed. She could not send Molly away. "I shall come directly."

She made her way down the hall. The drawing room door was shut: no one had used it since that day.

Molly stood as she entered. "I hope you don't mind, Miss," she said, in some confusion. "I heard you were sick."

Poor Molly; her face was drawn and her eyes shadowed.

"Sit down—please. It is I who should ask your pardon. I feel so guilty. If I had held onto Maria, she would still be alive."

"It's good of you to say so, Miss. But the pace that rider was going, no one could have kept their grip. Grieving won't bring her back." Impulsively Molly leaned forward and touched Flavia's arm. "You'll be married soon, and that will take your mind off it."

Flavia could pretend no longer.

"No, I won't," she said, shortly. "Be married, that is. I would not marry Bromley if he were the last man in the world."

Molly stared at her. Flavia stumbled on, groping for words. "When first I discovered you were with child, I condemned you as did everyone else. Now I fear I may be in the same way myself."

Molly looked up, startled. "By someone else than Mr Bromley?"

Flavia shook her head.

"Then why won't you marry him?" said Molly.

Flavia tried to speak, but the word "rape" stuck in her throat. Seeing her distress, Molly said softly, with a country-girl's directness: "Did he force you?"

Flavia nodded. One did not weep in front of servants. She rubbed her eyes and gulped.

"What will you do?" Molly asked quietly.

"I don't know," said Flavia with a sob. "That's the trouble: I honestly don't know."

"Poor Miss Flavia," said Molly, holding out her arms; and Flavia clung to the factory-girl, sobbing despite herself.

"Now," said Molly at length, dabbing at Flavia's hot cheeks with a red cotton handkerchief, "we need to come up with something."

"We?" repeated Flavia, stupidly.

"Look, Miss," said Molly firmly, "us poor people have our pride too. You stuck by me when nobody else did, not even my own family. I haven't forgotten. I'll help you if I can. I know what it's like to be on your own."

Flavia squeezed her hand in gratitude. Forming in her mind were the first outlines of a plan.

The parlour clock struck its hollow chime: half past eight.

"Please excuse me, I will retire," Flavia said. Marianne looked up. Flavia knew what she was thinking. *Tell me if you tire early in the evening…*

Flavia hated to deceive Marianne like this; but these good people did not know Bromley as she did. Still, it was a miserable recompense for their hospitality. Swiftly she changed into travelling clothes. Her portmanteau was already packed. She scribbled a final note: *Please forgive me. I must go away. Thank you for your many kindnesses.*

She eased the window open, let down her luggage, and climbed out. As she slipped through the trees she checked for the hard lump of Harriet's jewellery sewn into her jacket. *"Brides' jewellery"* indeed; Harriet would have understood that this was her only means of escaping an intolerable marriage. She thanked her cousin for her forethought.

Molly was waiting in the lane. She hefted the portmanteau, rather more easily than Flavia had done.

"Sammy's got a gig round the corner," she whispered.

"Thank you, Molly," said Flavia with feeling. "Goodbye. I shall never forget your help."

"Forget the goodbyes," Molly retorted, "I'm coming too. You need a maid."

Flavia felt a spurt of hope. "But what about your lodgings? Your work?"

"I can't stand it there, Miss, now that Maria's gone. I keep waiting for her to walk in the door."

Flavia was profoundly grateful. A lady travelling with a maid would attract far less attention than one on her own, and Molly had experience of supporting herself. Not that their escapade was likely to last long before their money ran out. She hardly cared, so long as they left Bromley and the wedding behind.

Lucius stood at the bottom of the staircase. He had just supervised the hanging of his mother's portrait. Reframed and cleaned, hung on the newly-painted wall cleared of Harriet's clutter, it gleamed with fresh colour. People had always said how much Lucius resembled his mother. He had her looks and while Flavia had Father's brains—and obstinacy. Still, in a few days she would no longer be his responsibility. She would be safely married off to Bromley, with babies before long to distract her from her foolish notions.

Lucius congratulated himself. Little Charles grew more rewarding every day. He had just bought him his first pony, a plump little creature the colour of butter. Caroline was in a much better humour now they had moved to London; she had shown it last night. Best of all, Mrs Lennox had stayed at Fontclaire. She had grown increasingly domineering since Charles was born, and always took her daughter's part. A gentleman should not be outnumbered in his own house.

His mind moved to the wedding. Tomorrow he must remember to have Caroline's new lace collected. He would never hear the end of it if he forgot. Caroline at twenty was much more assertive than Caroline at seventeen. His mind, unbidden, presented him a picture of Caroline at forty, sharp-voiced as her mother, opinionated and solid. No, he reassured himself; she is far too sweet a girl ever to coarsen like that. Never must she wear those ghastly turbans.

With a final satisfied glance at the portrait, Lucius climbed the stairs to his new study. It had once been Flavia's bedroom, but she would not need it again. Lucius had replaced the old-fashioned yellow wallpaper, and installed some comfortable modern chairs and a new writing-desk. He had just sat down and was opening his folio of investments when the candles jumped to a sudden draught.

"Bromley! I thought—"

"Where is she? Has she written to you?"

"Who?" queried Lucius, mystified.

"Your precious sister. She's vanished. What sort of a fool is she trying to make of me? Four days till the wedding and she runs away!"

"Did you quarrel?" Lucius ventured timidly.

Bromley glared at him. "I may have pressed my suit a little vigorously."

Lucius had expected Bromley to be more subtle. He should have known what a little prude Flavia was, and not frightened her off. "What the deuce did you do?"

"Don't come the injured brother with me," Bromley retorted. "You are in no position to complain. Don't tell me you hadn't bedded Caroline before you wed her."

Appalled, Lucius stood slowly. "Flavia wouldn't have run away if she had been willing," he said, thinking aloud. Vainly he searched the angry face before him for a sign of remorse. "Why did you do it? Couldn't you have left her alone for a week? This time you have gone too far. My sister's honour is in my hands. I demand satisfaction."

*"You? Honour?* Don't be ridiculous."

Lucius reddened. "This is not the conduct of a gentleman," he stammered.

Bromley turned on him. "You'll get no return on damaged goods! Be grateful I am still prepared to marry her—if I can find where she is."

Lucius sat down again, acutely uncomfortable. "How long has she been gone?"

"Three days. I tracked them as far as Chester."

"Them?"

"She had a maid with her. That country wench with the bastard child."

Lucius sighed. Trust Flavia to trail her lame ducks all over the countryside.

"I suspect they have taken the road west, but I have no time to go haring over North Wales. Flavia may be able to walk out on the wedding arrangements without so much as a backward look, but I cannot. I had hoped to retrieve her and talk her out of this folly before any more harm was done." Bromley pulled on his gloves. "She's your sister: *you* find her."

With a slam that sent the candlesticks jumping, he was gone.

Flavia sheltered in the lee of the cliff, watching the sea. She had never spent so long beside it before. She was fascinated by the play of the tumbling waves, their energy and heft; the lure of the faint gleam marking the distant horizon. The salt wind flowed past her face, clean and free.

The first days in the village she had been tense and short-tempered. She had slept fitfully last night, her mind churning; guilty for walking out on Marianne; fearful for her own future.

Today would have been her wedding-day. She had woken early, gripped by a dull cramp, and searched eagerly for the first spots of bleeding. The crimson stains had left her dizzy with relief. She had shaken Molly awake to tell her, whispering so their landlady in the other bedroom would not hear. Molly had got up in the grey light of dawn and made a pot of tea to celebrate. Tea and toast in a Welsh cottage at dawn: a strange wedding-breakfast.

Afterwards she walked the beach, her mind churning with snatches of thought and stabs of feeling which vanished before she could grip them. Ahead the sun glossed the wet sand. Seagulls circled screaming above. She lifted her skirts, stepping over a little stream that braided its waters with the beach. The row of footsteps behind her were dints in the slick crust. Every certainty of her past life was gone.

She had crossed her Rubicon.

# 40

## *England, October 1819*

The wind blew keen from the Irish Sea, blurred by the drizzle. With his horse up to its fetlocks in mud, Lucius followed the women's trail; finding a pawnshop here, slipping a shilling to an ostler there; self-consciously accosting coachmen and grinning carters outside low inns. Caroline had raged and sulked when Lucius cancelled their wedding trip to Manchester, denying him her bed out of spite. With each fruitless day of searching, his meagre sympathy for his sister abated, and his resentment of his wife's petulance grew. There was a chambermaid at Chester whose smile of invitation caught his eye. It would serve Caroline right if he took up her offer... but it was his wife's kindness he wanted.

Flavia answered the banging at the door. She was not surprised to see Lucius standing there, rain dripping off the brim of his hat; she had known they must be found eventually.

"Ah, Lucius. Come in," she said, calmly.

Lucius ducked beneath the low lintel, leaving muddy bootmarks on the flagged floor. "You're very cool about all the trouble you've caused," he said indignantly. He had rehearsed this meeting in his mind; but there was something unseemly about her self-possession. "You should be in a Roman *palazzo* on your honeymoon, not hiding in this dingy hole at the back of nowhere."

"A pot of tea, please, Molly," called Flavia, as though this were an afternoon call. If this was how she behaved with Bromley, thought Lucius, no wonder he lost his patience.

"Flavia," said Lucius, with an older brother's authority, "I deeply regret what has happened. But there is only one way you can salvage your reputation. Distasteful as it may seem, you must take up Bromley's offer of marriage."

"No."

"Come," he pleaded, exasperated, "you can't lurk here forever, like the Ladies of Llangollen! You have no money, and I will give you none. You have humiliated Bromley, had your revenge on him, if you like. His keeping open the offer is most forbearing."

"Forbearing?" Flavia exclaimed, stung to anger. "To legitimise with a licence what he has already taken without?"

Her intransigence provoked Lucius in his turn. "Don't carry on so!" he said bluntly. "You're not the first woman this has happened to!"

"How can you be so callous about your own sister! It may not matter to you, but it matters to me." She turned away.

Lucius reached out to her shoulder, but at its stiffness, his hand dropped away.

"Everything matters to you, Flavia: that's your trouble. You should learn to take things more easily. You're twenty-three now. Don't become a sour old maid."

"Hardly a maid," she retorted savagely, rounding on her brother. Lucius reddened. He looked like a wet dog, with his rain-darkened hair plastered flat against his skull. Flavia was incensed that Bromley's offer of marriage should exonerate him from all blame in her brother's eyes. How could Lucius consent to act as a lackey for the man who had so abused her! It was time her brother heard the truth.

"How like Bromley to bully you into doing his dirty work," she burst out, "and how like you to accept the obligation, then blame me for it!"

She paused for breath. "I will not creep, chastised, to the altar. The crime and guilt are Bromley's, not mine. He took my honour by force. You gave yours away. What would you not do for him, Lucius, if he asked you? Father would be ashamed."

His face paled beneath its sheen of water.

"I will collect you tomorrow at ten," he said, and walked out.

The uncertain summer lapsed into autumn. As they journeyed home it poured incessantly, the rain pelting down in hard drops that rattled the coach windows as they wrangled within.

"You have chosen your path," Lucius argued. "But don't expect the rest of us to suffer on your account. It is bad enough that you walked out so close to the wedding. If the real story gets out, your ruin will be absolute. Bromley will hold his tongue as long as he expects you will marry him. Convince him of your refusal, and there is no knowing what he might do."

"Is that a warning or a threat?"

"You may take it as you like," he retorted. "Remember that if you don't like your situation, you have the power to change it. I know a dozen women who would leap at the chance to marry Robert Bromley. But then, they are not so particular as you."

As soon as the rain eased, Lucius sat up with the driver. Flavia reflected that her words at their meeting must have offended him deeply; his manner had been distant since. After seemingly interminable days she glimpsed Beacon Hill on the skyline, followed by the familiar landscape of home. The horses jogged steadily through the village, past the turnoff to Ash Park. She remembered a tag from her father's favourite Goldsmith:

*Now lost to all, her friends, her virtue fled*
*Near her betrayer's door she lays her head.*

Why did the blame lie always with the woman? It was never the man who was cast out, to scavenge such scraps of charity as were tossed his way.

The lodge gates of Fontclaire Priory swung open at their approach, the trees of the avenue, their leaves brown now and falling, sombre in the rain. On her last visit Flavia had felt unwelcome in her brother's house. Now it would be little more than a familiar prison. Her choice lay between making a hateful marriage, a slow poisoning of the spirit; or being immured for the rest of her life as a sacrifice to propriety.

She felt a surge of anguish, daunted by a future severed from love, friends, children, any choice over how she spent her days. Should she not marry Robert after all? But the thought of submitting herself to his touch revolted her.

She felt a hand on her sleeve.

"Never mind, Miss," Molly whispered. "You'll manage, don't worry."

Mrs Lennox met them at the door, Vickery hovering behind her.

"Your old rooms are taken," she said briskly. "You will use the old nursery in the tower."

So that was to be her status here, Flavia thought: above the servants, but below the guests. The footman stared at her rudely as they started up the stairs.

"And silence that mangy bitch," Mrs Lennox called after her. "It's been howling in the yard ever since it arrived from Manchester. I won't have it in the house."

This was too much for Flavia. "Mrs Lennox!" The older woman wheeled on the narrow staircase, stern-faced as a gaoler, puffing from the climb.

"I lived in this house for twenty years. I know every brick and every stone. I was born here; I shall probably die here. And if I choose to take my dog from one room to another, I shall do so."

Flavia swept past her into the bedchamber. Stupid, narrow-minded woman, clinging to her scrap of authority, afraid I might snatch it from her. Or does she consider her daughter so perfect that she instinctively belittles everyone else? Caroline, with her doting husband, a son, a fine house—*two* fine houses; what possible threat to her did Flavia represent? If Alicia Lennox had calculated the true measure of her insignificance, she might have been more civil.

Next day Flavia took stock of her situation. She had a suite of sorts in the Abbot's Tower: her bedchamber, its thick stone walls whitewashed, with a deep embrasure for a window; a small dressing-room which Molly could use, and the old schoolroom, reached by a winding stair. This at least was lined, with shelves for her favourite books, and room for storage in the deep cupboard where she and Lucius had played hide-and-seek as children. Happier times: she remembered their excitement at discovering behind the loose boards at the back a cobwebbed passage leading onto the hall roof, and their father's quiet smile when they told him about it.

Now the room was empty except for her trunks and a heap of old furniture. She could clear part of it at least for a space of her own. She gave orders for her mother's pianoforte to be carried upstairs. Even Mrs Lennox could not deny her that.

Hester, muddy and pining, was retrieved from the stable-yard and scrubbed down. Thinner and more mournful-looking than ever, she followed Flavia everywhere, nails clicking on the floor. Whenever Flavia stopped, the dog collapsed in an untidy heap, scratching at patches of irritated skin. Flavia resolved to walk her every day. It would give her something to do.

Harriet's lilies, in their tarnished brass pots with the blue-and-white china handles, had been dumped on the schoolroom floor. The flowers had long withered to shrivelled black sticks. Perhaps she could plant out the bulbs in the spring; as she prodded tentatively at the loose soil, the dried stalks fell away. Something at least had survived, a wiry seedling, with delicate rows of rounded grey-green leaves.

It was unlike any plant that Flavia had ever seen. She was mystified until she remembered the seed she had thrust into this pot in Harriet's room in London, so long ago. She had not thought of it since. Whatever it was, it must be hardy, to have survived with so little attention. Harriet, she remembered, had meant to take it down to Kew. How desperately she now missed her cousin's good advice! Carefully Flavia watered her find; a libation to Harriet's spirit. She set the little tree beside the fire, where it would get some warmth. She remembered how cold these rooms grew in winter.

The following day she unpacked the trunks sent on from Manchester. There was no note with them; Flavia grieved for the severed friendship. She had hoped Marianne might understand how deep was the need which had driven her to flee. But Flavia had seen before how families closed ranks in times of trouble, even when their members were manifestly in the wrong.

Anything which had been bought for the wedding, she cast aside. Those afternoons of lavish spending, in retrospect, seemed unreal. Now the sight of the fine lace nightgowns, with their ruffles and ribbon inserts, chilled her. Molly pored over the boxes lovingly, unable to understand how anyone could throw way such beautiful clothes, all new.

"You take them," Flavia said. "We are near enough in height, and you may marry one day. Only don't wear them where I can see them."

Molly was overcome by her good fortune. Then her smile faded. "You might need them again yourself, Miss."

"Not I," said Flavia bleakly. "I shall never marry."

Molly pushed the stack of boxes aside, with the look of someone who has come to a decision. "Begging your leave, Miss, but it's not always like it was with Mr Bromley. You can't let that spoil the rest of your life."

This was too close to what Lucius had said for her to take dispassionately. She felt again the rush of anger that always accompanied any mention of Robert.

"You've little enough to thank men for," she retorted.

Molly went on undaunted. "It was different for me. I loved Jem and he loved me and I thought it was the most wonderful thing in the world. I wanted it as much as he did."

Flavia turned sharply away and stared out the window, but Molly continued. "We would have wed, but Jem was caught poaching and sent to gaol. He took fever and died. That's why I wouldn't say who Maria's father was; I didn't want her being jeered at for a convict's child."

"And I'll tell you something else. When I went to London and my sister and I fell out, I went with men for money to live. No one else would give me any. Mostly it was bad, with the men drunk and rough, and me feeling frightened and ashamed of myself. But even then there were some who were kind to me and made me laugh, and cared about whether I had food to eat or a coat to keep me warm."

When Flavia looked back, Molly had gone. Flavia let go the box of gloves she had been clutching. She had gripped it so tightly that the edge had pressed into her skin. She opened out her fingers and saw the white line cut across her palm.

Was this what Molly warned her against, clinging so tightly to her grievance that she became shaped by it? Already she was exhausted by the effort of holding in such anger. She felt no better for it; her memories of the rape had a stale momentum of their own.

How hard it was for Molly to admit she had been a prostitute! Of course this was the only way the girl could have supported herself. But by telling the truth, Molly might well have lost her position.

Flavia had no intention of dismissing her. In a world more just, women would not need to sin in order to survive. She could understand Molly's situation better, now she had suffered herself. If only she could comprehend her own.

Why had Bromley done this to her? It was not love, or even lust. Those she could understand. He had been cold and controlled throughout. That was why she felt so worthless and used. And if he wanted her now, it was only because she had refused him, and as he had said, he always got what he wanted.

With this understanding came a fragile calm, like the first skin over a wound. She would fight to safeguard whatever was left of her self-respect, no matter what pressure was brought to bear.

Brave words, she thought with a sigh. Robert would not give up yet.

Unpacking her piano music, she found her Beethoven sonatas. The ones she had learned before were too ebullient to match her mood. Here was an *Andante* that spoke of grief and plodding persistence. She played it over till she had it by heart. Someone else had felt as bereft as she did. Inside the music she was less alone.

By afternoon the drizzle had cleared and the sky was a light dove-grey. As Flavia tied on the dog's lead, she noticed that the leather of the collar was cracked. She must approach Lucius for an allowance. If only Father had left her money in her own right! But she suspected he had invested it towards her marriage-settlement; a sensible provision at the time when Ralph had been on the verge of proposing to her—or so everyone had thought. She could not beg for shillings. An income of her own, however modest, would give her some small measure of independence.

She walked the dog downstairs. Molly had just joined her in the corridor when the hall door opened.

"I'll tolerate the dog if I must," Mrs Lennox announced. "But that girl has got to go."

"She's my maid," Flavia argued, caught off-guard. "Surely I am entitled to one servant at least."

"She's a thief," Mrs Lennox retorted. "I threw her out once before and I'll do it again."

Flavia was dismayed. She could not lose Molly now.

"Wait for me outside," Flavia ordered, handing Molly the dog's leash. She turned back to Mrs Lennox, sour-faced and smug.

"I'll not have a common little piece like her about, breeding bastards."

Flavia, taken aback by the viciousness of this attack, was too overwhelmed by its implications to think quickly. But Molly confronted her accuser, arms akimbo.

"And how many men have you had to your bed, who've paid for the privilege? At least my Maria was an honest bastard, not like your precious grandson. I've heard how he was as well-grown at seven months as my babe at nine. Don't come the high-and-mighty with me, you nasty old cow!" Hester, caught up in the excitement, barked loudly.

Molly took Flavia's arm. "Come on, Miss," she said. "I'll lodge with old Sarah in the village. I wouldn't want to stay here anyway." She looked back over her shoulder. "She'd try to turn me into a frog."

Head high, Molly marched off, Flavia belatedly following, and the dog trailing behind in an undignified scamper. Once round the bend of the drive, they gave way to giggles.

"Did you see her face?" Molly exclaimed. "She looked fit to burst!"

"She would have turned you into a frog there and then, if she could," said Flavia. "But I am sorry you had to endure such abuse."

"It's not a patch on what my father said," Molly replied stoutly. "It was worth it, to tell her what I thought of her. I'm only sorry you'll have to deal with her on your own. She'll make your life a misery if she gets the chance."

Molly was right. She might be able to take such attacks in her stride, but Flavia felt cold to the stomach. She knew Mrs Lennox would never have treated her with such disrespect unless she knew what had happened in Manchester. Surely Lucius would have kept his mouth shut?

A thick wad of rotten thatch had slumped off the roof of Sarah's cottage. Long canes of raspberry straggled across the cobwebbed front windows. Flavia's shoes scrunched on the leaves drifted across the path. Even before she tapped on the door she knew the house was empty. What had happened? Betsy Turner would know.

"Fancy seeing you so soon, Miss! And you too, Molly!" Betsy exclaimed as she opened the door. "Do come in. We heard you was to be married, Miss."

"I changed my mind," said Flavia.

A look of mingled surprise and disapproval flitted across Betsy's plump features. "Whatever you think's best. I can't say I'm sorry, though. You'll not find a kind word here for that Mr Bromley, after what he done to poor Sarah. He heard as one of the lads in the hayfield was Sarah's grandson Luke; that nasty Frewin found out, sneaking about like a ferret, and told Mr Bromley. Luke were poaching; with that gang your Jem was in, Molly." She stopped, her hand flying to her mouth. Telling Betsy a secret was like pouring water into a sieve.

"It's all right, Betsy. I know."

Betsy's face suffused with relief. "Anyway, Mr Bromley had mantraps set and Luke got caught."

"What happened to him?" exclaimed Flavia. "Was he killed?"

"Oh no, Miss," Betsy explained in her maddeningly roundabout fashion. "But his leg was crushed, just under the knee, and now he's crippled. He can't work the farm any more so he's gone to the town, to beg. Sarah couldn't stay in the cottage."

"But what about the Poor Relief?" asked Flavia, horrified by the thought of that lithe young man, maimed.

"Mr Frewin's brother is Assistant Overseer, now." Betsy said knowingly, "and Mr Frewin does what Mr Bromley tells him. You have to sell everything you've got before you get the Relief. Sarah sold all her bits and bobs, but it didn't keep her long. Then she was off to the Poorhouse, or out on the road with the winter coming on."

Flavia remembered the old woman's few sticks of furniture, her few pots and plates and two garish vases, the pathetic accumulation of a lifetime's toil.

"Did you ask Mr Stanton for help?"

Betsy looked at her pityingly. "Mr Lucius don't look after us like your father did," she said. "And he'll not cross Mr Bromley. No: it's hard, but Luke knew what he was doing. He took his chance and paid for it."

Betsy might be able to accept the crippling of a fine boy as fair punishment for snaring a rabbit or two. Flavia could not. But at least she was able to arrange for Molly to lodge with Betsy in exchange for helping in her little shop.

Flavia was so preoccupied on her return to Fontclaire that she almost ran into someone coming down the steps. The dog growled softly.

"Flavia—" Bromley began.

"Let me pass."

He blocked her path. "Your brother agrees: you must marry me."

"Why?" She burst out. "You don't love me."

He went on as if he had not heard her. "I have never begged for anything in my life before. I am begging you now to be my wife." He spoke rapidly, in a low voice, as if afraid of being overheard. Had it been anyone else she could almost have pitied him.

"For the last time: *No.*"

His face was suddenly animated by more feeling than she had ever seen in it before. "No child of mine will be born a bastard!"

"There will be no child," she said, quietly.

"What have you done?" he shouted at her.

"What do you take me for?" Her tone cut sharper than the north wind. "You no longer have even that hold over me."

She wished he would go away. In this uncertain mood he frightened her.

"I can force you!" he cried.

"Force me?" she spat at him. "I loathe you! I would kill myself rather than marry you. You are obsessed. I wonder if you are quite sane."

For an instant his blue eyes widened; then his face settled into its customary hauteur.

"We shall see who is sane," he said quietly, and whistled for his horse. He touched his hat to her mockingly as he rode off.

Was this a sour joke? She thought over what he had said. Could he have her put away in an asylum? She felt the chill as this new menace sank in.

# 41

## *England, November 1819*

Ralph stepped from the rowdy warmth of the tavern into the dank London fog. Dull and bleary, it obscured the city surrounding him, huge and anonymous. His boots clattered on the uneven cobbles. Stone walls; iron railings; thick air heavy with the stink of coal; he thought he had left that behind him. He pulled up his collar, shivering. The penetrating November cold bit into his bad arm. It had healed, after a fashion, but he could move it only so far before it hurt. He rubbed it to ease the ache.

A whiff of gin and cheap scent: someone brushed against him. He flinched away.

"Madge cull, ye rip?" the woman sneered. "Or lack the mettle?" She flounced off, dissolving into the brown haze.

He walked on, faster. Little did she know how desire gnawed at him. But he could not bear to be touched. And he was ashamed. The scars on his back were a cage, and he was trapped in it. Pleasure lay beyond, where he could not reach.

Out of the fog loomed the portico of his club. Should he go in? Hardly, unshaven as he was, in his rough sailor's slops. What would he do? Play cards? He would win all right: any scruples about cheating were long gone.

He headed north, following the line of a new bridge across the Thames. After months at sea, the din of the City deafened him. All these people; too many to watch. The fog thickened into a blur. He turned west. He had all day. He would find his destination eventually.

The house was disconcertingly familiar, as though he had just returned from a month in the country. He had a sudden impulse to speak to Harriet. He had always admired her sharp commonsense. But it was not just his clothes that did not fit. Nothing about him matched her world any more. Once he would have stood at the piano to sing— but not the songs he had learned in the camps. The words she would not understand, and if he explained them to her she would be repelled. His stories were not fit for civilised society. He was more at ease in the company of felons.

Ralph strove to recall how he had filled his days when last he was in London, but these activities now seemed thin and insubstantial. Where he came from it was men, not foxes, who were hunted with dogs. Rather than fashionable amours, men groped at each other for lack of women. And how could the tawdry finery of the Opera compare with the drama of the Punishment Muster, with its scarlet jackets and gold braid under a blazing blue sky? In that theatre the blood and pain were real, not pretence enjoyed from the comfort of a box. No orchestra there, he thought: I acted my part at the triangles to the dry, insistent tap of a drum. What words could express this rage and shame to a cultured elderly gentlewoman?

And that was not the worst of it. That last night still tore at him. Donavan had pieced together what had happened, but he was a priest, used to confession. He understood something of the intolerable pain and exhaustion of spirit which had driven Ralph to breaking-point. But Ralph had not forgiven himself.

He heard a door closing, and a footman emerged up onto the pavement. Ralph trailed him until his hunger for information overcame his caution.

"Excuse me," he said abruptly. "Is Miss Stanton in town?"

The man turned. He looked puzzled. "Mr Lucius's sister?"

Ralph's pulse kicked.

"She's been gone for months, since the old lady died. Went to Manchester."

"Manchester?" Ralph repeated, uncomprehending. So Harriet was dead, but what was Flavia doing in Manchester?

"She went to get married. To Mr Bromley."

"When was the wedding?" he said hoarsely.

"Was to be September, but she took ill. Went upcountry to recover." The man peered at Ralph through the murk, trying to reconcile the voice with his shabby appearance. "I could take a message for Mr Lucius—" he suggested doubtfully.

"No, thank you." Ralph melted back into the obscurity of the fog. Flavia was too young for Bromley. She was only a girl—or had been— he had forgotten the four years between. If only she had waited! He remembered the words of her song:

*My heart is with Riley and I can't forget him*
*Although I may never see him no more*
No happy ending now, for the returned sailor:
*I am Riley, your long-lost lover...*

But he was not Riley, and she was not the girl in the song. She had betrayed him that night at the ball. Why? Jealousy of his mistress? Lucius had brought the note; the last thing he saw was the glitter of moonlight on her diamond clip. Had she and her brother laughed, as they dragged him away? How long until she sold herself to Bromley?

So that was all the faith she had kept: to ally herself to a man he despised. Damn them all, living high while Ralph slaved in the guts of the earth! He let out his breath in a long sigh. He was surprised that anything she could do could still cause him pain. Love had proved false. Now there was only *utu*, revenge.

Ralph drifted like a ghost through the sleeping house. A young woman in a portrait smiled at him as he passed. He had an irrational sense that only he was real, and everything around him was a trick of the light. These rooms had changed; his memory and what he saw as he turned each corner did not match. He ran his fingers over the gilded bronze flank of a table. What was it called? He had to search for the word: *Bühl*. He had forgotten that furniture could be elegant. But this show of wealth only fed his anger. While he had rotted, Lucius had waxed fat. It was the house that was real, and Ralph's memories only shards of a broken past.

This room had been Flavia's. He tried the handle on impulse; it held firm. He squatted before it, prying delicately at the lock with his picklock, as Clancy had taught him. He had acquired some useful skills in New South Wales.

The room was a study now. Even in the dark, the elaborate veneer of the desk gleamed as he moved. He snicked open the lock and eased back the lid. Opening a drawer he riffled through the papers, lifting the curtain a little way out from the window to admit a faint light. Bills, for the most part. Lucius had not changed. Carpets, furniture, building-plans—where was he getting the money? His luck at the gaming-tables must have turned.

Carefully Ralph set the papers back as he found them, and tried the matching drawer on the other side. It resisted; he drew his sailor's knife and prised it open with the tip of the blade. This was better: bundles of notes. Ralph stuffed them into his pockets. Empty, this drawer was less deep than the other. He puzzled over this for a moment. There must be a compartment at the back.

Footsteps approached from the staircase. Ralph froze into the shadows behind the door. The steps passed the landing, continued upwards. He relaxed, and lowered his knife. He returned to the drawer. The mechanism was hard to reach, but he sprang it in the end. Tucked in the recess were a little velvet bag and two pieces of paper, folded. He took his finds over to the window.

A note from Frewin to Lucius enclosing a receipt from Ralph's bank, for a thousand pounds. A slip of paper, torn off the bottom of a letter, with Ralph's signature. He tipped the bag onto his palm: a gold signet with a dark speckled stone. He did not need the light to read the motto: *Fortiter Ad Finem*: resolute to the end. The words were a reproach. But however tainted, the ring had been his years ago, when he was a gentleman, and he would have it back. He slipped it on his finger. Perhaps by wearing it he could again be Fairfax.

Shaved, hair properly cut, fashionably kitted out, Ralph regarded himself wryly in the mirror. Sir Ralph was ready to take the air. He had forgotten how constricting a dress-coat was. It felt ready to split across the shoulders the first time he turned. The elaborate necktie held his throat like a vice and his shoes pinched.

A face he did not know stared back at him from the glass; Fletcher's face, taut and wary, in borrowed finery. His mouth tightened in ironic acknowledgement. He had been innocent when he was shipped out of England; he was a thief now, if reclaiming your own property was theft. It was not a point he would like to argue before a court.

First, the bank. The manager looked surprised to see him, but enquired politely about his travels. If he could venture to suggest, the amounts withdrawn over the last few months had occasioned some concern, despite the increased income from the estate under the new system of management. Though of course the bank had been scrupulous about allowing withdrawals only upon receipt of Sir Ralph's signature and the validating seal, as per the letter of instruction.

Yes, he would prepare two drafts immediately. If the gentleman would sign here...

Ralph picked up the quill, dipped it, wrote "*Ralph F —*", hesitated, and completed the name "*—Fairfax.*"

Ralph handed over the two little packages, each stoutly wrapped, with a draft enclosed. In the first he had added a note *For your Tupara, as promised.*

The second note was blank except for his seal and initials. Donavan would know who it was from, and hopefully reclaim his mare, or at least buy another. He would be pleased that Ralph had kept his side of the bargain, and got clean away. The priest still had enough of the Irish rebel in him to rejoice that one victim at least had escaped the toils of English justice.

Ralph recalled Donavan now with an affection absent during their time together. What a pig of a patient he had been; half out of his mind with guilt and desperation, threatening to die at any moment. Well, he had sworn to stay alive, and stay alive he had. Donavan would be satisfied by that more than the money.

During his months at sea Ralph had learned that a man did not die of shame. Instead he came to terms with it, as a soldier will live with a twisted sliver of metal in his flesh. He had eaten his meagre fare, worked ship, slept, killed seals; in conditions barely less arduous, and among companions no less brutal, than those he had left in Newcastle. Only three things had been different: no irons; no friends; and he was heading home.

Now he was back in the England he had yearned for. But what to do next? Every decision was an effort. He found himself drawn back to the river, and stared up at the pale bulk of the Tower, that grim place of cruelty and death. Masters would be at home here, Ralph thought. He would have made a fine medieval baron, inventive in disposing of those in his way, and too cold-blooded for remorse.

A hand clutched his sleeve and he recoiled. It was a beggar, with lank black hair and ginger stubble. Dark eyes stared from a bony face.

"Go away."

The man did not whine, as Ralph expected, but made a peculiar moaning noise. For a moment, caught as he was in his dark imaginings, it seemed to Ralph that this was some doleful prisoner from the Tower, with his tongue cut out. But no ghost wore a coat in the faded dark green of the Rifle Brigade. Nor did one point with such meaning to the frayed regimental badge and then to his throat, with its star-shaped scar.

Even more compelling were the beggar's eyes. They bulged with the effort of expression, like those of seals under the club. His thin hands shook with his intensity.

The man's mute pleading touched Ralph with sudden pity. Ignoring the glances of passers-by, he gripped the man's arm.

"Nod if I am right," he commanded.

The man looked up at Ralph, his eyes those of a prisoner locked in a cell with no door.

"You were in the 95th, in Spain."

A nod.

Ralph pointed to his own throat. "Where did you get that?"

The beggar grunted, three syllables. His face twisted with frustration and he went to turn away, mouth set in bitter patience. Ralph tugged him back.

"Badajoz? You were there? At the glacis?" Clutching Ralph's hand, the man nodded again. His eyes, suddenly wide, locked onto Ralph's.

Ralph stared at him fixedly, his memory vivid with the midnight inferno of erupting stone and whining metal; green-coated soldiers clambering bloodied over the impaled bodies of their own dead.

A stocky boatman came up behind Ralph. "Shall I get rid of 'im, sir?" he said quietly. "He's a nuisance. Been hanging about for days."

"No—thank you," said Ralph hurriedly. Then to the man, "Do you want work? I need a manservant."

The sombre face quickened.

"Can you write? No. Your name—" Ralph snorted at the futility of his question. "I'll call you—Bob, at least for now. *Black Bob*, eh? Just like your old general, Crauford. I hope for both our sakes you've a better temper. Now let's get some food into you."

# 42

## *England, November 1819*

"What do you mean, *it's missing?*" Bromley snapped.

"It was here in the desk," Lucius insisted. "Locked away in a hidden compartment." He tugged the drawer to demonstrate. "Nobody knew about it but me."

"Somebody knew about it," retorted Bromley. "You should be more careful, with tradesmen in and out. Had I known you would be so lax, I would never have left it with you."

Lucius held his ground, feeling like an errant pupil berated by his headmaster. He wished now he had never borrowed the ring. Those bills could have waited.

"I am sure the staff is reliable," he replied stiffly. "And there were no tradesmen here that day."

"Tradesmen have tongues, and friends." Bromley stood by the desk, tapping it irritably with his thumb. "What else was taken?"

"All the money; about a thousand pounds. None of the documents."

"We can be thankful for that, at least." Bromley slid the broken drawer back into the desk. There was no external damage that he could see. "Obviously the work of a skilled thief, after valuables; frightened off when he heard someone coming."

Lucius was surprised by the other's coolness. He did not realise that Bromley, while pained by the loss of the ring, was far more relieved that the documents were still there. An investigation of the Fairfax accounts would be most embarrassing. Much as he regretted its loss, it would be simple enough to have another ring made.

"Give me those papers. I will take them for safe keeping. You had best return to the country and curb your spending for a while. At least you had the sense not to call the Runners."

Flavia returned from her morning ride to find Caroline sulking on the garden seat. Flavia's heart sank. She had not expected her back for another month at least. Now her armed truce with Mrs Lennox had changed into an offensive in which she was outnumbered.

"How was London?" she asked, endeavouring to be civil.

"Better than here," retorted Caroline, sitting on a damp patch, and flouncing further along.

"Did Lucius say why he returned to Fontclaire early?"

"You should know about that."

"What do you mean?" Flavia replied. "I had nothing to do with it."

"Yes, you did!" Caroline burst out. "Our visit to Manchester was cancelled because of you. I have been so humiliated! *Fancy Miss Stanton jilting that handsome Mr Bromley, on the steps of the altar too!* I must have heard it a dozen times. Now I am stuck here for months, because of the disgrace you brought on the family."

"My reasons for rejecting Bromley are no business of yours," Flavia replied sharply. "I trust you will not allude to the matter further."

"You'd like that, wouldn't you? Our season is ruined, and you want me to blame it all on Bromley! He's the second man you have scared off with your bluestocking ways! Mother always said you would end up a tart old spinster."

Flavia slapped the contorted face before her, and walked briskly back towards the house.

"You're jealous!" Caroline called after her. "You wouldn't know what to do with a man like Bromley!"

Flavia broke step; then, breathing quickly, strode on. As she reached her room she burst into humiliated tears. It had been a mistake to hit her sister-in-law. Caroline was a spiteful little cat; how much had Lucius told her? Not the full truth, surely; it would be all over the neighbourhood in a week.

At least she had Molly on her side. Isolated as she was, Flavia found herself relying increasingly on Molly for company, but she sensed a new reticence. Molly had been out when Flavia last called at the shop, buying eggs from Dennison's farm.

Through the narrow window of her bedroom the light failed early, blocked by the deep square-cut stones of the wall. Flavia kindled a fire against the afternoon chill, and pulling up her chair, spread her cold hands to the warmth. The dog, slumped along the hearth, was her only company. This was her life now. Flavia had set herself beyond the bounds of society, and must accept the consequence: an infinity of afternoons wasted in solitude.

She looked up from the interlocking flames as Molly burst in the door. "Miss, I must tell you first! Arthur Dennison has asked me to marry him!"

"I hope you said yes," said Flavia at her most rational, ignoring the pang of desertion.

No longer needing to hide her feelings, Molly was aglow. "We are to wed within the month, he says, and then d'you know what, Miss? We're going to New South Wales! He has saved up the fare, and his father is putting up the capital. Can you imagine it? Five hundred pounds!"

For Molly, Flavia knew, this was unimaginable riches. Young Dennison would be a good husband to Molly. He was intelligent and determined; with a modicum of good fortune, they would thrive in their new land. His mother would weep because she would never see him again, but she would be relieved he was now safe from informers and the threat of the rope.

Did he know about little Maria? Did he care?

"I am delighted for you, Molly," Flavia said. Soon, she knew, she would be a chapter in Molly's past, the kind lady who helped her when times were hard. Lucky Molly, fleeing this chill prison for a new start in the warm south! But envy would get her nowhere. This was the life Flavia had chosen; she would not give Bromley the satisfaction of knowing she was miserable. It was time to dress for dinner.

Lucius slammed the door and strode down the drive. The darkness and silence were a relief. Women! Caroline nagging endlessly about going back to London— he had presented her with as many alternatives to the truth as he could think of —she was satisfied with none of them. Her entire conversation was *Bromley this, Bromley that;* Lucius could have told her a thing or two about him! But you never knew where you were with Caroline these days. If he warned her Bromley could not be trusted in a room alone with a woman, it would only pique her interest. He loved her, paid out a fortune in clothes, bought more jewellery than he could afford. What else did she want?

And Flavia, trying to burden him with guilt over that old witch down in the Poorhouse; her grandson had known what would happen if he got caught. Lucius had been uncomfortable about the mantraps, but the poaching was so bad now that something had to be done. It was not just local men, but armed gangs, robbing to order from the towns: ruffians, escaped criminals, some of them...

Lucius stopped to tap the ash from his cigar. He had come further than he intended, down to the road. One of the lodge gates was open. He had given strict instructions to keep them locked. He grasped a bar of the gate to swing it to, but something held it back: a clenched hand.

Lucius looked up, startled. He could make out only a shadow against the black of the trees beyond. The hair prickled at the back of his neck. His voice trembled. "Who the Devil's ghost are you?"

"Why," Ralph replied, watching Lucius jump as he registered the voice, "Don't you remember an old friend, after all this time?"

*Fairfax!* The cigar dropped in a swirl of flaring ash. The gate clanged to. Lucius backed away, as though he expected Ralph to spring at him over the top.

"I must come to call. We have much to discuss."

Lucius broke into a run.

"And give my regards to your sister," Ralph called, as the crunching footsteps faded on the gravel.

Ralph had waited a long time for that moment, and he savoured it to the full. Lucius was terrified, every gesture betraying his guilt. A rogue of sounder nerve would have brazened it out. He would have a miserable night of it, Ralph thought grimly. He walked back to his mount. The branches around him stirred in the wind, dislodging flurries of dead leaves. There was a storm brewing. Swinging into the saddle, he headed for Longhallows. Time to go home.

The stone lion on the forecourt snarled down at him as a stranger; the blank windows offered no welcome. Ralph pressed his palm against the door, ran his thumb around the rim of a lion's-head boss in gilded bronze. Briefly he closed his eyes, recalling those nights on *Adelphi,* his ache for home.

His hand closed into a fist. "Open up!" he roared across the whistling of the wind, hammering the panels, jangling the bell. "Open up!"

The door creaked open a fraction, its edge defined by the lantern behind.

"What's all the noise? Who is it?" It was not the old doorman Ralph expected. He planted his boot firmly in the crack and forced the door open. The caretaker fell back.

"You can't come in, sir. Mr Frewin said—"

"Bugger Frewin. This house is mine. I am Sir Ralph Fairfax."

Nervously the man peered at him, holding up the lantern. "Why, surely, sir," he ventured uncertainly, "we were not expecting you—"

"Obviously. You will make up a meal and a bed for me; my man will bring my luggage in the morning. I do not know your face; I assume Frewin engaged you. You may go to him in the morning and take your wages. Your services will no longer be required. And you will tell him I wish to see him forthwith."

The man ducked off.

Where were the other servants? The place was deserted. By the light of a single candle, Ralph retraced Longhallows' empty passages and silent rooms. The dislocation that had seized him in London here wrenched more painfully. The high, painted ceilings, lost in darkness; the broad staircase with its elaborate balustrade; his father's portrait above; all were as familiar to him as the shape of his own hand. But the chandeliers which should have refracted the candlelight were bandaged and blind. In the Cabinet Room, covers shrouded the cupboards and chests. He ripped them free. White against the marble inlay, they looked like winding-sheets spilled from a tomb.

Perturbed, he continued his disconcerting pilgrimage. The reception-rooms, likewise draped in ghostly groups, were as he remembered them; in better condition, if anything, the carpets underfoot thicker than he recalled. In the long gallery his ancestral portraits still gazed down from their ornate frames, though oddly, his mother's picture was missing.

He had yearned for a triumphant return, but these mischievous changes, wrought by unknown hands, perplexed him. Ralph called for the caretaker, to question him further, but the man had gone: to the village, no doubt, to spread the news.

Instinctively Ralph made for his old bedroom. He opened the door and stopped. This room had been stripped; the floor was bare boards; the skeletal poles of the bed reared into the darkness. Only one picture remained, on the floor, face to the wall. The wire was snapped and the frame broken on the corner where it had fallen. As he picked up, it came apart in his hands.

It was his portrait, painted just before he left for Spain. The surface of the canvas shimmered in the poor light, the young officer's tight smile under the plumed shako disappearing into a blank glaze. Ralph picked away the broken frame and leaned the painting back against the wall. His father had commissioned the work; the artist, more faithful to his patron than his subject, had subtly emphasised their resemblance. It was recognisable, but Ralph had always felt it to be false: presenting him as the proud young officer his father wanted him to be.

Now he loathed it. The arrogant stance, the blue silver-laced officer's jacket, the furred pelisse with its heavy silver tassels, the carefully arranged hair: had he ever looked like that? It reminded him of Devereux. He shoved it out of sight behind a curtain, and stared around the room, the most altered of all he had seen. The painting had been wrenched off the wall so roughly that the hook had torn the plaster with it, exposing the lathe behind.

Ralph had anticipated comfort and safety, not a cold bed and more enigmas. But he was too tired to puzzle further tonight. He tugged half-heartedly at his boots and left them on; pulling at that angle set his arm aching. He wrapped himself in his cloak and curled up on the boards. This bed was enormous. Luxury, he though drowsily, was relative. On *Adelphi* a bunk this wide would have slept six. Here he had it all to himself.

Lucius fought his rising panic. Fairfax was back. He knew of Lucius's part in his abduction. He might walk through the door tomorrow. God! Flavia was implicated in this too. There was that note, and her things Bromley had given him, the brooch and the shawl. He had never paid them any attention before. What would Fairfax have made of them, all those years in prison? What would he do now? How far would he go? To violence? To both of them?

Should he send Flavia away—but where? What story could he concoct to persuade her? And what about his wife and son—would Fairfax avenge himself on them as well? He certainly had cause. But he was a gentleman—or had been …

Lucius raked his fingers back from his forehead, trying to press his frenzied thoughts into order. So much for Bromley's assurance, after that letter arrived from Ralph, that nothing like this would never happen, because Fairfax was safely in chains on the other side of the world.

Then there was the money. The builders were starting on the old refectory cellars next week. Lucius had committed the funds, relying on what he had drawn from the Fairfax estate to settle his most pressing creditors. But that money had been stolen, and there would be no more windfalls from that quarter.

Only now did Lucius perceive how clever Bromley had been. Nothing linked him to Fairfax at all. It was Lucius who had taken the message…a deeper horror gripped him. What if it was Fairfax who had broken into his study in London? Frantically he scanned his memory of that brief encounter in the darkness. Had Fairfax been wearing his ring? If so, he had read the letter, and Lucius's guilt was proven beyond exoneration.

He must tell Bromley. He would know what to do. Lucius seized at this avenue of escape. If he left now, he would be well on the way to London by daybreak. He should leave a note for Flavia, to warn her Fairfax was back. But the last thing he wanted was his sister sniffing around his affairs like a terrier after a fox. Lucius crushed a handful of incriminating receipts into a satchel. Flavia was forever asserting her independence. She could look after herself.

Bromley sat beside the fire in his study, a folded newspaper across his knee. So Vansittart had finally imposed his new duty on foreign wool. He must calculate what difference this would make to his returns from Longhallows. It would push up the price of the local clip; his gamble in evicting those useless tenants, and replacing them with sheep, had paid off. His father should have done it years ago. If Sir Everard had acknowledged him, and sought his advice in business, Longhallows would be worth a fortune by now.

It had been an inspired move, clearing his way to his inheritance by getting rid of Ralph. He would take his half-brother's place with Flavia, too, wear her down. With a pang of dark pleasure he remembered her body twisting under his, striving to escape. He had taken her then. She was his now; nobody else would have her. He could afford to wait. She would submit in the end.

"Mr Stanton to see you, sir."

This was an odd hour for Lucius to call uninvited; still in his dusty travelling coat, his face uncharacteristically pale.

"He's back. Fairfax. I saw him last night."

"Impossible!" Bromley returned, crisply. "This whole business is preying on your mind."

In his need to justify himself, Lucius's face regained a little of its colour. "I walked down the drive at Fontclaire and the lodge gate was open. He was on the other side."

Bromley frowned, still disbelieving. "Were you drunk? Had you a lantern? There was no moon last night."

"No."

"Then how do you know who it was? It could have been a poacher; anyone." Bromley stared at him intently, trying to ridicule the younger man into denial, but Lucius only grew more sullen. "It was Fairfax all right. I knew his voice."

"What did he say?"

"I can't remember exactly. Something about *'not knowing an old friend after a long time'*. His tone sent shivers down my spine."

Bromley bit back a derisive retort. Lucius was a weakling, too lazy to be moral and too squeamish to be resolute. He had none of the strength that made his sister a prize worth having.

Lucius caught Bromley's expression. "You don't believe me! This may not matter to you, but what if he blames me for sending him to New South Wales? And what if it was Fairfax who broke into my London house, and stole the ring and the money?"

Bromley felt the first stirrings of alarm. It had not occurred to him that the incidents might be linked.

"Now listen, Stanton," he snapped. "Go home, act normally, and keep your mouth shut. I shall come and see for myself. If you hint, by the slightest imputation, that I had anything to do with his disappearance; if you should be overcome by a sudden urge to confess; just remember who holds your bills. Do you want your precious Charles to grow up in the Marshalsea?"

Lucius cringed before so blatant a definition of their relationship. He stared at Bromley in horror. Good, thought Bromley; that threat struck home. He nodded his head at the door, and Lucius slunk out, like a hound shown the whip.

Bromley stared at the closed door. He was safe enough for the moment; he congratulated himself on the skill with which he had covered his tracks. If, by some extraordinary mischance, the story were true, he would commit himself to no action as yet, merely run Lucius as bait and see what happened. There was Caroline, too, giving him arch looks when last he had seen her. A little flirtation would pass the time agreeably, and perhaps provoke Flavia to jealousy.

Meanwhile, a prudent rearrangement of his resources...The even tenor of his reflections was cut by a sudden flash of hate. If Ralph were truly back at Longhallows, he would not stand in Bromley's way for long.

# 43

# *England, November 1819*

Flavia had resolved to ask Lucius to give her Harriet's jewellery that she knew he had redeemed from that pawnbroker in Chester. But when she came down to breakfast she was vexed to find he had gone, and had left no notice of his return. Looking out the windows to where the tail of last night's storm thrashed fitfully at the trees, she saw a woman's figure, well wrapped up, buffeting along the drive. Who would be out early on such a morning?

Flavia went upstairs to the nursery. She enjoyed playing with Charles; the one member of the family happy to see her. He was a pretty child, with his father's looks and charm, and the confidence of a three-year-old secure in love. Lucius doted on him, and found time each day to spend with him. That affection, Flavia thought sadly, was almost the last thing she and her brother had in common.

She folded him a paper hat, which Charles wore fore-and-aft like the Duke of Wellington. He was capering about on his hobby-horse when Molly slipped in, shutting the door quickly behind her.

"You look like you've seen a ghost. What's happened?"

"Could you come outside, Miss?"

"Has Lucius had an accident?"

"Mr Lucius? No, Miss. But there's someone downstairs asking for him. He says he is Sir Ralph Fairfax."

Flavia's heart lurched. "Fairfax? Asking for Lucius?" Surely she was mistaken.

"Betsy Turner told me he was back; turned up in the middle of the storm, she said, at Longhallows. She had it from the caretaker. I was coming to tell you, when he passed me on the drive."

Ralph! Here! The thought paralysed her. It was an effort even to turn her head as an agitated Mrs Lennox bore down upon them, glaring at Molly.

"Flavia! There is a man downstairs claiming to be Sir Ralph Fairfax, demanding to see your brother. I told him Lucius was not at home. He asked to see you."

Flavia could not face Ralph in this turmoil. "You claim to be mistress here," she replied. "Your responsibilities are not my affair. See him yourself."

Alicia's mouth pursed. She turned with a swirl of skirts. Molly looked at Flavia in concern.

"Thank you, Molly; leave me alone now, please."

As soon as the girl had gone, Flavia ran along the corridor to the library. She pushed aside a stack of papers on the window-seat to look down obliquely onto the entrance.

A dark-haired man came out the door. He paused. Even at this angle, she felt a kick of recognition. He strode across to where a groom held a restless black horse. Fairfax seemed broader in the shoulder, leaner in the body, than she remembered. His face, when he lifted it to look back at the house, was unexpectedly grim, his hair cropped short. He jammed on his hat and spurred away.

Those few seconds devastated her. Flavia had smothered her pain and walled it off, brick by brick. At one sight of him the whole edifice crumbled, leaving her as raw and confused as the girl of four years ago. After all that had happened, deserted and dishonoured, she was still deeply in love with him. She leaned her forehead against the lead bars banding the glass.

Ralph eyed his agent with distaste. His perceptions sharpened by years among rogues and thieves, he placed Frewin immediately. It could have been Thomasin toadying before him, obsequious and unreliable.

"May I venture to say, sir, what an unexpected pleasure—"

"Nonsense."

Frewin's smile wilted. His eyes flickered from Ralph's harsh face to his hands, and widened as he saw the ring.

"Just what have you been doing with my estate while I was away?"

The agent swallowed. "It was—not my idea, sir," he explained, thinking quickly. "It was Mr Stanton." Encouraged by some fractional shift in Ralph's expression, he went on more volubly. "He was using your ring, sir, with forged signatures, to draw money for his building schemes."

This was too glib. Another fright might shake loose more of the truth. "I will have you arrested. You will hang for this."

Frewin started at 'hang'; then his upper lip curled away from his teeth in an extraordinary gesture, part servile, part triumphant. "I wouldn't do that, sir."

Goaded by this insolence, Ralph snatched Frewin by the lapels, and jerked him forward.

Frewin gabbled in a high-pitched rush. "You wouldn't want people asking where you have been, would you, sir?"

Ralph shook him so hard his teeth clacked. "And what do you know about that?"

"N-nothing, sir!" Frewin replied, quick-witted for all his terror. "If you'll let me go—" Ralph's hands clenched again, twisting the collar tighter round Frewin's plump throat. "I can tell you about Miss Stanton—" he ended in a squeak.

Ralph paused, fighting the hot tide of rage. The man should be tried for embezzlement. Yet Ralph dared not risk exposure. Fletcher too could hang.

"I could kill you now," Ralph hissed, "and save the trouble."

"Bromley and Miss Stanton," Frewin spluttered. "They were lovers."

As if bitten by a rat, Ralph flung him aside. Frewin picked himself up and scuttled out the door. Ralph started after him but halted, panting. The words had stopped him dead, as they had been meant to do.

It must be true. Frewin had been terrified, searching for a scrap of information that would save his neck. Lovers! No wonder they were getting married, if Bromley had bedded her already. How could Ralph have been so wrong in his judgement of her?

He straightened out his arm and rubbed it, his hand shaking. His right cuff had ridden up; he tugged it down to cover the scar. Bromley was handsome, wealthy, successful, whole. Ralph was flooded by fierce hatred, visceral as that he had felt for Masters. He sat down, hunched, head in his hands, dry-eyed. She was not worth his tears.

"Why didn't you take me with you to London?"

"What on earth for?" snapped Lucius, preoccupied.

"You know how I long to go back!" Accusation brought no response. Caroline's mouth softened; she looked at him from under her lashes.

"What did you buy me, then? You always bring me a gift when you go away. You promised some new pearl earrings."

Lucius turned away wearily. "Wait until your birthday. You're not a child, Caroline; will you stop these ceaseless demands? I have just come back from a long journey, damn it! You could learn a lesson from Flavia. She doesn't hang on my coat-tails whining for gifts."

"Don't hold up your sister as an example to me!" Caroline retorted. "Everybody knows what she has done! No decent house in the neighbourhood will receive her!"

Lucius snatched her by the shoulders. "She is my sister, and you will treat her with respect!"

Caroline laughed in his face. "A bit late now, isn't it?"

His fingers tensed. "Go on," she taunted. "Play the rustic squire: hit me."

Lucius let his hands fall. Caroline bobbed him a curtsey and swept off.

There were two envelopes, neatly aligned, on the silver tray. His head still ached from the journey. He massaged his forehead briefly with finger and thumb, and slit the letters open.

The first was a milliner's bill for fifty pounds. He sighed and turned to the next. He recoiled from the familiar seal.

*Expect me for dinner tomorrow.*

"Give me back my jewellery."

"Yes, I've been meaning to," Lucius said distractedly. "I'll do it today. But there is something I must tell you."

"That Fairfax has returned?" Flavia replied with commendable calm.

"You know already?"

"The village is buzzing with the news, and his mute manservant as well."

"He will dine with us today," he said shortly. "Given the circumstances, you had better restrain your conversation to the barest limits of politeness."

He looked up uncomfortably to meet his sister's withering gaze.

"Don't worry, Lucius: I shall not shame you further."

Lucius extended his hand in an uncertain gesture and let it drop. *Act as normally as possible,* Bromley had ordered him before he left London. *Blame Frewin for any shortfall in the accounts. But don't let Fairfax alone with your sister. Play the overbearing brother, if you must; but keep them apart.*

Back in his dressing-room, Lucius spilled the brandy as he poured. Bromley might be able to do this sort of thing without a qualm… He tossed back another glass. Recalling the scorn on Flavia's face, Lucius despised himself.

At least he could give her jewellery back. But the box was gone: Madame had taken it.

He walked in on Caroline without knocking. She turned from the mirror, wearing a blue silk turban; the décolleté of her gown emphasised by the cascade of gem-studded gold held to her throat.

"Take that thing off," he ordered, frowning at the turban.

"Mother said it looked well."

"She would," he retorted. "They suit women trying to disguise their age. And hand over those jewels. They are not yours."

She slipped the necklace into a drawer and swiftly locked it. "Flavia didn't want them; she pawned them. And you didn't give me what you promised."

Lucius sighed, unwilling to trigger another argument. "'*They— are— not— yours!*' he said, with emphasis. "You must hand them over to Flavia."

"Why? Where will she wear them?"

"That's not the point. I promised."

"As you promised me those earrings?"

He fell back, defeated. "Just for tonight, then. But you must restore them in the morning."

She flashed him a smile of triumph. He kissed her longingly and hard, but she wriggled out of his arms.

"I must take back Mother's turban immediately," she said maliciously, "seeing you dislike it so."

When she saw Caroline wearing Harriet's bracelet and necklace, Flavia was bitterly angry. "It's only for this evening," Lucius whispered to her. This evening, indeed. That was what he wanted to believe, because it spared him a scene.

Flavia's glance kept sliding to the clock. Ten minutes, five. With reverberating chimes, the hour struck. Their guest was late. A brisk footfall on the marble flags of the entry-porch: Fairfax walked in. His skin was gypsy-dark and creased like a sailor's around the eyes. The mouth was hard, the eyes bleak, that she remembered for their ready humour. Even the way he held himself was different.

He nodded to her in curt acknowledgement and stood back. At dinner Flavia sat ignored by Mrs Lennox on one side and Caroline on the other. Their guest too behaved as though Flavia was not there, directing his remarks towards his host, who looked ill-at-ease.

Caroline was doing her best to attract Ralph's attention, reaching across in front of him for a bunch of grapes.

"What an unusual necklace," Ralph observed.

"It was left me by Lucius's cousin," Caroline replied.

Flavia made a sudden movement; Ralph glanced towards her; she looked down.

"Oh yes: I visited her house in London once or twice," Flavia heard him say. "A place full of unexpected curiosities."

Lucius choked on a slice of pear. He coughed and cleared his throat.

"You should take more exercise, Stanton. Join me for a bout at Angelo's when next we are both in London. Sabres, perhaps? You look pale. Are you unwell?"

Caroline spoke up brightly. "I'm afraid my husband will not be back in London for some time. He was there only last week."

"Was it about the pony-trap for little Charles?"

Alicia was unaware of having thrown her son-in-law a lifeline, but he seized it with both hands.

"Yes. I had hoped to keep it a secret."

"You have a son?" queried Fairfax.

"Yes," said Lucius, reluctantly.

"He is three years old now," chattered Mrs Lennox. "A beautiful little boy."

"My congratulations. Children are so precious, are they not? I should like to meet him. For you, these past years have not been wasted."

The footman Vickery leaned over and whispered in Lucius's ear. He rose from the table, his face slack with relief.

"Excuse me: Mr Bromley has arrived."

Flavia gathered herself to stand, but Lucius's hand pressed on her shoulder.

"Let me go," she whispered.

He leaned harder. His set smile did not change. "It would look bad if you left now," he mouthed at her. "You must stay." She sat down again, angry and humiliated, to see the rest of this disastrous dinner through.

She felt Bromley's eyes on her as he arrived. He turned to Fairfax. "Back from your travels, Fairfax," Bromley observed, taking a seat. "I trust the experience was interesting?"

"Very," murmured Ralph.

Lucius beamed at Bromley, cheered by this unexpected succour. "We must congratulate you: I hear you are a Member of Parliament now."

Bromley leaned back in his chair, every inch the affable country gentleman. "You have missed little of interest," he remarked to Fairfax. "There has been some disaffection among the lower classes; some disturbances in the North—"

Flavia interrupted in a low voice. "You mean the slaughter of dozens of innocent people, and the wounding of hundreds more."

Lucius cut across her. "We need not speak further of what happened in Manchester."

"Why not?" said Caroline loudly. "We all know your sister's interest in politics."

Flavia stared down at her napkin, silent and tight-faced. Ralph felt the wash of feeling around him. What had happened in Manchester? Bromley was watching her covertly, but she had not looked once in his direction. He continued smoothly.

"There are measures in train which will quash this nonsense of Reform." He glanced across at Flavia with a glint of triumph.

"Perhaps the ladies would like to retire," Lucius suggested hurriedly. Flavia stood immediately and left. Caroline curtsied to Bromley with a dazzling smile. "A pleasure to see you again, sir."

Bromley kissed her hand gallantly. "Perhaps you could all join me for a hunt next week? My gamekeeper has been troubled by a bold young fox; he promises good sport. You remember General Byng?" he said, turning to Ralph. "He will be there; he expressed a desire to see you."

Flavia confronted her brother, his hands clasped on the tooled green leather of his desk. "Give me my dowry," she demanded. "I wish to live alone."

His finger twitched. "We have discussed this before. It is quite out of the question."

"Good God, Lucius," she exploded. "I'm not made of stone! How do you think I feel mewed up in this house with your wife and mother-in-law sneering at me, and Fairfax and Bromley my only visitors! It is intolerable! I am amazed at your indelicacy that you do not see it!"

Lucius drew his hands slowly apart, clenching his fingers under his palms.

"I'm sorry about last night—"

"Sorry! You were so busy crawling to Bromley that I am surprised you noticed anything at all!"

"I have spoken to Caroline about her behaviour; it was unforgiveable."

"Did you get back my jewels?"

Shamefaced, Lucius stayed silent.

"You know what she is doing is wrong, yet you do nothing to stop her!"

Lucius looked at her, his face serious. "We are not all as strong as you."

This unexpected comment, half compliment, half plea, threw Flavia off her stride.

Lucius untucked one hand, his fingers playing with the silver sand-caster, tracing patterns in the spilt grains. "To be honest, I am unexpectedly short of money this quarter. If you can wait till next Quarter Day, I will see what I can do."

She was disappointed, but hardly surprised.

"Thank you, Lucius," she said coldly. His charm was wearing thin; anxiety showed behind his smile, like patches of brass under cheap gilding. He was a wastrel and a fool. "You have made your priorities plain: a stable for your horses ahead of a cottage for your own sister."

He trawled his mind for words to justify himself. When he looked up she had gone.

# 44

## *England, November 1819*

"I'm perfectly capable of shaving myself! Find something useful to do."

Bob set down the tray with its soap, opened razor and bowl of steaming water, and backed away. Vexed for no reason he could put a finger to, Ralph snatched up the towel. The first pass of the razor nicked his chin. He swore.

For months he had looked forward to a comfortable bed; proper clothes; decent food; freedom to do as he wanted. Now he had them they brought no solace. He slept badly, and woke tired. The smallest check irritated him beyond endurance, and he was short-tempered with Bob to the point of curtness. When these moods had seized him on the ship he had promised himself that once home, all would be different. Yet the burden on his spirit was the same. The past brought despair; the future no joy.

His lassitude frightened him. Masters had maimed more than his arm. By day he suppressed it, but the thought haunted his sleep. He dreamed he was pacing down the long gallery, past the portraits of his family. But each ornate frame, as he reached it, held not a canvas, but a glass: and the face sneering back from them all was Masters', not his own.

A single incident lightened his spirits. It had not taken Ralph long to realise how unpopular he had become during his absence. The villagers eyed him sullenly as he rode by; one morning Ralph opened the front door to find a sheep's head leaking bloodily over the flags of the porch.

He threw back his head and laughed, to the confusion of the men watching from behind a hedge. All morning his lip quirked whenever he recalled it; then, more seriously, wondered what had been done in his name.

Then there was the hunt. Ralph was in two minds about it. He feared Byng's sharp questions and observing eye. But the General knew

Ralph was back; to stay away would give rise to comment. Besides, Lucius would be there, and Ralph was far from finished with him yet. And there would be Flavia.

He did not know what to make of her. In place of the awkward, eager girl he remembered was a woman he did not know, remote and self-contained, dressed simply as a Quaker in a house garish with new furniture, wearing only a locket and chain while Lucius's wife queened it in Harriet's jewels. Why would Harriet have left them to Caroline rather than Flavia?

Nor did she match the bitter portrait he carried within. He expected guilt, even defiance, for her vile betrayal. And why was she so distant with Bromley? There was something between them; he could sense it in Bromley's possessive manner; the man had barely taken his eyes off her all night.

Down at the stables Ralph's mount was ready. Bob had shaped up well as a manservant; intelligent, prompt, and with no option but to be discreet. Ralph wondered what Bob had made of his scars, when first he saw them. Not that he was ever likely to find out. Ralph had sensed Bob's eyes on him rather more frequently thereafter, but his demeanour had not changed. Impassively he made the bed, bought food and cooked it, helped Ralph dress. The only thing he would not do was join him at table, even for a glass of claret the night Ralph offered it to him, guilty for his outburst that morning. Ralph had already worked his way through the first bottle and was feeling a little muzzy.

"Come and join me," he had said to Bob, patting the table. "No heeltaps."

Bob had shaken his head and withdrawn, leaving Ralph alone. He could have done with someone to drink with.

The horse tossed its head nervously as Bob led it up. Ralph mounted; the black tugged at the reins and Ralph swore as pain lanced up his arm. It was a hard-mouthed brute. He hoped the jumps would be straightforward. He could not afford to fall, and be carted off senseless to some apothecary.

"I shan't be back till evening," he called down to Bob. "Take the day off. Go down to the village, if you like."

Ralph glanced around sardonically. This was no Return of the Prodigal. He had not been so manifestly unpopular since Thomasin accused him of being an informer. At his approach groups melted away;

faces became backs, tense with urgent conversation. What was he supposed to have done?

Ralph cocked his hat unnecessarily against the pallid November sun and lounged in the saddle. He whistled under his breath, a coarse little ditty he had picked up in the mines.

"Why, Fairfax!" Ralph turned. "I would hardly have known you." It was Byng, trim in a brown coat. "When did I see you last? '15 was it, or '14?"

"'14, sir, before I left for Vienna."

"You intended to stay in the Army, I remember. You did not?"

"No." The answer was curt.

"A pity. We could have done with some steady Peninsular officers at Peterloo. You have not heard of it? A miserable business, hopelessly mishandled. The Yeomanry, and hussars who should have known better, charged a Radical meeting in Manchester. Scores were killed and injured. There was a neighbour of yours involved, Miss Stanton. Knocked down. Most distressing." Byng was silent for a moment. "You had an interest in the girl yourself at one stage, did you not?" he added, with the licence of superior rank.

Ralph's face hardened. "I prefer not to discuss it, sir."

"As you wish," said the other. "But you were a fool to go haring off with that *manquée* German woman."

Ralph was galled by the edge of contempt. "Thank you for your interest, sir," he replied, and spurred his horse away.

So that was the story Lucius had put about! How much more disgusted would the General be if he knew the truth. *Coward*: in Wellington's army there was no epithet more damning. The high summons of the horn cut across his thoughts.

The fox ran fast and well. Ralph glimpsed him on the edge of a fallow field, a russet flash against the tangle of brown and green. Then he went to ground, and the riders milled about while a pair of grooms stopped the earth and smoked him out. Ralph was hungry, as always; he dismounted for something to eat. He went to speak to Dacre, whom he remembered as an amiable nincompoop, but the young man turned aside, fiddling with his spur.

*"Hark forrard!"*

The fox was loose; the hounds streamed away. The riders mounted up again and rode off in pursuit. They galloped down a shallow valley, scrambled through the stream at the bottom, and laboured up the other side. Baying, the hounds poured through a gap in the hedge blocked by a fallen trunk. The Master's horn brayed. Chestnut and roan, the horses took the jump.

Ralph's black gathered to meet it, but as Ralph folded forward, rising in his stirrups, the horse twisted, neighing. Pitched from the saddle, Ralph fell heavily and lay still. Bromley, coming up, circled daintily round the unmoving body before urging his mount to a canter.

"I'll fetch a surgeon," he called back.

Lucius dismounted. Beneath his initial dismay was a crawling maggot of hope. Perhaps Fairfax is dead, he thought, ashamed of his gush of relief. He temporised, running first to catch the black horse. It backed away, flinging up its head and rolling its eyes.

Flavia had kept back from the body of the hunt, aware of Caroline's intense conversations with her friends, turning to stare. She wished she had never come, but rebelled against living immured like a nun in a Spanish convent. If they chose to regard her as a jilt, or worse, then the failure was theirs, not hers. But it did not make the eager, greedy glances easier to bear. For a moment Dacre had looked likely to address her, but a gesture from his mother had brought him to heel.

She crested the rise and looked across the valley. Someone was down; inexplicably, no one was offering assistance. She cantered closer, and saw, with a stab of alarm, that it was Ralph.

Anxiously she dismounted and knelt beside him. He lay still, a bright trickle of blood jagged down his face. She was acutely aware of the strong, dark lashes lying against the sallow tan of his cheek. With relief she saw the artery pulsing in his throat. At least he was alive. She looked around.

Lucius, halfway down the hill, was walking a horse on either side.

"Lucius!" she called "Hurry! Get some hurdles for a stretcher! Forget the stupid horses!"

Another rider reined in.

"Hadn't you better wait for a surgeon?" This was Dacre, peering down. He swung down from the saddle.

Ralph caught the word through a haze of pain. "No."

Flavia drew back. Dacre stared. "But Bromley's gone to fetch him."

"I said *No*." This time the tone was sharper. Ralph's head pulsed and he had jarred his bad arm, but he willed himself to sit up, fending off the young man's proffered hand. Dacre hovered, concerned. "At least let the fellow have a look at you."

This was the last thing Ralph wanted. "When I want a damned surgeon I'll ask for one!" He made an effort to be polite. "Really there is no need. You will lose the hunt." He stood up, trying to ignore the hammer thudding inside his skull. He touched his head gingerly; he must have caught it where Masters hit him.

Flavia fell back, rebuffed. The onlookers dispersed as Ralph walked over to his mount. As soon as they were out of sight he slackened the girth-strap, traced back the drops of blood and eased out from under the saddlecloth a wicked spur of thorn. Someone had planted it there at the last halt. It had needed only a shift of pressure to drive it down into the horse's back. He could have broken his neck. He looked around, saw Flavia hesitating, and flung it towards her.

"Which of you put it there?" he shouted. "You or your brother?"

Too hurt to reply, she turned her mount homewards. Why would he accuse her like that? She was only trying to help.

On her way she caught a flash of mulberry in a little copse. Only one man was wearing that colour: Bromley. But surely the surgeon's house was in the village, not back the way they had come?

Flavia's mind churned with the events of the morning. Seeing Ralph again evoked her misery at his desertion; those unending nights lost in weeping; the sting of the cold water she had splashed on her hot, swollen eyes in the morning. She must not slip back into that gulf of sadness, burdened as she still was with guilt over Maria's death, and the shock of Bromley's rape. And what was Robert planning next, to compel her to his will? She was friendless and deeply uncertain, and the man her heart clung to against all reason treated her with despite.

To distract her thoughts she took Charles out walking. She had brought a slate to amuse him, and a bag of apples. With the rest of the neighbourhood still off chasing foxes, she should be safe from interruption.

Little Charles stumped along manfully for some ten minutes and announced he was hungry. She sat him on a tree-stump and gave him an apple.

"Auntie draw," he demanded in his high, clear voice. This was a game he enjoyed, where Flavia sketched a picture on the slate, Charles guessed what it was, and Flavia wrote the name underneath. Charles had already learned to recognise three words, and was vastly pleased with himself.

"Shall I draw the apple?" she asked.

"Draw *Lion*," cried Charles, clapping his hands. 'Lion' was one of his words. Flavia sketched rapidly, the slate-pencil screeching as she changed the angle. "But you'll know——" she began, and looked up.

Charles sat very still, his blue eyes wide in alarm. A man confronted them, dark and gaunt, with an intense stare. Flavia backed away, all her fears flooding back, acutely conscious of how far they were from help. He gestured, with a strange animal sound. Flavia's arm went out to gather the boy to her. Charles's lip trembled.

"Auntie," he piped in his carrying voice, "Why is he making that noise?"

If he is a lunatic about to attack, thought Flavia, he will do it now. He gestured again and grunted. Flavia looked more closely, remembering, now the first shock had passed, the gossip from the village.

"I think he has hurt his throat, Charles," she said as calmly as she could manage. "You're Fairfax's servant, aren't you?" she asked, gathering courage. He nodded. "Your master has taken a fall by Whitmonk's Brook. Look, I'll write it down for you——" She stopped as he shook his head.

"You can't read?" She looked again in pity at the mangled throat and pleading eyes. Already the village girls derided him as some sort of monster, aping his attempts at communication with mingled cruelty and alarm. "You can't speak and you can't read," she repeated, almost to herself. His eyes rested on the slate, wistfully. To be shut up inside yourself, with no means of expression at all... it was intolerable, a sentence of solitary confinement.

Flavia came to a sudden decision. "I can teach you to write," she declared rashly.

He looked up in disbelief.

"Charles: read that word." She held up the slate.

"That's *Lion*".

"You see?" she challenged him. "If I can teach a three-year-old, I can teach you. You would like to read and write, wouldn't you?"

The man nodded eagerly. "Be here tomorrow, at the same time. Charles and I walk out most days, unless it rains. Meanwhile you had best tend to your master."

Brushing away the rough ends of sawn bark, Flavia sat down beside the little boy. How Harriet would have chided her. "Another lame duck! You can't change the world, you know!" But she could change some small part of it, and find some thread of purpose within the constraint of her days. She was already so far beyond the pale that nothing else she might do would make any difference.

Ralph awoke drenched in sweat, fighting for breath, shuddering in a tangle of sheets. This was the fourth time since the hunt. The headaches had subsided, but the nightmares would not go away: sometimes trapped in the mine, sometimes trying to wrench free of his torment, ending always in this overmastering horror. Some trapdoor in his memory had jammed open, and no effort could force it shut.

He had even exiled Bob to the stables, afraid of what he might hear. He must have hurt the fellow's pride, because he was gone, now, almost every afternoon. Perhaps he had a girl down in the village.

Ralph lay back and closed his eyes, his heart still thudding. But the landscape that formed in his mind's eye was not the winter-muted valley of his home, but the hot river-flats of the Nepean where he wandered in fever, with the ramparts of the Blue Mountains beyond. He knew what would come next if he lapsed into sleep: the shouting rider charging him down; the dead child.

He got up. Walking might tire him enough for the rest he craved.

The night air was sharp and cold. He shrugged his collar over his ears, and glanced at the sky. On a wrack of cloud, the moon rose. Beneath the stark branches of the trees the ground was dappled in shadow. He cut through the oak-wood towards the stream that marked his boundary. Gabled and peaked, a little Gothic folly stood on the other side.

He reached the eaves of the trees, his ears full of the chattering of the brook. Before he moved into the open ground beyond he looked about. There had been one attempt to kill him. There could very well be another.

Ralph shrank back against the tree-trunk. Just ahead a man, heavily caped, was handing a woman up onto her horse. The scene was all black and silver, drained of colour in the moonlight. The woman's hair gleamed as the hood of her riding-cloak slipped back. It was Caroline, and the man kissing her hand was Bromley. She urged her horse to a trot. Bromley passed not ten feet in front of Ralph, his boots heavy on the icy ground. With a jingle of harness, he rode off.

Ralph eased his stance. So Lucius, poor, devoted Lucius, was being cuckolded by his patron. It served him right. Ralph had a weapon, now, to exact retribution. *Utu.*

Ralph felt a twinge of distaste. Once he would have scorned to gloat over another man's humiliation. Now he sneered at such qualms. His years as a felon had coarsened him; Lucius had only himself to blame for that. His wife was promiscuous; she was so by nature, and Lucius was deluding himself to believe otherwise. So Ralph had chanced upon a midnight tryst... it was less degraded than the sordid couplings of which he had been the unwilling witness, and nearly the victim.

Ralph rubbed his eyes and leaned back. He had tried to concentrate on the estate accounts, but his newfound secret wormed at his mind. He pushed aside the heavy volume with its yellow calf binding. After so long struggling barely to survive, he had no patience for calculation. Money had been transferred, in large sums; but where, it was impossible to trace. Ralph had checked last month's accounts, but could find no record of the thousand pounds remitted to Lucius which he had inadvertently recovered. Frewin must have been running two sets of books.

Ralph had ridden to his house yesterday, to demand an explanation, but the man and his wife had disappeared. He would never be brought to account; he had covered his tracks too well. There were important decisions to be made about the estate, but Ralph shied away from them. He felt taut and overburdened enough. This craving for revenge was an itch that must be scratched. Until it was satisfied he could settle to nothing else.

He rang for his servant, and waited, tapping a pen-knife on a box of quills. Ten minutes. Bob was gone again, just when he needed him. Exasperated, he snapped the haft of the knife. He shoved back his chair. He would have to saddle his horse himself, an awkward business. By the time he rode out, he was short-tempered and sore.

At a little coppice he reined in, astonished. There was his valet, sitting on the trunk of a fallen tree, next to Flavia, bent over a slate, while a little golden-haired boy played at their feet.

"Will you kindly tell me what this is about?" he asked with heavy courtesy. "When I require the services of my servant, I do not expect to have to come and fetch him."

Flavia challenged his angry gaze. "I am teaching him to read and write."

If the man could write, he could give Ralph away. He had hired him for his silence.

"My servant's accomplishments are no business of yours," he snapped. "Bob, come with me." He tugged the reins left-handed, to turn the horse about.

The man gathered himself to rise, but Flavia stood first.

"His name is not Bob," she said.

The horse sidled at her sudden movement, jolting Ralph's arm. "Oh?" he replied sarcastically. "I suppose he told you so himself?"

"He has ears," she rebuked him quietly, "even if he lacks a voice. He wrote it down. Show him," she ordered. "A man has a right to his own name."

Nervously, glancing from one to the other, his servant held out the slate. On it were large, wavering letters: *JOHN VERCOE.*

Ralph had been ready to berate Flavia for her interference, but her words checked him. *A man has a right to his own name.* How could he, of all people, quarrel with that? His anger cooled to shame as he saw the fear in the man's eyes. Ralph remembered what it was to cringe.

Grim-faced, he looked down. "You had better come along—" he said shortly, "—Vercoe."

A sudden smile lit his servant's face. The two men turned back down the bridle-path, leaving Flavia looking after them, clutching the slate.

"Why is that man mad at us?" Charles asked.

"I don't know," said Flavia. "I really don't know."

# 45

## *England, November 1819*

Flavia had just reached the stable yard when Lucius overhauled her, panting.

"What's this I hear from Charles?" he said urgently. "Have you been speaking to Fairfax?"

"Yes," she replied, puzzled by his tone.

"What about?" he demanded.

"I don't see what concern it is of yours."

Lucius seized her by the arm. "Tell me what he said!"

Flavia pulled free. "What is the matter with you, Lucius! We argued over his servant, if it means so much to you."

"That valet you've been giving lessons to?"

"Did you get this from Charles, or have you spied it out for yourself?"

Lucius let this pass. "Have no dealings with Fairfax. The man is dangerous."

"You certainly seem to think so," she retorted. "So why do you let him call? I can only assume you owe him money. Nothing else would make you so abject."

Lucius glared at her, breathing hard. "You shall not drag my son around the countryside to clandestine meetings with idiot serving-men! You have only to look at the fellow to see he is as warped as his master! Anything could have happened to you. Really, Flavia, there are times when your conduct defies rational explanation. I sometimes wonder if Bromley is right!"

"What has Bromley to do with it?" she asked swiftly.

"He says your nerves are strained. He knows of a place at Shillingthorpe, with private apartments, very well appointed, where you could rest until you feel better."

"Lock me up in a madhouse, he means, until I agree to marry him!"

"Flavia, you exaggerate," Lucius said reasonably. "But you must see how readily your behaviour can be misunderstood. I should not need to remind you that people of our rank do not associate with servants. Were you to act with more propriety, you would show Bromley's suppositions to be baseless. And I mean what I say about Fairfax. There are things about him which I am not at liberty to disclose; but I assure you he is no friend to this family."

*Hobson's Choice*, thought Flavia. "What are your terms?" she said, dully.

"You may continue your outings with Charles, but stay close to the house. And keep clear of Fairfax. As a near neighbour, some contact is unavoidable, but I am sure you would prefer not to be exposed to more of his boorishness."

"You have made your point, Lucius. You need not repeat it endlessly. When do you next expect him?"

"This afternoon."

"That problem is solved, then. Molly's wedding is this afternoon. I shall attend that instead—that is, if I have your permission, given your concerns over my associating with servants."

Lucius shifted uncomfortably under the weight of her irony. "Of course," he said. "That was not what I meant—"

"I know precisely what you meant," she said.

"Goodbye, Molly."

"Are you sure you won't come up to the Farm, Miss, for a bite to eat?"

"No," said Flavia gently. "It would only make the Dennisons uncomfortable. You have a new life to lead, with a fine young man. Both of you deserve to be happy, after his first wife dying so young, and you losing Maria." Flavia gave her an impulsive hug. "I wish you a safe journey to New South Wales. And here is a gift for your husband: Mr Wentworth's book."

"You'll be all right, won't you, Miss?" Molly said in a low voice.

"Of course," she replied with a heartiness she was far from feeling. "Off you go."

Tears came to her eyes as she watched Dennison proudly hand his pretty wife up into the gig. Molly lifted her hand in a last wave. Flavia walked away from the crowd, around the back of the church, chiding herself for her self-pity. Her feet rustled through the fallen oak-leaves, cracked and brown. Molly had been her friend. She had needed Molly more than Molly had needed her. She had done the right thing in letting her go, but now she felt utterly alone.

Sitting on the bench by her father's grave, her chin on her hand, she stared at the grey granite slab, its edges crimped already with lichen. No strong arms for her; only a relentless pursuer. No children to the man she loved, twisted now into a dark twin of himself, sharp, suspicious, ungrateful—and left-handed, she realised, unlike the Ralph she remembered. Yesterday he had not used his right hand once. And at the hunt, when he shouted at her, his face had taken on a look almost of Bromley.

Was he a stranger, or some kind of madman, as Lucius implied? What if he had simply forgotten what they had meant to each other? Worst of all, what if she had been wrong from the start, and he had never loved her? Then she would have lost not only the future, but the past as well. She could not force Ralph to love her; love cannot be compelled. That was what Bromley could not understand.

Should she ignore her brother's sanctions, and have it out with Ralph? But had she the courage? She had challenged him readily enough over his servant. But that was over a principle, and for someone else. Where she herself was concerned, she had too much to lose.

She stood and dusted the wet grass from her skirt. It was a long walk back to the house, and a cold welcome once she got there.

Chill despite the fire blazing on the broad hearth, Lucius fixed his eyes on Ralph like a sheep circled by a wolf. For the first half-hour he had been quite civil. Then Caroline had joined them, flaunting those damned jewels again, even though Lucius had commanded her outright not to wear them. They had caused him enough trouble already. She was rattling them almost in their guest's face, simpering at him. What demon of perversity had got into her today? Now she had slipped the bracelet off, and was holding it out for him to admire.

Ralph ran his fingers over the elaborate gold chasing. "Very pretty, particularly as I'll wager it's not yours." He tugged it from her grasp and held the embossed monster-heads up to the light. Their eyes glowed pink, reflecting the flames.

"Give it back, sir!" She looked challengingly across to her husband. "He insulted me!"

"Come on, man," said Ralph, expectant beneath his mockery. His hand holding the bracelet tightened.

Lucius refused to meet Ralph's stare. "Look, my dear," he pleaded with Caroline, his voice strained, "I told you to return it to Flavia. You make things very difficult for me."

His restraint fed her rage. "And where would *she* wear it?" She snatched as Ralph dangled the bracelet just beyond her reach. "Give it to me!" She rounded on her husband. "Won't you stand up for your wife's honour?"

"Harangue him as you will, Lucius will not fight me," Ralph stated. "And as for your honour, you might ask Bromley about that."

"What do you mean?" Lucius's eyes moved from one to the other, stricken.

"He's lying," Caroline snapped.

Lucius whispered: "Please leave Caroline out of this. I know you have little love for me, but don't drag in my family."

Ralph weighed up the words in his mind, sharp as a blade. "Tell him where you were the night before last," he said to Caroline. "And how you got those grass stains on your skirt."

Instinctively she glanced down. Ralph watched Lucius turn ashen as the significance of her gesture sank in. Having achieved what he came to do, Ralph flung the bracelet back at Caroline and strode out the door.

Lucius stood in front of his wife, hand held out. "Give me the bracelet," he ordered. "And the necklace."

Caroline undid the catch but held up the necklace, admiring her reflection in the mirror. She shrugged her shoulders and passed it over. "I don't want it any more. Every time I wore it I would remember how my husband stood by as I was humiliated."

"Humiliated!" cried Lucius. "How do you think I feel! Why did you do it, Caroline? You know how much I love you!"

"Love?" she said, peering again at the mirror as she dabbed perfume behind her ears. "What thrill is there in your devotion? You fawn to me as you do to Fairfax. You are like a spaniel, Lucius; you cannot help yourself."

He seized her shoulders to turn her round. "Look at me, damn you!"

"Why?" she said. "I know what you look like. Really, you are tiresomely earnest, Lucius. Most of my friends have affairs. Fashionable people do it all the time. But they do not draw attention to themselves as you are doing."

"Is that all our marriage means to you? Answer me! Would you stand by me if I lost my money, or got into trouble?"

She giggled. "What a silly question! Why pretend we are going to be lovers in a cottage! I shall not run away with Robert, if that's what you mean. I would not behave so foolishly as that."

"Thank you, my dear, for your regard for the proprieties," Lucius said bitterly. "And to think how cruelly you treated poor Flavia, after what happened to her—"

"Your sister is even more old-fashioned than you are," Caroline interrupted. "I'm married; I have given you an heir. So long as I am discreet, nobody minds. Flavia is a spinster, with her head full of odd notions. She jilted a most eligible match. Now her honour is compromised, nobody wants anything further to do with her. She is as much a pariah as that mangy old dog of hers."

Lucius slapped her pretty, complacent face. "You make me sick."

She stared at him, angry and frightened, her hand over her cheek. He turned to leave.

"Where are you going?"

"To Ash Park," he called back.

Lucius, his head bursting, ran up the shallow stairs to the portico. He would knock Bromley down. The man was a satyr: first Flavia, now Caroline. He would tell him exactly what he thought of him. He would threaten to go to Fairfax and tell him the truth. Then at least his conscience would be clear. Fairfax was destroying him. He could bear the tightening band of guilt no longer, the uncertainty, not knowing where Ralph would strike next.

Mr Bromley was in London, the footman said smoothly. Lucius turned away, rigid with frustration. As he rode home, the old doubts seeped back. Why should Charles suffer for his father's mistakes? How could he meet his debts? If Bromley's money dried up, Caroline would surely leave him; if they stayed under the same roof, her infatuation might pass.

The mood in the house was so unpleasant that Flavia was pleased to be out of it. Charles skipped along beside her as Hester cast about, sniffing along piles of stacked stone. This had been part of the old orchard.

"I shot a pistol here, once," Flavia said, smiling at the recollection. Charles looked up, round-eyed. "I hit a bottle. Your father was astonished. So was I."

"Did Father shoot, like Dick Turpin?"

"Fight a duel, do you mean?" She smiled down at him reassuringly. "Gentlemen don't fight duels any more." Charles picked up a bent twig, and banged away noisily, prancing on an imaginary Black Bess.

The old monastery kitchens were half-demolished now. In the pointed archway the door to the old cellars hung on one hinge. Before it the workmen had propped a flimsy barricade, a board against two barrels.

"Look! Black Bess can go fast!"

Flavia was distracted by a sudden squawk as Hester slunk from behind a box of old rope, with a duck flapping in her mouth.

"Give it to me!" The dog retreated, guilty. "Naughty dog! Give!"

Hester stood abject, tail drooping, as Flavia retrieved the protesting bird. It flapped off, unscathed but for some loose feathers. Flavia looked around for Charles, but the rutted yard was silent.

"Charles?" No answer. The board lay flat, the makeshift pistol on the other side.

Her tone was urgent now. "Come out at once!" She lifted the board aside and pushed past the broken door. Pray God nothing had happened to him. She had already lost one child in her care.

A faint noise sounded from ahead. The trapdoor over the stairs was open. She climbed down to the cellars. It was quite dark. Once she turned the corner the blackness closed her in. She felt her way along the wall in the gloom, her fingers tracing arched openings and locked doors. Then the floor underfoot gave way and she tumbled down a scree of earth and fallen stones. She sat up, rubbing a skinned knee. She could smell damp, and hear Charles whimpering. All she could see looking up was the hole in the floor above, through which she had fallen.

"Charles!" she cried.

"I want to go home." His voice was plaintive in the dark, and oddly resonant.

"Where are you?"

"I'm scared."

She groped towards the sound. Her fingers touched something smooth and slimy; flagstones, in a regular pattern, with a cover of planks. As she leaned closer, she knocked loose a pebble. It rattled past her, and landed a moment later with a deep *plunk*.

This must be the old well. There was a gap where the lid had decayed. She could smell the rotten wood, dank and sour. Charles had slipped as she had, but rolled further, through the lid. How far had he fallen?

"Don't move!" she said sharply. "I know where you are." She lay at full length and stretched down as far as she dared over the edge. She could just feel the top of Charles's curly head.

Could she climb down to rescue him? She knelt on the rim, seeking a foothold, but the rotten timbers sagged under her weight. Quickly she pulled back.

Again Charles whimpered. Once more she lay flat and reached down to touch him. If only she had a light, or a rope!

"Hold hard, dear. I won't go away."

More stones pattered down on top of her. Twisting around, she saw Hester's inquisitive head at the edge of the cellar floor above. The dog whined.

"Go home!" she hissed. "Bad dog! Home!" She shied a stone at the dog and turned back.

"Let's play a game," she said. She must keep from panicking. "You are Dick Turpin, and we are hiding in a cave. We must be very still."

"I don't like that game." His voice wavered.

"It's not for long. Hester will be Black Bess. She has gone off for help." If only it were true.

Ralph dismounted in the stable-yard. He had not bothered, this time, to make an appointment; he had come to demand his money back.

He heard a yelp behind him as Harriet's dog cringed from the ostler's kick.

"Beg pardon, sir, but she's a right nuisance. Been howling for the last ten minutes. She won't leave us alone."

Recognising Ralph, the dog crept over to him, not with her tail between her legs, as he would have expected, but pressing herself low on the ground, then jumping back, whining and yapping, and running up again. He looked down at her, troubled by her persistence.

"Have you seen Miss Stanton?" he said, reluctant to become involved, yet remembering Clancy and his dog Gyp.

"She was here half an hour ago, sir," said the ostler doubtfully, "with young Master Charles."

That would be the boy he saw, Lucius's son. The dog gazed up at him, distressed. Abruptly he followed her.

The ostler called across to the groom. "D'ye think something's wrong? You'd better go up to the house and check the two of them are back."

"Who's there?" Ralph called, hoarsely.

A sound came back, eerily, from deep in the earth. His skin prickled. Beckworth would have laughed at him.

Again it came: a woman's voice, urgent. Following the sound, he found the trapdoor. As he reached the bottom of the stair it hit him: darkness, damp, stale air. His body refused to move. He felt suddenly faint and his left hand came up to clutch his injured arm. Another wave of fear washed over him and his heart hammered. You're not in the gallery, buried alive, he commanded himself. He willed one leg to advance a step, then the other. The dog whimpered and Ralph forced himself to follow as the wash of panic subsided. The palms of his hands were damp.

He moved on warily. The dog stopped in a frenzy of barking. Ralph could taste the water on his palate before he reached the hole in the floor. Gingerly he peered over.

"Lucius? Is that you?" Flavia's voice reverberated from below, magnified by the shaft.

"Fairfax," he replied, curtly. "Where's the boy?"

"He's fallen down a well. He can't hold on much longer. Can you get help, please? I can't leave him."

His eyes adjusting to the gloom, Ralph instinctively placed the faint shapes and deeper voids within the room beneath. Below him was Flavia, stretching dangerously across a broken cover of old boards. If the child slipped, and she snatched after him, they would crumble.

"There's rope outside," she called, her voice strained. He turned and ran back to the light.

"Have you a message from Miss Stanton?" asked Lucius impatiently. The groom shifted from one foot to the other.

"No, sir. The ostler sent me to ask was she back yet, with Master Charles."

"Of course they're not back yet," cut in Mrs Lennox. "Nurse has been waiting with the bath drawn this last half-hour."

The lad looked more uncomfortable than ever. "It's almost dark, and the dog was acting strange, and the gentleman from Longhallows said—"

"Fairfax?" Lucius said sharply. "Where is he?"

"He was at the stables, sir, and he followed the dog 'cause it was whining."

Lucius stood up.

"It's all right, sir," the groom called after him. "The gentleman is looking after it."

Appalled, Lucius dashed from the room.

With unthinking competence Ralph knotted the rope into a loop and coiled it over his shoulder. He would have preferred to rig a support over the well-head, but there was no time. A ringbolt, ridged with corrosion, was set into the floor; he would have to trust to that.

"Get back," he ordered Flavia. "Jump clear if that bolt gives, so the rope doesn't whip around your ankle. I'll pass the child up to you."

As he stepped backwards a cold breath enveloped him. The child's fair head shone faintly.

Ralph felt a beam angled beneath him, lodged across the shaft. The boy must have landed on it when he fell. The slightest pressure from Ralph would send it crashing down.

"Charles," he said softly. "Can you see me? Hold onto me, now."

The child clung to his beam, too scared to let go. Ralph leaned down, but he could not reach with his left hand; it would have to be his right. As he moved a spatter of little echoes came from below.

He stretched down and wrenched the child free. His hiss of pain as the weight tore at his muscles was masked by the rustle and crash as the beam fell away. Ralph grabbed with his good hand, pressing the boy to him to stop him slipping from his weakened grasp. The rope quivered, taut. The child clung to him, pinching like a frightened monkey. His hair smelled sweet, like wet wool.

"Have you got him?" Flavia was crouched at the top.

Ralph hauled himself up, the child a dead weight round his neck. With a final heave he was over the edge, disentangling the boy from his shirt. He felt a sudden rush of exhilaration. In some way he could not understand he had laid one of his ghosts. He handed Charles over to Flavia, who hugged the boy with a sob.

"Thank you," she said shakily.

He looked across at her in the gloom. She was filthy and dishevelled; he heard the catch in her breathing. He was close enough to sense the warmth of her body and the sweet remembered tang of lily-of-the-valley. She had been afraid; but she had stayed, so the boy would not be alone in the dark.

"Flavia—" he began.

Footsteps clattered down the passageway above. Dazzlingly bright, a lantern jigged as Lucius slithered over the edge of the hole. Ralph stiffened; then continued coiling the rope in silence.

"Is Charles hurt?" Lucius said urgently, darting a look at Ralph half distracted, half relieved. Ralph read it exactly. He flung down the rope, shouldered Lucius aside, and pushed tight-faced through the gaping servants.

The lantern swung again, throwing a beam of light across Flavia's face. Through the dust on her cheek ran a track of tears.

# 46

## England, December 1819

Rubbing his gloved hands together against the cold, Bromley straightened up from the parapet of the new Waterloo Bridge. Today his mind was on more pressing matters than its fine proportions and superb shallow arches. He had already dealt with his first item of London business. Frewin, arriving panic-stricken from his bruising interview with Fairfax, had been deeply grateful for the hundred pounds and offer of accommodation while arrangements were made for his new life in America.

Arrangements had indeed been made, but with the proprietor of *The Split Crow*, proving his usefulness yet again. It was two of his men who had taken Fairfax, four years before. Bromley relished the irony. Now Frewin's fears, and the threat he posed, were alike irrelevant; somewhere downriver the naked bodies of a man and a woman slopped in the tide, their faces smashed in.

The second item was more challenging. By the end of the morning he would either have an elegant solution to his problem, or be thoroughly compromised. He gave a thin smile. He was prepared for that eventuality as well.

Someone had been making discreet enquiries about Sir Ralph Fairfax around the City. Bromley's interest, already roused, had been further piqued when he heard that their originator was a gentleman newly arrived from New South Wales. Hazarding a guess that a friend of Fairfax's would have approached him directly, Bromley had made an appointment "to discuss a matter to our mutual advantage". This gentleman must have a very compelling reason indeed, to follow a runaway convict halfway round the world.

Fairfax had to be got rid of; he was too unpredictable. The thorn under the saddle had come within a whisker of success, but Bromley could not afford another failure, not with Stanton threatening to crack at any moment. If the morning's meeting went well, Bromley would have only one more call to make upon Lucius. He would accede to it readily enough, believing it to be the last. And with Fairfax gone, he could make the next move in the endgame he had planned for Flavia.

"Mr Bromley?"

The man before him was shorter than he, and older, with black hair turned to grey; dressed respectably but without obvious distinction. He could have been any man of business in the City.

"At your service, sir," replied Bromley, aware of a sharp scrutiny in his turn. This was no fat grazier. He had a politician's tight mouth, that gives away no secrets. "Are you the gentleman I am expecting?"

"Masters," confirmed the other, with a hint almost of amusement. "I am the man you are looking for."

Disconcerted, Bromley led the way. They had crossed two spans of the bridge before he noticed a low-looking, hard-faced man keeping pace with them.

"Never mind him," said Masters. "That is my servant. He lacks polish, having been a convict. Would you agree that *nothing can wash away the convict's guilt, or obliterate its brand?*"

Bromley darted a keen look at his companion. This Masters was both audacious and acute. If Bromley had read this conversation aright, he was as eager to be rid of Ralph as Bromley himself. Why, he wondered. Had Ralph, impertinent as always, but no longer protected by his rank, provoked his betters once too often?

Bromley decided to wager all, and put to this Masters the scheme he had devised. But it was as well, when commencing negotiations, not to admit enthusiasm; so he addressed the manservant, staring blankly at the incomparable vista of the Thames. "What's your name, my man?"

The man touched his hat. "Pryor, sir," he grunted.

Flavia leaned over the keyboard. The day after her nephew's accident Lucius had replaced the broken door with a new one, fitted with a strong bolt and padlock. He kept the key in his desk. Flavia had been curtly informed there would be no further outings with Charles. Both Caroline and Mrs Lennox forbade it, as they were concerned for the child's safety. Arguments had not moved her brother. She would not stoop to tears.

Music was now her only solace. In this private world she could give some vent to her feelings; feel beauty quicken under her hands. At a knock at the door she glanced up.

It was Lucius, with a smile such as she had not seen for weeks. "You have a visitor from London," he said.

"A visitor? For me? Who is it?"

"A Mr Wentworth, who says he was a friend of Harriet's. He is gathering information on sheep-breeding. He has brought you a copy of his book."

"How kind of him. It will replace the one I gave Molly."

Down in the hall, Flavia welcomed Wentworth with unfeigned warmth. His red hair and familiar slouch recalled happier times. An old friend was a treasure indeed at this nadir of her fortunes. She wondered how he had survived his mauling by the gossips. He appeared a little chastened, but still had the look of being charged with more energy than the air around him could comfortably hold.

"I must apologise for not coming sooner," said Wentworth. "I was ill in Paris when your cousin died; then there was the book to finish, and certain—er—family matters. I daresay Bromley wasted no time acquainting you with them."

Flavia had never seen anyone both downcast and pugnacious at once. "He told me when I first met you about your father's youthful scrapes," she replied. "And as for your parents not being married: that is a circumstance you share with many people of higher rank than ours. You would have heard no more of it, had there not been a political advantage in disclosing it. Why else libel a woman dead these many years?"

Flavia was surprised at her own heat. Now she had felt the censure of society, she sympathised with others who had suffered its sting. "But please do not call Bromley out, as I understand you have done with some connected with this affair. He would probably fire at the count of two."

Wentworth gave her a strange look. "You never cease to surprise, Miss Stanton."

"I take it your understanding with Miss Macarthur is at an end?"

"Since September," he replied shortly.

"But—" she suddenly realised, "that was before..."

He looked uncomfortable. "Her father objected to a squib I penned some years ago. He discovered only recently that I wrote it."

Flavia smiled despite herself. "Mr Wentworth, you are impossible!" She could think of no one else who would lampoon his prospective father-in-law, and not expect him to be angry about it.

He grinned reluctantly. "Earl Fitzwilliam has stood by me, so I am not entirely disgraced. I shall return to Australia, and the Exclusives shall hear of me yet." He handed over the parcel under his arm. "I hope you will enjoy my *Description of the Colony of New South Wales.*"

"The *Edinburgh Review* spoke very favourably of it."

"*Piquant oddities of antipodean society?*" he quoted. "When will they see beyond the oddities to the opportunities? New South Wales is no longer simply a gaol; they must encourage more free emigration."

"Ever the Australian patriot! I have gained you one convert at least," said Flavia. "My lady's maid has just wed a local farmer; they sail for your homeland within the month. I gave them my copy of your book, so I am pleased to have another, especially from the author's own hands."

"I would happily sail with them, to escape this dank December weather! But too much is happening here for me to leave now. The Select Committee on the State of Gaols is packed with Marsden's supporters; and Bigge's report, when it comes, will be the end of Old Sandy."

"How can they act on his conclusions," Flavia objected, "before he has submitted the report? Why should it end Macquarie's career?"

"His successor has already been named: Brisbane, who has the interest of the Duke of York. No, Macquarie will go; you may take my word on it. There is talk of him putting up Redfern as a magistrate. The Exclusives will never stand for it."

"You have lost me," said Flavia. "Who is this Redfern?"

"He is a top surgeon in the Colony and the Governor's close friend. But you must understand: he is a pardoned convict. He was transported as a youth for giving advice to the mutineers on the Nore."

"But that was years ago!" Flavia exclaimed. "Surely his labours for the general good would atone for a single youthful folly."

"So you might think. I was told Mr Bigge's opinion: Redfern is *a traitor guilty of the most foul and unnatural conspiracy that ever disgraced the page of British History.* His appointment as a magistrate would *contaminate the office of justice.*"

Flavia was silent for a moment. "I must confess I am taken aback by such vehemence," she said. "I have met Mr Bigge. He seemed to me mild, almost prim."

"Prim in everything but denunciation," declared Wentworth roundly.

"You hardly do the Commissioner justice."

"Justice?" he echoed. "When was the Government of New South Wales concerned with justice? Slavery, more like; a slavish system of begging for rights which, as British subjects, we ought to possess. But enough of politics. I shall be staying for some days in the town—"

"In the town? You must stay with us," said Flavia, warmly. "I am sure Lucius will make no objection. We have had few visitors of late."

Indeed Lucius pressed Wentworth to accept. Even though he proposed to spend most of his time visiting the local farmers, Lucius was relieved by even an occasional presence, seeing his guest as a bulwark against the next visit by his neighbour.

Lucius folded the letter that had just arrived from London. It was from Bromley, instructing Lucius to invite the local gentry to a Christmas Ball, and confirming that thereafter, Fairfax would trouble him no longer. If only it were true! He would do anything to escape this nightmare. Knowing that Ralph had saved his son's life only made it worse. How thank the man who had exposed him as a cuckold? Caroline still denied him her bed. Lucius suspected that Bromley meant to have Ralph done away with, but preferred not to think about it. He went to lock the letter away. On second thoughts, he fed it into the fire.

Ralph reined in his horse sharply, and twisted in the saddle to stare down the village street. The object of his attention, a stocky ploughman, nervously touched the rim of his hat. Ralph's eyes told him this was only a rustic; but a ripple of fear had made him shiver. It could not possibly be Pryor: the notion was ludicrous.

It had started two nights ago, when he was riding at dusk and saw—or thought he saw—a man in the lane. He could have sworn it was Pryor. But when he looked back the road was empty.

What was wrong with him? He had solitude at last, and his thoughts were driving him mad. Sleep only loosed the terrors he suppressed by day. He had blighted Stanton's marriage, but after the first surge of triumph he felt more wretched than before. Now he was drawn back to Fontclaire Priory. At least with Lucius he could drop the strain of pretence.

From the tower, Ralph caught a wisp of music; its raw tension echoing his distress. For a moment he was lost in it. Then he remembered Limeburners' Creek, the price he paid when last he halted for a haunting strain. He spurred his horse on.

"Sir Ralph Fairfax, a neighbour—Mr Wentworth, a guest from London, studying for the Bar." Lucius saw Ralph frown as he registered the name. This afternoon he would get some of his own back. "Mr Wentworth describes himself as an *Australian.*"

"A homesick one," his guest put in, smiling. "I have been gone some three years."

"We were just discussing the London papers," Lucius said blandly. "Orator Hunt has been arrested."

"That news will distress your sister," said Wentworth. "She has a partiality for the Radical cause. Where is she?" he said, looking around.

"Banging away on that old pianoforte, I expect," said Alicia Lennox. "They should have called in the Military long since. A dangerous agitator like Hunt deserves to be flogged. No doubt you, Mr Wentworth, would agree with the need for strong measures to keep order. Look how necessary they are in your own country."

"I beg to differ, Ma'am. The flogging of free men is an act of arbitrary despotism. And I would further say, from my experience of Government men—what you would call convicts—that flogging ruins a good man and drives a bad one to desperation. I know no case where a man was improved by it."

Surprised at Wentworth's robust reply, but too obstinate to abandon her position, she turned to Ralph. "And you, sir? What is your opinion?"

For a moment Ralph was back in Coal River, the realm of King Lash, one of thirty-odd brutes being served out their necessary chastisement on a Sunday morning. He took a deep breath. "I have been away some time," he said with restraint. "If there are men rioting from hunger, give them full bellies, not sore backs."

Mrs Lennox blinked. "But how else enforce respect for the law?" she exclaimed, indignant. "Surely steps must be taken, as a salutary warning—"

*You and Morisset together.* Ralph's temper flared at this ignorant, vindictive woman, oblivious to the agony of those she so casually condemned. "Madam," he began, his voice growing rougher as he went on, "have you ever seen a man strung up and flayed like a side of beef? What possible satisfaction could any *gentlewoman* derive from it?"

There was a ringing silence. Mrs Lennox stood, her cheeks flaming. "Good day, sirs," she announced, glaring at Ralph. "This conversation is no longer fit for a lady." She swept out.

Flavia passed her in the doorway. Her glance flew to Ralph; she had not expected him to be there. Her smile faded. "I am interrupting," she murmured.

"Not at all." Lucius jumped up, eager to dispel the mood. "Shall we show Mr Wentworth the conservatory? My father had an interest in rare plants; he collected botanical prints as well, some quite valuable, I believe." Chattering to his guest, he led the way out of the room.

Ralph had not seen Flavia since the rescue. The image of the woman in the cellar had lingered in his mind. She might have been Bromley's mistress in the past, but each time Ralph had seen them together, she had kept a careful distance from the man. She was afraid of him. Ralph knew fear: none better. He recalled how her playing had touched him, and the warmth of her body in the cellar, so close.

"Hullo!" exclaimed Wentworth, a little way ahead. "Here is an old friend a long way from home. How came you by this, Stanton?" He squatted down by a sapling.

"I don't know," said Lucius. "It's new to me."

Craning forward, Ralph was astonished to recognise the feathery leaves of a golden wattle. He crumbled a piece in his fingers, releasing a pungent scent. The memory rushed back of that last night in Sydney, shielded by boughs dusted with blossom as Donovan talked to the night-watchman, and the dark waters of the harbour glittered beyond.

"Oh, that was Harriet's." Flavia exclaimed. "It outgrew the old pot so I moved it here. You never saw it, did you, Lucius? I meant to tell you: remember that odd letter to Father? We didn't open it, but a seed fell out as Harriet read the direction. I pushed it in with the lilies and forgot about it. Surely you recall it? It was about a year after Father died. What was it about?"

Ralph's hand tightened on the crumpled twig. "Yes, do tell us," he echoed. "*What was in the letter?*"

Lucius flushed. "Really, I cannot recall." He shrugged nervously, with an attempt at a smile. "Some routine matter, I expect."

Quickly he turned into the next path.

"How remarkable!" said Wentworth. "It's a golden wattle all right." He stared at it with longing. "I know this is asking a great deal—there are so few specimens in England—but might I have it, to keep in my rooms? I promise to tend it carefully. It reminds me of home."

"By all means," came Lucius's voice from the other side of the stand, well beyond Ralph's reach.

Ralph felt a race of anger. The bastard: the callous, crawling bastard. For years he knew where I was. He knew about the punishment camp; and what did he do? Stole my money, and left me to rot.

"It was probably just a begging letter," he said loudly. "I have a friend who gets them all the time, from the most disreputable people."

He turned on his heel and strode outside. If he stayed there any longer he would give himself away. *Fiat justitia et ruat coelum. Let there be justice, though the heavens fall.* Now he would destroy Lucius utterly.

"Miss Flavia!" Betsy Turner waved an agitated arm. She hurried up, cheeks flushed, labouring for breath. "It's about Sarah," she wheezed. "She's asking for you."

Flavia had heard the old woman was ill, and had meant to visit. But the near-disaster in the cellar had distracted her. "I don't know—" she began, doubtfully.

Betsy clutched her sleeve. "You'd better hurry, Miss. She's dying. It's terrible bad luck, to thwart a dying wish."

Flavia looked around. Wentworth had gone off to commune with his tree, like an Arab with his horse. Lucius and Ralph had disappeared. She had caught the menace in that last exchange. Lucius had started the afternoon in higher spirits than she had seen in weeks, but had left the conservatory as scared as a rabbit.

Flavia sighed. "Very well," she said. "I'll fetch my cloak."

They walked along the path, Flavia only half listening to Betsy's chatter. Then a name snagged in her mind: *Fairfax.*

"You know what they're saying in the village now, Miss?"

"No," said Flavia, wishing she could leave the subject alone, but knowing she could not.

"They say it's not Sir Ralph at all. They say he was killed overseas, and this other man came back in his place."

"That's ridiculous," said Flavia sharply. "Anyone can see it's Fairfax."

"But he's very different, isn't he? So hard and rude, and the old Sir Ralph would never have put off all those people. This one never goes anywhere but Fontclaire. And he's strange. Two of the lads killed a sheep to give him a scare, and when he found it he just laughed."

"Perhaps it was to show he was not afraid," Flavia objected.

Betsy shook her head. "It wasn't that sort of laugh." She tapped her head expressively.

Was Lucius right, insisting Ralph was dangerous? But no madman would have acted as he did in the cellar. He could have left the child to die. He could have killed them both, had he wanted to. For all his brusque manner, something had touched his pity. If only Lucius had not arrived when he did…

Stop deluding yourself, she corrected. Fairfax, whatever he is, has shown only hostility towards you. The Ralph you loved is dead, if indeed he ever existed. She stepped out briskly, pulling her green cloak about her, wishing she had dressed more warmly against the chill fingers of the wind.

# 47

## *England, December 1819*

Bromley surveyed the great hall, satisfied by the hubbub of voices. He checked the hour and snapped shut his watch. Lucius had assembled a suitable audience at Fontclaire for the last act of this little melodrama.

Only three of the players had so far been rehearsed: himself, Masters and Pryor. Bromley would be happy to see the last of this ill-assorted pair. Pryor was a brute, as out of place in a gentleman's house as a wild boar with its hooves clagged with dung. If one must employ a creature for one's darker dealings, then let it at least be one with intelligence, like Frewin. Masters, too, irked him by his casual assumption of authority. When Bromley had queried this, Masters had replied with a tag from Goethe: *You must either command and rule or serve and lose, suffer or triumph; be the anvil or the hammer.* Bromley was happy for Ralph to be the anvil. But was there room for two hammers? Still, for this evening at least he required Master's cooperation. After that he would never see him or his half-brother again.

There in the far corner sat Flavia, alone. Good: Lucius had done as he was told, insisting that she attend. Bromley needed her to witness Ralph's humiliation; besides, he had news for her.

"Good evening, Miss Stanton." He bowed over her hand with relentless politeness, gripping her wrist so tightly that it hurt. She tried to pull away.

"Knowing your interest in politics, I must tell you that Lord Sidmouth has passed his Six Acts. I voted for all of them."

Flavia stared blindly ahead.

"In view of your manifest enthusiasm, let me explain. Now the Government has power to prevent bodies of men drilling; to raid houses for arms; to forbid public meetings; to imprison those who preach sedition and to tax the Radical press out of existence. Your reformers are utterly crushed; their leaders broken or in gaol. Perhaps now you will admit what a fool you were." He leaned closer, his head and hers almost touching. "And don't think we have finished with each other."

He dropped her hand and walked back to the sideboard, gaudy with its banks of candles. Rubbing her wrist, Flavia rocked in silent grief. Despite the ruin of her own hopes, she had drawn solace from this yearning for reform. That had been part of Wentworth's charm: his brave talk of the rights of free men.

But the Radical cause had been only that: brave talk. The ramparts of reaction would not crumble at the mere waving of banners. No amount of principled argument would induce Bromley and his ilk to concede one iota of their privilege. What had Castlereagh said, when accused of ignoring the people's distress? *Time alone can bring an effectual remedy.*

Time! It stretched before her endlessly, each day as empty as the last, as void of hope as the well over which she had hung. Bromley would never let her go: she had hurt his pride too deeply to be forgiven. What new scheme had he devised, to manipulate her spineless brother? What escape did she have, other than killing herself? She let out a long sigh, her head bowed and hands clenched on her lap, fighting down the tears that choked the back of her throat.

Ralph had arrived just as Bromley left her. For an instant her face was unguarded, desolate. With a visible effort, she straightened her shoulders and composed her features. She turned to the passing footman. "A glass of punch, Vickery."

From beside the fireplace, Mrs Lennox raised her hand in summons.

"Can't, Miss. I'm busy." Vickery made to edge past.

Instinctively Ralph barred his way. "Attend to Miss Stanton," he ordered.

"I'm doing what my mistress said," the man retorted, reaching for a bottle of champagne.

Ralph struck it out of his hand. "Forget the old bitch, you useless shit-sack!" He filled a glass from the punchbowl as Vickery gaped, astonished, from the dark splashes on his livery to the shards on the floor. The footman jumped as Ralph clanked the glass down on his tray. "Take this to Miss Stanton, now."

Scared, Vickery backed away.

Ralph took a deep breath. He had not meant to react so strongly.

Lucius appeared at his elbow, nervous and angry. "What are you doing?" he hissed.

"Teaching him manners."

"Don't speak of my mother-in-law in that fashion!"

"Why not?" Ralph replied, more loudly. "Is she any less a procuress than Emma Hamilton's mother? Or did you think Caroline had succumbed to your manly charms? She would have leaped into bed with the first man who asked, provided he was wealthy and stupid enough."

Lucius looked about anxiously. "For God's sake lower your voice!"

"Why?" demanded Ralph. "It's the truth, isn't it? That's what you're afraid of: the truth—" he had a sudden incongruous memory of the Parramatta courthouse "—the whole truth, and nothing but the truth."

He gave an ugly laugh. "A toast." His eyes glinted. "To old friends, happy memories."

Thoroughly alarmed, Lucius hurried over to Bromley.

"You must silence Fairfax," he whispered urgently. "He's in a freakish mood. There's no knowing what he'll say next."

Bromley patted his arm reassuringly. "All will be attended to."

"He has already attacked one of the servants. You must get rid of him now before he ruins the evening."

"Not yet," said Bromley with emphasis. "I have everything in hand. He will be gone in under an hour. Start up the dancing."

Uncertainly Lucius obeyed, darting occasional glances at his unpredictable guest. Flute and fiddles struck up a lively quadrille. Flavia still sat like a statue; she had not moved since the evening began. He went over to her.

"Come on—" Lucius began.

"I wish to go to my room," she cut in. "Whatever game you are playing with Fairfax has no place for spectators." She went to rise.

Her brother was suddenly mindful of his instructions. "You can't leave yet; the dancing has just begun. People will talk. Stay till supper. Please."

Flavia's shoulders were rigid with the effort of self-control. "I cannot bear it!" she burst out. "Do you know how it feels to sit here like a pariah? Bromley came only to gloat. Is this why you force me to stay?"

"Don't say that," Lucius pleaded. "Look: I'll lead you out for the next set, and take you into supper. Then you may go."

She was grateful for even this small gesture. "Very well," she said, trying to smile. "Just till supper."

"There," said Lucius, giving her a quick hug. "Everything will soon be well. Just you wait and see."

Ralph would have preferred to drink alone. He tensed as Wentworth loomed beside him.

"I hear you were some years overseas," he remarked. "Did you by any chance reach New South Wales?"

"I spent some time there," said Ralph carefully.

"And what was your opinion?" Wentworth enquired with enthusiasm.

"What I saw I did not like."

"Come, sir: it is the finest country in the world!"

"It all depends on your point of view." Ralph went to shake off his unwanted companion, but Wentworth was not letting him go so easily.

Colouring, he placed himself squarely in Ralph's way. "I mislike your tone, sir."

Ralph snorted and moved to pass, but Wentworth, his temper stirred, put out his arm. "Tell me: to what did you take exception?"

Ralph was in no mood to justify himself. How much of the coal he had hacked, sweating, had gone into D'Arcy Wentworth's free allowance? He eyed Wentworth with a convict's sullen contempt. "There's your father's hospital, for a start."

Wentworth's shoulders hunched pugnaciously. "Pray what do you mean by that?"

"It's filthy; it's corrupt. I wouldn't send a dog there."

He could hear Wentworth's faster breathing. "Come outside, sir." Ralph ignored him. Wentworth snatched at Ralph's arm; the bad one. Ralph jabbed him left-handed, and Wentworth staggered back to collide with Alicia Lennox.

Lucius rushed over from the dancing-floor. "Fairfax!"

Ralph, rage boiling inside him, snatched up a knife from the sideboard.

Lucius backed away. "Quick! Help!"

A woman screamed. Flavia pushed her way towards the commotion as the guests scrambled clear. She stared unbelieving as Ralph circled her brother and lunged. Lucius clutched his wrist, his other hand tearing at the buttons of Ralph's waistcoat, struggling to fend him off. Bromley knocked Flavia aside. As Ralph's eyes flicked to his new antagonist, Lucius struck the knife spinning.

The music lapsed into silence. Lucius and Ralph grappled; from behind, Bromley wrenched down Ralph's coat to pinion his elbows. The punchbowl clanged to the floor, gouting over the tiles. Bromley seized the back of his shirt. As Ralph slipped, it tore with a grating rip that set Flavia's teeth on edge. Lucius flung his weight across his legs to hold him down. As Ralph strained away, Lucius, fist raised, stopped in mid-movement.

"Dear God," he said.

Ralph lay still except for the rise and fall of his shoulders as he fought for breath. With a shock like a blow to the stomach Flavia saw that his back was seamed with thick intersecting weals. Lucius shifted; the trapped man realised suddenly what had happened; the muscles tensed; he froze.

A clock ticked in the hush. Ralph moved; the restraining hands fell away. He crouched and shrugged on his clothes. The crowd that had pressed forward to stare now shrank back. Shame tainted his mouth like bile. Fool, he thought; you should have left Wentworth alone.

No one would meet his eye. Flavia was white; Lucius looked sick. Wentworth's hostility faded to understanding. The rest were puzzled, scared. Bromley had gone.

Ralph caught the tread of approaching feet.

Flavia, still numb, saw him stop, taut-faced, as the crowd parted. A voice rang out, commanding.

"Ralph Fletcher, alias Fairfax: I arrest you in the King's name as a transported felon, unlawfully at large."

She expected Ralph to protest but he stood mute: he knew this man. Bromley watched from the doorway as a hard-faced guard stepped forward, swinging a pair of fetters on a chain. Ralph inched back.

"Come on, Fletcher," Pryor coaxed. "Don't pretend you haven't seen these before."

Ralph's face drained; so pale Flavia thought he would faint. Slowly he brought round his hands. As the guard reached out, Ralph snatched at the chain, and leapt for the door. But as he reached it the older man spun him round and slammed his shoulder against the jamb. Ralph winced as his wrists were twisted back, lashed together, and the loop hauled tight. Pryor snapped one fetter around the prisoner's wrist, the other on his own. He whipped a short club from his belt as Ralph twisted to face him.

"No!" Flavia dashed in his way, revolted.

"Stand clear," Masters snapped. "This man is dangerous."

"This is my home!" she cried, "not a prison yard! There has been enough violence here!"

She held her ground. Master's mouth hardened. He gestured down; slowly the club descended. She felt the current of air as the man behind her breathed out.

Pryor yanked the chain. It rasped cold against her skin. As Ralph brushed past, his left hand closed round her fingers, pressing into them something round and hard. She stood back.

Lucius hesitated by the door, grey-faced and no longer young.

Ralph spat in his face. *"Judas."*

The room exploded into babble. Questions, snatching hands; Flavia pushed through the blur of faces, the echo of voices fading as she sought the silence of her own room. Her stomach heaved. She was violently sick in the wash-basin.

Who was Ralph? What had they done with him? Where had he been, these last four years? Grief desolated her. Those scars were not new. How desperately he had deserved her pity, while she gave only blame.

She could keep the ring safe, at least. She tried to slip it onto the chain round her neck, but fumbled the catch. It took three more attempts to secure it. Her eyes spilled hot tears.

Lucius knew what this was about. She dashed water on her face. The room was chill; she changed quickly into her riding-costume, snatched up her cloak and ran to find her brother.

From outside she heard the rumble of coach-wheels on gravel as the guests streamed away. The connecting door to the hall was shut. As she reached it she caught the sound of raised voices and checked, recalling the casual violence of the men who had dragged Ralph away. She stooped with her ear to the keyhole.

Bromley was arguing with her brother. Their voices rose in pitch, then ceased. Lucius's rapid step faded. She heard Bromley's short, dismissive laugh; then his steps grew louder. She tried the handle of the door, but it was locked. She was trapped in the tower.

As lightly as she could, she raced up the worn stone steps, past her own door, to the dark schoolroom above. Only one way could she cross to the body of the house. She dragged aside the broken chair blocking the cupboard door, and ran her fingers along the top of the frame.

Caked in spiderwebs and grime, there was the key. The door was stiff;
but it creaked open. She clambered in, locking it behind her. She felt for
the loose panel at the back and crawled through, feeling her way in the
darkness, fending off the sticky tendrils that clung to her face and hair.
Then with a heave she was out through the trapdoor and onto the roof.

Up here the air bit her lungs with each breath. It was coming on to
snow. She edged precariously across the leads, not daring to look over
the side. It seemed so easy when she was a child. Then, with two tugs
on the rusty bolt she was back inside, shaking off the cobwebs and dust.

As she had guessed, Lucius was in the library.

"What have you done?"

He swallowed, refusing to look at her.

She tried again. "For God's sake tell me what this is about!"

"I dare not." His voice was a whisper.

Her sorely-tried allegiance to her brother snapped. "You have
made your life. What about mine? Who are those men? Why do they
call Ralph 'Fletcher'? Where has he been?" She shook him by the
shoulders, compelling the words out of him. "If you won't tell me
yourself, let me ask him! Where is he?"

"Yes." The answer was less to her than to himself. "This is the
best way." At last he met her eye. "They are holding him in the cellars
while they change the horses. There's a guard on the door. Try the coal-
hatch."

He clutched at her hand. "I'm so sorry, Flavia. It was never meant
to happen like this."

Wordlessly she pulled away.

# 48

## *England, December 1819*

Snow fell in cold flurries, plucking her cloak as she hid behind the stacked blocks of stone. A lamp glimmered inside the refectory porch. Against the arch a dark shape stood in silhouette, looking out: the man with the club. He turned his back to the weather and she dashed across the yard.

Now she was in the angle of the wall, sheltered from the worst of the wind. Set into the flagstones was a heavy iron grille, secured by a loop of rusty chain. She raked away the litter of twigs and dead leaves, so that the barred oblong stood stark against the lantern-light within. Flavia knelt at the edge.

Ralph sat hunched awkwardly below her, his arms twisted behind him. She tossed down a stone; he looked up; she heard the clink of a chain.

"Who is it?" he whispered.

"Me. Flavia."

"Has your brother sent you to gloat?"

"No," she replied. "He would tell me nothing. I have no part in this. All I know is that you deserted me after Bromley's ball, and reappeared six weeks ago. Surely you owe me an explanation."

"Owe you? When you lured me outside to meet you and stood by while I was knocked over the head? Don't deny it: I saw your shawl and that jewel in your hair. If you are innocent, why did you send Lucius with the note?"

The cold of the iron bars seeped into her hands. "I sent no note. I left directly we quarrelled. The shawl and the diamonds were on my dressing-table in the morning; I never missed them. I swear it!"

His voice was bitter. "Doubtless your brother would swear just as readily."

"I am not Lucius. Disbelieve me if you will, but I have told the truth. I would swear it on my father's grave."

The wind sobbed in the long silence.

"Well," he said heavily, "someone has made fools of us both." There was too much to explain; no time. "Lucius brought me a note: from you, he said. I wanted to apologise and—" it was too painful now to tell her about the ring that had been in his pocket. "From the path I glimpsed a woman wearing your shawl, and those diamonds. I thought it was you." Did it matter any more? He would be dead before dawn. "Then someone knocked me senseless. When I came to I was Ralph Fletcher, convict, on the prison transport *Adelphi*, bound for New South Wales."

"When I saw you using your left hand, instead of your right, I thought you might be someone else."

"My arm was broken in an—accident. Is it so obvious?"

Not all looked as closely as I, she thought. Then she realised: "Masters: you knew him in New South Wales."

"And Spain before that: he was the Frenchman I told you of at Badajoz. I escaped him then, and again, at a price. But when next I ran from Newcastle he knew that I was not the convict he had believed me to be, and that he had seen me in Spain."

Suddenly the past Ralph had tried so hard to suppress burst open like a wound. In brief, disjointed sentences he told her what had happened that night: "Beckworth: where are you meeting him? When?" Merciless fingers probing the shattered bone. Choking as a bucket of water doused him chill and coughing out of the welcome darkness. His desperate cry: "Stop! I'll tell you…" Shame, rising like vomit: then the brief, exquisite respite.

With Pryor gone to the rendezvous, Masters' questions had started again, more urgently. "Who are you? Who have you told about me? What were your duties in Wellington's army? *What is your name?*" His name: the one thing he had kept to himself through those years. The searing iron biting into his wounded shoulder; heat beating upon his face, the incandescent glare closing intolerably on his eyes: "Ralph— *don't!* Not Fletcher. Fairfax." Then a blast of cold air as the trapdoor opened, and the grating crack against his skull as he pitched into the void.

Huddled over the grille, Flavia shivered in the grip of so much evil. Her words sounded thin and inadequate. "What can I do?"

"Nothing. Once they reach the high road they will shoot me and claim Fletcher was trying to escape. Masters will have letters. What coroner would question that mine was a convict's corpse? I will end up anatomised, or in a pit of quicklime." Then sharper: "Someone's coming."

She cringed back against the wall, straining to hear. Who was it—Lucius? Masters? No, Bromley, the blond head gleaming in the faint light.

"Where is it?" Bromley demanded.

"What?"

"The ring."

"So you're in on this too. Another jackal snatching his share of the spoils?"

Flavia flinched at the crack of bone on flesh. "You never could keep a civil tongue in your head, Fairfax; I thought they would have flogged the insolence out of you. But I see they failed."

"Amateur." Ralph's voice was heavy with derision.

Flavia could not bear to listen any longer. Shaking, she turned away. The wind shrieked, hurling the snow stinging into her eyes as she ran to the stables.

"You're wasting your time." Ralph grinned as he was roughly searched. "I haven't got it."

Bromley's temper rose. "Quite the hardened old lag! You would never throw that ring away; did you give it to Flavia? Only a fool would trust another man's leavings. I thought that would wipe the smile off your face. I had her first. She likes her wooing rough."

Ralph leaped at his tormentor, but the chain pulled him up short. Bromley laughed in his face.

"You still blame Lucius, don't you? You will go to your grave not knowing." The door slammed behind him as he walked out.

Ralph flung his weight against the shackle. Damn the chain, damn Masters, damn Flavia's jealousy and his own pride; damn Bromley and crawling Lucius. All that pain, and why? It made no sense.

His wrist was raw; his arm ached fiercely. His hands pulsed from the tight lashing; he was hungry and very tired. Poor Flavia; he could see now the pain beneath her fragile composure. Jealousy tore through him. Was this how Lucius had felt, when Ralph had told him—with what satisfaction—that Bromley had taken his wife? Chilled and despairing, he slumped against the stone.

The click of the lock alerted him as the door opened.

Masters set down the heavy pistol. He snapped at the stable-boy struggling cold-fingered with a length of harness.

"Faster, boy! Can't you tie a buckle quicker than that?"

"It's not just the buckle, sir; looks like someone's cut the traces. I'll have to fetch another set."

"Get Pryor to help you! Hurry!" He picked up the powder-horn, squinting in the poor light as he tilted it carefully into the firing-pan.

Flavia, slipping quietly through the back door, lifted the side-saddle down from its peg and hefted it into Zobeide's loosebox. She saddled the horse as swiftly as she dared. Ralph's big black stamped nervously in the next stall and sidled back, banging against the wall.

"What's that?" Masters' voice, suspicious. She crouched beneath the manger.

The boy's voice came fainter from the tack-room. "Must be a rat, sir. Get them by the grain store."

She huddled, devoured with impatience. The boy emerged, burdened with the heavy harness, and they made for the yard. As soon as they had gone she cut back along the servants' path to the house.

Lucius must still be in the library; she could see the light under the door. Panting, she pushed it open.

He was asleep, his head on the table.

"Lucius! Wake up!" Impatiently she shook him by the shoulder. He slid forward. She saw the damascened barrel of the pistol in his hand, the dark mess at the back of his head, blood pooled on the green leather.

She felt the bile rush to her mouth. *Judas!* Oh Lucius, why did you do it? Was it shame or a muddled kind of reparation? Ralph's flayed back must have driven home just what you had done.

His tumbled curls were still warm. She dared not look at his face, but there was something beneath his left hand: a paper, stained down the edge.

*"My Dear Flavia,"* she read. *"I let Fairfax go. There is a note for you in Father's favourite book. Take care of Charles. Forgive me."*

There was a gap as if he had been searching for more to say. Then a final, sprawling line: *"This at least I had the courage to do."*

She turned to the bookshelf. There in its place was *The Vicar of Wakefield*, a folded paper inside the front cover. She opened it out. It was all there without extenuation: Bromley's plot; Lucius's acquiescence; his admission that he had received funds drawn by Frewin from the Longhallows accounts; dated and signed. Proof of Ralph's innocence. Hope.

She looked up as the floorboards creaked.

Bromley advanced, his hand outstretched. "Give it to me."

She clutched the note to her.

"Lucius was a fool. Give me that letter, and I will not trouble you again."

She backed round the other side of the desk. She knew too much; Bromley could not risk her telling the truth. She confronted him across her brother's body.

"Get out of this house. You have done enough harm here. You destroyed Lucius, battening onto him like a leech. Everything that was good you drained out of him."

He gave a stifled laugh. "You cannot haunt me with a brother's ghost." He was smiling, excited. She slid the letter into her pocket.

He saw the movement; as he snatched at her she scooped up the glass inkstand and flung it in his face. Instinctively he put up his hand. She slipped past him out the door, swung it to and, turning the heavy key, locked it from the outside. For a moment she leaned against the wall to regain her breath. As she dashed, almost tripping, down the stairs, she heard Bromley hammering at the stout panels.

In the stable she stumbled on something yielding and still warm. Ashamed of her relief, she recognised the man as he stirred: Vercoe. There was blood down the side of his face: he tried to stand.

"*You* cut the traces! They caught you? Did Ralph get away?"

Vercoe nodded. "Where did he go?"

With his bloodied finger he made two strokes on the white-tiled wall: one down, one across.

"Longhallows!" He squeezed her hand in confirmation, pointed across the yard. Lights. Men running.

Vercoe dragged himself back into the shadows. Hurriedly Flavia tossed two armfuls of hay to hide him. She led out her horse at a run, flung herself into the saddle, and kicked Zobeide to a gallop as she heard a shout behind her.

From the shoulder of the drive she glanced back. One horse and rider was out, circling; two, then three. Masters, Bromley, Pryor. She must reach Ralph first, with the letter. The trees flashed past as she turned off the road, down the quicker forest path. She knew the way, had a good horse and was lighter. She urged her mount into the flurrying darkness.

The bulk of Longhallows reared above her. Turning Zobeide to the dark stand of trees on the right, she tethered her where she would not be seen. In all that array of blank windows, one light gleamed. The high studded door swung open at Flavia's touch. She pushed it to, and shoved home the bolt.

Ahead of her the great staircase rose in twin curves, meeting under a portrait on the landing. She recognised Sir Everard even in the gloom. Beneath the left-hand door-sill a faint light flickered.

"Ralph! I must speak to you!"

The door opened just enough for Flavia to see a fire flaring in the room beyond, echoed in the bevelled glass panes of a cabinet. Ralph's face was in shadow.

"What are you doing here?" he said sharply.

It was a discouraging beginning. But she must deliver Lucius's last message, or his death would be wasted.

"Lucius shot himself. He left a letter proving your innocence. I have it here."

"Innocence!" he said, obliquely. "So Lucius is dead. I did my best to destroy him. I suppose I have succeeded."

His tone angered her. "Do you feel better for it?"

"No. But you had better come in," he added as an afterthought. He squatted in front of the fire and stirred the embers, then piled on another armful of wood. "I feel the cold," he added, unnecessarily.

As he turned his face to the flame she saw the broken skin high on his cheek.

"Did Bromley hurt you?" she asked, quickly.

"Oh, that. It's all a matter of knowing where to hit."

She could make nothing of this answer, or of his distant manner. Unsure what to say, she handed Ralph the letter.

He scanned it quickly. "Bromley implied it was his doing," he said, dully. "What I cannot understand is why. Not that it matters now."

A fragment of meaning teased at the back of her mind. Someone had hinted something about Bromley, not long ago, but as she strained to recall it, it vanished.

"It was Vercoe who cut the traces. He was injured but alive when I last saw him. Bromley and the other two will be here any minute." She yawned. In the warmth of the room she was beginning to realise how tired she was. "You have just enough time to get away."

"I'm not going." He handed back the letter, and squatted before the fire, his shackled hand between his knees. He picked up a file and rasped awkwardly, left-handed, at the iron gripping his wrist.

She saw the blood down the back of his hand.

"You can't fight three armed men!" she exclaimed.

"I am not unprepared." He jerked his chin to the left and she saw a cavalry sabre, its hilt worn, lying on the table. A steel-shafted pike leaned against the wall.

"But they have guns!" she pleaded.

"I'm not running any further. Thank you for what you tried to do, but go."

She had come so far to help him. Now he was driving her away. A shout came from outside, cutting across the surge of the storm-tossed trees.

"You must leave now," Ralph repeated, brusquely.

"But surely—"

The front door boomed under the weight of blows.

Ralph threw down the file and twisted to face her. "I don't want you here. Don't you understand? What can I say to convince you?" His chained hand clenched to a fist. "Do you want Pryor to do what Bromley did?"

She flinched. She had not thought he knew. A shot echoed as they shattered the lock. Boots clattered up the stairs. The old panic rose within her.

"For God's sake, go!"

Ralph shoved her through the far door and snatched up his weapons. No time now for the hurt in her eyes. He checked the stairway door was locked. *Fortiter Ad Finem.* He remembered Everard at Waterloo, spurring into the lowered lances.

"Fletcher! Come out!" Master's voice was muffled by the thick oak.

"My name is Fairfax," Ralph called back. "And tell Bromley to come first. That is, if he has the stomach to fight a grown man, not just women and half-grown boys." The door shook. Bromley always used others to take the risks.

Pryor was the strongest and most expendable; he would lead the charge. Ralph had a score to settle with him for Beckworth as well as himself: Pryor had told him exactly what he had done to Beckworth, and how long it had taken him to die. Quietly Ralph turned the key and eased the door a fraction. He braced the butt of the pike under his boot.

Gasping for breath, Flavia halted in the trampled snow at the foot of the steps. Until Ralph had so brutally pointed it out to her, she had not realised her danger. He knew from terrible intimacy what these men could do. She could not face that again.

A long, sobbing shriek rang out. She pressed her hands to her ears. Ralph did not want her there. He had ordered her to go. He was half-crippled, fighting three angry, resolute men.

A shattering crash. They would kill her if they found her. She was the only witness—she must get away. She cast a terrified look at the splintered door.

Three horses stood tethered to a pillar. You said you loved Ralph, she taunted herself; but you are leaving him to die. He does not want me, she argued. Any minute they will be after you, Bromley and the torturer and his brute. Zobeide was too far away. Flavia was at the first horse now. She need only mount up, and ride away: a man's saddle, but she could manage... It's not his love at issue, said a voice in her head with a clarity she recognised as Harriet's, but your own.

A leather holster hung from the pommel. She wrestled with the buckle at the top. Inside was a long, heavy dragoon's pistol; loaded. She seized it, gathered her skirts, and raced back up the stairs.

Ralph dropped the haft and leaped back as Pryor, screaming, clutched at the pike in his belly.

Masters jumped clear. Ralph cut at him two-handed, but the Frenchman blocked the blow. Their blades clashed. Ralph dodged a movement to his left. A pistol cracked and the crystal panels shattered beside him. His ears sang. He caught an acrid whiff of gunpowder. He lunged at Bromley, who fell back.

"Get behind him!" Masters shouted.

Masters attacked again, driving always from Ralph's right, every parry jarring his arm. The fire flashed past him as he gave ground. Where was Bromley? His knee crumpled under a sudden blow; he stumbled and put out his hand to break his fall. A heel crunched down on his fingers; his sabre was kicked away.

Masters lunged again, arrow-quick, aiming for the heart. Ralph rolled desperately, but came up hard against the wall. The blade scored along his ribs and he curled, clutching at the wound. Bromley stamped down on the trailing chain. He wrenched Ralph's head back against his knee.

"Hurry up and get it over with," snapped Bromley as Ralph threshed in his grasp. "We must find the girl."

Flavia edged through the open doorway. She could hear grunts and the thud of feet. She slipped on something wet; Pryor lay staring, propped up by the shaft protruding from his stomach. The air stank of sweat, and blood, and the tang of gunpowder.

In the firelight a dark slick of blood soaked Ralph's jacket. Bromley had him fast on the floor; Masters straddled him. As Flavia watched, stricken, the point of Master's sword poised under the angle of Ralph's jaw; hesitated; dipped. She realised: he is going to gut him, like a fish.

She lifted the heavy pistol two-handed, as Lucius had taught her so long ago: cocked it; sighted: fired.

The shot rang out: the blade jerked wide from its killing-stroke. Masters flexed back, twisting, black, like a broken spider.

Her hand numb from the recoil, the pistol clattered to the floor. Flavia stepped forward and her eyes met Robert's.

"You interfering bitch!" Bromley flung Ralph aside and lunged at her. As she shrank back Ralph snatched Bromley's ankle and brought him down. Robert was taller, heavier and whole. But Ralph was desperate, fighting for his life with all he had learned from his vicious scraps in the camps. He hammered Bromley left-handed with savage chopping jabs and kneed him in the groin. They rolled back towards the fireplace. Ralph cracked Bromley's head against the stone sill.

Ralph, head hanging, dashed the sweat from his eyes with the back of his hand. The flames leapt as he pulled out the neglected poker, glowing now. He pinned Bromley down.

As the two faces stood in relief Flavia's memory flared: *No child of mine will be born a bastard! Still Ralph, after all these years!* Abruptly she understood what Sarah had tried to tell her, saw the kinship in the bones.

Half-crazed, Ralph held the hot iron to Bromley's cheek. Robert screamed.

"Stop!" Flavia cried.

Again Ralph brought down the poker, his hand shaking.

"Ralph! He's your brother!"

He checked. "Is this true?" Ralph's voice was thick, as though speech were an effort.

"Go on, little brother. I did my best to kill you."

Again Ralph raised the iron.

Flavia could stand no more. She turned and stumbled away.

"Why?" Ralph could not keep the pain from his voice.

"I hated you from the moment you were born. You took what was mine."

"But why that name, *Fletcher*? The tattoo?"

"What tattoo?" said Bromley, blankly.

Ralph swayed on a wave of dizziness. No answers, even now. He raised the poker to smash the face below, but saw in it a reflection of his own. He remembered the stink of his own seared flesh. Disgusted, Ralph flung the poker aside. He punched Bromley on the jaw, with all the strength left to him. His brother's startled face slackened into unconsciousness.

# 49

## *England, December 1819*

Ralph stood up stiffly. His side ached fiercely and his shirt clung, cold and wet with blood. He swore as his leg almost gave way beneath him, and headed unsteadily for the door, skirting Masters' backwards-sprawled body, and the pooling stain where Pryor had twitched and jerked, shrieking like a stuck pig. Halfway down the stairs he clutched at the rail to keep from falling. His father's portrait loomed splendid above him.

"Flavia!"

From where she stood, numb with shock, she heard him call. She turned, taking his weight as he lurched. His voice was so low she could barely hear it.

"Get me away from this place."

She did not ask what had happened. All that lay between them could wait.

She braced herself as Ralph leaned more heavily, stumbling across the courtyard to the tethered horses, picking out a mare which might be chestnut, a well-formed animal with the strength to carry two.

"Are you fit to ride?"

"Yes."

"I'll mount first, and hand you up."

She slipped from under his arm and swung into the saddle, hitching up her skirts to ride astride. "Up you come, now."

He looked up, remembering another mare, another Christmas, the priest's stubborn promise.

"Donavan was right," he muttered.

"What was that?"

"Nothing." He pulled himself up, wincing.

"Shouldn't you stay here?" she asked over her shoulder as she turned away from the house.

"With Pryor and Masters?" He spat out the names as if they were tainted, dead or alive. She urged the horse on in silence, making as rapid a pace as she dared. Ralph's head weighed increasingly on her shoulder; she feared he would slip. Twice she felt his grip tighten as though he had jolted awake. He was in no state to travel far. Yet she could not return to Fontclaire. By now the news of his arrest would be all over the neighbourhood. Ralph was to all intents a dangerous escaped criminal; there would be parties of soldiers out before dawn, scouring the countryside. They needed somewhere close, quiet, with shelter and warmth.

The night was well advanced; she wondered what hour it was. She felt buoyed by a force frozen deep inside her which had now been freed. The air of the snow-patched valley hung in icy silence as she made for Dennison's barn, its ranked buttresses reassuring before them. She led horse and rider into the building's shelter, offering thanks to the ghosts who kept the villagers away. By the door she found a lantern and flint, and lit it carefully. The flame glowed.

Ralph lay slumped over the horse's neck. She shook him awake.

"Mmm?"

"We're here." She tugged and he slithered down. Somehow she had to get him up to the loft, where it would be warmer.

She hitched his arm again about her shoulders, ignoring the dark smears on her riding-jacket. "Can you climb a ladder?"

"If I must."

Half-climbing, half-hauling, they made it to the top. Here, under the arched beams of the latticed roof, the air was sweet with the scent of last summer's hay. There was a pile of sheepskins in the corner. She spread them out into a bed. Ralph slipped down, letting out his breath. She turned back to the ladder.

"Where are you going?"

"To find water."

Her head vanished below the level of the floor. Ralph eased out his stiff leg. In what seemed only an instant she was back, balancing a tin jug in a chipped basin. He snatched the jug and tilted it back, gulping; he had not realised how thirsty he was. It clattered as he set it down. After a moment's hesitation she poured the rest of the water into the basin.

"What's that for?" he asked sharply.

"To clean up that mess," she stated. "You can't sleep covered in blood."

"Why not?" he said flatly. "I've done it before."

"You're not doing it again!" she said fiercely, angry and distressed.

Ralph stared gracelessly away from the light, reluctant to be touched. She looked at him, unsure, then slipped off her petticoat and tore it into strips. Dipping a rag into the water she dabbed first at the raw skin on his shackled wrist, wrapping it in a strip of cloth, then his stiff, unresponsive hands with their bruised knuckles. The water grew darker. She eased off his ruined shirt; her hands shook as she saw the raw gash along his ribs. She shrank from touching it, but the gaping cut was scummed from the fight on the floor.

Delicately she started to wipe it clean. He swore under his breath and set his jaw in stubborn silence. She felt him shivering. When she was finished she set down the stained rag and drew the rough bandage round his ribs as tightly as she dared. She sat back on her heels and looked at the taut body now exposed, with its knots of muscle, sharply defined bone, and the ravaged back, scarred beyond hope of healing. She saw the exhaustion in cheek and jaw; the shame in his averted head.

She bent and kissed his back.

The dried grass rustled as he turned, his eyes seeking hers. His bruised fingers reached out to touch her wet cheek. "Are those tears for me?" His voice was a cracked whisper.

"For both of us. I never stopped loving you, even when they said you had deserted me."

"Even when you agreed to marry Bromley?" He could not hide the pain in his voice.

"They told me you had fled with that woman, and I would never see you again."

He drew loose the coils of her hair, as he had wanted to do, years ago by the river. They fell like heavy silk into his palm. His fingers traced the line of her neck. He had forgotten how to be gentle. Her skin was so soft, so flawless: he marvelled at its warmth, the curve of the hollow above her collarbone; the delicate line of her breast.

"I'm sorry," he said, jerking his hand away. "I have no right to do that. After what Bromley did—"

"I didn't love Bromley."

A moment passed, of dragging tension, as he understood what she was saying. Then, with a long sob, he drew her into his embrace.

Afterwards he slept, his head heavy over the beating of her heart. The candle in the lantern had gone out; she lay warm and comfortable in the darkness, her body singing.

Rain drummed gently on the thick thatch. Ralph moved in his sleep; the chain on his wrist chinked and he awoke. She saw the gleam of his teeth as he grinned.

"Docking a scapegallows. It will be the wreck of your reputation."

"It was gone already. I am twice a fallen woman." Now that wasteland was behind her.

He drew her hands together and kissed them. "But the second time was better than the first?"

She caught the undertone of seriousness. "Next time will be better still."

She was aware of how much he still withheld from her; behind what formidable reserves lay the prize she sought. She was seized by a fear of how much she had staked on this strange and difficult man; how deep was her need to love and be loved by him. She knew now how much she had to lose.

"Flavia—my manners have decayed of late. I have not thanked you for saving my life." He sat up, catching his breath. "Have you my ring?"

She slipped it off the chain and passed it to him. He rolled it between fingertip and thumb.

"There's something I didn't tell you," he began, "about the night I was taken. I was going to ask you to marry me. Through my foolishness and pride that did not happen. Many other things did, none of them pleasant. Everything I put my hand to, I misjudged. I betrayed my friend and myself. I meant to return and exact punishment on whoever had done this to me, but I was so blinded by vengeance I got that wrong as well." He paused. "Since all else has failed, I shall have to trust to love. God, I put that badly. I don't know what to say. How can I ask you to marry me—" his voice roughened "—when I am ruined whatever happens?" She went to move and he snatched to restrain her. "Don't go."

The desperation in his voice moved her more than any words could have done.

She knelt beside him. "I will be your wife, and bear your children, and forsaking all other, keep only unto you, as long as we both shall live—what is the phrase? *With my body I thee worship—*"

"*And with all my wordly goods I thee endow,*" Ralph went on, "*to have and to hold from this day forward, for better for worse, for richer for poorer, in sickness and in health, to love and to cherish, till death do us part.* Death came very close, tonight." His voice shook. He slipped the ring on her finger.

"There, Lady Fairfax. This will have to do until I get another." He kissed her, lingeringly. Her lips tasted of salt. "It's too cold for a wedding tomorrow; shall we continue the honeymoon?"

"You will set that gash bleeding again."

She sighed as his fingers tracked down her spine.

"Tell me when to stop," he said.

Ralph woke first. He had dreamed of the sleek wet head of a seal cleaving the calm morning sea, its wake leading him home. From a narrow window, high in the end wall, light poured down on him like a blessing. Flavia lay curled beside him, her long brown hair tumbled across the fleece that served them as a pillow. She had wrapped one lock around her eyes, to keep out the light.

He savoured this idiosyncrasy, treasuring it as the first of her secrets he would come to know. What folly had so long blinded him to her generosity and courage? She would never know how much she had restored to him, opening her body to him last night.

His knee was bruised and stiff, but he could bend it, and the deep cut on his ribs, though still fiercely sore, had not started bleeding again. He would check the horse had food and water, and look for some way to remove this accursed iron. As long as he wore it, Masters' hand was still upon him.

Quietly he made his way down. He brought the horse an armful of hay. There must be water nearby; he would not disturb Flavia to ask. He eased open the door to go outside.

He sensed a movement. Instinctively Ralph seized a stirrup-iron dangling from the wall.

"Steady on, old fellow; it's only me." Wentworth walked forward into the light. "After Miss Stanton's horse came back riderless to Fontclaire, half the countryside turned out to hunt you down. I came to warn you. I carry no arms. See for yourself." He held out his hands. Ralph's wary expression eased a little. "I brought some items you might find useful. Here."

He tossed over something small and hard. Ralph laughed as he caught it: a key. He unlocked the shackle with a sharp click, opened it out and flung it, rather too vehemently, as far as he could.

"Here's your cloak. And a shirt, too."

"You thought I might need them?" Ralph said wryly. "Thank you." Gratefully he slipped them on. "Now I can appear decently dressed before the good folk of the county, and not scare them into fits.

I once dug coal for your father's fires. I expected you to be out with the rest, tracking me with musket and hounds."

"We Currency lads have a different attitude to authority to that which prevails here," Wentworth replied evasively. "You might say I am putting the Governor's Emancipist theories into practice."

"Macquarie? I saw him once. A good man, I thought."

"They have him on the run, now; it will not be long before they write his epitaph."

"He found Sydney wood, and left it brick?" suggested Ralph. Unexpectedly he found himself liking this brash Australian.

"Ralph! Are you—" Flavia appeared around the edge of the door. "Oh." She blushed crimson.

Wentworth smiled broadly. "Good day, Miss Stanton," he said blandly, doffing his hat. "I trust you are well."

Ralph drew her close. "Miss Stanton and I are to marry."

Wentworth's smile broadened. "Please accept my felicitations. But there is something else I must tell you," he went on, suddenly serious. "There has been a fire at Longhallows. Most of the house is destroyed. It was thought, to begin with, that you had all perished in the blaze; but Bromley turned up at Fontclaire in the early hours of the morning."

"He must have torched Longhallows after we left," said Flavia. "If he could not have it, neither would anyone else."

Ralph was surprised by his indifference. The house had always been a dead weight of tradition around his neck; a burden of expectation. In one way, Bromley had been right. He had the taste, the money and the connections, to restore Longhallows to its former glory. Thwarted, he had burned it down out of spite.

"What did Bromley do?" asked Flavia, concerned for Lucius's child.

"No harm, if that is what you are afraid of. He asked Caroline to run off with him, and she did."

"And Charles?"

"They left him behind. You will be pleased to hear that that Mrs Lennox was packing as I left, surely an example of every cloud having a silver lining. And one further point. I slipped away, Fairfax, just after you had done your best to knock me through the mantelpiece. I misliked the look of the whole business, so I took the liberty of sending a message to General Byng. He should be on his way now. It would be wise to secure your position with him before some enthusiastic yokel blows your head off, expecting a reward."

"You have been most kind," said Ralph, shaking his hand. "I apologise for swinging into you like that, last night."

"Don't trouble yourself about it," Wentworth replied courteously. "We shall have a return bout one day, if you promise to fight clean." He touched his hat to them and rode off.

Flavia walked slowly back into the barn and looked up. In the cool winter daylight the loft was only a high shelf spread with hay. Sheltered there for one night, they had possessed each other utterly. Now they must confront a hostile world.

Ralph saw her sombre expression. "Look! It's gone!" he said, lifting his freed hand; but he had caught her mood of constraint.

He had shared the joy of his release with the woman he loved and a man he felt to be his friend. Now he must argue his innocence, and bare his scars of mind and body to men less warm in their sympathy; cruder in understanding. Masters was dead, but he would have left letters to authorise Ralph's recapture, potent still with the venom of his record, that convict-shadow that had tracked him from the ends of the earth. For a moment he chilled to sudden panic and was again Fletcher the absconder, the sheep-stealer, the name on the punishment lists. He took a long, shuddering breath.

What had been done to him would always remain. His trust would always be wary; his friendships few. He looked at Flavia and the grimness about his mouth relaxed. I am not alone any more.

They led out the horse as a glimmer of sunshine lit the valley, silvering the puddles which he was alive to see, and Masters was not. *There is light on your path, though you cannot see it.*

A file of riders was approaching; sighting the fugitives, they quickened to a canter. The dragoons closed round them, staring curiously, weapons at the ready. The sergeant trotted up with a spare mount. Pale but composed, Ralph handed Flavia up onto the mare, and swung into the empty saddle, already turning over in his mind the words he would say to Byng. Saluted by distant rooks, the little cavalcade set off down the long slope, back to the road.

# Acknowledgements

The author acknowledges use of the following copyright material:

Details on the betrayal and capture outside Badajoz in April 1812 of Colonel Colquhoun Grant, then Wellington's Chief of Intelligence for the Army, taken from *Wellington's Spies*, Mary McGrigor, Leo Cooper 2005, Copyright © Mary McGrigor 2005.

Interior layout and shipboard working routines of my fictional convict transport ADELPHI reproduced from *Convict Ships* by Charles Bateson by kind permission of the publishers, Brown, Son & Ferguson, Ltd. I have also brought forward the reference to the suspected mutiny on the (actual) transport *Chapman*, which occurred early-mid 1817.

The work of M.H. Ellis *Lachlan Macquarie, His Life, Adventures and Times*, Angus and Robertson, 1978 (contemporary attitudes to the Rev Samuel Marsden, quotations from his sermons, and Bigge's opinion of the appointment of Redfern as magistrate) reproduced courtesy of HarperCollins Publishers Australia. Due diligence was made in getting permission from the relevant rights holder in regards to digitally reproducing this work. If the current rights holders have any objections, they can contact myself or HarperCollins Publishers.

Transportation as deterrent, Marsden "The Flogging Parson", capital required by free emigrants for land grants taken from:

C.M.H. Clark, *A History of Australia: vol 1: From The Earliest Times to The Age of Macquarie*, Melbourne University Press, 1962, and

C.M.H. Clark, *A History of Australia, vol 2: New South Wales and Van Deiman's Land 1822-1838*, Melbourne University Press, 1968.

Miner's warning rhyme (p. 238), Earl Fitzwilliam's wealth based on control of the Barnsley coal seam (p. 244), Shillingthorpe aristocratic asylum for the insane (p. 405) taken from Catherine Bailey, *Black Diamonds: The Rise And Fall Of An English Dynasty*, Penguin, London, 2008.

Copyright © Catherine Bailey 2007.

Reproduced by permission of Penguin Books Ltd.

Descriptions of, and traditions associated with, Indian jewellery taken from *Indian Jewellery* by Nick Barnard, V&A Publishing, 2008.

Status of Specials, workings of the Pass system, pervasive sodomy, psychological effects of flogging, details of the disfigured Newcastle commandant Morriset and his regime taken from *The Fatal Shore* by Robert Hughes, published by Vintage Books. Reprinted by permission of The Random House Group Limited.
Permission sought from Knopf Doubleday Publishing Group, Random House Inc. New York.

Details of shipboard scrutiny and official convict indent, also pervasive influence of convict's bureaucratic record drawn from *Chain Letters: Narrating Convict Lives* by Lucy Frost and Hamish Maxwell-Stewart, Melbourne University Press, 2001.

Extracts from the *Authorized Version of the Bible* (The King James Bible), the rights in which are vested in the Crown, are reproduced by permission of the Crown's Patentee, Cambridge University Press.
Extracts from *The Book of Common Prayer*, the rights of which are vested in the Crown, are reproduced by permission of the Crown's Patentee, Cambridge University Press.

There are instances where I have been unable to trace or contact the copyright holder. If notified the publisher will be pleased to rectify any error or omissions at the earliest opportunity.

*Also cited:*

*Ralph Rashleigh, or The Life of an Exile*, James Tucker, Angus and Robertson, Sydney and London 1952.

*A Regency Visit: The English Tour of Prince Pückler-Muskau Described in his Letters 1826-1828*, trans Sarah Austin, ed E.M.Butler, Collins, London 1957.

Foreword, Max Harris, *1811 Dictionary of the Vulgar Tongue: A Dictionary of Buckish Slang, University Wit and Pickpocket Eloquence* London 1984.

*The Making of the English Working Class*, E.P. Thompson, Vintage 1966.

*The Australian Legend*, Russel Ward, Oxford University Press Melbourne 1996.

Psalm 24: 1-3 *Ad te levavi animam meum* from Introit, first Sunday of Lent, from *New Marian Missal* by Sylvester P. Juergens, Michelin 1957 Tridentine Rite, English translation from the *Douai Bible*.

Breton folktales *Le Chateau de Crystal; La Princess de Tronkolaine; Le Fille Qui se Maria à un Mort; N'oun Doaré* translated by the author from Luzel, François-Marie: Contes Populaires de Basse-Bretagne http://www.legendesbretonnes.fr, after the edition of Maisonneuve & Ch Leclerc, 1887.

www.ingramcontent.com/pod-product-compliance
Lightning Source LLC
Chambersburg PA
CBHW020922020726
47495CB00002B/310